WINDHALL

WINDHALL

Ava Barry

PEGASUS CRIME
NEW YORK LONDON

WINDHALL

Pegasus Crime is an imprint of
Pegasus Books, Ltd.
148 W 37th Street, 13th Floor
New York, NY 10018

First Pegasus Books cloth edition March 2021

Interior design by Timothy Shaner, NightandDayDesign.biz

Library of Congress Cataloging-in-Publication Data is available.

ISBN: 978-1-64313-626-4

10 9 8 7 6 5 4 3 2 1

Printed in the United States of America
Distributed by Simon & Schuster
www.pegasusbooks.com

For Marsh

PROLOGUE

I dreamed of that night a hundred times. The gates of Windhall thrown open to greet a procession of ghostly cars, dazzling apparitions gliding up the drive. The garden, filled with deadly flowers and orange blossoms, the night sky a bowl of stars. And Windhall itself, blazing with light, all the windows thrown open to the summer air.

Most of all, I dreamed of Eleanor. She arrived late to the party that night, hours after the band had switched from lively swing to something sweet and melancholy. There wouldn't be very many details of that night that the papers missed, since the host was one of the most famous people in Hollywood. Reporters would obsess over the attire, the music, the guest list. I had seen hundreds of pictures of the attendees, the giddy starlets and men in their tuxedos, eyes bright with alcohol and opportunity. They had always reminded me of the doomed aristocrats in some wicked fairy tale, all those gods gathered in one place, unaware that one of their own would shortly be killed.

There were no neighbors around Windhall that year. A decade before, in the 1930s, that part of Los Angeles was still sleepy orchards and farmland dotted with health clinics. Pale young women had wandered in the dusty California sunlight, bruises blooming against their milky skin. There had been more invalids than movie stars, with tuberculosis and polio patients coming out to the West Coast to strengthen their bones with sunshine and calcium. In the last decade, however, the land had been claimed by the Los Angeles elite. The orchards had yielded to wild, secretive mansions with deep windows and heavy doors. Windhall was one of the biggest.

I knew the script for the evening by heart. At seven, shortly after sunset, the first of the guests arrived. Men had been hired for the evening to park the expensive cars in the orchards that surrounded Windhall. That month was filled with garden parties that lasted until daybreak, beautiful women with ebony hair and alabaster skin traipsing down the garden paths, weaving poisonous flowers in their hair. The glittering actors and actresses of the silver screen would pile into cars, draped in furs and diamonds, then drive up Benedict Canyon and arrive at the gates of Windhall.

The evening continued. Twilight gave way to night, a collision of stars against a black landscape. The band began to play, something hopeful. The host of the party, Theodore Langley, had not yet made an appearance. There had been rumors about his latest film, trouble with one of the producers. Still, Theo was not one to be deterred by a little trouble at work. His name commanded respect, and it wasn't just because of his legendary skills as a host. Theodore Langley was a talented director, one of the best.

More guests arrived. On that night, they were invincible, the rulers of a young kingdom. Their names and faces claimed every marquee in Hollywood and beyond, into the vast gray hinterland of unknown Middle America, dusty hamlets with little more than a main street and two stop signs.

The band continued to play. Nine o'clock. The night was a masquerade, filled with men accompanied by dates in silk dresses, all dark eyes and bright smiles. They drifted inside the house in a haze of cigarette smoke and expensive perfume, gliding down the halls of Windhall and trailing their fingers along the walls.

And finally, she arrived. Eleanor Hayes, queen of the silver screen, the type of femme fatale to be described by poets and yet never captured. She eluded description. That evening, she wore a green silk dress with a black sash; after her death, it would become emblematic. Her graceful throat was draped in pearls. The weekend before, she could be found pilfering hand-rolled cigarettes on the beach, but on this night, she was elegant.

There were stories about what went on behind the scenes, of course, but most of it remained unsubstantiated. There were stories of dark-eyed beauties who dipped their hands in rosewater and made animal sacrifices, then drank the blood. Chambers and death rooms beneath those big, crazy houses. Nighttime parades, swimming pools filled with champagne and drops of human blood. It was the golden age of Hollywood, after all, where the sins of a few went pardoned, if they were wealthy enough.

Ten o'clock. Someone suggested a game of hide-and-seek. All the guests ran to find a hidden space in that sprawling, somber house. Too many doors, too many windows, so many places to hide. One of the men began to count while the other guests vanished. *One, two, three . . . eighty . . . one hundred . . .*

The first guests were picked off quickly, hiding behind the grand piano. Some of them had hidden in the hedges of the garden, the night swollen with the scent of magnolia and jasmine. Greer Garson, Robert Taylor, Clifton Webb; each returned to the house and poured themselves another drink.

It was mid-May, coming up on the scalp of summer. Heat lingered in the bones of the valley, malignant and cruel. Coyotes had left the hills and wandered through the streets like crooked phantoms, looking for something to eat. Nothing was sacred, nothing was safe. The air was sweet with the smell of eucalyptus, burning olean-der, salty earth, and chaparral. That late at night, the city took on a magical glow, wavering between black magic and a spell of sleep.

Two hours passed, and nearly every guest had been found. The only ones missing were Theo and Eleanor. Titters, rumors, and gossip: perhaps the pair had found something better to do with their time. There had always been rumors about Theo and Eleanor, work-ing so closely on all those famous movies. If there was something going on behind the scenes, nobody would be surprised.

A waiter made another round with a tray of drinks, and talk idled. The first guests peeled off, heading home. Still no sign of the host and his leading lady. Three women remained, and two men. One of them made a lewd comment, a suggestion for how to fill the rest of the evening. Another guest complained about the heat.

And then Theo finally reappeared, standing in the door of the living room. His face was ashen, his hands shaking.

"There's been an accident," he said. "She's in the garden."

Later, after everything that happened, these words would become so famous that they were nearly always misquoted. They became a cliché, synonymous with broken Hollywood dreams and failed romances.

They found Eleanor in the bed of trampled rosebushes, lying in a dish of concave dirt. *There's been a fall.* Even in the darkness of the garden, shadows collapsed all around the cast of characters, they could see it had not been a simple fall. A bloody star upon Eleanor's chest, a badge of misplaced honor. The fabric had been torn.

One guest knelt beside her and tried to take a pulse.

"I can't feel anything," he said. "God, she looks awful. What happened?"

"It was an accident," Theo repeated.

Eleanor's head rolled upon her neck. A woman in a silk dress knelt in the dewy grass. "There's blood on her chest," she said, then gasped. "Eleanor!"

"Theo," the man said softly. "I think she's dead."

At some point, the police arrived, but nobody was quite sure who had called them. The guests were questioned, but politely, of course; the police knew all their faces. There were no accusations, not that night; the accusations against Theo would begin to leak out the next day. It was the stuff of movies, after all: a famous Hollywood starlet, all dark eyes and long lashes, killed by her strange lover.

That year would raise questions without very many answers. Theo's trial stretched on for the better part of a year. Private lives were thrown into question, and the members of Hollywood's upper crust were forced to descend from their secret world to take part in the trial. Alliances were tested, secrets revealed.

The first policemen to arrive on the scene said that the cause of death was immediately apparent; even though the medical examiner was called for, his presence was almost unnecessary. Eleanor had been stabbed through the back. Her heart had been impaled; she had probably died right away. The garden was searched for weeks, but ultimately, the search was abandoned. They never found the murder weapon.

Eleanor Hayes, dead at twenty-six, never to age another day. I came to know her face by heart, the famous dark eyes and bowed lips, which were her trademark, the languorous gaze she cast upon her victims. At the peak of her career, she was the wealthiest woman in California, but this distinction did little to raise her social habits: weekends found her dancing barefoot in dim little bars of downtown Los Angeles, between smoky ghosts and Philip Marlowe types, or else up in the hills, riding bareback through the gorse and sagebrush. At night, they pitched tents and fell asleep to the sound of coyotes calling, waking up to see a glorious sunrise break over the dusty hamlets of Los Angeles.

And Theo. As the years faded away and the murder went unsolved, Eleanor became the woman in a myth, the details of her life blurred. Theo was released, in the end; the case fell apart. He was a secretive man with too many stories to tell, someone for whom the past and future could be rewritten. Still alive, all these decades later, but unseen since the trial.

As the years passed, Theo joined the ranks of true-crime lore, a cabal of wife-killers and opulent eccentrics whose names were tossed around as gossip rather than injunction. The '60s passed, and then the '70s; his legend was replaced first by the death of Marilyn Monroe and then the Manson killings, the deaths of Elvis and John Lennon. Home televisions replaced the fanaticism of classic movie theaters. Fans became caged by domesticity and the Internet. Celebrities shrank to fit the size of a mobile phone, easily tucked away for cigarette breaks at work. Theo was forgotten, mostly, relegated to a past of black-and-white movie screens; the grand old days. And then, late one autumn, he came back to me.

ONE

I had been staring at my computer screen for hours in frustration. A nasty bitch of a storm had knocked out the power a few hours before, and I'd only been able to get back online in the last twenty minutes, siphoning off my neighbor's Internet. I was an expert at guessing passwords: they were usually obvious number combinations, boring monikers, sexual innuendos, or anatomical terms spelled out with zeroes and eights. My neighbor had used his cat's name.

I hadn't written so much as a paragraph when Madeleine called.

"Have you seen pictures of the dead girl?"

"Which dead girl are you talking about?" I cradled the phone against my shoulder and feigned ignorance.

"The girl who was killed Tuesday." She waited. "It's Eleanor all over again."

I knew who she was talking about, of course; the girl had been all over the news for the last two days. A dark little slip of a thing, probably didn't weigh more than a hundred pounds. Details about the girl and her life came filtering out in the aftermath of her murder: an art student, barely twenty, scientist father and philanthropist mother. Nobody cared about the rest. The only thing anyone could see was the dark green silk dress, the puncture wound through the left chest cavity, the wilted hair. She'd been found laid out in a patch of wildflowers, her left arm draped across her brow. *Just like Eleanor.*

To make matters worse, the girl's body had been found a stone's throw from Theo's house. A jogger had found the girl's body on a derelict fire trail that wound up behind the mansions, where you could still see wild scratches of California. I had been to the trail myself, dozens of times, because it offered the best view of Windhall.

I hadn't read the story when it first came out. There had been splashy headlines all over Facebook and the *New York Times*, so I was aware of what was going on. But instead of reading the news, I had laced up my running shoes and plugged in my headphones, blasted early Led Zeppelin, and pounded the pavement so hard that I knew I'd have muscle spasms the next day.

These murders always unfolded the same way. Headlines were inundated with salacious details about the victim's circumstances, doe-eyed photographs from happier times accompanied articles, and then, later, came the stories about the impact on the family.

Her parents were absolutely shattered, the newspapers would say, or *They had no idea how she earned her money, until the call came.*

Everyone loves a beautiful dead girl. The rest of the murders go unacknowledged by the media or the world at large: the stories of old women, for example, living with their killers for the last fifty years, subjected every day to countless untold horrors.

"Max?" Madeleine's voice brought me back to reality. "You okay?"

"Sorry, Mad," I said. "You know I hate these stories."

I had known Madeleine for so long that I didn't have to explain myself to her. She knew that the anniversary of my grandmother's murder was coming up and that these stories were more upsetting to me than usual this time of year. It had only been seven years, but it felt like a minor eternity since my gran had been killed by her ex-husband. She had left him when I was ten years old, after he hit her one time too many. We considered ourselves lucky when he got locked up for something unrelated, a failure to pay a back balance of taxes. Once he got out, freshly paroled, he headed straight to Gran's. The irony is that I had just sewn up some legal troubles of my own, and we thought we had some peaceful times coming to us.

No matter how long I put it off, though, I always ended up reading the stories, devouring them alongside the rest of the general public; in the end, I was no better than anyone else. The fact that Theodore Langley had been looped into this particular story made it irresistible, even though I knew he hadn't had anything to do with it.

There hadn't been any photos of the dead girl until early that morning. The photos hadn't been of the body, but of the girl in the year leading up to the murder, just as the formula demanded. Pretty young thing, dead too young, so much wasted promise. Everyone pretended to mourn even as they ate up the details. My attention, however, was riveted more on the connection with Theo and Eleanor Hayes. Most of the bloggers and Internet trolls who had filled the comments section of the *New York Times* probably had no idea that this was a re-creation, an homage, some might say, to something that had happened sixty-nine years before.

Madeleine must have known what I was thinking.

"Sloppy tribute," she said. "If someone was going to pay homage to Eleanor, shouldn't they have killed this girl on the same date? I mean, Eleanor was killed in May, and it's October."

"No," I said, and I suddenly felt filled with dread. The date had just clicked in my mind, and I knew it wasn't an accident: whoever had done this had planned it exactly, and what's more, they had known more about the case than the commonly acknowledged date of Eleanor's murder. "It wasn't a tribute to Eleanor. It was a tribute to Theo. October third is when Theo was released from all charges. It's also when he disappeared."

As much as I hated myself for doing it, I had followed reports of Theo throughout the years. I'd kept track of all the sightings, no matter how loony and desperate they sounded. There were claims by people who had seen Theo in supermarket checkout lines, windsurfing in Monterey, hiking in Canada, and even one improbable story about Theo snatching someone's child from a secluded picnic area. The claims were sporadic, and there was never any concrete evidence that Theo was still alive. Sometimes there were photographs, sometimes not, but the question lingered in the back of a lot of minds: How did someone so prominent manage to stay completely off the grid for more than six decades?

The stories grew wilder as the years continued to unfold. After Eleanor's murder, the accusations, and the prosecutor's failure to convict Theo, had vanished. To all known accounts, he hadn't set foot in Los Angeles since. The case against him had been summarily dismissed, due to evidence tampering. He had been allowed to leave the city and, in addition to everything else, this made people very angry.

For one, there was the fact that Windhall was allowed to remain standing, despite all the protests over the years from the neighbors who wanted to see it torn down. After someone finally threatened to take matters into their own hands, Theo's lawyers produced documents that stated that Windhall was a historic building and therefore protected from demolition. There was the fact that Theo's friends, the elite and wealthy of Hollywood, had been treated with kid gloves. Some left the city to avoid testifying in the murder trial, and they weren't so much as reprimanded.

The parties at Windhall dried up after Eleanor was murdered, of course, and after Theo left Los Angeles, the great house sat collecting dust. While the manors and secretive estates of the other great old stars gently faded away and disappeared, Windhall endured. The bougainvillea and roses shriveled up and died, replaced by spiky plants and weeds that grew ten feet high. The fig trees in the garden became wild things, like nightmare plants. Yet Windhall remained intact.

With the passing years, the truth about Theo faded away, replaced with what he came to represent: a wild misanthrope with too much money, a creative fiend who had killed and gotten away with it. Decades of feminists saw something else, a theme much more transparent with the evolution of Western society: a man killed a woman and got away with it. As a lifelong feminist myself, I hated Theo, but I couldn't help obsessing over him. I hid my fascination behind contempt: *Trust the fucking system to protect a predator.*

What I didn't say: *I'd give anything to see inside Windhall.*

"There's something else," Madeleine said. "About Windhall. My boss said that someone was arrested for breaking in."

"When?" My heart jumped. "Who was it?"

"Some vandals. It's not important; I just thought you should know."

"Did they take anything?"

"I heard the story secondhand, Hailey, I don't have details. It'll probably happen again, though. This story has renewed interest in Windhall."

Windhall. Unoccupied for six decades, virtually untouched since Theo's departure in the '50s. The house was a vacant ruin, presiding over the Beverly Glen neighborhood above lower Sunset. From the fire trail where the girl had died, you could see the upper spires of the Victorian gables, the sun glinting off the windows.

My grandmother was the one who introduced me to Theo's story, and she had always warned me not to visit Windhall. After her death, however, I started driving out there to see it for myself. From listening to her stories, I had imagined the walls crumbling from years of untended wild roses, the garden like some terrible, savage thing. There would be broken glass and signs of vandalism, the silk organza curtains gone ragged in the desert air.

The first time I went to see Windhall, I saw that my imagination had been wildly off-base. Not a rotting shell of a house, nor a decaying bramble of thorns. The main house still stood over everything like an aging monarch, resilient yet faded, the windows unbroken and the paths quiet and undisturbed by uninvited guests. The driveway wound up through the gardens and decaying terraces, weaving past the gardener's hut. The cracked tennis court lay on the right, faded and overgrown from disuse. The empty swimming pool came next, guarded by a clutch of old pool chairs.

In some ways, it looked like a kingdom left undisturbed for three hundred years. One might enter the house and find the guards still clad in their brocaded vests, nodding off against stone pedestals. I pictured children in diamond garters and woven braids, playing with polished stones in the garden.

It wasn't until my third visit to the property that I actually sneaked inside Windhall, and instantly, I wished I hadn't. There was a sense about the house, and even for all my dexterity with words, I couldn't name that feeling until a few days later. I had been sneaking into buildings for years, but none of the other abandoned structures had felt quite so occupied. In a way, it was as though Theo had never left.

"You still there?" Mad's voice brought me out of my reverie.

"Yes," I said, thinking quickly. "Where are you right now?"

"Home. What's up?"

"I'm coming over," I said. "I have to see it. We have to go to Windhall, tonight. There's no telling what might happen the next time someone breaks in."

Gran had been an actress herself, and even though she stopped acting once she had children, she never forgot that world. She'd even worked on one of Theo's films, playing a young shopgirl without any lines, but she said that Theo treated everyone on his set like equals.

The stories about Theo weren't the only stories she liked to tell. I grew up on tales of the aristocrats and royals who fled to America and ended up penniless, begging for work in the film industry. There were stories about actresses hanging out in full costume jewelry, drinking milkshakes at a soda fountain on Vine Street. In those days, you could climb on a trolley headed for Sunset Boulevard and find yourself in the company of pirates, kings and queens in thick furs, and young Swiss children in full Alpine garb.

In all of Gran's stories, Los Angeles was a faded city built on the edge of a desert, once filled with beautiful women but now overrun with ghosts. I pictured smoky corridors and doors hanging open, women with sad eyes lingering at the bar until last call. I longed for the days when young starlets filled swimming pools with champagne, then stripped off their silk robes and waded in up to their elbows.

For years, I had dreams about the parties at Windhall, strolling through the grounds, perhaps lobbing a tennis ball across the decaying tennis net. In some of my dreams, Theo came out to greet me himself; in others, blind faces came toward me, folding in succession, and then dozens of hands, like the detached limbs of some Cocteau nightmare.

Theo's neighborhood was quiet when we arrived. Windhall's main gate opened onto Sweet Briar Lane, but since the parking nazis in Beverly Hills were especially vicious, we parked off Benedict Canyon, then walked toward the fire trail where this new dead girl had been discovered.

We were quiet as we made our way through the underbrush to the lookout point. Once, we had to stoop to get under a cat's cradle tangle of "Do Not Cross" police tape. Since the fire trail was still officially a crime scene, there was a chance that we might encounter police, but I doubted it.

Madeleine broke the silence first. "Are you going to write about this for the *Lens*?"

"It's not really my genre," I said. "Dead girls are probably Brian's specialty."

"Your Jenner-Foster story wasn't really genre-specific."

"That was the article of a lifetime. I made an exception."

"What about this?" she said, stooping to get under a diagonal section of tape. "You've always been obsessed with Theo. What if he's back?"

"He's not," I assured her. "It's a copycat crime, I guarantee it."

I was cranky that the murder had happened on the trail, because up until that point, it had been a nice little secret. Finding the trail had been a lucky break, something I had come across on my third or fourth visit to Windhall. The fact that the trail had stayed under the radar for so long was almost too good to be true: Windhall was in one of the most expensive neighborhoods in Los Angeles, a zip code that had once been home to Jack Warner, Harold Lloyd, Valentino, and Mary Pickford. Every time I walked along the fire trail, I felt a little bit like a peasant slipping through the palace gardens.

Even though the fire trail was technically a public easement, it was so small that it was almost off the map. Unlike Elysian Park or Runyon Canyon, runners who spent their mornings here were usually locals, and most of the time, I had the trail to myself. Since I found Los Angeles runners to be lower on the food chain than gelatinous invertebrates, the lack of joggers worked out nicely for me.

The discovery of the art student's dead body two days before changed everything. Overnight, pictures of the trail and the surrounding neighborhood were all over the news, and suddenly my trail was blocked off by TV crews, police officers, and plainclothes cops turning over rocks, checking under leaves, and using their black lights and other technology to find traces of human matter.

The worst part of the whole ordeal was the fact that the newspapers kept dragging Theo's name into the stories about the girl. COLLEGE SOPHOMORE DISCOVERED TWO HUNDRED YARDS FROM SITE

OF FAMOUS WINDHALL MURDER, one newspaper proudly declared. *Similarities found between young, helpless women who died at the pinnacle of youth.* Once again, Eleanor's murder became a front-page headline. Parallels were drawn between how Eleanor's body was found tangled in the rosebushes, murdered at a fabulous golden age party while her friends danced mere feet away from her body, unaware.

WILL THEO RETURN TO WINDHALL? queried another newspaper. *Now in his nineties, the elusive Hollywood director hasn't been seen in over ten years. Where is he now?*

The last reported Theo sighting had been in New Mexico. A blurry photograph had surfaced a few hours after the claim: Theo exiting a laundromat, wearing a pair of sunglasses. He was half-turned in profile, and most of the people who still zealously tracked his sightings were convinced that it wasn't him at all. Nevertheless, I'd clipped the photograph and added it to the wall in my office.

"Hailey," Madeleine said softly, shaking my arm. "There's someone up ahead."

I peered into the darkness, but I couldn't see anyone. High above the city, the path didn't benefit from the light of streetlamps or passing cars, and the stars overhead were so faint that the trail was nearly pitch black.

"I don't see anyone," I whispered.

"Shh!"

We pressed against each other, shoulders touching, eyes trained in the same direction. I had been visiting abandoned sites for so long that I didn't spook easily, but there was something eerie about the silence of the trail. It was rare to find silence in Los Angeles, a city with four million beating hearts, where the hum of electricity and tires and city noises drowned out most thought.

Madeleine and I stayed there for a good three minutes before I put my hand on her shoulder.

"It's fine," I said. "Let's go on. It's probably just an animal."

"Yeah," she said sarcastically. "With any luck, it's a friendly little mountain lion."

Madeleine was the only one who I had ever taken to see Windhall, because Windhall was special and I felt that only a few people should be able to see it up close. She was the closest thing I had to a best friend, and even though we were unlikely candidates for each other, we got along so well it was almost like we had grown up together. We'd met while I was doing research for an article on the Victorian homes in Boyle Heights and had stayed close when we figured out that we had a lot of other interests in common, most of which involved creepy Los Angeles legends. She had a lot of information to draw from, because she worked for a historical preservation society that purchased old houses and prevented them from getting torn down.

Madeleine was the only one who knew that I had dropped out of college halfway through my first year, then done a quick week in jail when one of my excursions went very, very wrong. The lead prosecutor called it arson. My lawyer called it a youthful mistake. It was a weird point in my life, one that I almost never talked about, since it was the same stretch of months that had seen my grandmother put a second mortgage on her beloved home in order to finance a good lawyer.

Madeleine was also the only person who knew why I had missed two years of junior high, which was the same reason why I was a grown man who still didn't know how to swim. I could count on one hand the people who knew about my time in the hospital, aged eleven to nearly thirteen, helpless on a hospital bed while doctors tried to figure out what was wrong with my spine. I endured endless tests and false prognoses, then three or four surgeries that worked, but I wouldn't ever really be a complete human being.

By the time I went to high school, I was half the size of other kids my age and smarter than most of my class put together. Thanks to my grandmother, I'd managed to keep on top of my schoolwork through one of those homeschool programs for child actors and other shut-ins who can't make it to a regular classroom.

It was a good thing that I hadn't met Madeleine until after college, because if we had gone to high school together, I probably wouldn't have even registered on her radar. Madeleine had gone to school with the younger Geffens, Weinsteins, and Gettys. I had seen pictures of their weekend get-togethers: all dressed up in their raggedy thrift-store finds, unwashed hair piled on top of their heads like young bohemians, crouched on the balconies of million-dollar penthouses in Malibu and the Palisades. There was an artfulness to even the throwaway shots: painfully beautiful high school boys, long curly hair tumbling down around their shoulders. All of them with perfect skin and cigarettes balanced between their fingers, sleepy eyes and worn-in T-shirts on private planes. The message was clear, again and again: *It's ours, we've grown accustomed to it, we're not afraid to lose it.*

I had devoured Mad's stacks of disposable camera photos with something akin to obsession, angry and envious of all these wealthy children who could be so blasé about the stained, secondhand clothing that they wore like some kind of private joke. I coveted their looks and the way they could make ripped T-shirts look glamorous, then hated myself for feeling that way. Second- and thirdhand clothing in my house wasn't a joke; I had been lucky if I got something that came close to fitting.

I could pick Mad out in all the photos, a thin girl with an explosion of curls, sometimes down around her ears like an Italian model in the early '80s, and an overlarge sweater or T-shirt. No matter where she was in the photograph, she always seemed to be the center of attention; while most of her friends looked complacent or wary in the photographs, Madeleine was always smiling. It was radiant, that smile, and I wanted to pluck young Mad out of the photos and carry her away to safety. *Don't hang out with these people, you won't talk to any of them in ten years.*

I might have envied her for the deep, cool private pools flanked by palm trees, elegant friends that gathered around the lip like off-duty swimsuit models, but there was a darker side to that life. There had been an eating disorder and then, in college, a dalliance with cocaine. She never called it an addiction, but her older sister had intervened and made her check into rehab. Neither of her parents got involved; I came to understand that was customary in wealthy Los Angeles families. Daddy had been off in the Swiss Alps at the time, mummy somewhere in London.

"With all the snow in LA, you would think people would stay for the winter," Mad said about it all, wry as usual.

She hadn't had contact with any of her old friends for years, but there were still elements of that lifestyle sprinkled around her house. I found Polaroids jammed into her kitchen drawers, holey T-shirts from an Italian regatta in the '90s, which could have belonged to her father or else have been scooped up from a thrift store. You could never tell what was authentic and what was merely ironic.

By the time we reached the lookout and Windhall came into view, the hairs on the back of my neck were standing up. We hadn't passed anyone on the trail, but I still felt like someone was watching us. If they were hiding in the bushes, then we were sitting ducks. For the first time, I questioned whether it had been a good idea to come out that night. If someone had killed the girl on the trail, and he hadn't been caught yet, there was a chance that he was waiting for the chance to strike again.

The sight of Windhall calmed me a little bit. Even though most of Los Angeles thought of it as a creepy old murder site, it had become so familiar to me that I almost considered it a second home.

"Look," Madeleine said, pointing toward Windhall. "Someone's in the garden."

"Where?"

"In the yard," she said. "Can't you see him? He's standing by the swimming pool!"

As Madeleine spoke, the shadowy figure turned in our direction. It was too far for our quiet conversation to carry, of that I was almost certain. The lookout was on a cliff above Windhall, and there was a steep drop down the cliffside, at least sixty feet. The cliff tapered out into crumbled rocks and sedge, which collected in a drift at the back of Windhall. The back gate was fifteen feet high, edged with Victorian iron spikes.

We remained very still. As we watched, the figure stepped away from the pool and then meandered in the direction of the house. He disappeared beneath a warped fig tree, and we lost sight of him.

"Who do you think it is?" Madeleine asked. "It can't be Theo, can it?"

"No way," I said quietly. "Theo has a limp, remember?"

"Right. A friend, then?"

"Not a friend. Someone must have found a way to slip past the wall," I said, and I felt angry. "It's probably another vandal. We have to get inside."

"What?"

"That person we saw," I said. "What if he's going to break in?"

"Have you thought this through?"

"You don't have to come," I said. "Stay back here and tell me if anyone comes."

"How do you plan on getting down the side of the cliff?" she asked.

I shrugged. "I've done it before. It's not so bad down the path. There's a section where it's just trees and brush. I know this trail pretty well, you know."

Her eyes glittered in the darkness. "I'm coming with you," she said.

"You sure?"

"Absolutely."

I turned away from the lookout and headed down the path. The altitude dipped as the path wound down through the trees, and the chalky cliffs yielded to dirt clods and chaparral.

"Here," I said. "We'll have to go down here. We go any further, we'll wind up in someone's yard."

Madeleine was quiet as we picked our way down the hillside. I wasn't scared of heights, or spiders, or things that might be hiding in the darkness, so edging my way down a steep cliff wasn't a big deal for me. Being in the hospital for so long had numbed my scare reflex, in a way, and that was probably the only positive side of it. The idea of climbing over the fence of Windhall and facing off against another interloper didn't scare me, either; I was too fueled on the adrenaline of confronting someone. I had come to think of Windhall as my house, and I didn't like the thought of someone else setting foot inside without my permission.

As we made our way toward Windhall, we passed above the yard of the next-door neighbor. The elaborate swimming pool was illuminated, and the yard was immaculate. Sandstone lined the patio, and I could see the flicker of a television through one of the windows.

"Do you know who used to live there?" I asked, pointing.

"No idea."

"Otto Preminger," I said. "It was a beautiful estate, but they tore it down."

"You're awfully sentimental for someone under thirty," she said.

"Someone's going to tear Windhall down, too," I said. "They'll replace it with a garish monstrosity, something with an aggressive security system and absolutely no personality."

"Maybe you should buy it."

"Sure, let me take out a third and fourth mortgage."

We reached the back wall of Windhall.

"It's just here," I said, making my way over to the pile of rocks. "It's a bit of a climb, but if you let me get up, I can try to help you over. You have to be careful about the spikes, but there's a magnolia tree on the other side, and you can climb into that."

"Hailey," Mad said softly.

"If you've changed your mind, it's okay," I added.

"Hailey, *shhh*!"

I started to turn around, but before I could ask her what was wrong, someone clicked on a flashlight and shone it in my face. I was temporarily blinded by the beam and threw my hand up over my eyes.

"Who goes there?" called a male voice.

I eased myself in front of Madeleine. The voice was about fifteen feet away, standing at the base of the cliff. The beam was so bright that I couldn't make out anything but dazzling rivulets that shot off the side of the light.

"Get that out of my face, would you?"

The man wielding the flashlight hesitated, then aimed the light away from our faces. As my eyes recalibrated, I could see a vague silhouette behind the light.

"I'll ask you again," he said softly. His voice had a Southern lilt. "What's your business here?"

"We were standing on the fire trail," I said, pointing up. "I saw someone sneaking into Windhall."

The man mulled over the information. "What's your name?"

"Max Hailey."

"And your friend?"

"Madeleine Woolner," she spoke up. "Who are you?"

The man was silent for a long moment. "There's been a murder," he said. "A girl died up here a few days back. It's dangerous to be out wandering at night."

"The same could be said for you," I argued.

"Don't you worry about me," the man said, then laughed. "I'm the most dangerous thing out here tonight."

His voice was genteel, easy but polished. East Coast Southern, either South Carolina or Georgia, maybe Kentucky with a Yale education. My eyes had adjusted enough to see that he wasn't a policeman, or, at least, not a cop in uniform. He wore a linen shirt and slacks, a dark wool sweater. I couldn't see his face against the darkness, but I could see a sweep of dark hair. Without fully realizing it, I had edged in front of Madeleine again, in case the man proved to be dangerous.

"Go on, now," the man said. "It's time you headed home."

Madeleine and I didn't speak as we made our way back up the crumbling cliffside toward the fire trail. I kept my hand on her elbow, gripping her every time she stumbled or came close to falling.

By the time we reached the trail, I was angry.

"Let it go," Madeleine said, turning and seeing my face. "Let's just go home."

"He shouldn't be down there," I said. "He's not even a cop."

"How can you tell?"

"Trust me, I can tell. College wasn't too long ago."

"Right, sorry," Madeleine said, catching on. "You think he was the one to kill that girl?" She was only half serious. "I don't think he'd want to get bloodstains on those clothes."

"He's probably a neighbor," I said. "One of those people with too much spare time on his hands, making sure nobody trespasses."

"Let's go home, Hailey."

We walked back toward the car in silence, then climbed in and drove toward Los Feliz. When I dropped Madeleine off at her house, she turned to give me a sympathetic look. She squeezed my arm but got out of the car without a word.

Even after I dropped Madeleine off at home, I couldn't stop thinking of the man behind Windhall. It didn't matter to me who he was, or what he was doing there, so much as his air of entitlement. I had been surrounded by rich assholes my entire life, people who thought they could tell me what to do.

As I drove home, I remembered what my grandmother had told me about Theo.

"A gentleman, Max," she had said. "That's the thing I remember the most, in spite of all the other things that happened afterward. I can't shake the memory from my mind. Theo always treated me like a perfect gentleman."

TWO

The next morning I called Thierry as I drove to work.

He picked up after two rings.

"Hailey."

"Hey, Thierry," I said. "I need a favor."

There was a pause. "Am I on speakerphone?"

"I'm driving, T."

"You ever heard of Bluetooth?"

"Can't afford that shit. I'm a writer."

"You don't make enough money working as a writer, come back and work for me. I paid you good money."

"We're getting off topic," I said. "I need you to look into Wind-hall again."

"I've told you, Hailey, you need to give that shit up."

Here's what you need to know about Thierry: even though he was inching toward thirty-four, he looked like he'd woken up on the wrong side of middle-aged. Squat, with a pale face and a generous bald spot, T was the son of Polish immigrants. He spoke English with no discernible accent, though occasionally an off-phrase would slip in, like the way he referred to the epicenter of Los Angeles as "the Hollywood" and cobbled phrases together in the manner of someone who's learned English from a '70s sitcom.

Thierry was a friend and someone I turned to in emergencies, because his web of underground contacts was one of the most extensive networks in the city. I'd met him after dropping out of college. I'd come back to Los Angeles and found that my grandmother couldn't support me, so I got a job with an estate sales company owned by Thierry's uncle. The job was pretty simple: someone would die, and their kids or grandkids would hire us to come in, clean stuff up a bit, and sell it for a tidy bundle. My coworkers were a bunch of illiterate ex-cons for whom conversation was limited to the type of fractured run-ons you see printed on the wall of a restroom, but we got along well enough.

Thierry was our boss, and he ruled over us with aplomb. Here's something else to be said about Thierry: in a city filled with pretentious assholes who can't tell a Klee from a finger painting, Thierry managed to sort through all the bullshit and make a serious amount of cash. He might've seemed rough around the edges, but if you wanted to sell your stuff for the right amount, Thierry was your guy.

Thierry and I had stayed in touch after I saved up enough money to go back to school, and he'd even been one of the few guests at my grandmother's funeral. When I came back from Illinois, a journalism dropout with a stack of bills and not much else, Thierry had reached out and offered me a place on his team. I'd declined, but Thierry had become an important contact nonetheless, and he'd even been partially responsible for the story that had started my flimsy career and earned me a contract writing for the *Los Angeles Lens*.

Thierry knew that I was fascinated by Windhall, but it had been a matter of debate between us for years. It wasn't unusual for people who grew up in Los Angeles to have a strong opinion about the Langley trial: you were either convinced that he did it, or adamant that he'd been framed. Thierry didn't entirely approve of my interest in Theo and Windhall, but he still kept an eye out for anything that came from Windhall.

"Look," I persisted. "Madeleine and I went there last night. Something's going on, but I'm not sure what it is. You heard anything from your contacts?"

"Take me off speakerphone, Hailey," Thierry said. "You know I hate that shit."

"Still driving."

"Is the phone sitting in your lap? I'm in your fucking lap, aren't I?"

"'Course not," I lied.

Thierry's voice went quiet as he muttered something, and I realized he must be talking to someone at work. I could hear other voices in the background, and then Thierry came back to me.

"Someone called me about a month ago." His voice drifted up from my crotch. "Wanted to sell me something that belonged to Theo. Or maybe it didn't belong to him, but it had to do with him. Said it was some kind of missing film."

I frowned. "He's full of shit," I said. "Everyone knows that Theo's last film is gone. If it still existed, it would be worth a fucking fortune."

"Yeah, I blew him off. Guy seemed a little weird. He's a professional magician, for fuck's sake."

"You haven't heard anything else?"

"That's it. I'll send you the guy's number, if I find it. He lives with his mom, you guys probably have a lot to talk about."

"I live in my gran's *house*, asshole, there's a difference."

"Yeah, yeah, Hailey, single white males living rent-free. Sounds the same to me."

"Speaking of Theo," I said. "You hear anything about the journals?"

"*No*, Hailey, Jesus Christ. Those journals don't exist. I'm telling you, someone burned them but good."

"They exist," I said. "I'm going to find them."

"Yeah, yeah." I could almost hear him rolling his eyes.

"Put me in touch with that magician, would you? I'd like to check it out, just in case." And with that, I hung up.

Theo's last movie was called *Last Train to Avalon*. The film had been mid-production when Eleanor was murdered, and for many Langley fanatics, it was the holy grail of iconography. All of Theo's infamous team had worked on it, including Eleanor as the leading lady. Stories and snatches of what the film had been about were open to speculation; since Theo always kept his films under a tight protective seal until they were finished, nobody outside the production had been allowed to see the script before he started filming.

Last Train to Avalon had always been a hot topic of debate in Los Angeles, and over the years it had become a kind of urban myth. Even those who were convinced that Theo had killed Eleanor were forced to concede that *Avalon* would have put Theo up there with the rest of the great directors: your Hitchcocks, Capras, and Langs. Even though the movie had been shut down and locked away after Eleanor died, stories had leaked about production. All remaining copies of the script had been destroyed, but I had heard enough about it to know the gist of the story: a hapless actor comes out to Los Angeles, hoping to strike it big in the film industry. When he gets there, of course, he finds that the whole place is smoke and mirrors.

If this sounds tame, stay tuned. It soon becomes clear that the only way for the young man to succeed in Los Angeles is to partake in an ongoing cycle of abuse involving the wealthy men who run Hollywood and the desperate young women who are powerless to protect themselves. In addition to being a revolutionary statement, the script made no secret about who it was condemning.

According to popular belief, Eleanor had been killed because she was one of the writers behind the film. Some people maintained that Theo had been the studio lackey who had done the job; others said that if the death hadn't gotten so much attention, Theo would have been the next one to be killed.

I had always been curious about the movie, but I was just as curious to see the set that Theo had built for it. Avalon was reportedly a miniature scale model of Los Angeles. It was made of tiny buildings and wide boulevards, crooked alleyways and pepper trees hanging over Hollywood Boulevard, back when that part of town still had a bit of green. Gran explained that Theo was so precise in shots that when he was in the planning stages of a film, he liked to have a miniature set to refer to. Sometimes these sets made it into the film itself, used in establishing shots and overhead angles.

Before the murder, people called Theo a magician, and in the 1940s, his kind of talent would have seemed like magic. While most sets were made of plywood and sealing wax, Theo's sets took months of painstaking labor and attention to detail. For *The Queen's Shadow*, Theo had ordered a miniature Versailles built in a warehouse in Glendale. His production assistants scoured Los Angeles, buying up mirrors of every shape and size to line the fabled hallways. Gold leaf and trinkets of every shade of yellow were purchased for the set walls. Old windows were broken apart to construct the miniature chandeliers that adorned the ceilings, and all the frescoes were painstakingly re-created by one of Theo's favorite set designers.

Theo was adamant that no spectators or guests ever intrude on his filming, and in that way, his sets remained among the most exclusive rooms in Los Angeles. His protocols didn't necessarily change after a movie had wrapped, either: those sets that were able to be disassembled were packed away in crates and relegated to a top secret storage facility, while the larger, freestanding sets had a mysterious way of disappearing.

Avalon was fascinating, that was for certain, but there was something else that I was keen to get my hands on, and that was Theo's journals.

If Theo's journals still existed, and I was almost positive that they did, there was a chance that they could prove who killed Eleanor. The journals were the reason the murder trial had been thrown, and Theo had been allowed to walk free. During the trial, the prosecution had felt that the case was on the verge of being dismissed, and so the chief trial prosecutor had done something very, very stupid: he hired someone to break into Theo's house.

What they were looking for was never clear, but what they found were Theo's journals. An avid registrar, Theo was known for writing down every mundane detail that happened on and off set. His journals were always the same; slim parchment notebooks purchased from a drugstore on Vine Street.

And inside of them, the prosecution insisted, was the key to why he had murdered Eleanor.

———————————

My office was in Hollywood, just off Sunset and Wilcox. The office took up the whole second floor of a run-down apartment building done up in the classic Spanish hacienda style that had been popular in the late '20s and '30s. Spiky palms and banana plants littered the courtyard with leaves that looked like moldy strips of wallpaper, and at least once a week, some homeless guy would pass out there. Once, thirty or forty years before, an aspiring actress had leaped from a fourth-story balcony to her death, and that meant that every once in a while, ghoul crews came to visit the spot and ogle the dent in the ground where her head had smacked the pavement.

Once you got past the homeless people and the suicides, our building had a lot of charm. The lobby still had an old reception desk, complete with pigeonholes and mail slots. Old wallpaper and crown molding that needed to be replaced lent an eerie air to the lobby, which was always empty. The elevator had an intersecting iron door, but it hadn't worked in the last decade, so everyone took the stairs. It was all a bit macabre, but most of the time I felt like I worked for the last decent publication in Los Angeles.

The *Los Angeles Lens* was a quirky magazine that highlighted the underground, the bizarre, and the outright disturbing. It had been founded in the mid-'70s, and, once, it had real clout. The couches in the lobby had been occupied by the likes of Eve Babitz and Marcel Duchamp, and nearly every left political rally began in the court-yard of our building. We championed the neopolitical losers; the left-wing nutcases; gay, trans, and gender-queer quasi terrorists who wouldn't blink at the thought of bombing out the office building of a racist, rightist regime. The Laurel Canyon crowd used to get stoned and drop acid in the office of Ford Fordham, our editor in chief.

When Ford had announced his retirement three months earlier, everyone wondered if the magazine would finally go under. We'd made the switch to an online format six months before, and Ford had insisted he wasn't the right man for the job anymore. The magazine had changed a lot since its inception. We still had healthy cultural and political sections, but our readers were mostly interested in cult: strange murders, spooky history, speakeasy bars, and boarded-up hotels. We wrote about places like Necromance and the Museum of Jurassic Technology. The most hits our magazine had gotten was the creepy story about the Cecil Hotel, where a Canadian tourist had mysteriously drowned herself in the rooftop water tank.

The office itself was a tribute to everything weird in Los Ange-les. Taxidermied animals sat on a shelf in our entrance room, which was ruled over by an enormous secretary desk. One of the old editors had scored the desk from a massive drug-bust estate sale in Cala-basas, and when he had disassembled it to fit it through the door-way, he'd uncovered eight bags of cocaine tucked up inside the legs.

We'd taken the doors off all the bedrooms and turned them into offices, and even though we suffered from the occasional bit of loose ceiling plaster, everyone who worked at the *Lens* loved their job.

Ever since Mad and I had gone to see Windhall, I had been thinking about the dead art student. I hadn't wanted to write about it, not at first; I didn't want to pick up some pulpy piece of murder gossip bound to pull readers from *TMZ*. The more I thought about it, though, the more it made sense that I should be the one to unspool this new story. Nobody else at the *Lens* cared about Theo, at least, not to the degree that I did. There was only one person I was going to have to convince, and he had about as much sense as a three-day-old corpse left out in the sun: my new editor.

When Ford retired, he told us that he had chosen a replacement, someone much more culturally attuned and capable of steering the magazine toward a younger audience. The new editor in chief was nearly the exact opposite of everything that Ford had represented, and I tried to keep this in mind as I walked through the lobby.

I reached his door, and found that it was open.

"Right, Pulitzers. The only award that Los Angeles cares about is the Oscar. Golden Globes? Don't make me laugh. Grammys, maybe, but you want respect, you need a big O."

I rapped on the door, and my editor turned to give me a thumbs-up.

"Gotta go, Dad. Yeah, yeah, see you there."

Brian turned off his Bluetooth and grinned at me. "Hailey's comet," he said. "What's good?"

"I've got an idea for a story."

"Well, step on in, brother."

Brian was a full six inches shorter than me, with a defiant red pompadour that could, on a day without humidity, raise his height a good two inches. Brian wasn't a bad guy, per se, but when I met him, he wasn't even vaguely interested in writing. His mother's side of the family was heavily invested in NASCAR, and up until six months ago, that's where Brian's life had been headed. The fact that he was Ford's son didn't seem to imbue him with any bohemian leanings, either. The *Lens* had even done a piece about his racing career—in one of the photos, he posed with a former Playmate of the Month; in another, he did loops around a track in San Pedro that Marty, our staff photographer, captured.

"Dude sprayed himself with Axe body spray before every lap," Marty had complained, and all the underlings at the paper had laughed. Still, nobody had really had a problem with Brian until he decided to take over his dad's position at the magazine.

Brian had been editor for only three months, but he had already made some drastic changes. Even though Ford had assured everyone that his son would continue to guide the magazine in a similar direction, their taste in stories was so vastly different that sometimes I felt like the office was being featured on a bad reality show. While our magazine had once felt like a sagging mansion filled with precious, broken objects, Brian's influence had already begun to present itself in the form of sports banners, advertisements for nightclubs and new deejays, and a collection of Jason Statham movie posters in Ford's old office.

Still, I could see that Brian had incredible business acumen, and in brief, startling moments, I felt that he might actually be able to salvage the *Lens* from bankruptcy.

"What's on your mind, my little asteroid?" Brian asked.

"I want to write about the dead girl," I said. "I think that Theo might be back in Los Angeles, and if I can connect this new murder to Theo, it would make a great story."

"Which dead girl are we talking about?" He took a sip of coffee.

"The art student who was found dead outside Windhall." I patted my chest. "You know, the one who got stabbed?"

"Right, right. I've been reading about that."

"The murder is a tribute to Theo Langley," I said. "You know that, right?"

"Who?"

"The director who killed his leading lady in the middle of filming a movie," I said. "Back in the forties. Trust me, you know who he is."

Brian narrowed his eyes and took a sip of coffee. "Langley," he mused aloud. "The name rings a bell."

"That Nirvana song 'Dead Roses'—it's all about the murder."

Brian's eyes lit up. "Shit, yeah, I know that song! That was my ringtone for two years. 'Down in the thorns, Macy . . . Macy . . .'"

"'The girl with no shoes, hazy, dark skies . . .'" I tunelessly joined in, mildly resenting the fact that it might count as a bonding moment with Brian.

"Yeah, man, I know it! That's about something that really happened? What were the words, something about climbing a tall tower to fill a basket with stars? The thorn king catches her in his claws?"

"Yes," I said. "The thorn king is Theodore Langley."

"Huh. So, what's your story?"

"He's been gone this whole time," I said. "But if there's even a slight chance that he's back, and nobody else knows about it, we can run the story before anyone else does."

Brian narrowed his eyes. "What makes you think he's back?"

"All right, I don't have any proof," I said. "But I'm working on that."

"I don't want any wild speculation or conspiracy theories," he said. "Come back to me when you have some proof."

"Sure. Look, I have a list of people I can interview. This could be a huge story, Brian."

I could sense that he was losing interest.

"There used to be a reward for information leading to Theo's arrest," I went on. "Something like fifty thousand dollars."

His eyes widened. "You should have led with that. Is there still a reward?"

"No," I admitted. "The guy offering it died a few years ago. Reuben Engel, he was the producer of Theo's last movie."

"Cool story. Hey, I have a little announcement. I'm going to tell everyone officially on Monday, but I figured I could tell you now, since you're sort of senior here."

He steepled his fingers and grinned at me. I was annoyed that he had interrupted my pitch, but I decided to play along. Placating Brian was a good step to getting story approval.

"What's the announcement?"

"It's gotta be secret, though. Can you keep a secret?"

"Sure."

"We found a buyer," he said. "That's why we have a bunch of money. We paid off a stack of old bills and everything. Man, I'm killing it at this editing job."

It took a moment for his words to register. "Brian, what do you mean, you found a *buyer*?"

"Time Inc.," he said. "They bought the magazine. We're now under the Time umbrella."

"You're shitting me."

"It's great, right? No more bankruptcy, my friend. Out with the old, in with the new. Now that we have some money, I'm thinking about renovating this whole place."

"Brian, Time is going to fold us up into another one of their origami animals and put us on a shelf. We'll be plastic. They'll strip every ounce of character from the *Lens*, and we'll be just like everybody else."

"You don't need to worry about that."

"The only difference between the *Lens* and the *Huffington Post* is that we've got goddamned integrity," I said. "Why didn't you call a meeting and consult the rest of the editors?"

"I'm editor in chief," he said, and his smile began to fade. "I'm the *boss*, Hailey. Sometimes the boss has to make tough calls. If you ever rise above the position of ground-level employee, you'll probably come to understand that."

"People are going to be pissed."

"They're going to get paychecks," he said, tapping the side of his head. "Integrity isn't worth more than a place to sleep. We done here? I've got real work to do."

I rubbed my jaw. "I'm going to go ahead and start researching the Langley story," I said. "It's a good piece."

"No, you're not," he said. "You have plans tonight?"

"No, why?"

"You're going to see a band in Echo Park," he said. "Kind of electro-soul. They're called Rigor Mormon. I need a thousand words by Monday."

"But—"

"Marty's going along as your photographer."

I tried not to sound exasperated. "Brian," I said. "Ford used to let me choose my monthly feature. I want to get started on the Langley story before someone else gets the jump on it."

"You're not writing the Langley story."

"Why not?"

"I'm not interested," he said simply. "Sounds kind of dull. Here are the tickets for the show, by the way. Get there early. I want you to talk to the band before they go on."

THREE

I was at my desk, packing up my things, when the phone rang.

"Max Hailey."

"Yeah, this is Dexter," came a man's voice. "I'm at your house."

I frowned. "I think you have the wrong number."

"We had an appointment," he said, annoyed. "I'm here to inspect your roof."

"Shit! Sorry, I forgot. Any way we can reschedule?"

"Can't come back for at least ten days," he said. "You know there's a storm coming on Thursday, right? The whole city will be underwater."

I cursed under my breath, then glanced at my watch. Four-fifteen. Getting to my house in Laurel Canyon would take twenty minutes without traffic, but I didn't know how long the roof inspection would take. If it went past six, I would be late getting to the show in Echo Park.

"Stay there," I said. "I'm leaving my office right now."

I made good time, and when I pulled up in front of my house, I saw a beat-up blue pickup truck blocking the drive. I parked behind it, then climbed out of my car and walked up the drive.

"Sorry I'm late," I called.

The man standing on my footpath turned and shrugged. "Look, we charge by the hour," he said. "I've already been here for an hour, and I could technically charge you for that, but I'm not going to."

"Thanks," I said, slightly suspicious. "Why not?"

"I can tell you're going to be a valuable customer," he said, then reached up and tugged on a clump of morning glory. "Your roof has completely gone to shit."

I ran a hand through my hair. "Look, I don't need a new roof," I said. "I really just called about the hole in the kitchen ceiling."

"You ever go to the dentist for a cleaning and leave with a root canal?"

"Come inside," I said. "Let's talk in there."

The house had belonged to my grandmother. It was designed as a sloping Alsatian cottage, the type you might see in a forest after losing the path. A witch might live inside, or a band of elves. Every single Halloween, I got the most trick-or-treaters out of anyone in my neighborhood, because the nearby dwellings were, on one side, a boring house of glass and concrete and on the other, a squat row of '70s flats made out of cheap stained wood.

If I weren't nostalgic, I would sell my property and cash in early. My gran had bought the place with cash in the 1940s; back then, land was affordable and houses had a way of getting vacated without notice. Theater troupes would blow in from out of town, stay for a week or a few months, then depart, usually leaving half their things behind. Stars had more money than sense, and when film studios made the transition from silent movies to talking pictures, a whole rash of silent gods went bankrupt. Gran bought the place from one of these silent divas who went broke on opium and alcohol; the actress had purchased it from the man who built it, who was a set designer at Metro-Goldwyn-Mayer.

It had never been a completely solid house, even when I lived there with Gran. With every rain, a spate of leaks would open up throughout the house. We had a special collection of thrift store pots and pans stashed away in a box for storms, and at the first sign of cloudy skies, we'd break out the box and position our cache in all the usual spots.

I'd been working so much lately that I hadn't had a chance to fix the roof, but the week before, a great big hole had opened up in the kitchen ceiling. I hadn't realized that there were holes in the main roof until sunshine came streaming through, and tendrils of morning glory started to poke down among the cabinets. I could almost hear a mental cash register *chinging* away in Dexter's mind as I led him through the house.

"All right," Dexter said, as we moved into the kitchen. He looked up through the hole in the ceiling, which had grown at least three inches in the last few days. "We've got a problem."

"Just one problem?"

"You're going to have to replace the entire roof," he said.

His words didn't register right away.

"It's just a little hole. Can't we throw some duct tape and shingles on it?"

"I'd say the problem's at least a decade old," he said. "You've got dry rot and a whole dynasty of termites living in your roof."

"Shit. How much does a roof cost these days?"

"We can talk about that," he said. "The roof is separate from the ceiling, of course, and you'll have to replace that, too. How do you reach the attic?"

"I used to use the stairs, but now we just need a ladder," I said, gesturing to the hole in the ceiling. "I'll give you a leg up, you can hoist yourself the rest of the way."

"You think this is funny?"

"No, of course not." My smile evaporated. "This way."

It was hard not to feel a certain amount of pride in the house, even as Dexter went looking for problems. First-time visitors usually got a kick out of the uneven gingerbread portholes, the sloping walls and the hardwood floors inlaid with little mother-of-pearl diamonds. Bookcases were built into at least one wall in every room, and the stairs leading up to the attic were a particular point of pride. The original owner had stashed the staircase behind a small rounded door in the library, the type Snow White's dwarves might have departed through each day.

Dexter didn't find it cute. "You expect me to fit through there?"

"It's the only way up."

"For the love of God," he muttered, getting on his knees. "If I find out this is some kind of practical joke, I swear to you—"

After ten minutes of awkward maneuvering, Dexter and I emerged in the attic. A blotchy constellation of light shone through pinprick holes in the roof, and I sighed, looking down at the floor. I could see termite damage left and right, and tried to remember the last time I had come up here.

"You'd better not step anywhere," I said.

"I realize that. You're going to have to find some way to get all this stuff down, and soon, or it's going to fall through." He narrowed his eyes at a set of trunks in the corner. "Those boxes heavy?"

"Probably."

"Let's go back down," he said. "I'll give you a quote."

Once we were standing back in the kitchen, Dexter took out a notepad. I discreetly glanced at my phone and saw that it was almost six o'clock.

"I have to go soon," I said. "Any idea what it might cost to fix this?"

"We're looking at about fourteen grand," he said. "Of course, that only covers the damage to the infrastructure. You want someone to come and fix this little gingerbread cottage roof, it's probably going to be another five."

"Jesus."

"Can you afford that?"

"Not even close," I said.

"Might be cheaper to tear the place down and sell it," he said.

"I grew up here," I said quickly.

"Well, you could consider taking out a second mortgage," he said.

"It's already got a second mortgage."

Dexter sighed and tore off the sheet of paper, then handed it to me. "You don't have many options," he said. "If you wait for a miracle, you're going to lose the entire house. Give me a call when you've had a chance to think about it."

Echo Park wasn't too far away, but traffic in Los Angeles was unpredictable, and there was no telling how long it might take me to find a parking space. The venue would undoubtedly have an overpriced valet service, but it was a point of pride for me that I almost never paid for parking.

I made it in twenty minutes, then found the venue and started the parking search. Since it was Friday, the neighborhood was hopping, and most of the streets were packed. People walked in pairs and threesomes down the sidewalk, laughing and leaning against each other, gearing up for a night out.

A parking spot appeared on the block ahead of me, and I headed toward it and hit my turn signal. I was starting to reverse into it when a motorcycle swooped in.

"Hey! Asshole!" I jammed on the horn, but the motorcyclist pretended to ignore me, then climbed off his bike and started to remove his helmet. Hitting my emergency blinkers, I put my car in park and climbed out. Cars honked as they passed me, because I was blocking the street, but I was too indignant to care.

"Hey!"

I walked toward the motorcyclist, but the man dug in his pocket for something, pretending not to see me.

"I'm talking to you," I said. "That was my spot!"

"Oh, was it? Did you put your little beach chair next to the curb to indicate that it was yours?"

"I see how it is," I said. "You're one of those entitled biker assholes who splits lanes and sticks his dick into every non-permitted bit of curb. Congratulations on being superior to everyone else in the city."

He gave me a pitying smile. "Well done, guy. You've figured me out."

All through high school, I'd managed to stay under the radar and avoid fights by being smarter than the other boys. I didn't have too much trouble, since my high school was filled with stoners and the children of hippies, but on the few occasions when someone did try to start shit with me, I'd cut him down to size with a few acidic remarks. It had never failed, but now I was out of practice, and I couldn't help feeling lame sparring with the motorcyclist.

"Move your bike," I said.

"Enjoy your night," he replied. Plenty of paid parking around here."

He started to walk away.

"How do you know I won't do something to your bike once you're gone?" I called after him, and I was pleased to see that this stopped him. He turned around and started walking back toward me, taking his phone out of his pocket. He moved past me and bent in front of my car, then took a picture of my license plate.

"Thanks for the warning," he said, patting me on the shoulder as he walked past.

Traffic had started to pile up behind me, and the air was filled with the sound of honking. I was so pissed off when I climbed back in my car that I almost reversed over the man's bike, but since he had a picture of my license plate, it was no longer an option. I gave myself a moment to breathe, then started my car up again and continued looking for parking.

The man's remarks stayed with me as I scanned the streets, too distracted to even think about heading to the show and working that night. I was starting to feel like I was out of touch with the rest of Los Angeles, the bearded hipsters with leather jackets and worn-in denim shirts; the artisanal coffee drinkers and people who could afford overpriced yoga and stand-up comedy classes. What made it worse was that I wasn't yet thirty and already committed to a house that was falling apart. I couldn't afford to fix it, couldn't bear to part with it, and now I was virtually stuck in a career track that was starting to feel a lot like dancing for an idiotic royal regime while wearing bells on my ankles.

I was so distracted that I turned a corner and nearly slammed into the back of an SUV. I stomped on the brakes and sat there for a moment, gathering my wits. Before I could change my mind, I hit my turn signal and flipped my car around. I wasn't going to make it to the show that night, Brian's wrath be damned.

I crested a hill and headed toward the freeway leading away from Echo Park. I felt a thrill down my spine as I saw the city glittering in the distance, freeways streaming in and out like arteries of some black heart. There were glowing lights and ribbons of road, buildings and towers like dark cathedrals. It was intoxicating and beautiful, the cars slipping in and out of lanes beside me like darting fish. It was my city. I still felt the same thrill of possibility that I had felt when I was a kid, driving out of the valley in the nighttime.

Beneath the freeway, all the houses winked and bowed their heads and disappeared into nothing, a swirl of gray and black. Traffic was light heading north, since it was well past rush hour. I took the Vermont Street exit, then turned onto Beverly Boulevard. *Seven fifty-two.* I was definitely going to miss the Rigor Mormon show. I could only hope that the band had enough decently filmed YouTube videos for me to half-ass an article to go along with Marty's photographs. *Rigor Fucking Mormon,* I thought to myself. *Only in Los Angeles.*

Outside my window, expensive designer brick-and-mortars yielded to apartments, then cute bungalows with small gardens. The houses suddenly evolved into mansions, austere mock Tudors and Spanish colonials fringed by palm trees and perfect lawns. I drove up to a stoplight across from the Beverly Hills Hotel, then the light changed and I drove across Sunset, up into one of the wealthiest and strangest neighborhoods in Los Angeles.

It's notoriously difficult to trespass in Beverly Hills, unless you're a marathon walker or an ace on roller skates: "No Parking" signs are posted every ten feet for almost two square miles, which makes unexpected visitors extremely unlikely. Nobody who lives in this part of Los Angeles needs to leave their car on the street, anyway: they've all got long, luxurious driveways and three-car garages hidden behind thick hedges.

There are five parking spots—I'm not kidding, and you can believe I've done my research—where you won't be ticketed, towed, or bullied by the neighbors. Three of them are next to a little public park that's smaller than my yard, and the other two are on a dead-end lane guarded by a big weeping willow. Those two spots are a ten-minute walk from Windhall, and since I couldn't park anywhere near the great house itself, I had parked under the tree whenever I wanted to see Theo's house.

I was in luck: the dark little lane was empty, and I parked, then switched my phone to silent and tucked it in my pocket.

It was easier to sneak into Windhall over the back wall, but this time, I didn't want to risk running into the man with the Southern accent, on the off chance that he had come back. I was going to have to risk going over the front wall.

The wall was topped with a row of gothic iron spikes, but the vines had grown over them in sections, making it possible to surmount the wall without stabbing a hand or leg in the process. I found a thick branch in one of the sections of ivy, then hoisted myself up slowly, grabbing other branches as I went. I reached the top of the wall and swung a leg over, and was nearly across when my leg caught and I felt an awful scrape. There was a tear and then a feeling of wet warmth, and then I fell headlong over the wall, into the garden.

I lay there for a moment, praying that I hadn't broken a limb in the process, then gingerly patted myself down and decided that everything was fine. When I sat up, I realized that I was lying next to a pale statue of a young woman, who gazed down in blind consternation. Six inches to the left, and I might have paralyzed myself by falling on her. Sobered slightly by this fact, I sat up and took inventory of my surroundings.

The main house crouched in the garden as though it knew that I was coming. It was a sprawling, curious thing, with windows for eyes. I had landed just behind the gardener's cottage, which was seated at the base of the drive, and just beyond it, I could see the three-car garage. The apartment above the garage had once held Theo's household staff before he let them all go.

I started walking across the grounds, keeping my eyes on Windhall. The upper gables loomed against the night sky, a staggering dark form. The house looked the same as it did in the nightmares I used to have; the towers of Theo's castle piercing a wounded sky, the leering doors, the broken paths. I imagined the night of the party, all those years ago, all the Hollywood royalty gathered beneath one roof, spilling out into the gardens below, toasting to their shared successes and never dreaming that one of their own would die before morning.

As I crossed the garden, I started to feel the tingling anticipation I always felt right before I sneaked into an abandoned property. The grounds had gone wild in the decades of solitude. Foxtails grew up to my chest, strange wild things that belonged on a foreign planet. Deep holes marred the ground around the path from the gardener's cottage, as though someone had dug in, actually believing that Theo kept buried gold in his yard. It was one of the many rumors that had come out around the trial, adding to the public's convictions against him. Windhall was one of the few places in Los Angeles that didn't change every few years, which was a nice bit of relief in a constantly shifting city.

Beyond the carriage house lay the garage, which I could barely make out in the deepening gloom. It looked too austere to hold anything but ghosts, and I pictured a chauffeur rolling up the doors to let out an expensive car. When Theo still lived at Windhall, all the staff had worn crisp, customized uniforms; I had seen pictures from some of their gatherings. They always lurked in the background, hands folded in their laps or at their sides, mouths turned down in the suggestion of unease and propriety.

I lingered in the garden for a moment to make sure that nobody was watching me, then made my way toward the main house.

The front door was carved with the faces of angels, but the sun had done its damage, and their eyes had faded into blank, staring orbs. The wood bore deep gouges, as though someone had slashed the door repeatedly. They had wanted to draw blood. I thought of all the dazzling gods and starlets who had made their way across the threshold all those years before.

I made my way around the side of the house, through the weeds and bracken, toward the kitchen. The path was made of broken cobblestones, and I nearly tripped a few times before catching myself.

Last time I visited Windhall, I had sneaked into the house through a servant's entrance, which stood at the end of the cobbled pathway. Besides the path, an overgrown kitchen garden had gone ragged in the abandoned decades, and only scraggly weeds remained in the dirt. The original stone perimeters were still in place, and I could see that the garden must have been large enough to feed a Victorian family of a modest size. I suddenly remembered that Windhall had been built as a rehabilitation facility for young women recovering from tuberculosis, a few years before Theo bought it and converted it into a dwelling.

I put my hand on the kitchen doorknob, expecting to find resistance, but it was unlocked. I stood there for a moment, contemplating all the implications of an open door. I thought of the man outside Windhall who had told me and Madeleine to leave. There was a chance that I would find someone waiting in the house for me. But that thought wasn't enough to bar my entrance.

I opened the door and paused, then stepped inside.

A gust of warm air washed out. I coughed on the smell of mold and slow decay, then blinked into the dimness. I turned on my phone's flashlight and passed it around the room. Last time I had visited, the cups and saucers had all been in their individual cupboards, hidden behind dusty panes of glass. Stacks of white plates had stood against the back counter, as though waiting for a Sunday afternoon lunch that would never come.

Now, however, I could see that changes had been made. All the dishes had been packed away in boxes, some of which sat on the floor and counters, flaps open. The dust had resettled. *Someone has been here, and recently, too.*

I lingered in the kitchen for a moment, wondering if the packed plates were a sign that I should leave.

I had once pored over a glowing editorial in *Architectural Digest*, published a year after Theo had first moved into the house and started to renovate. The article showed a dozen or more photographs of the host and his house, accompanied by staccato praise and flowery sentiments: *Windhall's grand foyer welcomes guests into Theodore Langley's updated California Victorian*, one caption read, while according to another, *The ballroom summons up images of bejeweled maidens lingering at the edge of the room, waiting for a dance with their handsome beaux*.

Unable to tear myself away, I moved forward, through a set of swinging doors that led into a long room lined with windows. Had it been daytime, the windows would have shown the garden, toward Westwood and Brentwood, and beyond that, out of sight, the ocean. This was the dining room.

The dining room had also been lavished with high praise, and photographs showed the long antique table holding court over the stately room. In the pictures, high-backed chairs stood at attention, carved from mahogany or some other dark wood. The room was illuminated from the west and north by banks of windows.

It took a moment for my eyes to adjust to the gloom, and I could immediately see that someone had been in this room, too. The chairs were set on the side of the room, and the great table had been cleaned with furniture polish. Last time I had visited, some poor creature had crawled atop the table and died, wearing its own collapsed skin like a mantle. The creature and its bones had been summarily cleared away, however, and all signs of death in the room had vanished.

I was about to move on when I noticed a stack of papers on a small bench at the edge of the room. The papers did not interest me as much as what sat atop them, and I let my eyes adjust to the gloom once more to be sure of what I saw. I was looking at a slim black iPhone. Whoever owned that phone was probably still inside the house.

A gust of wind rattled the windowpanes, and I jumped. The sounds of wind and branches prevented me from hearing anything else, but I hadn't sensed that anyone else was inside the house. It was possible that whoever had cleaned up had simply forgotten their phone, but seeing the purged state of the kitchen and the dining room made me think twice. A change had happened, and for the first time in a long time, I felt afraid.

I waited for a few minutes to see if I could hear anyone moving around, but there were no voices or creaking floorboards. After deciding that I was alone, I crossed the room and picked up the iPhone. The battery was low but still had juice, low enough that it was possible that the man had left the phone the previous night. The phone was password protected, and the lock screen image was a generic photo of bamboo. I stuck the phone in my pocket and left the dining room.

Next to the dining room was the fabled grand foyer, and beyond that, a small, empty room. I pushed open the door and walked through a hallway that split off into three different directions, choosing to go down the path on the right. I shone my flashlight through the room to illuminate walls lined with bookshelves. I was in the library. The floorboards were still in good condition, but a thick green rug had been tossed aside and lay in a heap at the edge of the room. *Discarded skin.*

The light from my flashlight flickered over walls shot through with cracks, over the gilded ceiling and the furniture. Faces peered out of the woodwork, and seeing them gave me a nasty shock. They were carved into the mantel of the fireplace, their sunken eyes seeming to beg me to go no further. I stumbled over the carpet and then regained my footing, and shone the light across the crumbling silk curtains.

I stopped when I saw a painting resting against one of the shelves. I wouldn't have recognized it if it weren't for my grandmother, because she had always loved the painter. It was a Paul de Longpré print, roses sketched against a brown background. I had seen it before, because she had had a print hanging in her kitchen, and it was one of the things that I had kept when she gave me the house. I had always liked it because it looked like a work in progress, less refined than some of his other works, and yet still so effortless. I liked to imagine that Longpré had sat down to breakfast one morning and started etching something, and beauty came so naturally to him that the roses had simply bloomed out of his fingertips.

The painting was small, and before I could second-guess what I was doing, I tucked it inside my satchel. If the house was getting cleaned up to be sold, I wanted to claim a piece of it for myself.

The house still had a pulse, even after all this time. I could almost hear voices echoing down the hallway, laughing and moaning softly by turns. There was a round window on the stair landing, and panes of glass were missing. The night sky was trapped in the window spokes. Starlight spilled onto the walls and the floor, painting everything blue gold. Skeleton moon, devil moon. *I see you.*

I made my way upstairs, to the second floor, and followed the feeble light of my cell phone through the second-story hallway. The light illuminated the peeling wallpaper, dazzling and strange; twirling flowers against a red background. A door leaned open at the end of the hallway, and I headed toward it. After a moment's hesitation, I stepped forward and pushed the door open.

As soon as I stepped through, I felt like I was falling through empty space. A small light glowed in the corner of the room, and two silhouettes crouched beside it. I had been right in thinking that someone else was in the house, someone who had left the kitchen door open and forgotten their cell phone downstairs.

A brief moment collapsed in which it was still possible to turn and erase my steps, charge headlong back down the hallway, and crash out of the house before they realized that I had ever been there, but I hesitated. One of the figures turned, and then it was too late.

"Max Hailey," he said, then stood and stretched his arms. "I thought you might come back."

It was the man with the Southern accent. A freestanding plastic lantern stood on the floor of the room, projecting light against the wall. I could see now that they were working to patch up the fading wallpaper.

"Hello," I said, hoping a confident voice would hide my trembling hands.

The other man stood from his position by the wall, then stuck his hands in his pockets and glanced between us. He was average height, somewhere in his late fifties, with the salt-and-pepper dark hair to prove it. His sweater looked expensive, maybe cashmere or angora.

"Who's this?" he said to his companion.

"It's a journalist," said the man from the South. "He came here with his friend last night."

It took me a moment to catch his meaning. He knew that I was a journalist: he had investigated me after our encounter the previous evening. I wasn't too hard to find online, because some of my articles for the *Lens* had gone quasi-viral. I wondered how many Google pages he had gone through; if he had discovered my arrest record. Even though the light in the room wasn't great, I had a much better view of his face than I had the night before. He had light eyes and a square nose, and the corners of his mouth turned up a little bit, as though he was on the verge of smiling.

"Call the police." This was from the man with the dark hair. He cocked his head and looked at me. "You're aware that you're trespassing, aren't you? Of course you are. The gates and doors were locked."

"Someone forgot to lock the door downstairs." I narrowed my eyes at him. "Let's not be pedantic, though. Who are you?"

The man gave me an indulgent smile. "Leland, where's your phone?"

The Southern gentleman patted his pockets. "I must have left it downstairs," he said.

I realized that the phone in my pocket belonged to the Southern gentleman, who now had a name. *Leland.*

"Look, Ben, I don't think it's necessary," Leland went on. "I'm sure that Mr. Hailey was just leaving."

I should have taken the opening, but I couldn't resist. "I'll leave when I'm good and ready," I said. "Tell me what you're doing here. Are you going to tear this place down and turn it into a tacky apartment complex?"

Ben frowned at my satchel. "What do you have there?" he said.

I remembered the Longpré painting from the library with a sick little jolt. "My bag is my business," I said.

"No, let me see that," he said, crossing the distance between us.

"It's nothing," I said, stepping backward, even as Ben reached for my satchel. Clouds of dust rose up into the light from the lamp on the floor, and our shadows made crazy dancers against the wall.

Before I could stop him, Ben deftly reached into my open satchel and snatched the painting. His eyes narrowed when he saw what he was holding.

"This belongs to Windhall," he said. "I'm calling the police."

"Ben, wait," Leland said. "We don't need to make a big fuss over this. We've got the painting now, and there's been no other harm done."

"We don't know that," Ben said. "He should be arrested for breaking and entering."

"Think about the press. Police reports mean journalists. We're not ready to sell yet, and we could use the extra time."

Ben gripped the painting, and I could see him deliberating over his choices.

"How do we know that he won't talk?" he said, keeping his eyes on me.

"Mr. Hailey already has a criminal record," Leland said. "A fire, wasn't it, Mr. Hailey? I can't remember all the details, but it was somewhere in Covina."

My jaw was tight. I hoped my face didn't give anything away.

"Judges in Los Angeles have long memories," Leland went on. "I'm sure you don't want to come face-to-face with the same judge on a charge of breaking and entering. Isn't that right, Mr. Hailey?"

I mulled over what he was saying.

"Fine," I said. "I won't say anything. I'm not entirely sure what I'm keeping secret, though."

"It's simple," Leland said, giving me an easy smile. "Just don't say anything at all."

Leland escorted me all the way to the end of the drive, then unlocked the chains linking the gates together. He nodded his head as I slung my satchel over my shoulder and made an unhappy exodus down the drive.

Before I had reached the street, he called out to me.

"Mr. Hailey," he said. "Don't ever come back to Windhall. You've had two friendly warnings, but you won't get a third."

And with that, he withdrew behind the gates and locked the chain once more.

FOUR

I knew that I couldn't hack into Leland's phone at home, because if his Find My Phone feature was activated, it would lead him straight to my house. I turned the phone off and drove to Brite Spot, a little diner on Sunset Boulevard. When I got to the parking lot, I pulled out my own phone and glanced at the screen. I had put it on silent when I got to Windhall, and I now saw that there were four missed calls from Marty, the photographer from the *Lens*.

The events of the last two hours had taken me out of the present, and I had forgotten about the fact that I had blown off Brian's assignment. Brian was going to be pissed when he found out that I had gone off to pursue a story he had rejected instead of writing about Rigor Mormon, which made it all the more important for me to actually produce something worth writing about.

Brite Spot's turquoise walls and pine furniture reminded me of my grandmother, because she used to take me there for grilled cheese sandwiches and hot chocolate. In the last few years it had become a haven for hipsters and fashion interns, but it still reminded me of my childhood. I knew most of the waitstaff by name, and I considered the diner to be a part-time office.

The soda fountain bar was empty when I sat down. Casey, an architecture student who worked late nights, came over and passed me a menu.

"Dinner?"

"No, thanks, Case, just coffee tonight."

I probably only had ten minutes before Leland realized his phone was missing, possibly another ten minutes before he realized that I had it. If he drove fast, it would be another twenty minutes before he arrived at the diner, potentially with police in tow, calling for my arrest.

I had to work quickly.

Keeping Leland's phone turned off, I scrolled through Google on my own device. The location feature on Leland's phone wouldn't work as long as the phone was off; I knew this from experience.

After Casey brought me a cup of coffee, I started looking for Leland in the most obvious places, pinging Google with the keywords "Leland" and "Windhall." The top search results for that query all had to do with the dead girl found on the fire trail, but Leland's name was missing from all of them.

Since my job relied heavily on research, I was pretty good at finding things through a simple process of Google queries. The fact that Leland's name was eluding me was more than a little frustrating, and after a bit of fruitless searching, I sat back and thought.

Casey returned with her own cup of coffee and leaned against the counter. "Working tonight?"

"I blew off work, actually," I said. "Something better came up."

"Oh yeah?"

"I have a huge favor to ask," I said. "If a really angry-looking man shows up, would you warn me?"

"That sounds like half our late-night customers, Hailey."

"He'll be wearing an expensive suit. Blond, somewhere north of sixty."

"I'll do my best."

I struggled to remember the name of Leland's companion at Windhall, and after a moment, it came back to me. *Ben*. Leland and Ben had clearly been trying to hide something, but I wasn't sure what it was. It seemed like they were trying to get the house ready for a sale, and maybe, by conjunction, the fact that Theo was back in town.

A bit more research finally revealed that Leland Bates was the name of Theo's lawyer. A Wikipedia article gave me Leland's birthday, which was March 10, 1967.

Bingo.

I turned on Leland's phone and tried a few configurations of his birthdate. On the fourth try, the password went through.

"Silly boomer." I kept my eye on the clock as I went to Leland's email folder and began scrolling through his emails, looking for evidence. The most recent emails had nothing to do with Theo, but it didn't take long for something to turn up.

The email's subject line read "The Dead Girl," and it was dated three days before, just after the art student's body had turned up on the fire trail.

> L—
>
> Have you seen the news? How is this going to affect the house? I know that you've mentioned taking the house off my hands for a while now, but I imagine interest will be especially high after such a high-profile murder case.
>
> I'll be in town this weekend; we can talk then.
>
> Theo

My hands trembled as I read the email. It was from Theo; Theo was back in town. I grabbed a napkin, located a pen in my satchel, and quickly copied down Theo's email address.

"Hailey," Casey called. "Is that your angry man?"

"Shit," I muttered. "Two seconds, I'm almost finished."

"You must have pissed him off something good," she said, leaning against the counter. "Need me to dig out the baseball bat?"

I glanced over my shoulder and saw Leland crossing the parking lot, about to reach the front door. I got up and came around the counter, then ducked down by Casey's legs.

"I'll be out of here in two seconds," I whispered. "Just buy me another minute, if you can."

I didn't have time to scroll through Leland's other emails, but there was something else that I did have time for. I went into Leland's contact folder and searched for the name "Ben." To my dismay, the search returned nineteen results, and only a few of them had photos.

My hands trembled as I worked through the contacts one by one. I had an anonymous email account that was untraceable, and I sent each contact to this email. I had barely had time to email myself the last of the Ben contacts before the door swung open. The last thing I did was send myself Leland's own contact card, so I could get in touch if I needed to.

I couldn't see him, but I could hear Leland walking up to the counter. Judging by the sound of his footsteps, he was standing in front of Casey.

"Good evening," he said. "I'm looking for a phone."

"You need to make a call?" she replied. "There's a pay phone on the next block."

"I'm looking for *my* phone," he said. "I have it on good authority that it's somewhere in your diner. Have you seen a man with dark hair and bad posture? Somewhere around thirty? His name's Max Hailey."

"I haven't."

"Would you mind letting me use your phone to call my phone? I'd be happy to pay for the privilege."

My hands shook as I turned off Leland's phone.

"My cell phone's dead," Casey said. "I'd be happy to check in the lost and found, though. Someone might have turned it in. Why don't you take a seat, I'll see what I can do."

I heard one of the bar chairs creak as Leland sat down. Praying that he couldn't see me, I crawled into the kitchen behind Casey, and then, when the door was shut, stood up.

"Hailey, what kind of mess have you gotten yourself into?"

"Tell him you found it," I said. "Please. Say a homeless guy turned it in half an hour ago." I handed her a folded-up fifty. "I'll see you in a few days."

Thierry called me the next morning as I was making lunch.

"You still interested in Windhall?" he asked.

"Always."

"I might have something for you," he said. "I found that guy's number in my Rolodex."

"Which one?"

"That crappy magician, the one who says he has some kind of film. Said it has to do with Theo. He's having a show tonight in Hollywood; he told me to stop by afterward. You game?"

"Yeah, of course," I said.

"I can't vouch for him," he warned. "Could be a nutcase."

"Let's go," I said. "I have to stop by the office, but I'll give you a call afterward."

I had woken up early that morning, unable to sleep any longer. The first thing I did was go to my computer and start going through the contacts that I had stolen from Leland's phone, but I hadn't figured out which Ben had been at Windhall. I had been on the verge of anonymously calling them, one by one, when Thierry's call interrupted me.

The Bens could wait, though, because there was something more important that I had to deal with first. I knew that if I didn't stop by the office that morning, I would risk losing my job. The fact that I had blown off the Rigor Mormon show had landed me in deep shit, as evidenced by a barrage of missed calls and text messages from Brian and Marty.

I packed up my computer and then headed toward Hollywood.

It was a Saturday afternoon, so the office was fairly quiet. Many of our staff were freelancers, and we didn't adhere to a strict nine-to-five schedule, but people still liked to spend their weekends out of the office.

When I stepped in, I saw that the secretary's desk was occupied by a young woman with dark eyes. Her dark hair was cropped in a chic, short cut, and she wore a loose-fitting tunic. When she heard me come in, she glanced up from a book.

"Welcome to the *Lens*," she said. "How can I help you?"

"You're not Jordan," I said. "Who are you?"

"Petra," she said. "Can I help you with something?"

"I work here," I said. "Are you new?"

"I'm an intern."

"Max Hailey."

"Ahh," she said. "You're the infamous Hailey."

I leaned against the wall. "If you've been talking to Brian, allow me to disabuse you of a few things."

"No, you wrote that story," she said. "The one about politicians selling works of art and then pretending that they were stolen. What was it called again?"

"The Jenner-Foster case," I said.

"That was really impressive," she said.

"Thanks," I said. "That was back when I could afford to let my morals dictate what I wrote. Now I have a roof to replace, and a four-foot gremlin riding my ass."

She blinked.

"That was a metaphor. Brian in?"

"I think he's expecting you."

Brian's door was open, and he was on the phone when I reached the door. I could see him, leaning back in his chair and gabbing away with someone about a party from last night.

"I swear to God, Rihanna was there," he said. "You can ask Jackson! He went up to talk to her!"

I waited a moment, then knocked on the door. Brian kicked off the wall to spin around in his chair, wearing a goofy grin on his face. The moment he saw me, the grin vanished.

"Gotta go," he said, then hung up without waiting for a response. "Hailey."

"I missed the show last night," I said. "I'm sorry about that."

"You missed the show. You missed the show! You don't think I already know that?" He stood up. "This is the hot new band of the year. They're supposed to be the next Tame Impala, and you weren't there to cover them."

"Who's Tame Impala?"

He stared at me for a moment, then shook his head and slipped his phone in his pocket. "Look, my dad's always liked you," he said. "I don't get it, personally. You're lazy and disrespectful, and you have a massive problem with authority."

"Sorry, I drifted off for a second. What were you saying?"

He glanced at something on his desk. "You're not very popular here, Hailey," he said. "This isn't coming from me. People find you abrasive and condescending."

I didn't respond.

"Your contract's coming to a close," he said. "Dicking around and blowing off articles isn't going to improve your chances of staying on."

I will not kiss ass, I won't, I won't . . .

"I hate to pull this, but you haven't given me much of a choice," Brian said. "I gave you an article to present to Alexa on Monday; you decided not to cover the show."

"Alexa . . . ?"

"Alexa Levine. She's our new editor."

I laughed. "You expect me to believe that Alexa *Levine* is coming to edit the *Lens*? Now I know you're bluffing, Brian—she used to cover things like Sarajevo and the Madoffs. Plus, everyone knows she stopped writing years ago."

Brian gave me a bland smile. "You're right, Hailey, I'm *bluffing*."

"Look, Alexa aside, I'm sorry about the show. Really. Something else came up, but I'm happy to write a different story."

"What came up?"

I weighed my options, then decided to go with the truth. "I went to Windhall," I said. "I think I have a good angle on a story."

"Fuck, Hailey. Seriously? *Seriously?*" He pressed his fingertips together. "You write what I tell you to write. Nobody cares about dead people and old houses."

"Windhall is a better lead than a band called *Rigor Mormon*. If it makes you feel better, I watched some of their clips on YouTube, so I could probably write something vaguely comprehensive."

"What was the name of the guy? The one who supposedly killed his actress?" Brian snapped his fingers. "It wasn't Hitchcock, was it?"

"Theodore Langley. He's back," I said. "I can prove it, too."

"Oh yeah?" Brian feigned interest. "How's that?"

I decided not to mention the stolen phone. "His lawyer is fixing up the house so they can sell it," I said. "This is incredibly pertinent to what's going on with that dead girl. We can write a story about Langley, then tie in the current story. If we can get an interview with Theo, he might be able to shed some light on what's going on now."

He was quiet, and for a moment, I thought he might actually be considering my story.

"I know it sounds crazy," I said. "But I've always thought that if I could get Theo alone in a room, I could prove that he killed Eleanor. They were so close to proving that he did it. If the trial hadn't been thrown—"

Brian raised a hand to cut me off. "I'll let you finish your contract," he said. "But after that, I'm going to have to let you go."

The little shit. I could feel the color rising in my face, but I couldn't bear to debase myself further by arguing with him.

"I still have three weeks," I said.

"I know that, and like I said, you can finish out your time here," he said. "I'll be using that time to interview people to replace you. I've got a stack of résumés about a mile high."

I was silent, and he laughed. "Come on, this is Hollywood, Hailey. Don't feel too bad; people struggle to reach their dreams every day. I've got another meeting."

He grabbed some papers and his glasses from his desk, then walked to the door.

"Up you get."

I followed him out of the office, so pissed that I couldn't articulate a good response.

"I'll see you Monday, hey? I'd say enjoy the rest of your weekend, but if I were you, I'd start looking for another job."

There was a bounce in his step as he walked through the office and headed toward the stairs. I stayed there for a moment, waiting for him to disappear, because I knew that if we left the office together, only one of us would emerge. I waited in the lobby, counting to twenty to try to calm myself down.

"I want to help you."

I turned to see the dark-haired intern.

"Help me with what?"

"I heard that you're going to write a story about the Langley trial," she said. "I've read every book on the subject. I've been to Windhall a few times, too. You're wrong about Brian, though. He's not bluffing. Our new editor is actually Alexa Levine."

"Were you eavesdropping just now?"

"Yes." She didn't blink, and I had to admire her grit.

"Alexa Levine," I said, then whistled. "Not *the* Alexa Levine, though?"

"The one and only."

"Look, the last thing I heard, Alexa was either in jail or on the run. I mean, she dropped off the face of the earth after that whole thing in Burma."

Petra frowned. "Did she actually go to jail for that?"

"She was definitely on trial. You know what I'm talking about, don't you?"

"I read the news." Petra seemed offended. "It was all my parents could talk about when it happened."

"Man." I stuck my hands in my pockets. "I don't like Brian, but I've got to hand it to him. If he got Alexa to come out of hiding, he's really doing something right."

"Ford gets all the credit for that," Petra said quietly. "Brian had nothing to do with it."

"Anyways," I said. "I'm going to go home and try to save my job. It was nice to meet you."

"I think that Brian is rude to you because you have a reputation around here."

I couldn't help laughing. "What kind of reputation?"

"A reputation."

"You don't happen to have a law degree, do you?"

"No," she said. "I was serious about Windhall, though. I'd really like to help you. Eleanor never got any kind of justice, because women were treated so badly back then. If there's one time to prove that Theo killed her, it's now."

"Look, thanks for the offer, but I don't think this story is going to go anywhere."

"If we work together, we can pull together a proposal this weekend," she argued.

"At this point, I have no leads," I said. I didn't want to mention the stolen phone and Theo's email address, because I didn't know how Petra would react. "I doubt I'll be able to get inside Windhall again. You know I've got a record, right?"

Her expression didn't change. "Yes, I do."

"Keep your head down; you'll do fine here," I said. "Have a good weekend."

———

I had been fired before, but in the past, I had always deserved it. There were one or two restaurant jobs where I got fired for stealing food, and then there was a time in high school when I was fired from a bookstore because I'd gotten drunk and fallen asleep in the nonfiction section. Those times hadn't really bothered me. This time, though, it was personal.

Ford had given me credit for saving the *Lens* twice; once with a legal connection that helped us dodge a lengthy lawsuit, and the second time by publishing the Jenner-Foster story under our masthead. We'd made enough money from the traffic off that story that we had been saved from the brink of bankruptcy.

Now I was short a mortgage payment, and it looked like I was going to miss the next one as well. I had no idea how I was going to save my roof, and it looked like my only option was to put my house on the market. The worst thing about the whole situation, however, was the fact that Alexa was about to start working at the *Lens.*

If there was one editor who would champion a story about socioeconomic injustice and the disparity between male and female scrutiny under the American legal system, it was Alexa Levine. I was intimate with Alexa's work, because she had been the topic of my senior research project at Northwestern. If I had to pinpoint a single person who had inspired me toward journalism rather than writing fiction, Alexa would be it.

Alexa herself was a somewhat polarizing force in the field of investigative journalism, which was still by and large an old boys' club. At twenty-three, Alexa had infiltrated a New Mexican drug cartel with ties to two Republican state senators, and when her senior editor pressured her to sit on the story until the senators' families could be moved to safety, she went ahead and sold it to a different newspaper. It had gone on to reach the Pulitzer shortlist.

A few years later she shaved her head and went to Israel, posing as a young man and fighting alongside the Jewish Resistance Movement. No one ever suspected that she might be a woman, or even American. Alexa was half Mexican and half Jewish, giving her a fairly ambiguous look that could be attributed to a wide variety of countries. Her strong facial features and thick eyebrows lent a certain androgyny to her appearance, which she used in her favor.

Her career continued along a highly unorthodox path, and she refused to be limited by her gender or background in a field mostly dominated by white men. She pissed off her superiors and challenged people who threatened to stifle her, but she was able to impress the right number of people to rise through the ranks. There were countless awards and accolades, but Alexa further infuriated the powers that be by gracefully rejecting a nomination for the Goldsmith Prize, citing various ways in which the nominations were unfairly biased, then went on to suggest a list of journalists worthy of consideration.

All of those things seemed like childish acts of rebellion compared to what happened in Burma, which is what finally ended Alexa's career.

Anyone who's done their homework will immediately link Burma in 2007 with two things: the oil shortage and Alexa Levine. When the local government raised the price of fuel in Burma, setting off a massive series of protests throughout the country, Alexa turned her attention elsewhere. Although she had a desk at the *Los Angeles Times*, she flew out to Washington, DC, to find out why the *Washington Post* had been sitting on a story about the events of the crisis, when two of their reporters had gone out to Burma to see things firsthand.

After that, it becomes a matter of national security, and most of the details are kept in some locked vault on the other side of the country. But after Alexa was turned away by the *Post*, she flew out to Burma, impersonated an American senator from Massachusetts, and discovered that the *Post* had been bribed or threatened to keep their mouths shut about an international crisis partially engineered by American oil conglomerates. Two senators had financial stakes in the debacle, including the woman Alexa had impersonated.

She returned home, intending to leak the story, but was met at the airport by federal marshals. The rest is cloudy. Her editors didn't stick up for her, that much is common knowledge, and editors are always supposed to stick by their reporters. She went on trial for the crime of impersonating a politician, and she spent some time in jail, but ultimately got off lightly on a plea bargain.

And then she disappeared.

Right after she disappeared, speculation was rife about what might have happened. She was killed—or, at least, that was the most popular theory. Taken out by government agents for threatening national security. The Bush administration was embarrassed, even though the story never went to print.

I followed the whole thing religiously, and I still held out hope that she might have gone underground to work on an important story. Other possibilities were more likely, like that Alexa had gotten tired of fighting everyone and disappeared to have a family. I secretly hoped that wasn't true, because there weren't enough powerful female journalists willing to fight the corporate hierarchy.

Hearing that she was back in Los Angeles and coming to work at the *Lens* was sort of like finding out that Orson Welles was still alive and he was going to be signing books at Barnes & Noble. I couldn't figure out why she would accept a position as editor in chief of the *Lens*, or how our dingy little zine would have even contacted her. Our magazine had gained a reputation for covering historical and cultural news, but with the direction that Brian was pushing, I didn't see why Alexa would be interested. The previous year, the story that pulled in the most traffic on our website was about a Puerto Rican drag queen who dressed up as Beethoven for Pride and deejayed a set of baroque music.

I mulled the thought over as I headed home. If Brian was going to be my boss forever, I would be tempted to quit the *Lens*, but if Alexa was taking over, I definitely had a change of heart.

FIVE

That evening, Thierry and I met at the little Gower Gulch strip mall. I had spent hours researching Leland's list of Bens, but so far, I hadn't figured out which one had been at Windhall on Friday night. After deliberating the pros and cons of contacting Theo, I had fired off a quick email from my work account, asking him if he was in town, and whether or not he would be willing to grant me an interview. I didn't really expect to hear back from him. I also knew that without a solid lead or something to bring to the pitch meeting, there was no chance of salvaging my job. The magician was probably my last shot.

The magician wasn't the first person Thierry had unearthed for my benefit. Throughout our entire friendship, he had occasionally come across weirdos and fanatics who claimed to have information on Theo. Years before, I'd let myself get optimistic about meeting them, but now I sat through their spiels and rants with something less than enthusiasm. Regardless of the dubious authenticity of their claims, however, I'd gotten into the habit of bringing cash to the meetings, on the off chance they had something I wanted to buy.

Thierry was dressed up for the occasion, which meant that he was decked out in cowboy duds. He was wearing a black suede jacket with studs and embroidery along the shoulders, and a pair of black corduroy pants. I'd known Thierry long enough to know that the getup had nothing to do with the Western-themed location; Thierry had always been obsessed with cowboy garb and had a closet full of Western-inspired clothing. When I walked up to him, he was admiring his ten-gallon hat in the rearview mirror of a Subaru.

"I guess we're not being inconspicuous tonight." I clapped a hand on his shoulder.

"Inconspicuous? What are you talking about?"

"You look like you're about to call the cows home."

"Hailey, you know I hate the Hollywood. I'm doing you a favor by coming here, you don't have to be an asshole."

I lifted my hands. "Apologies."

"By the way, you need to get your phone fixed."

"What are you talking about?"

"Half the time I call you, it gets picked up by some Chinese lady," he said. "She doesn't speak English, but, boy, she likes to yell."

"Jesus, I thought they fixed that," I said. "Never mind, I'm not dealing with it now. Let's go."

Gower Gulch was an embarrassing little strip mall, bracketed off between a Starbucks and a Rite Aid, but it had its charms. Since it had once been the hangout of cowboys and ranch hands, the mall was decorated like an old Western outpost, complete with fake cacti, wagon wheels, and an old stagecoach.

"Let's get this show on the road," Thierry said, adjusting his hat one last time.

"Road? Don't you mean stagecoach trail?"

"Not another word, Hailey, I am warning you!"

I followed him into a restaurant with a narrow shopfront. Inside, the decor was kitschy Hollywood: a warty candle on every table, glittery drapes on the walls, faded murals depicting cacti, ranch hands, and blowing tumbleweeds. A small stage occupied a corner by the back wall of the restaurant, and an emcee cradled the microphone. He was a slender, gawky man in a crimson jacket with matching pants, and the light glanced off his thick spectacles.

"Ladies and gentlemen, you've just been dazzled by the amazing hands of Raymond Chandelier," he said. "Let us take a step further into the strange, explore a bit more of the mystique, as we welcome to the stage . . . Tyko Lightwood!"

A smattering of applause filled the dingy restaurant, and the emcee bowed his way off the stage.

Thierry edged his way along the back of the restaurant, and I followed him. The emcee was chatting up some of the waitresses, and Thierry approached him, then put a hand on his shoulder. The emcee bowed his head to listen to what Thierry was saying, then nodded and turned to look at me.

"You're here about Theodore Langley?" he asked. All traces of his self-conscious stage persona had disappeared. He leaned in. "Can we trust you?"

"Trust me with *what*?"

"This is highly confidential information," he said. "Will you respect that?"

"You don't need to worry about my discretion."

The emcee studied me for a long moment. "This isn't Club 33 at Disneyland," he said. "We're talking about the most famous unsolved murder in Los Angeles. If I don't feel that you can be respectful, I'm going to have to ask you to leave."

I struggled not to roll my eyes. "I get it, champ. I'll keep your secrets, and later we can discuss how Katy Perry is really JonBenét Ramsey, all grown up."

The emcee squinted at Thierry. "Is he making fun of me? I really can't tell."

"Hailey, fuck off!"

I raised my hands in surrender, and the emcee sighed.

"Come with me," he said, then turned and walked away.

We followed him down a narrow corridor, past the dingy bathrooms, and up a set of stairs. At the top of the stairs was a cramped office, filled with lost jackets and purses, cubbyholes for the staff, cardboard boxes containing cups, napkins, and other restaurant detritus. A slender man sat before a mirror, cleaning makeup from his face. When the door opened, he glanced up to look at us.

"Some friends," the emcee explained. "I've gotta get back onstage."

After the emcee departed, the man in front of the mirror turned to greet us. He had only cleaned the makeup from half his face, which gave him a skewed appearance. His left eyebrow was still etched in dark pencil, sharply drawn to indicate mystery, and his cheekbones were highlighted in rouge.

"You must be Thierry," he said. "Who's your friend?"

"Max Hailey," I said. "Are you Raymond Chandler?"

"Chan-*de-lier*," he said, exasperated. "It's just a stage name. You can call me Ray."

"So, you have something belonging to Theo Langley?"

Ray leaned back against the table and gave me a dubious look. "What's your interest in Theo, anyway?"

I showed him my palms. "I've always liked dinosaurs."

"Do you think he killed Eleanor?"

"Did OJ kill Nicole Brown? Of course Theo killed Eleanor. The only reason he got off was because the prosecutor tampered with evidence."

"I think we're done here." Ray turned back to the mirror and continued cleaning his face.

"Whoa, what? You made me drive out to some hack magic show in Hollywood for nothing? Thanks for wasting my time."

"Your friend has bad manners," Ray told Thierry.

Thierry rolled his eyes. "Hailey, don't be a jackass."

"I grew up poor," I said. "*Dirt* poor. I have no sympathy for rich sociopaths like Theo who can hurt women and get away with it. If he didn't kill her, why did he vanish after the trial? If he were truly innocent, wouldn't he stick around and try to pick up the pieces of his life? Clear his name?"

"He didn't do it," Ray said, then turned around and faced me. "Someone framed him."

"Look, I'm a journalist," I said. "I believe in cold, hard facts. There are a lot of urban legends floating around this city, and most of the time, they don't lead to anything. Why are you so convinced that he's innocent?"

"Theo was a magician," Ray said. "Those sets he built. People still haven't managed to create anything similar. Hot-air balloons that rose without strings. Smiling, waving people, less than an inch tall. Those sets were from another world."

"Agreed. And?"

"Someone who devotes his life to beauty isn't capable of that kind of violence. Theo was an intellectual."

"The two aren't mutually exclusive. Where's your evidence?"

Ray sighed and turned to Thierry. "I thought you said he was looking to buy," he said.

"I make no guarantees on my friend's behalf," Thierry said. "I told you he was interested, that's all."

"What are you selling?" I cut in.

"I don't go showing this to just anyone, you know. If you're interested in buying, I need you to show some respect for the process."

"I appreciate that."

"Are you willing to put your convictions aside and look at new evidence?"

I scratched my head. "Yeah, yeah. I'm open-minded and all that."

Ray crossed the room to a bank of lockers against the wall. He guarded the padlock with his left hand while he spun the dial with his right. After opening the door, he withdrew a metal box the size of a shoebox. He carefully set it on the table next to him and, with a smile and a flourish, lifted the lid.

"What is that?" Thierry asked.

"It's an old film reel," I said. "What's it show?"

"It's proof that Theo was framed." Ray removed a set of white gloves from his pocket and took a black metal film canister from the case. It was old footage, I could see that much just from the container that it was in. It was a bit wider than a CD case, flat, small dents in places.

"Can I see the film?"

"No can do, friend. If I take it out of the canister, the oxygen in the air will start to deteriorate the film panels."

I sighed, exasperated. "How do I know I want to buy unless I actually *see* the film?"

"You're just going to have to take my word for it."

"What word? You haven't even told me what's on it."

Ray crossed the room and opened the door to look out into the hallway. Satisfied that we were alone, he returned to the chair in front of the mirror and took a deep breath.

"Theo didn't kill Eleanor," he said, "because someone else *did*. That's what this film shows. It's a man, strangling Eleanor."

"Aw, bullshit."

"It's true!" The color rose in his cheeks.

"If that's on film, it was part of a movie or something. Back in those days, they didn't waste valuable footage. Plus, nobody left their recording devices on by accident."

"It wasn't an accident," Ray said. "That's what I'm trying to tell you. Someone filmed this shot and tried to make it look like it was Theo."

"If you can't show me the footage, I'm leaving. I'm not going to hand over my money on the strength of your convictions."

"Fine!" Ray pulled out another set of gloves and handed them to me. "You have to wear these, though."

I pulled on the gloves. Ray carefully removed the lid from the film canister and handed it to me.

"Be careful," he said. "This is priceless evidence."

I could see that the film hadn't been properly stored, and it had deteriorated quite a bit. There were yellow spots on some of the cells, and the base was brittle and curling in on itself. I held it up to the light, and the first thing I saw was Eleanor. She was smiling, and she was alone. A script rested in her hands.

My breath caught in my throat. I had seen all of her movies, watched them again and again. I'd always had a soft spot for tragedy, the thought that someone else's family was as fucked up as mine was, and a small part of me was convinced that if I had been able to reach out to Eleanor, I could have stopped everything.

I moved along through the panels slowly, aware that Ray was watching my every move. As I progressed through the cells, Eleanor looked up from the script. A man crossed the room and began gesturing, and Eleanor shrank against the wall. He gestured, then knocked the script from her hands. She threw up her hands over her face, and after a moment's pause, the man reached for her and wrapped his hands around her neck. Before I could make out any identifying features, the film reel ended.

"Well?"

Thierry and Ray were both watching me.

"I need to look through it again," I said, winding the reel up.

"No, no, that's all you get. I don't want to damage the reel."

"What am I supposed to do with this? Write an article about a decomposing film strip and convince people that Theo is innocent?"

I knew that I sounded like an asshole, but I couldn't calm myself down. I had spent too much time trying to convince Brian that this story was important, damn it, and I had just been fired, and now I was having a fight with a part-time magician.

"Hailey," Thierry said quietly. "What's wrong with you?"

And then I thought of my gran: a memory from when I was nine years old. I had woken up in the middle of the night to hear an argument downstairs, between her and her husband. An image: *a pattern of bruises, increasing in size. Pale yellow, brown, and purple. Never where anyone could see, of course, always under her clothes. And she always wore those long-sleeved shirts.*

"Nothing's wrong with me."

"Give me the reel," Ray said, taking it from me. "You don't look so good."

"I need to see it one more time," I said. "Just let me borrow it. I'll take it to my office, make a few copies."

She never stopped wearing those long-sleeved shirts, buttoned all the way up to the bottom of her neck. I knew why she wore them, of course, even though I was too young to understand that kind of violence.

Ray was shaking his head. "I don't think you're the right buyer," he said. "I've changed my mind. You need to leave."

"Thierry, why did you even bring me here?"

Thierry gave me a wide-eyed look. "Don't blame me, pal. I told you this guy was a nut."

I tried to compose myself. "How much are you asking, anyway?"

Ray had turned back to the mirror and continued to remove his makeup. He glanced up at me in the reflection.

"Fifteen thousand."

"Fifteen . . . ! You're out of your mind." I couldn't afford fifteen thousand on a good day, but the fact that my house was falling apart and I was on the verge of losing my job meant that the figure wasn't even in the realm of possibility.

"I should mention that you're not the only one who's interested," Ray said. He traced a finger around the lid of the canister. "I spoke with a woman this morning who is *very* interested in seeing this reel."

"If you're asking fifteen thousand, at least let me see it one more time."

"Sorry, pal," he said. "Now, if you don't mind, I have to finish my shift."

He cleaned off the rest of the makeup from his face, then stood up and put on an apron.

"Wait—you're a server?" I asked. "I thought you were some kind of hotshot magician."

"We all have to pay the rent." Ray gave me a dirty look, then walked to his locker and stashed the film reel back inside. He made a big show of locking it again. "I think you can see yourselves out."

"Give me until tomorrow morning," I said. "I'll come up with the money."

"We'll see," Ray said, then stood by the door and indicated it was time for us to leave.

———

Once we were outside, Thierry turned to me. "What the fuck happened in there?"

"What?"

"You turned a weird color. I thought you were going to cry or some shit."

"I get claustrophobic sometimes."

"Bullshit, you get claustrophobic. We've done jobs together, I've seen you climb into a crawl space tighter than a worm's asshole."

"I don't want to talk about it."

"You don't have fifteen thousand dollars, Hailey."

"I know that. Don't rub it in."

"I could give you some work," he said. "We're doing a house near the reservoir tomorrow."

"I'll think about it."

"Look," he said, gesticulating. "There's one more thing. When I was making calls about this magician, I remembered this other guy. Said he had something that belonged to Theo, or Eleanor, I can't remember. If you want, we could check it out tomorrow, before I go to the reservoir."

"Thanks," I said. "Yeah, let's check it out."

"You need a ride? You going to be okay to drive?"

"I'll be fine. I'm just dehydrated, don't worry about me."

I watched him get in his car and fiddle around with the keys. Thierry was good at sniffing out bullshit, and I hated to lie to him, but I knew he wouldn't approve of what I was planning to do. I needed to see the reel one more time, needed to hold it in my hands.

Once Thierry had left the parking lot and driven down Hollywood Boulevard, I walked around the back of the restaurant and let myself in through the service door. I knew from experience that these doors were usually cocked open an inch or two, so servers could sneak out for cigarette breaks without getting locked out.

Another magician had taken the stage, and I watched him pull a bouquet out of a top hat. Listless applause from the audience. Ray was taking an order from a table in the corner, and his back was turned to me. Glancing around to make sure that I hadn't been detected, I made my way up the stairs to the office.

It was empty. I crossed the room to stand by the lockers, then took out my phone to do some research.

Raymond Chandler had been born in 1888 and died in 1959. Neither of those dates worked. I cursed softly under my breath. I didn't know anything about Ray the magician, and I wouldn't have time to stalk him online before someone found me in the office.

I was at a loss. I pulled out my phone and called Madeleine, who was the biggest Raymond Chandler fan I knew.

"I can't talk long," I said, as soon as she answered the phone.

"You called *me*!"

"What's the best Raymond Chandler novel of all time?"

A quick pause. "*Farewell, My Lovely.* No debate."

"Any idea when it was published?"

"Google that shit."

"Cheers, bye."

I did as Mad suggested and Google coughed up the result: 1940. After tucking my phone back into my pocket, I spun the combination lock: one, nine, four, zero. I tugged on the cheap lock, but it didn't budge.

"Some Raymond Chandler fan," I muttered.

There were voices in the hall, and I ducked behind the door until they disappeared. I was running out of time, and I knew that I already looked like a crazy person. Worse than losing my reputation would be dragging Thierry into a convoluted criminal trial regarding a theft of some ancient, worthless footage. I was quick with words, but I knew that I wouldn't be able to come up with an excuse to protect myself if someone walked in now.

And that's why I didn't give my next action another thought. The staff room was messy, and an open tool chest sat in the corner of the room. I walked over and dug through until I found a screwdriver. The lockers were cheap, flimsy metal, probably purchased from some old high school teacher on Craigslist. I jammed the screwdriver into the little clip that the lock held shut. A few cantilevered shoves of the screwdriver, and the clip snapped. The locker groaned open.

I opened the locker and grabbed the film reel, tucking it into my bag. For a moment I thought about leaving the contents of my wallet in Ray's locker as a form of contrition, but then I remembered that he was an asshole and, furthermore, I didn't really care.

After making sure that the hallway outside the office was clear, I walked down the staircase, then paused once more to make sure nobody had seen me. When I was certain that the path to the back door was clear, I walked toward it in quick strides, then made my way out into the night.

———————————

My nerves were buzzing by the time I got home. I'd nicked a few things in my lifetime, but that's a phase that every poor kid goes through. I had never taken anything worth more than a hundred bucks, and I had certainly never taken anything that might land me in jail. My plan was to look at the reel, take a few notes, and get it back to Ray before he could press charges.

I went into my kitchen and pulled out my gran's old Atomic coffee machine, then put it on the stove and waited for it to heat up. The hole in the ceiling was slightly bigger than a soccer ball, and there were cracks shooting out from it. It looked malignant, but thankfully, Los Angeles didn't get too cold, and I felt like I could put the repairs off for another few weeks. I had no idea where I would get the money, though; my best option at the moment was patching up the thing myself until I found another job.

While I waited for my coffee to percolate, I went up into the attic and dug around until I found Gran's old film projector. I set up the film projector on the living room table, then aimed it at the wall opposite, bare of decoration, because I tried to live a mostly sparse existence. My hands trembled. I knew what I was going to see when I turned the projector on, because I had already looked at the cells back at the restaurant, but the idea of seeing it life-sized on the wall of my living room was something else entirely.

The reel was in bad condition, and I fed it into the projector with great caution. Once the film had been set up in the projector, I turned it on. There was a soft shuffling sound as the projector hummed and whirred, and then the images began dancing across the wall.

Eleanor stood in her dressing room, rehearsing her lines. I could see her lips moving as she read them to herself, frowning in concentration.

"Eleanor," I said softly. "Get out of there."

She continued to read, then gestured at something. There must have been a sound; she looked up.

A man stood just before the camera, partially blocking the lens; for a moment, I could see nothing more than a full head of dark hair. He was tall, probably taller than the average movie star. I mentally flipped through images I had of Theo: tall and dark, yes, but was this him? *Wouldn't he have known that the camera was there?*

I frowned at the image as the man advanced toward Eleanor, and she looked at him in fright. Suddenly, he attacked her. And then I noticed something that hadn't jumped out when I viewed the slides in the restaurant—Eleanor crumpled before his hands reached her throat. She wasn't surprised by the attack; she had been expecting it. There was another thing that bothered me, and this one bothered me more—the man in the clip didn't seem to have a limp. It was one of the things that I knew about Theo, after all: as a result of a childhood accident, he had always walked with a pronounced limp. It had saved him from going off to fight in World War II.

"Fucking magicians," I muttered.

After I had given myself a moment to mull over the reel, I watched the clip three more times, taking notes.

When I had taken notes on everything in the clip, I went into the kitchen and made myself another cup of coffee. While I was waiting for it to brew, I turned on the radio to listen to the Sound, my favorite radio station. A track by Blue Öyster Cult was playing, and I tried to lose myself in the music. I felt strangely removed from what I had watched. At worst, it seemed like inconclusive evidence. Any defense lawyer today would claim that this was a scene between two actors, rehearsing a scene. Added to a greater case, though, it could be damning evidence. As much as I hated to admit it, the first inklings of doubt crept into my mind. Was it really Theo in the clip? I had never given myself room to consider other suspects, and I didn't relish the prospect of doing so now. I wouldn't have the first idea of where to begin looking.

When the song ended, the deejay cleared his throat.

"Someone with a sense of humor requested that one," he said. "You've been listening to '(Don't Fear) The Reaper,' which goes out to Eleanor Hayes. Just a quick recap for those of you tuning in now: Eleanor was murdered in 1948, and to date, it's one of the most popular unsolved murders in Hollywood. Apparently someone has been re-creating the original murder. For those of you who live under rocks, a young woman was murdered near Theo's creepy abandoned mansion."

"'One of the most popular unsolved murders'?" Another deejay chimed in. "And I don't know about unsolved. Everyone knows that Theo did it, right?"

"Sure, sure, and he got away with it because that's what rich white dudes have been doing for centuries. Anyway, the police have just reported that a *second* body was found earlier this evening, and even though nothing has been confirmed, our sources tell us that it might be connected to the murder that happened three days ago."

I moved closer to the radio and turned up the volume, convinced I had heard wrong. I grabbed my phone and pulled up *TMZ*: if you wanted to be thorough, you could go to any number of investigative websites, but if you needed quick, fast, dirty facts, *TMZ* was the go-to.

Sure enough, there was the big, bold headline: SECOND BODY FOUND NEAR THEODORE LANGLEY'S HOME.

"We've got a caller on line one," the first deejay said. "Where do you weigh in on Theo Langley?"

"He did it. There's no question in my mind." The caller's voice was refined, and I guessed that it was an older woman.

"So you think he's back in Los Angeles?"

"I certainly hope not," she said. "But most violent offenders usually come back to visit the scene of the crime, especially if they got away with it."

"Thanks for calling," he said. "For those of you just tuning in, there's been another murder tonight in Beverly Hills. It looks like it might be the same culprit as the person or persons responsible for the dead art student earlier this week. We don't know whether or not a suspect has been apprehended—"

I grabbed my keys from the stand by the door, then ran out and got into my car.

SIX

If the newest murder was another tribute to Theo, I knew that the body would have been found somewhere near his house, just like the first. It didn't take long for me to find police cars and yellow tape, only three blocks away from Windhall.

I parked haphazardly and got out of my car, but no sooner had I approached the yellow tape than I was stopped by a cop in a bright yellow vest.

"Can't let you past."

"You gonna tell me I can't stand right here? It's public property, isn't it?"

I could tell that he was not in the mood to be messed around with. "Your vehicle's in violation of the parking code unless you've got a Beverly Hills permit. Do I need to have you towed?"

I took out my press pass and waved it at him. "Can you tell me anything about this new victim?"

"Move your car, sir."

He started to walk away.

"He's back, you know," I called. "I know how to find Theo. The murders aren't going to stop on their own."

"Fantastic," he said, turning around to give me a sarcastic look. "Write up your little report for the *National Enquirer*. I'm sure your fans will be thrilled."

"I work for a highly respected online magazine!" I called, but this time he didn't turn around.

A small crowd of people had gathered, pressing against the yellow tape. I could see the flares of the police, the bright lights and vehicles, but nothing beyond that.

Two people near me were having a heated conversation. The woman, a middle-aged blonde with a streak of gray through her bangs, was gesturing toward the police.

"They're saying it was another young woman," she said. "The same age as that art student who got killed on the fire trail. They were both wearing the same green silk dress."

"Just like that dead actress," her male companion said. "What was her name again?"

"Eleanor Hayes," the woman said. "I've been reading all about it. They were both stabbed through the heart. It's kind of poetic, don't you think?"

"It's tragic."

"And apparently Theo what's-his-face is back," she went on. "The director who killed the actress in the first place."

"There's no way that dude is still alive," the man replied. "Didn't the original crime happen in like, the thirties?"

"Forty-something. And yes, he's in his nineties. I don't know if he's spry enough to go around killing young women. Maybe someone's helping him."

I stopped paying attention to their conversation, because I had just noticed someone familiar in the crowd. His face was turned in profile, his hands were shoved in his pockets, and he didn't look as eager and curious as the rest of the crowd. Dark hair, somewhere in his fifties. I struggled to place him until he turned and I saw his face.

Ben, the man from Windhall.

If I needed any more confirmation that it was him, I got it a moment later, when Leland appeared at his side. I slipped my phone from my pocket and snapped a few pictures of the two men. Ben listened to something that Leland was saying, then nodded. He scanned the crowd and did a double take when he saw me.

I put my phone away and headed toward them, but before I could get close enough to call out Ben's name, he turned and vanished into the crowd.

"Shit," I muttered.

Leland spotted me and frowned. He turned on his heel and followed Ben.

I tried to push through the crowd, but a police officer grabbed my arm.

"This is an active crime scene," he said. "We're asking everyone to move backward!"

I might have argued, but Leland and Ben had both disappeared. Frustrated, I turned and headed back toward my car.

———————

My phone rang early the next morning. I glanced at the screen and saw that it was Thierry.

"It's five o'clock, T," I mumbled into the phone. "This better be important."

"You asshole!" he shouted. "I get a call at midnight last night from that shitty magician. He accused me of stealing that movie or whatever, and it took me about five seconds to figure out it was you."

I bolted upright. "T, I can explain."

"I don't need to hear an explanation," he said. "Next time you think about asking me for a favor, think again. I'm not going to help you out if you drag my name through the mud. He said he's going to have me arrested if that reel doesn't turn up! Next time he calls me, I'm going to give him your number—and your address!"

"I'll take it back to him this morning," I said. "I had to take a closer look."

Thierry had already hung up. I swore to myself and realized that it had been selfish to steal the movie when the magician might blame Thierry.

I rolled out of bed and went into the living room. I had to figure out a way to get the reel back to the magician without incriminating myself, which wasn't going to be easy. I doubted that I would be able to sneak back into the restaurant without being detected.

I carefully unwound the reel from the projector and placed it back inside its case. While I was trying to decide how I should proceed, I went into the kitchen and started up my Atomic.

———————

Thierry's car was in front of his house when I pulled up an hour later. I hopped out, carrying a sack with breakfast burritos and french fries. Thierry was an insomniac, and even if he hadn't called me at dawn that morning, I knew that he would have been awake.

He opened the door a few minutes after I knocked.

"Go away," he said. "I don't want to hear your bullshit excuses."

"Come on, T," I said. "I got your favorite from Los Nopales."

He eyed the bag. "Set it on the stoop and walk away."

"Come on, fat man. I got fries on the side."

He growled and moved to the side, and I walked in. We moved into the kitchen and Thierry fetched plates, then we sat down to eat in silence.

When we finished, Thierry wiped his hands with a napkin and pointed at me. "It's back by tonight," he said. "Or you never ask me for a favor again."

I raised my hands. "You got it."

"My client by the reservoir asked me to stop by early," he said. "Gotta go soon."

I cleared my throat. "You still going to take me to see that collector today?"

"You think that's still on the table? After that shit you pulled?"

"C'mon, T."

"I can't take you anywhere. You got sticky fingers."

I raised my hands. "Think of this as getting me out of your hair," I said. "I make the connection between Theo and Eleanor's death, you'll never have to do me a favor again. I'll be doing you favors."

He looked at me skeptically.

"Otherwise I'm going to be some unemployed would-be writer, always knocking on your door and asking for handouts—"

He waved the comment away. "Jesus," he said. "Wait for me in Silver Lake. I'll call you when I'm heading over. Gotta go see this other client first."

———————

Two hours later, I was hunched over a lukewarm cup of coffee in a cute little café in Silver Lake, still waiting for Thierry. I was itching to meet up with Thierry's lead, but when Thierry made up his mind to go at his own pace, there was no rushing him.

I didn't know how much money Thierry's lead wanted for their information, but I had stopped at the ATM to get some cash, just in case. The machine had outright rejected my request to take out three hundred dollars, then balked as I dropped down in increments of twenty. A line of people formed behind me as I took my card out and inserted it again and again, and finally managed to take out two hundred dollars.

Not wanting to spend more than five dollars while I waited for Thierry to show up, I had ordered an eight-ounce drip coffee and mentally calculated how I was going to afford to eat for the next two weeks.

I was idly scrolling through the list of Leland's Ben contacts when a text message appeared on my phone. It was from a number I didn't recognize, but I opened it anyway.

Call me as soon as you get this – Petra

My thumb was over the "call" button when the door of the coffee shop opened and Thierry came bursting in. He glanced around and then spotted me.

"Come on, let's go, what are you waiting for?" he said, coming over to clap a hand on my shoulder. "I told this guy we'd be at his house an hour ago."

"You mind if I make a quick call?"

"Yes, I mind," he said. "Let's get going. I'll drive, you can't navigate for shit."

"T, this is important."

"I'm not your fucking secretary, waiting around for you to make phone calls. Either *we're* leaving or *I'm* leaving."

"What does this guy have, anyway?" I said, getting to my feet. "I don't want to buy crockery or pillowcases."

"Nah, it's not pillowcases," he said. "The guy's wife was some kind of crime fanatic. She had some stuff that came from the crime scene, that's what the guy said on the phone."

The house was only a few blocks away, in a quiet neighborhood of sloping streets and comfortable, sagging Craftsmans. Thierry parked outside a narrow brick building in a row of shops touting vintage wear. The building's bottom floor was a little coffee shop with gold lettering in the window, and there was a community garden next door.

"Try to be sensitive," Thierry said, as we walked toward the building. I could see that he was still irritated with me, but I knew that he would cool off in an hour or so. "This guy's wife just died. He's selling off some of their stuff."

An upstairs window opened, and someone whistled.

"Up here," called a man, and I looked up to see a waving hand. "Come up the stairs in back."

At the top of the stairs we were met by a thin blond man with a bow tie. His outfit was straight out of the 1950s: suspenders, knit tie, vest tucked into gray wool pants. There was something a bit disheveled about him, though, and I wondered if he had fallen asleep in his clothing. He shook hands with Thierry, and then with me.

"Kent."

"This is Max Hailey," Thierry said.

"Thanks for meeting with us," I said.

"Not a problem."

The apartment was small and cozy. Old hardwood floors stretched the length of the space, and a bookshelf was decorated with narrow, wooden shoes. Kent saw me looking at them and nodded.

"Lasts," he said. "For shoes."

The home had a warm feeling about it, and it was also slightly anachronistic, in a very pleasing way. The sound of ticking clocks filled the air, and framed vintage maps decorated the walls. There were no television screens or modern gadgets available, not even a microwave.

"You make shoes?"

"This whole building belonged to a cobbler," he said. "Very successful business in the early days of Hollywood, but he ran out of clients in the eighties. Nice old man."

"And he lived up here?"

"It's sad, you know? People want to buy cheap these days. They just go to the mall and buy Adidas, things that will wear out in a year's time. You want something that will last, you have to pay good money for it."

"I'm sorry to hear about your wife," I said.

He nodded and looked out the window. Then, "I hear you're interested in Langley stuff?"

"Always have been." I thumbed my phone anxiously, wondering what Petra wanted to talk about. "So, what do you have? Thierry said your wife had something from the crime scene?"

"I think so, but I'm no expert," he said. "My wife was into all those murder stories, loved to collect crazy deaths and ghost stories. She would take rocks and stuff from murder scenes. Kept them labeled in jars. I have a box of stuff. I want to get rid of it. Too many creepy memories. It was one of her hobbies I never understood."

Thierry and I followed Kent through the apartment, which was nicely illuminated in the afternoon sunlight. I discreetly looked at my phone again, in case Petra had texted, but there were no new messages. We emerged in a cramped office at the back of the apartment.

"Here it is," Kent said, lifting the flap of a cardboard box. "The silver's gotta be worth something, but I don't know about the rest of this junk."

I picked up a salad fork and tilted it under the light. The tines were mottled with age, but the *W* etched into the bottom was unmistakable. A slight chill ran through my fingertips, and I could imagine a dinner party at Windhall from years before.

"How did your wife get this stuff?" I asked.

"She was a collector," Kent said, and shrugged. "She had some of Nicole Simpson's old shirts, too. She got a lot of it on eBay, thought it was all going to be worth a fortune someday."

"And this is all from Windhall?" I asked, looking into the box. There were some more pieces of silverware, a pair of cups and saucers, even a few broken-up pieces of wood.

"You bet. My wife always thought Theo was innocent, though. Thought he was framed. She had all these theories about how the film industry was changing and the old players were getting thrown under the bus."

I thought about telling him that his wife was wrong, but it seemed cruel under the circumstances: the man was clearly still grieving. I had also been having trouble shaking the feeling of doubt that lingered in my mind since watching the magician's film reel.

Under a set of empty frames was a teapot and matching saucers. I skipped over the tea set and pulled out a tarnished locket. "What's this?"

"Oh, that's kind of creepy," he said. "There's a lock of Eleanor's hair in it. Some kind of old Victorian custom."

Another box of worthless stuff. "I appreciate you taking the time to show us this stuff," I said. "It's not really what I'm looking for, though."

Thierry scratched his head and appealed to the man. "Don't you have a bloody knife, something a bit more crime-scene related?"

"Not that I know of," Kent replied.

"Thierry, I can't use this," I told my friend.

"These are good teacups," Kent offered, then looked stumped. His face brightened, and he snapped his fingers. "Oh! There's one more thing."

He vanished from the room, and Thierry turned to look at me.

"What do you think?" he asked.

I shrugged, uncomfortable, then scratched my neck. "Most of this looks like mementos." *And I'm fucking broke.*

Kent returned, carrying a beat-up leather satchel. "This belonged to Theo," he said. "Who knows what it might contain? An unfinished screenplay, perhaps some important papers."

"Open it up, let's see what's inside," I said.

"I've got no idea where the key is. You can take it home and cut the thing open."

The leather was stiff and damaged with mold, and the lock was rusted shut.

"If there's a key, it's in the box with the teacups," Kent went on. I could tell that he was starting to get impatient.

"How do you know it was Theo's?"

"What else does *T.L.* stand for?" He took the satchel and pointed to a tiny, faded monogram on the front of the satchel. "Theo Langley. Theodore, whatever his name was."

The idea was probably too good to be true. But if Theo had left Los Angeles very quickly, there was a possibility that he had left a lot of valuable stuff behind. An unfinished script might not be enough material for a front-page article, but it could at least be enough to get a conversation started with Theo.

"You're selling everything together?" I asked.

"Sure, the bag, the silverware, you can take it all," Kent said. "Let's call it three hundred."

"Dollars?" I glanced at Thierry, who shrugged.

"It's probably worth more than that," he said. "I'm eager to get rid of all this stuff. A lot of bad energy I don't need."

"Let's call it two hundred."

"Ahh . . . two fifty."

"I don't have a cent above two hundred," I said.

"Right, they never do." Kent rolled his eyes and then gave me an impatient gesture. "All right, two hundred. It's yours."

I waited until we were in the driveway before I turned to look at Thierry. He was shaking his head and grinning in disbelief.

"You're a shit hard bargainer," he said. "Nice bluff."

"It wasn't a bluff, but thanks." I thought wistfully of my last two hundred dollars, and the unpaid mortgage popped back into my head.

"You know those are Meissen teacups, right? A whole set could be worth something like three grand. Your boy Theo has taste."

"Tell you what," I said, lifting the cups from the box. "Take the cups and we'll call it even. Thanks for your lead."

"You're ripping yourself off, you have to know that."

"I could care less about cups," I said. "I'm after a big fish, and this time, I'm not going to let him go."

SEVEN

As soon as I got home, I called Petra.

"Hey," she said. "I'm just leaving the office."

"What was that text about?"

"You know about the second dead girl?"

"Yes, I do," I said. "What does that have to do with me?"

I could hear her shifting something, and then a car door closed. "Brian met with Alexa Levine today," she said. "He's going to write the story himself."

"Which story?"

"The Langley story," she said. "Brian's going to write about the connection between Eleanor's murder and the murder of these two girls."

"Like hell he is! That was my angle!"

"I'm sure a lot of people have drawn the same conclusion, Hailey." I could hear the sounds of Hollywood in the background, cars and arguing. A snatch of music played. "He did say something about Theo returning to Los Angeles, though. Weren't you the one who told him that?"

I rubbed my eyes. "What did Alexa say?"

"She's interested. I only heard part of their conversation."

"Why are you telling me this?"

"Windhall has always fascinated me," she said. "And I've been following your pieces for a few years. When I got a job working for the *Lens*, I didn't think it would be quite like this."

"Like what?"

"Like the rest of Hollywood," she said.

"Is this your first job in Los Angeles?"

"Not even close."

"Look, I appreciate the call," I said. "Thanks for looking out for me. I'm not really in a position to help you, though. I'm on my way out. My contract's almost up."

"Maybe I could help you. We could research this story together."

"Thanks, but no. I always write my stories alone."

"Suit yourself," she said. "Let me know if you change your mind."

After hanging up with Petra, I went to my office in the greenhouse out back, taking the box of artifacts with me. When I inherited the house, one of my first orders of business had been to clean out the greenhouse and convert it into my office. It held some fond memories for me, because after my time in the hospital, I had moved in with Gran, and she would potter around in the greenhouse, smoking cigarettes and poking at various plants. She didn't have any real talent for gardening, and most of the time, plants would grow for an inch or so before withering and dying. But her lack of talent didn't seem to bother her. She'd go on watering plants that had died months before as though she never even noticed their shriveled stalks.

As such, the greenhouse had been filled with clutter when I inherited it. The shelves were lined with cracked terra-cotta pots, the tables in the back held one or two dusty urns, and half a dozen broken lattices were leaned up against the walls. I had spent three days emptying pots filled with dirt and scabbed algae, then lost a week scrubbing mold off the windows. I'd salvaged one or two glazed pots, which I'd repurposed for Kentia palms.

With Madeleine's help, I'd taken out the old flagstone floor and replaced it with brick, then removed all the cracked panes of glass and moved my grandmother's kilim rug collection into the newly renovated space. From then on, it was my office, and I spent more time in there than in any other part of my house.

Settling in at my desk, the large wooden table that had once held my grandmother's plants, I thought about how it wasn't the first time I had seen things from Windhall. But if everything had really come out of Theo's house, then it was the biggest single collection that I had come across so far. Most of the items I had seen in the past were offered like illicit goods, because that's what they were: a pilfered fork, a napkin stitched with the Windhall monogram, a book discreetly tucked into the pocket of a onetime dinner guest. Each item was interesting in its own right, but they were all one-dimensional: none of the items did anything to illuminate the bigger picture, or give me an idea of what life at Windhall was like.

I should have been more excited about the haul, but the news about Brian stealing my story had taken the wind out of my sails. Now, sitting at my table in the greenhouse, staring at a pile of lifeless objects, I felt hopeless. I had been chasing a fantasy for years, and I had finally run out of time. If losing my writing contract didn't signify that, then the crumbling roof and the rotten foundations of my grandmother's house certainly did.

I picked up one of the Windhall forks and then reached over and picked up the locket. Keeping hair in a necklace was definitely a spooky old Victorian custom, but it wasn't the first time I had seen it. There was a store on Melrose that specialized in strange old memorabilia, and they had drawers full of them. As I picked up items and set them out on my desk, I remembered the satchel. I had left it in my car.

It was unlikely that the satchel would contain anything of value. Working with Thierry had taught me all the old tricks: a con artist, some distant member of the family, would arrive before Thierry and his team got in. He'd slip a decent knockoff of a lesser-known work of art in with the rest of the garbage, and he'd materialize just as Thierry and his team were discovering it. One of the crew might notice it and estimate some value, but the con artist would insist that it wasn't worth anything. This denial would only make Thierry's guy more certain, and he'd work himself up into a state of excitement, thinking of the commission. Sometimes, there was even a headline to go along with it: LOST WORK OF ART FOUND IN HOARDER'S BASEMENT. You can imagine what the auction would be like.

Since Thierry knew his Caillebottes from his Morisots, he was always able to nip these scams in the bud, but he hadn't examined the satchel. And he didn't know that much about Theo, so I was going to have to rely on my own judgment about the provenance of the satchel.

Once I returned to the desk in my office, I brought the lamp over and examined the bag. It was good-quality leather, probably bespoke, and still intact, despite all the mold and ill treatment. I tested the seams. It was a solid piece of workmanship, which meant that I was going to have to force the lock if I didn't want to destroy it to get inside.

Before I turned my attention to the lock, I rooted around in the box to ensure that the key was really missing. My search didn't turn anything up, and I doubted that a key would have made a difference anyway: the lock was so rusty that it seemed unlikely that a key would have been able to open it.

The satchel had a leather flap held down by twin buckles. The lock holding it shut was in between them, stitched into the main flap and the base underneath. After picking at the lock for a few minutes with a screwdriver, I abandoned the project and grabbed a pair of kitchen scissors.

I cut a small section from the top flap and freed the satchel from its lock. The buckles on either side of the lock were rusted shut, but

I was able to get them open without destroying the bag further. I gently opened the main flap, then looked inside.

There was a bit of ink on the inside edge of the flap, as though a pen had leaked on the leather and the owner had never managed to get it out. I picked through the rest of the satchel—it was filled with writing implements, pens and a moldy pad of paper, some personal memorabilia, and a few coins. I took out an old set of keys and put them to the side; I would try to figure out what they opened some other time.

In the back section of the satchel was a notebook, most of which was waterlogged and stuck with mold. I coughed as a few spores drifted up through the air, and then found a book stuffed in one of the pockets. It was *Ethan Frome* by Edith Wharton.

I turned the satchel over again to make sure that I hadn't missed anything, and noticed that there was some writing on the inside flap. *Theo is a big fat jerk!* it read. The writing was faded and slightly blurred. It was only a small consolation to know that the satchel did, indeed, belong to Theo.

The notebook proved mostly worthless, since all the pages were fused together. They fell apart when I tried to unstick them. The writing was completely washed away by the years and whatever moisture had gotten to the satchel.

Disappointed, I turned my attention to the copy of *Ethan Frome*. The pages were stuck together there, too, but with the aid of a letter opener, I managed to slide some of them apart. A photograph fell onto my desk, and I picked it up.

In the photo were a man and a woman, dancing in front of a row of buildings. He was ducking his head and grinning, and her back was to the camera, but I could tell by their pose that they weren't very good dancers; they were just doing it for fun. The buildings in the background were cream-colored Victorian terrace houses, with lace curtains in the windows and a rocking chair on each porch. Blue hydrangeas lined the sidewalk in front of the houses, and in the background, an old woman peered at the two dancers. They didn't seem to know that their photograph was being taken.

The photo was old and square, faded, probably taken sometime in the '60s. I made a mental note to ask Marty if he recognized the type of camera that had been used, and when it might have been taken. The lens must have been damaged; in the upper right-hand corner of the photograph, was a small mark like a crooked, backward *J*.

I turned the photo over and saw that someone had scrawled a quick phrase in blue ink: *Lucy's with Connie.* Beneath that, a serial strip of letters and numbers that read 021664GFNVT. There was nothing else to elucidate the identity of the dancers, or where the photo might have been taken.

I flipped the photo over and stared hard at the man. With a shock, I realized that I was looking at Theo. He was much older than he had been in other photographs that I had seen, but then again, all the other pictures had been taken before the murder and resulting trial. His skin was tanned and lined, but the smile was unmistakable.

The woman was harder to make out, since I couldn't see her face. She was as tall as Theo, but whether that was the result of genetics or high heels was impossible to say: the photo cut off the dancers at mid-thigh. Her dark hair was pinned at the base of her neck and she wore a multicolored dress.

Connie. Could have been short for Constance, or Consuela. Regardless, it was impossible to say if she had anything to do with Eleanor's murder, because she could have been someone Theo had met after leaving Los Angeles.

The satchel and its contents had a mild amount of interest, but without a bloody murder weapon, as Thierry had suggested at Kent's, I was no better off than I was before. I left everything on my desk, then turned off the lights in the office. After a moment's hesitation, I went back and grabbed the photograph of Theo and Connie.

The dregs of a bottle of Jameson sat on my kitchen counter. I looked at the bottle for a long, hard moment, then grabbed it, too, and took it into my bedroom.

The first shot burned, and the second warmed my chest. I felt magnanimous and numb, the way I usually did with alcohol. After sitting on the edge of my bed for a moment and staring into space, I took out my phone.

I had looked at Leland's phone number so many times that I had committed it to memory. If he ever did call me, I would probably be too wracked with anxiety to answer it, but now, edged toward comfortable alcoholic numbness, I wasn't afraid. For a moment, I thought about emailing Theo directly, but he hadn't responded to my last email, so I decided to text Leland, instead.

I want to talk about Connie, I typed. *Tell Theo I know.* I thought about sending him a picture of the photograph, but then decided against it.

The message sat there for a moment, innocuous and disposable, and then I hit "send."

———

I must have fallen asleep at some point, because my dreams were gently interspersed with the sounds of harps, strings, and then a plaintive trumpet. Jerry Goldsmith's theme from *Chinatown*; it was my ringtone. I blinked awake and rolled over and found my phone under my bed. The call was from a private number. My heart jumped. I knew it must be Leland. I picked up.

"Are you ready to talk?" I asked.

"Have you found him yet?" It was a woman's voice, one that was vaguely familiar.

"Found who?" I rolled onto my back and stared at the ceiling. The smell of mildew had crept into my bedroom, and the cold had seeped in under the door. "Who is this?"

"Have you found Theo yet?" the voice said impatiently. There was something pleasing about the way she spoke, husky with rounded sibilance. I couldn't place it, but I knew that I had heard it somewhere, like seeing a bit actor in a film. "You are still looking for him, aren't you?"

"Tell me how I know you."

"Never mind about me," she said. "Tell me if you've found Theo."

"Is this Connie?"

"What?"

"I'm not in the mood for playing games," I said. I glanced at my watch. "It's past one in the morning. Good night."

I hung up. A moment later, my phone began to ring again.

"Listen to me, Mr. Hailey," the same woman said, and I could hear the taut wire in her voice. "This question happens to be worth a lot of money to me. I know that you're about to lose your job, and your house is in a bad state of disrepair."

I sat up.

"Do I have your attention now?"

"If you were trying to threaten me, you'd come directly to my house," I said.

"I already did," she said, then laughed. "I stopped by earlier, but you weren't home. If I were trying to threaten you, believe me, you'd know it."

"What do you want?"

"I can answer some of your questions," she said. "Theo is back, for one. You're not going to find him by buying up his old junk."

A chill ran down my spine. "Have you been following me?"

"I can tell you how he's connected to all those dead girls. Have you found out who Ben is?"

"Look, I'm done—"

"I can pay you for your time, but I need to know if you're worth the investment. Now, have you found Theo?"

"What makes you think I'm interested in working for you?"

She cleared her throat. "Your house is falling apart," she said. "And you're about to lose your job. I believe I already mentioned that."

"Good night," I said again.

Before I could hang up, she said, "I have something you want. You're certainly not going to find it by speaking to amateur collectors."

"I'm about to hang up," I said. "You'd better get to the point."

"I have the journals," she said. "The reason that Theo's trial was thrown. You do remember them, don't you? The prosecution broke into Theo's house to find them. They can tell you everything you want to know."

"I don't believe you," I said, but I could feel my heart rate accelerating.

"Suit yourself," she said. "Half-rate journalists are a dime a dozen in this city."

She hung up.

———————

The next morning, I woke up with a sour taste in my mouth. Weak daylight filtered in through the window, and I mentally replayed the conversation with the anonymous woman. I found my phone and checked to see if there were any messages from Leland, but there was nothing.

I dragged myself out of bed and padded into the kitchen, blinking sleep away. I pulled out the Atomic and scooped coffee into it, then put it on the stovetop and rubbed my eyes. When the coffee was ready, I diluted it with cold milk, then drank it in one quick jolt. The vines creeping in through the ceiling looked healthier than they had the last time I had checked, and I briefly contemplated the merits of growing a garden in my attic.

When I was feeling more awake, I turned around to grab something from the fridge, and then I saw it sitting on the counter.

My kitchen was always tidy, roof deterioration aside. If anything had been sitting on my counter the previous evening, I certainly would have noticed it, especially if that something was an expensive bottle of whiskey.

I crossed the kitchen and picked up the bottle, turning it to examine the label. Macallan whiskey, aged twenty-five years, unopened. Underneath the bottle was an envelope of thick, expensive parchment, embossed with a return address in Pasadena. I slipped it open and found a single sheet of paper inside.

> I know about the film you stole from that magician, Max. He's planning to press charges, but I've convinced him to let me speak to you first. I have something else that you want instead.
>
> We want the same thing. Meet me at my house on Tuesday, at 11 a.m.
>
> Heather

I flipped the envelope and studied the return address, then turned on my computer and searched for it. The satellite image showed a sprawling Spanish mansion on about three acres, protected by a high, smooth wall.

After a moment of consideration, I went back to Google and searched for "Spanish colonial estates in Pasadena." I scrolled through the results until I spotted the house from the satellite image, then clicked on the article.

Annesley presides over Sausalito Avenue in Pasadena, read the caption. "Built as a summer house for the DeMille family in 1914, the stately home has retained its original charm even as the town evolved around it."

I assumed the bottle and note had come from the woman on the phone. Could she be a descendant of Cecil B. DeMille?

I was stumped for a minute, and then I had a different idea. I searched for "Annesley" and "Pasadena," and this time, I hit pay dirt.

Heather Engel-Feeny hosts a black-tie gala at her estate, Annesley; Hollywood elite attend, began one article. I clicked on the link, which took me to *Vanity Fair*. The party was an exclusive affair to raise money for the J. Paul Getty Trust, of which Heather was an executive chair.

I couldn't help feeling impressed, but the pictures gave me no indication of who Heather was, or why she might want to talk to me about Theo. All of her guests were the power brokers of Hollywood and Los Angeles, the top-tier financial executives, art dealers, influential architects, and movie producers.

I finally found a picture of Heather herself and stopped to study her face. She was an attractive redhead who looked like she might be in her early sixties, but she had an unnaturally smooth complexion. In one photo she spoke to Tim Roth; in another, she smiled and spoke to a man with silver hair, whom the caption identified as developer Linus Warren. I spent an hour reading up on some of the other guests who were at the party.

When I finished clicking through the *Vanity Fair* gallery, I went back to the search bar to see what else I could find out about Heather.

The next article showed some more of Heather's humanitarian work, but the third article indicated that she had recently fought against a Los Angeles County proposition that prevented one person from buying multiple historic homes in a certain period.

Historic homes. Bingo. I picked up the phone and called Madeleine.

"It's early," she said.

"I know you don't sleep. Have you ever heard of Heather Engel-Feeny?"

"Yes!" she said. "She's a legend. Why do you ask?"

"What do you think of her? Dark and ominous? Vaguely threatening?"

"No, not at all," she said, perplexed. "She's kind of a hero around the office. I've never met her, but she does some great stuff. Lots of preservation work."

I thought for a minute. "You think she's the type of person to pick a number from the phone book at random, and fuck with whoever picked up?"

"I'm at work. Is there something you need?"

"You said Heather's a legend," I said. "How'd you like to meet her?"

"Are you interviewing her for the *Lens*?" Madeleine sounded dubious. "That seems . . . beneath her."

"Thanks for the vote of confidence. But no. One more question—does she have any connections to the film industry?"

"She's the head of a huge charity," Madeleine said. "She works with a lot of celebrities."

"Anything else?"

"She might have gotten her start working in film," she said. "No idea. Hey, I have to go. Call me when you meet up with her."

"Will do."

After hanging up with Madeleine, I went to the J. Paul Getty Trust website and found a page with Heather's biography and background information. *Descended from Hollywood royalty, Heather is intimately familiar with the history and rich cultural background of Los Angeles. Her family was one of the first families to arrive in Los Ange-les, back in the days when Hollywood was nothing more than a cluster of farmhouses among the orange groves . . .*

The pieces were starting to fall into place, and I had a feeling that I knew what I was going to find before I got there. It only took a few more minutes of searching through websites for me to find the name of her parents: "Heather Engel-Feeny was born to Norma Lisbon and Reuben Engel."

I stopped reading, because I had made the last connection between Heather and Theodore Langley. Reuben Engel had been the producer in charge of *Last Train to Avalon*, and he had worked with Theo on a number of other movies, as well. His name hadn't endured in the way of Lang or Hitchcock, but I had always been a fan. He and Theo had been a team for years, like Wilder and Diamond, making a slew of successful films.

Most people who remembered Engel's name in the present day remembered him for something else, though: in the end, he had stood on the witness stand for the prosecution, declaring that Theo was absolutely, irrevocably guilty.

As I studied Heather's image and wondered where I might have heard her voice before, it came back to me. Her voice had been the one I heard on the radio, weighing in about how Theodore Langley had killed those girls.

EIGHT

It was Monday morning, which used to be reserved for our weekly pitch meetings. When Ford was still editor in chief, pitch meetings had been a lot of fun. The *Lens* staff would sit around and debate conspiracy theories for hours, talking about unsolved murders and weird mysteries. Ever since Brian had taken over, however, things had soured a bit. Instead of listening to writers pitch their stories, we'd all sit around and listen to Brian detail his weekend activities, and then there would be a fifteen-minute freestyle session (Brian versus Brian), where he would try to remember the names of various people he had partied with.

"We ended up at a mansion in Venice," Brian had said during the last week's meeting. "There was a hot tub on the roof. The place was massive—the guy who owned it was one of the founders of Yahoo! I was so wasted, I spent the whole night throwing up over the side of the roof. Thank God Venice is built along canals, right?"

After confirming Heather's identity, I had grabbed the stack of notes that I had already compiled on Theo, then got in my car and drove to Hollywood. When I got to the office, I ran up the stairs to the second floor, then burst through the door, into the office.

Petra looked up from the secretary desk, and her eyes widened. "They're waiting for you."

"Wait, what? Who's waiting for me?"

"Alexa and Brian," she said. "Ford's here, too. They're all in Brian's office."

"Do you know what it's about?"

"No idea."

I made my way down the hallway, and knocked on Brian's door but didn't wait for a response. I opened the door and stepped inside to find Brian and Ford, and across from them, the one and only Alexa Levine.

"Ford," I said, catching my breath. I was sweating from my run up the stairs. "What are you doing here?"

"Hailey," Ford said, smiling. "Take a seat."

Alexa turned to look at me, her expression neutral. It was unreal to see her sitting ten feet away from me, the same high cheekbones and hooked nose, the sharp eyes I had seen in all of her photos. Her dark hair was pinned back, but I could see a few streaks of gray. She wore no makeup, and she looked just as distinguished and fierce as I had always imagined her to be.

"Ms. Levine, it's a pleasure to meet you," I said, walking across the room and offering her my hand. "My name is Max Hailey."

There was an awkward moment, and I realized that they were all waiting for me to sit down. I took a chair next to Brian.

"I want to talk about Theodore Langley," Alexa said. "Brian said you have some information about him."

I tried to remember everything I had told Brian.

"Is Theo back in town?" Alexa prompted.

"I have reason to believe so."

"What reason is that?"

I didn't want to mention the fact that I had stolen Leland's phone. "His lawyer is in town," I said.

"Leland Bates?" Ford asked.

"Yes," I said, perplexed. "How did you know that?"

"Brian has been doing some research on his own," Ford said. "He's put together a few theories."

"I'm going to write about the dead girls," Brian said. "I've already met with the father of the dead art student. He's pissed off, as you can imagine. He wants Windhall to be torn to the ground."

"Alexa," I said, trying to keep my voice even. "I'd like to write about Theo."

"That's not an option," Brian said, cutting in. "Alexa, I've given Hailey notice. He's going to finish any stories that he's working on, but he'll be gone in two weeks."

Alexa didn't even look over at him. "No."

Brian laughed. "Sorry, no to what?"

"Max isn't fired," she said. "If he has information on Theodore Langley, it's an incredible lead. It would be incredibly shortsighted to let that lead go."

"I've already terminated his contract."

"So draft another one." She met his gaze with cool eyes. Brian's face had turned red, but he finally backed down.

"Hailey's a great reporter, Bri," Ford murmured.

"Whatever, *Dad*."

Alexa turned to me. "You're also interested in writing about the dead girls?"

"No," I said. "I think I can prove that Theo killed Eleanor. That's the story I'm interested in."

Brian snorted. "I doubt that, my friend. Also, I haven't given you permission to write the story."

"You don't know anything about Leland, or Theo," I said. "Petra's been doing your research for you."

"Leland's dad defended Theo at his first criminal trial," Brian said. "I know that much. And, yes, Petra has been helping me, but it would be stupid not to use all the resources available."

The color rose to my face. "Ms. Levine, with all due respect, this is my story," I said. "I'm not going to relinquish my contacts or my information so that Brian can write it."

"It's not your decision," Brian said. He leaned back in his chair and grinned. "I'm the editor in chief."

"You're not," Alexa corrected him. "I'm taking over that position. You're an editor, but you're not the top editor."

"That's fine," Brian said. "I'm still writing the story on Theo."

"Actually, Brian, I think it's best if you let us finish this conversation privately."

Brian shot to his feet. "Dad!"

"She's right, Bri," Ford said. "I'll talk to you afterward."

Brian gave me a filthy look, then stalked across the office and paused at the door. "This is *my* office, you know," he said. "You're the ones who should be leaving, not me."

Alexa fixed her eyes on him and said nothing. Brian stood there, wavering, and then left the office, slamming the door behind him.

"Now," Alexa said, turning her gaze to me, "I'd like to know what information you have. Is Theo back in Los Angeles?"

"I think so, but I don't have any definitive proof yet."

"Max, I'm going to level with you," she said. "Theo had nothing to do with the murders of those two young women. It's the work of a copycat, there's no doubt about that."

"How can you be sure?"

"I've seen this before," she said. "Besides, Theo's too old to inflict this kind of damage. He's in his nineties."

"Ninety-three," I said quietly.

"There you go. What's your angle?"

"I want to know why he did it."

"I want you to be completely honest with me," she said. "How do you know that Theo is back in town?"

"I went to Windhall," I said, then hesitated. "I broke in, and I found Leland's phone. I took the phone and went through it. There was an email from Theo."

Ford bit back a smile, and I couldn't read Alexa's expression.

"There's no statute of limitations on murder," I said. "We could get a retrial."

"He was acquitted," Ford said. "You can't be tried again if you're acquitted."

"He wasn't acquitted, the case was dropped," I said. "The prosecution team never got enough evidence together to launch a new case. Shortly thereafter, a new district attorney was appointed, and the case eventually got swept under the rug. If we were able to produce enough evidence to pull together another trial, that would be huge."

"Hailey, Hailey," Ford said. "Let's not go gallivanting off too quickly. None of us have law degrees, and even if we did, how would you go about gathering evidence?"

"Isn't Lapin going to law school?"

Lapin was Ford's boyfriend, and also a law student at UCLA.

"He's in his first year," Ford said. "Besides, he's studying antitrust, not criminal law. Lapin's out."

Alexa leaned back in her chair. "You're a skilled journalist," she said. "I've had some time to look at your portfolio. You're not the first one to try to prove Theo's guilt, however, and so far, nobody's proven anything."

"The entire Los Angeles prosecution team couldn't come up with anything," Ford added. "They had warrants."

"I've known a few people who have tried in the past," Alexa said. "Theo's the holy grail of true crime. Wasn't there a reward offered for a while?"

"Reuben Engel was offering fifty thousand dollars for a while," I said. "But that's over, since he's dead."

"Remind me who Reuben Engel is."

"He was the producer for *Last Train to Avalon*," I said. I debated telling them I had gotten a phone call from Engel's daughter the night before, but decided that I should see what Alexa wanted before I mentioned her name. "Theo's last movie, the one that never got finished. Reuben lost a ton of money after Eleanor died."

"You have a backward way of doing things, but I miss that spark of yours," Ford said. "You're one tough bastard, you know that, Hailey?"

I couldn't resist my next comment. "I think it was a mistake to hire Brian, Ford. He doesn't have the same eye for a story."

Ford and Alexa exchanged a look, and neither one of them said anything. I wondered if I had put my foot in my mouth.

"Look, Hailey, I don't want this information to get spread around," Ford said. "So don't tell anyone else. There's a reason I stepped down."

"Okay, you can trust me."

"I had some tests done," he said. "I kept getting these awful headaches. Turns out I have some aggressive form of cancer in a part of my body I don't think you need to know about."

"Come on."

He was smiling, but it didn't quite reach his eyes. "You were always my best reporter," he said.

"Ford, you're not serious," I said. "Are you really sick?"

"Afraid so, old chap." He tried another smile. "That's why I brought Alexa in. I taught her everything I know, once upon a time."

I could see that he was getting emotional, and it embarrassed me. Without saying anything, Alexa rose from her chair and exited the room, so that we were alone together. There was an awkward moment, and then Alexa returned, carrying a glass of orange juice. She went over and sat next to Ford on the couch, handing him the glass.

He accepted it with shaking hands, and Alexa squeezed his shoulder. She sat there for a moment, until some of the color returned to Ford's face, and then she returned to her chair.

"I'll level with you, Max," Alexa said. "I think you're overreaching by trying to get an interview with Theo."

I waited.

"It's a story I'd love to see, but right now, Brian has a better angle," she went on. "He has leads. He's talking to the families of the dead girls, and that's the hot topic. It'll sell ad space."

"Ad space." I failed to hide my disgust.

"Haven't you heard? The *Lens* is coming back from bankruptcy."

I saw a flash of annoyance across her face.

"So you don't want my story," I said. "That's what you're saying."

"I'm saying that if you can't prove that you've got a lead, I'm going to run with Brian's story," she said. "And then your story will probably be redundant. I'll give you both until the end of the week before I decide which one to go with. Thanks for coming in today."

She turned her attention to some papers in front of her. It seemed clear to me that the conversation was over, so I left the room.

It had been almost twenty-four hours, and Leland hadn't taken the bait on my Connie message. I only had one last option, and before I could talk myself out of it, I climbed into my car and headed south, toward the city.

I knew that I was playing with fire by going back to Windhall, when Leland and Ben had both warned me not to, but I had to give it one last shot. If Brian went ahead with his story about the dead girls, it was only a matter of time before Windhall became the center of a shitstorm. I didn't want all that extra attention directed at the house before I'd had one last go at it.

I got my first surprise when I reached the edge of the property and saw that the gate was open. Something inside me warned that it was a bad sign, but I pushed the feeling aside and slipped past the heavy iron barrier. Leland was probably at the house, that was all; he had forgotten to close the gate. It hadn't yet occurred to me that they might be expecting a visit.

As I walked up the cracked, overgrown driveway, I saw that there were lights on in the house. The windows weren't completely illuminated; the light seemed to emit a hollow glow, a feeble beating heart within the walls. Lanterns, then, or maybe a strong flashlight.

I approached the front door and lifted the heavy knocker, then banged it against the door three times.

A small eternity passed before I heard a noise from within the house. A voice, and then a reply. I couldn't make out the age or sex of who had spoken, but at least I knew that someone was there.

The door finally swung open, and Leland stood before me.

"I don't believe it," he said. "I thought you were smart enough to stay away from here."

"I want to talk to Theo."

He took his phone out of his pocket and waved it at me. "A homeless man found this near a diner on Sunset. Anything you want to add?"

I shrugged. "Some people have integrity."

"I'm going to give you about thirty seconds to vacate the property before I call the police—"

"I want to talk about Connie."

Leland was quiet. He still held the phone in the air, but I could see that I had caught him off guard. Recovering, he tucked the phone back in his pocket, then smiled.

"Connie," he said. "I don't think I know what you're talking about."

"Sure you do," I said. "Theo and Connie were at Lucy's together. Didn't you get my text message?"

"What do you want?"

"I want to talk to Theo."

"Why would I agree to that?"

"I'll sit on the story about Connie," I said. "We're prepared to run it this weekend, but we'll hold it, if you agree to let Theo meet up with me."

"One interview?"

"Two," I said. I was gambling, here, but I wasn't about to go all in unless I knew that I could get something solid from Theo.

"I'm calling your bluff. Run an article, if you like. You might have some information, but it's equally possible that you've just come across a lucky piece of memorabilia and you don't actually have a story. I'd be willing to bet the latter."

"I thought you might say that," I said. "And if that's how you feel, I'll have to go ahead and run the article without your input."

"As you wish."

"But you should know," I went on. "I know about Ben. I know why he doesn't want me to come back to Windhall."

This comment was followed by a steep silence. "All right, Mr. Hailey," Leland said. "I'll hear your terms, and see what I can do about them."

"I want to see the inside of the house," I said. "Every room of it."

"I thought you already had."

"I'd like a personal tour."

"We'll see about that. Next?"

"I want two interviews," I said. "One won't be enough."

He was quiet for a long moment. "I can get you a meeting with Theo. I can't promise two. It'll have to be here, though, I don't want him walking into some kind of media ambush."

"That's fine." I was afraid I might burst into song if I kept talking.

"Thursday. I'll send someone to your house to pick you up."

"I don't mind driving over."

"That's not necessary. I'll send a driver to pick you up at two."

"Okay, let me give you my address."

"I know where you live, Mr. Hailey."

A chill ran down my spine, and I tried to sound casual. "Great," I said. "I'll see you Thursday, then."

"See you then."

I was practically skipping as I made my way down the driveway. When I hit the curve in the driveway, I turned to look at the house before it disappeared from view. There was a light on in the library, which had tall windows overlooking the yard. A figure stood in the window, watching me. It was a slightly stooped figure, tall enough, I could see that even from that distance.

Could it be Theo?

As I stood there wondering, the figure turned and retreated, and then the light vanished.

———————

The next morning, I woke up bright and early, then went to my computer and compiled a list of notes for my meeting with Heather. I didn't know what she'd want to talk about, but I wanted to be prepared. I scanned back through the articles that I had already read about her, boning up on information about her social circle and possible business acquaintances.

Afterward, I headed over to Los Feliz. Madeleine's favorite café, an old brick fire station that had been converted into a coffee shop, was located two blocks from her house. There were always lines out the door.

I resented the artisanal coffee culture that had taken over Los Angeles in the last few years, since I had always been a shameless devotee of instant espresso. If I had been the type to hole up in a café for a few hours, though, I would have chosen to work at Sparks. With the high, round open doors and the vines swarming all over the brick, it was a hospitable place to get work done.

I picked up two cappuccinos, then headed over to Madeleine's house.

"You're too early," she said by way of greeting when she opened the door.

"It's ten o'clock. We're supposed to be in Pasadena at eleven."

She stared at me. "It's the middle of the day," she said. "We won't have to worry about traffic."

"I got you coffee. I'll give you ten minutes to get dressed, and then I'm leaving without you."

"Jesus," she said, swiping the coffee. She wandered toward her bedroom.

"I'm serious!" I called after her. "You've got ten minutes!"

Madeleine's house was one of my favorite houses in Los Angeles. In some ways, it was in worse shape than my house was, but it had a lot of charm. The three-room cottage had sloping ceilings and holes in the walls, and Madeleine hid the worst of the damage to the floorboards with some creatively placed rugs. The door leading out to the back garden didn't open, so whenever we wanted a bit of fresh air, we'd climb out through the kitchen window. Once a year, a developer tried to talk Madeleine into selling for the land value alone, but she refused on principle, because the house had a lot of history.

The rambling little cottage was a former Raymond Chandler residence, and Madeleine had it on good authority that he had written at least three chapters of *Farewell, My Lovely* while half-tanked in the back bedroom. Living in a Raymond Chandler house isn't a huge claim to fame in Los Angeles, because Ray and his wife were fairly transient, but I had always been a Philip Marlowe fan, and I got a small thrill every time I came to visit Madeleine.

Madeleine finally reemerged, rubbing her eyes.

"How do I look?"

"Great," I said. "Let's go. You can navigate."

We got on the I-5 North, which drove past Griffith Park. It was a splendid morning, with only a few benign cumulus clouds pinned above the horizon. Baked summers and mountain haze could make you question why you lived in Los Angeles, but a blue sky and early-morning outing could sort everything out again.

"You want to go to the York for lunch this afternoon? My treat," I offered.

"I could kill a burger," she said. "You're on."

I got on the CA-134 East, toward Pasadena. The San Gabriel Mountains were pristine in the morning light, and once again, I felt filled with optimism.

"Why does Heather want the reel?" Madeleine asked.

"She didn't say."

"Take the next exit," Madeleine said, looking at her phone.

"You sure?"

"That's what my phone says," Madeleine read. "I think there's an accident up ahead."

I turned off the freeway and wound through a shady, tree-lined street. The oak trees created a thick canopy of leaves, and the houses stood behind long, sloping lawns. The houses were friendly, Craftsman-style mansions, fringed with geraniums and pine trees. Practical houses, intellectual houses. There were no frivolous Swiss chalets or Moroccan temples, no spindly turrets with sugar glass windows.

"Sausalito Avenue's going to be in two rights," Madeleine said. "Also, my phone would like to know whether you're carrying any weapons, and if you have the right to breathe the air in this part of the city?"

"Laurel Canyon isn't exactly a slum, thank you very much," I said.

"Compared to this neighborhood, everywhere is a slum."

Madeleine was right; we had left Los Angeles behind. The Craftsman houses had given way to luxurious, imposing estates, some as big as museums. On the left sat a house so big that it looked like it might have been a hotel, its upper terrace supported by thick Ionic columns. The next house resembled a French palace, complete with flowing gardens and fountains in the front yard.

"Here we are," I said, as we pulled up in front of Heather's house. I recognized the house from my earlier Google stalking.

We had reached a smooth, white wall. I pulled up to the gate, which was fitted out with an imposing security system. A decorative sand strip fringed with native California plants stood between the street and the edge of Heather's property.

I punched the button on the box of numerals, and a moment later, a singsong voice came crackling through.

"Ye-es?"

"Max Hailey to see Heather," I said, then added "Engel-Feeny."

"That's her!" replied the voice. "Do come in."

With a tiny click, the gate retreated into the white wall, and we were confronted with Heather's mansion. It was much more impressive than the photos I had seen in the *Vanity Fair* article, which hadn't quite managed to convey the warmth and grand scale of the thing.

Heather's wide, well-groomed lawn was decorated with palm trees, bougainvillea, and jacarandas. The gardeners must have been extremely diligent, because not a single blossom or leaf marred the stretch of clean, white stones that expanded up to her front door. A wide brick pathway led up to the house itself, a spacious Spanish hacienda.

After parking, we approached the front door and I knocked. The door swung open to reveal a young man with dark hair and perfect teeth. A Bluetooth glinted in his ear.

"Max," he said warmly, taking my hand in both of his. "I'm Barney. And who's this?"

"Madeleine Woolner," Mad said, stepping forward.

"She doesn't like apples," Barney muttered. "And she's allergic to cinnamon."

"Excuse me?"

"Oh," he said, waving his hand at me. He pointed to the Bluetooth. "Caterers."

"Got it."

We stepped into the foyer, which was suffused with warm light. The walls were cream-colored cob, and the floors were made of dark wood. All the doorways were arches into other rooms, and I looked up to see vaulted ceilings.

"Follow me," Barney said, then turned and looked at our shoes. "Are your feet clean?"

"Yes . . . ?"

"You can take your shoes off, then."

Madeleine and I stooped to remove our shoes. We exchanged a look, then made our way through the foyer behind Barney, who was delivering lines in a dreamy monologue.

"Heather's particular about who she lets into her house, as you can imagine," he said. "She has some dogs, which won't interfere with your business; they're locked up in the nursery. Also, Heather has an appointment this afternoon, so she might have to cut your meeting short."

"Got it," I said.

"Now, is there something we can do about that ridiculous color? Heather finds yellow to be confrontational."

I glanced down at my outfit. "Are you talking to me?"

"No," Barney said, irritated. "The caterers' uniforms are offensive to anyone with eyeballs."

"Max Hailey! Is that Max?"

Heather emerged in the hallway before us. She looked the same as she had in the photos that I had seen of her, but it looked like her red hair had been recently permed. She wore a crisp oxford shirt and slacks, and a small dog quivered in her arms.

"Barney," she said, turning to address the young man. "Did you lock the dogs in the nursery?"

"They were highly animated this morning."

"Well, one of them's done a shit in the vintage bassinet. You're going to have to clean that up."

"Of course, Heather."

"It looks runny," she said. "Have you been giving them lamb again?"

"We were out of kibble," he said, lowering his voice.

"No lamb!" she snapped. "Pedigree can't take anything but mince. Take care of that now, please."

Barney disappeared, and Heather turned her attention to Madeleine.

"Who's your friend, Max?"

"I'm Madeleine," she said, stepping forward to offer Heather her hand.

"Are you a journalist? Do you write?"

"No, I work with a historical conservation society."

"Which one?" Heather narrowed her eyes.

"Aiden-Harms."

"The Jewish one." Heather pursed her lips, then noticed our bare feet. "You took your shoes off."

"Barney asked us to."

"I'd watch your step, if I were you," Heather said. "Barney gave the dogs lamb this morning, so all bets are off."

We followed Heather toward the back of the house, and I tried to absorb as much of our surroundings as possible. The thick walls of the estate managed to keep out the heat of the day, and the tiles were cool against my bare feet. Each room followed the same basic color scheme: cream and dark wood. We passed a living room lined with French windows and a formal dining room with a modern art chandelier, and I caught a glimpse of a library down another long hallway.

Heather opened a set of double doors, and we emerged into the backyard. There were paths of swept marble and another tidy, immaculate lawn. Chaise longues were gathered around the lip of a marble swimming pool, and I couldn't help wondering when someone had last gone swimming.

"Do you swim?" I asked.

"Not *here*," Heather said. "I have a personal trainer and a gym membership."

"I see."

"Pools have a ghastly history in Los Angeles," Heather said, turning to look at us. "Did you know that Cecil DeMille's grandson drowned in his neighbor's pool? Maybe it was a duck pond. Charlie Chaplin nearly *died* in the swimming pool at Pickfair—oh, he was a devout atheist, he was trying to make some point about the lack of God in Hollywood."

"Didn't Cecil DeMille live here?" I asked.

"You've done your homework," she said, impressed. "The accident happened near Los Feliz, though. This was the summer house. I've done some extensions and renovations, as you've probably noticed."

Heather set down the dog and found her keys. We stepped into the pool house, and I felt a surge of envy when I saw the interior.

One wall was just windows, looking out toward the San Gabriel Mountains. The other walls were covered in framed posters of old movies.

Heather followed my gaze. "My father's pictures," she said. "He was a prolific producer."

"I've seen some of them," I said. "*Last Train to Avalon* was supposed to be one of his best."

Heather pressed her lips together, and I realized that I had broached a taboo subject.

"His other movies were great, too," I added hastily. "*The Queen's Shadow* was excellent."

"It was," Heather said warmly. "You like movies?"

"Of course. Los Angeles would be nothing without the film industry."

"Moving on," she said. "Did you bring what I asked for?"

"I did," I said. "But first, you said you have something for me."

I had miscalculated my advantage. Heather narrowed her eyes and laughed once, without mirth.

"You listen to me," she said. "That reel doesn't belong to you. Ray wanted to call the police, but I talked him out of it. You're going to hand it over, because if you don't, I'm going to have to call the police myself."

"What?"

"I don't like to play games, young man," she said. "You're a guest in my house, and you're overstepping your bounds."

I stared at her, mute.

"Max," she said, and her voice had softened. "Have you seen the reel? You took it home, so you must have had a good look."

I nodded.

"Surely you realize," she said, "how damaging it would be for MGM if the reel got out. My father's name would be tarnished. It's a producer's job to protect his stars, you know."

"Your father is dead."

"It's my job to protect his legacy."

I reached into my satchel and took out the reel. Before I handed it over to Heather, I hesitated, stalling for time.

"You said you had something for me," I tried again.

"The reel, Max."

I handed it over, and Heather smiled. "Thank you for that."

"You should be careful with that film," I said. "Nitrogen film is highly flammable. That magician's lucky it didn't set fire to his restaurant."

"Hailey's a pyromaniac," Mad said helpfully. "Went to jail and everything."

Heather ignored her. "I'm aware of the dangers of nitrogen film," she said. "My father used to tell me stories about how old studios would go up in flames because of it."

She knelt by a safe and punched in the code. The door opened, and she withdrew a metal box. With a smile, she set the box in front of me.

"Go ahead," she said. "Open it, don't be shy."

I flipped the latch and opened the metal box. Inside was a sheaf of papers, tidy black notebooks, and a few old photographs. I was suddenly short of breath.

"What is it?" Madeleine craned her neck to see.

I picked up the top notebook. Beneath it was a stack of similar notebooks, as well as various photographs, clippings, and bits of memorabilia. *May 12, 1944*, began the first line. I flipped through the first few pages of the notebook, which was filled with the same, whimsical script. Page after page of meticulous, careful notation.

I turned to Heather. "Where did you get these?"

"Does it matter?" Heather smiled. "They're authentic. I had them tested for fingerprints. Not that it matters, but the handwriting is a perfect match. There's no faking this stuff."

"But . . . how did you get them? I thought they were destroyed a long time ago."

"Someone kept them safe." She shrugged. "They weren't cheap, but I knew that they were valuable. They'll give you a lot of insight into Theo's life back then. I think they can help you prove that he killed Eleanor."

"What do you want from me?"

"Information," she said. "That's all."

"You already have Theo's journals. Can't they tell you everything you need to know?"

I counted the notebooks—there were six of them. Madeleine's hand was on my arm, and I turned to look at her.

"What is it?" she asked.

"These are Theo's notebooks," I replied. "These notebooks are the reason that the trial was thrown."

"That's not entirely true," Heather interrupted.

"Well, the judge threw out the case because he found out that the district attorney paid someone to sneak into Theo's house and steal these," I said. "Apparently he thought they were valuable enough to risk the case."

I rested a hand on top of the journals. I felt like I was vibrating at a low frequency, and my feeling of boundless optimism had returned. A long time had passed since the last time I felt so carefree.

"The journals are yours," Heather said. "If."

"If?"

"In exchange, I need you to do something for me," Heather said.

"I'm not sure I can offer you anything." My hand was still on the journals. I had never allowed myself to really believe that they still existed, and now I wasn't going to let them out of my sight. I already knew that I was going to agree to whatever Heather asked of me, no matter how ridiculous.

"I heard that you're trying to get in touch with Theo," she said. "You've been speaking with his lawyer."

"I can't confirm that."

"Cut the shit, Max. I've got connections, I hear things. I don't expect you to understand this, but my father's career was nearly ruined because of Theodore Langley. I want to see him brought to justice before he dies."

"You think I can make that happen?"

"When you meet him," she said, "and I'm sure you will, because you're resourceful—I want you to find out how he did it. I get first dibs on any evidence you find. I don't want movie posters with Theo's signature, I want proof that he killed Eleanor. If you can get the district attorney to open a new case, I'll pay you handsomely. Let's call it thirty thousand dollars."

"And the journals." I was having trouble wrapping my head around the agreement.

"And the journals. It should go without saying that you can't publish an article until I've looked at it."

"Thirty thousand is tempting, but that would last—what? A year? This story would make my career." I lingered on the thought. "I'm thinking long-term, here. Money runs out; I'm more interested in keeping my job."

"You're forgetting the journals, Max," Heather said. "You won't get anywhere without them."

I reached into the box and picked up a stack of photographs. I recognized a lot of the players in the shots—Errol Flynn, Jean Harlow, Mae West; Rita Hayworth posing next to Porter Hall and Jimmy Stewart. Some of the shots were at Windhall, but others were in the Hollywood Hills, when they were still somewhat wild, or else on the beach.

There were also quite a few shots of Eleanor, sometimes alone, and sometimes with others. I flipped through pictures of Eleanor wearing a tennis outfit, a racket swung over her shoulder, or Eleanor and another woman brushing a horse, so absorbed in their task that they didn't even seem to notice the photographer. There was a photo of Eleanor standing in a garden, her hair pinned at the base of her neck. I peered closer and recognized the hedges of Theo's garden, and a shiver went down my spine.

I stopped on a photograph of Windhall. Some dark-eyed stars languished around the lip of Theo's pool, social malaise written across their features. I frowned and held the photo closer. I could make out Barbara Stanwyck, and it looked like Robert Taylor was shading his eyes against the glare of the sun.

"There's one more thing," Heather said. "I expect you to give me weekly updates, let me know what progress you've made."

"Why can't we just meet at the end of the month? I'll tell you everything then."

She wagged a finger at me. "I'd like to know everything as it comes. Anything you learn about Theo, you tell me straight off."

I couldn't take my eyes off the journals.

"Thirty thousand," Heather repeated. "I'll give that to you once you've fulfilled your end of the deal, of course."

"Hailey—" Madeleine started, but Heather cut her off.

"Do we have a deal or not? I have a very important meeting in a few minutes." Heather was starting to sound impatient.

"Can I take everything in this box?" I asked.

"You may, but only if you sign something."

I hesitated, looking at Madeleine for confirmation. She looked exasperated, and I felt like I must have missed a hidden signal at some point.

"Look, I can't promise not to run the article," I said. "If I find something conclusive, I can show it to you, but I can't promise to sit on the story."

"Promise me seventy-two hours," Heather said. "Give me the information seventy-two hours before you run the story. I'll take it to the district attorney, and we'll get the case reopened."

"Hailey, can we talk outside?" Madeleine gave me a hard look.

"Max, this deal evaporates once I walk out that door." Heather glanced at her watch. "You've got about thirty seconds before I change my mind."

"Forty-eight," I said. "I'll give you forty-eight hours with the evidence before I run my story."

"Excellent." Heather walked around her desk and opened a drawer. She pulled out an iPad and swiped the screen, then made a notation. "I've got a contract for you right here. I'll just make a note on here that we've changed the terms, and my lawyers can go over it and send you a new copy. Sign with your finger at the bottom of the screen."

I took the contract and scanned it. It was disheartening to see that for all my strong words and negotiations, Heather had known that she would get things on her terms in the end.

I signed at the bottom of the paper, then picked up the box of notebooks.

"Thank you, Max," Heather purred. "I really think we'll do well together."

NINE

Madeleine waited until we reached my car before turning to me.

"What was that?"

"This is an incredible opportunity," I said. "Reading through these journals might give me motive, and it also might shed some light on how Theo planned to kill Eleanor."

Madeleine looked at me like I was crazy. "How long do you think Heather has been holding on to those journals?"

"No idea."

"Don't you think she might have already looked through them? They're clearly worthless, Hailey. Heather hasn't found anything, so why would you?"

I hadn't considered this, but I wasn't willing to admit defeat. "Well, they might give me an upper hand on Theo," I said. "Maybe I can find something in here that will convince him to confide in me."

"Oh, Hailey." Mad sank her head into her hands. "I know you don't like taking advice, but damn. You played right into her trap. Do you even know what happened back there?"

"It's cute when you explain my job to me."

"Don't be an asshole," she snapped. "Thirty thousand is Heather's annual hair budget. That money means *nothing* to her. Her assistant probably spends more than that on drugs. Heather thinks she owns you now. You're never going to get that article."

"You know what?" I snapped. "I'm not hungry anymore. You can eat lunch by yourself."

"That's mature."

"I didn't ask you to come along so you could Madsplain things to me."

"She was patronizing you," Madeleine said, exasperated. "You work for a progressive, quasi-queer online magazine. You might as well have walked into her house wearing a rainbow flag and a T-shirt that reads CLIMATE CHANGE IS REAL. Any deal that you make is going to be to her benefit, fuckwit."

"You wanted to come here, remember?" I retorted, trying to hide my hurt feelings. "You said that Heather was a legend for history nerds."

"She was," Madeleine said. "But I got a bad feeling, Hailey. Right off the bat, she made some racist comment about my conservation society. *Oh, the Jewish one.* What a bitch."

"You're imagining things."

There was a click and then a pressured release as the front gate opened. A moment later, Heather's gate retracted, and a sleepy black MG convertible rolled on through. Madeleine and I watched as the car drove past us and parked in front of Heather's front door.

A man with thick silver hair climbed out, adjusted his jacket, then glanced over at us. He looked like an age-progressed Bruce Wayne. The man raised an eyebrow, then walked toward the door. Before he could knock, the door opened, and he vanished inside.

"I know him," I said.

"Who?"

"That guy," I said. "I've seen him somewhere."

"Been attending a lot of black-tie orgies lately?"

"His name is on the tip of my tongue," I said. "Oh my God, it's going to drive me crazy."

"Whatever," Madeleine said. "Let's go. I'd like to get away from here."

We drove back into Los Angeles, and the car was silent all the way to Madeleine's house. When I finally reached Los Feliz and pulled up in front of her house, she turned to me.

"You're one of my best friends," she said. "But honestly, Hail, fuck you. Don't drag me into your schemes anymore."

It wasn't until almost an hour later, when I had pulled up in front of my own house, that I realized who the man at Heather's house was. I had seen pictures of them talking at Heather's fundraising gala, and when I remembered that, the man's name came back to me.

Linus Warren. Billionaire developer and notorious capitalist. His name was attached to half the new developments in Santa Monica and Malibu. I dug into my memory to see what else I could recollect about him, but the worst thing that came to mind was the fact that he had ousted a colony of pied-billed grebes. The reason that he had looked familiar to me was that even in a photograph, he looked like a gay, off-duty superhero.

I had more important things to think about, namely Theo's journals, and I put Linus Warren out of my mind.

I didn't bother going into my house; I went straight to the backyard and set myself up inside my office. After carefully unpacking all six notebooks from the box, I reached in and pulled out the collection of photographs that had sifted to the bottom.

The photos showed the other side of a life lived in public. These were the private moments that had managed to stay encapsulated in film but protected from the outside world, rare moments of solace in a world of chaos.

I stopped when I found a photo of Eleanor leaning against the shoulder of a handsome young man with dark hair. Neither one of them was looking at the camera, and they weren't looking at each other, but their heads were bent toward each other in the suggestion of intimacy. I tucked the photo aside and made a mental note to find out the young man's identity later.

Another photo of Eleanor caught my eye, but this one was familiar. I had seen copies of it in the newspaper and, more recently, on Google Image searches. It was a photo of Eleanor and a young man bending to tie his shoe while Eleanor rolled her eyes. The young man had always been identified as "Eleanor's friend," but I flipped the picture over to see if there was a caption. Written in an unidentified hand was *Eleanor and Theo pause between games of tennis*. I turned the picture over and marveled at this younger Theo and wondered what this version of Eleanor would have said if I had revealed the outcome of her life to her.

I finally turned my attention to Theo's journals. I spent a good ten minutes flipping through the pages, admiring Theo's consistent, dreamy script. I was almost too excited to begin reading, but I finally sorted back to the beginning and found what seemed to be the first journal. The date was in 1944, which was right around the time that Theo had started working on his first film, *She's Got Moxie!*

I began to read.

May 12, 1944: Hollywood, California—

It's a dim little place, but it's cheap. Stanley in the art department gave me the address on a recommendation, and I moved in two weeks later. Only half the doors lock properly, the walls are thin enough to hear your neighbors breathing, and you can count yourself lucky if you don't wake up to find strangers waltzing in your living room. On at least two occasions I've come home to someone sleeping in my bed, and last Wednesday I went into my bathroom to find a well-dressed stranger enthusiastically cleaning his teeth with my toothbrush.

The bungalows look like they might have been taken from a movie set, because they're flimsy and romantic. The owner of the complex is an old movie star from the twenties, who hasn't made a film since movies switched to sound. She's got a thick accent—maybe Russian, I'm not sure—and you never see her without an elaborate getup, complete with makeup and jewelry.

I can't get a fix on my neighbors. Most of them seem to be creative—actors and clowns, some dancing girls and theater types. On a few occasions I've caught glimpses of some boarders who seem rather out of place, including morose businessmen and sleepy doctors, and once, a young priest.

And then there are the stars. I've been in Los Angeles for a month now and I can't help staring when I catch sight of them around the studio, but Stan tells me this excitement will pass. It's one thing to see them moving about the studio in costume, walking between their dressing room and the sets, but I don't think I'll ever grow accustomed to the sight of them lounging around the swimming pool of my apartment complex.

Stan told me about this when he gave me the recommendation. He told me that the Garden of Alla was a bit seedy, but it had its own reputation around Hollywood. Everyone's lived here at some point, apparently, for a few months while they find their feet.

The arrival of even the most famous faces from the silver screen—Humphrey Bogart, Lauren Bacall, Gloria Swanson—is never met with cheers or fanfare. When they come to the Garden, they're just like the rest of us, and more often than not, people fail to notice their presence. Some of them seem to be more like obnoxious house pets than guests, asking to borrow tweezers or pens, bending to sniff our drinks, falling asleep poolside for the entire world to see.

The pool seems to be the social center of the whole complex. It's a kidney-shaped pit in the middle of the bungalows, and a magnet for everything: celebrities, tourists, lost crazies, drunken revelers, late-night stargazers. It also seems to draw in lost items, from diamond earrings to gold bracelets to pairs of shoes, all of which can be seen winking up from the depths of the pool like some strange breed of fish.

When work settles down a bit, I'll go for a swim.

August 2, 1944—

I've fallen head over heels in love with Hollywood. In some ways it feels like the whole town was built yesterday. It's not so much a place as a state of mind, and it changes every single day.

I can be a cynical person, but I still can't help admiring the geraniums and date palms on every street, the pepper trees on Hollywood Boulevard and the smell of oranges on the breeze. The world is seeping in around the edges of Hollywood, and all we have to do is catch it on camera.

When we need cowboys for a shoot, we drive over to Gower and Sunset, where all the unemployed cowboys hang out, waiting for work. They drift in from the desert between jobs wrangling cattle, because they know that film people pay a lot more money for a lot less work. The same goes for Indians and churchgoers, cops and priests— if you can't find an actor to suit your needs, you drive around town looking for the real thing. He'll turn up, sooner or later.

I've been working under Walter Thomas, one of the best producers Hollywood has to offer. He's a generous man and everyone seems to love him—actresses, stagehands, even the studio heads. I keep pinching myself and wondering how I got to be such a lucky son of a bitch.

I love the way that actors can sink into a script and warp the characters in ways that I haven't even considered. Inspiration is everywhere if you have the presence of mind to capture it. Sometimes people outside the film industry have trouble distinguishing between reality and fiction, and I can't blame them, because the film industry can hardly be contained within the walls of the studios. We're a restless, wild bunch, sometimes with no more discretion than children. Traffic gets frequently interrupted throughout town by floods, fires, fireworks, exploding buildings, men running around waving swords and daggers, damsels caught high up in the branches of trees—all of which disappears as soon as the cameras stop rolling, of course.

Characters and stories come leaking out of the studio walls faster than the residents of Hollywood can slap down new laws, but they put up a valiant fight, all the same. Life explodes in every direction, and it's hard to determine what's real. You might go to buy milk from your corner drugstore and find Lon Chaney trying horror makeup on in the mirror, or else you might stand in line behind a family in Tyrolean garb, waiting for the pharmacist. You might go to the park on your lunch break and see a British nobleman wandering lost beneath a canopy of palm trees, only to look again and see that he has disappeared.

We design life the way we want to see it. We have the best wardrobe designers, diction coaches, language consultants, dance teachers; the best screenwriters and storytellers. If we want you to believe something, you'll believe it. We could dress your mother up in men's clothing and send her round, and you'd be convinced that your father had come back from the dead.

Our talents are wasted on the original residents of Los Angeles, however, who seem hell-bent on getting rid of us. There are protests every day, as the citizens of Old Hollywood try to reclaim their quiet town. Cecil DeMille, one of the top directors around, carries a gun to work, because someone once shot at him on his way home.

They call us charlatans and heathens, claiming that we've warped God's creation to suit our fancy. The original residents are a dying breed, however, and they're slowly being edged out by Hollywood's next chapter. Even the loudest voices quickly fade into echoes, no louder than mumbled recitations as they tell us that we've created our own, sinful religion, and that one day, we'll pay for it.

August 18, 1944—
This was meant to be a straightforward account of my days in Los Angeles, but even a few months in, I can see more potential here. Whenever I get a spare moment I write down everything—the snatches of conversation, the weather (report: unchanging), and even the goddamn outfits of the people walking by.

I never meant to be a novelist, per se—but is there potential for a film here? Could this be the beginning of a scenario? Either way, I want it all on record.

September 2, 1944—
I thought I was going to die last night.
The evening began like any other. I came home late from work, exhausted, prepared to drop into bed. As soon as I walked into my

bedroom, however, I realized that the bed was already occupied by a young couple who proved impossible to wake up.

Frustrated, I wandered outside and headed toward the pool, hoping that someone could tell me the identity of the people in my bed, or else help to wake them up.

Someone was playing piano; I could hear them as I walked down the path. It wasn't unusual to hear music at all times of day in the Garden. People frequently played accordions, horns, trumpets, harmonicas, sometimes banjos. All the music contributed to a strange cacophony that wasn't altogether unpleasant, though it did make it difficult to get work done.

When I reached the pool, I saw that the piano music was actually coming from a piano that had been moved next to the pool. A young man sat on the bench, almost jumping up and down at the keys, trying to keep up with his own fingers. My attention was drawn to the young woman beside him, however, who was managing to match his tempo.

Her dark hair was loosely pinned at the base of her neck, and a few damp strands stuck to her skin. She smiled as she played, as the music climbed and tumbled over itself, stirring the energy into a near frenzy. A small crowd pressed in around the two players, but their concentration remained fixed, their melodies winding in and out of each other. The music was so beautiful and effortless that they might have been performing on a stage.

When the music was over, the crowd stomped and cheered, then pressed in to congratulate the musicians. I waited until the commotion had settled a bit before going over to introduce myself to the young woman. She smiled as though we had met before, and I couldn't help feeling that she looked familiar.

I introduced myself and asked her if we had met.

"Don't think so," she replied. She had green eyes and a very pretty smile, with a slight overbite. A pair of emerald earrings winked from beneath the strands of hair that fell down to frame her face. Elegant and understated; most people wouldn't have noticed the jewelry. The thing that really caught my attention was the fact that she wasn't wearing any shoes.

"Are you an actress?"

"Well, mostly theater," she said. "I've done a movie or two."

"I'm Theo," I repeated. "I live here . . ."

But just at that moment, a young man came over and put a hand on her shoulder.

"We're about to hit Mulholland," he said. "You still want to come? Oh, hullo," he said, turning to me and offering me his hand. "I'm Jules."

"Theo," I said. "Pleasure."

"You know, I have no idea where I left my shoes," the girl said, glancing around. "I shouldn't have taken them off!"

"Might be dangerous to go without," Jules said.

"Maybe I'll find some along the way. Token."

"Tokens are small, you're not supposed to wear them."

I tried to follow their conversation, but I had no idea what they were talking about. They squabbled for a while, and then the girl turned to look at me. "You coming?"

"Wait, wait, wait," Jules said. "No newcomers. Sorry, pal."

"Errol was new."

"Yes, but we know him. You think he's trustworthy?" He motioned me with a jerk of his head.

"Who's he going to tell?"

They both turned to look at me.

"Right," Jules said to me. "You're riding in the trunk."

We walked toward the street. I had a hundred questions, but I had the feeling that if I seemed to inquisitive, my invitation might be revoked.

"Are you a good climber?" Jules asked.

"Moderate to decent."

"Are you afraid of dogs? Are you a fast runner?"

"I can run if I have to."

We reached Sunset. Ahead of us, on the sidewalk, two men shared a flask of something. They both wore expensive suits, and when they turned to look at us, I saw that one of them was Errol Flynn, Hollywood's most famous pirate. I did a double take to make sure that I could trust my eyes.

The other man was diminutive, with close-cropped gray hair and a black mustache. A bloody gash stood out on his forehead, and I tried not to stare at it, but I couldn't tear my eyes away. Even more remarkable than the bloody scrape was the fact that nobody else seemed to notice it. The man's eyes flickered up to meet mine, and he gave me a slight nod.

"Hello, hello," Errol said, wiping his mouth with the back of his hand. "Whose turn is it?"

"Mine," said the young woman. I still hadn't caught her name, but I felt like it was too late in the conversation to ask; I would have to wait until someone addressed her. "There's a place on Benedict Canyon."

"Ah, Benedict's boring," Errol said. "Just a bunch of paranoid housewives."

"Low risk is good for you, since you're clearly drunk."

Errol winked at her, then turned his attention to me. "Who's this? I thought guests weren't allowed."

"This is Theo," Jules said. "Nora's friend."

Nora. I made a mental note.

Errol fixed his eyes on me for a moment, then passed me his flask. "Take a drink," he said. "Mandatory rite of initiation."

I accepted the flask and took a swig.

"Okay," Errol said. "Into the trunk with you. We'll let you out when we get there."

Before I could ask where we were going, I was ushered into the trunk and boxed up in the complete darkness. The car started, and I grasped about wildly for something to hold on to. I didn't know who was driving, but by the bumps and swerves, it must have been Errol. Something kept hitting me in the head, and there was nothing to hold on to, so I held my hands over my head and hoped that it would be over as soon as possible. There were a few stops, some longer than others, which I guessed to be traffic lights. After an eternity and no small amount of quiet praying, the car stopped and the trunk popped open. Four faces peered down at me.

"There he is, still in one piece," Errol said. "Come on, out with you. We've only got a few hours."

I climbed out to find myself standing outside of a sprawling Victorian mansion. The upper gables and spires rose against the blue-gray sky, watchful and austere. A single light burned in one of the lower windows, but other than that, there were no signs of life.

The neighborhood around us was sparse and populated with the heathen scrubs that I had already come to associate with wild California. A few skeleton forms of houses yet unfinished stood on the lower reaches of the mountain, eerie in the night stillness.

I turned to find Jules arguing with Errol, who was taking another swig from his flask. The third man stood away from everyone else, and when he noticed me, he ambled over.

"It's strange, isn't it?" he said.

"What is?"

"All of it. This town. This world of images. We're adults playing make believe."

"Yes," I said vaguely. "Are you an actor?"

"He's Bill," said Nora, who had come up to join us. "Bill, meet Theo."

"Pleasure."

"Count No-Count!" Errol called, and Bill turned to look at him.

"Yes?" he said.

"Will you be in charge of time?"

"Oh, I suppose."

Errol handed him a pocket watch, then clapped a hand on my shoulder. "Pal," he said. "Which studio do you work for?"

"MGM."

"Writer?"

"Yes. How did you know?"

He waved the comment away with his hand. "Do they know your face? You have a recognizable face?"

"Not really, I'm new."

Errol wheeled around to face the rest of them. "It's him," he said. "He'll go first."

Everyone cheered. Nora came over and linked her arm through mine. "I'll go with him," she said. "He has no idea what he's doing."

"Look, I think it's high time that someone told me what's going on," I said.

There was a sustained silence, and then everyone burst into laughter.

"He's scared, look at him; he's so scared." Nora smiled.

"It's not every day you come to Hollywood and find yourself abducted by the screen elite!" Errol joined in.

Nora smiled at me. "We like to play a little game," she said. "There are no rules, except not getting caught. If you get caught, we're all done for."

"What sort of game?"

She shrugged. "We break into people's houses while they're sleeping. Sometimes we take things."

"That's absurd."

"Isn't it!" Errol waved his flask at me, grinning wildly. "I guarantee you've never had so much fun in your life."

"Whoever finds the most interesting token wins the game." Nora started up the drive, then turned to face me. "You coming?"

I couldn't see her face, just a flush of moonlight that stretched down the driveway and made shadows of everything.

"Yes," I said faintly. "I'm coming."

It was unnaturally quiet, no traffic sounds or shouts of laughter from late-night revelry. Nora was always two steps ahead of me, and I had to marvel at her lack of fear.

"Wait up!"

"Shhh!" she said, turning to put her finger to her lips.

I followed her as she tiptoed through the garden. My attention was fully riveted on the window with the light on; I could hardly focus on anything else.

"What happens if they catch us?"

She shrugged and smiled. "Hasn't happened yet."

I waited by a patch of hydrangeas as Nora strolled up to the front door and gingerly tested the handle. She tried it again, then turned around and shook her head. Before I could follow her intentions, she walked around the side of the house and disappeared.

There was only a moment for me to decide what to do. If I was caught in the garden alone, I would seem like a common thief. I could hardly expect a wealthy homeowner to believe that I had been talked into the act by Errol Flynn and the three others, because I could hardly believe it myself. I lingered a moment longer, then ran after her.

She was nowhere to be seen. I looked around frantically for a moment, then heard a small noise above me. Nora had scaled a latticed portico on the side of the house and was straddling an upper balcony.

"Nora!"

"Come up here!" she whispered. "This one looks promising!"

Before I could say anything else, she climbed over and disappeared once more.

It took me a good ten minutes to climb up the lattice, and by the time I had finally reached the balcony and peered through the windows, there was no sight of her. Trying to be as quiet as possible, I slipped through the balcony doors and nearly had a heart attack when I realized what was in front of me.

I was standing in a bedroom, and by the size of it, it looked to be the master bedroom. Right next to the balcony doors were two sleeping forms, and as I watched, one of them rolled over to face me.

Five minutes passed before I could fully convince myself that the man was asleep. I finally summoned the courage to tiptoe across the bedroom and into the hallway, which lay beyond an open door.

Nora stood at the end of the corridor. She looked up and smiled when she saw me. With an excited motion, she called me over, and I went to join her.

Even in the darkness, I could see that the room at the end of the hall was a nursery. It had a slanted ceiling, and a mobile hung with moons and stars. Against one wall lay a crib, and next to it, a fancy perambulator.

"He's asleep," Nora said. "Let's take him with us."

It took me a moment to realize that she was talking about the baby. "No!" I hissed, under my breath. "Are you crazy?"

"C'mon, Theo, he's so cute." Nora walked over to the crib and leaned on her forearms. "I'm good with babies."

"Nora, this is too much," I said. "I'm leaving."

"Relax, Theo," she whispered. "I'm joking. We'll find a different token."

We tiptoed out of the nursery and made our way toward the stairs. Following Nora's lead, I placed each foot on the stairs with absolute care, not wanting to make a sound. It took forever to descend to the bottom floor, but when we finally did, I allowed myself my first real breath.

"Find something, then let's go," I said.

Nora gave me a sly grin. "You're nervous, aren't you?"

"It's no big deal if _you_ get caught," I said. "You're a beautiful young woman. You can say that you were lost. If I get caught, I'll go straight to jail."

"Is that a compliment?" She touched my chin, then walked past me. She peered into the dimness of the living room, then turned around and walked into the foyer. After a few steps, she turned to look at me.

"What are you waiting for?"

"I think we should leave."

"So, go." She shrugged, then disappeared.

I watched her vanish into the dimness of the house. A moment later, there was the sound of creaking wood, and a soft _phwoosh_, and then silence once more. As I listened, a gentle, mocking melody came floating out of the silence, followed by a dizzy sequence of notes that dissolved into a lilting crescendo.

I lingered there for a moment, frozen to the spot, and then ran down the hall to find Nora. To my immediate horror, she was seated at a grand piano, playing a whimsical ballad with the effortlessness of a sleepwalker.

"What are you doing? They'll wake up!"

She ignored me. A moment later, a light snapped on upstairs, and then I heard a voice.

"Marvin!" came a voice. "Marvin, there's someone downstairs!"

Nora only played faster. The ceiling shook as someone heavy hopped out of bed, and the baby began to wail.

"Nora, please! I don't want to leave without you!"

Her hands danced along the keys, scaling the high registers with precision. I could see a slow smile curling up at the edges of her mouth, and she swayed gently as her hands climbed over each other to head toward the lower keys.

"Who is that?" a man's voice called. "You've been warned—I have a gun!"

I crossed the room and grabbed Nora's shoulders. She looked up at me with a smile.

"I'm leaving," I said. "Let's go out through the back."

Thunderous footsteps came down the stairs as Nora stood up from the piano. I crossed the sitting room and threw open a door. It opened into a little servant's corridor. I could hear the man turning on lights, and I could tell that there was very little time to get out of the house before he caught up with us.

Without further ado, I grabbed Nora's hand and pulled her down the corridor.

"I know you're in here," the man said. He flicked on the sitting room lamp, and light flooded in beneath the doorframe.

I could hear him stomping around the room, throwing furniture aside and bending to look behind the piano. Nora pressed up against me, and I tried not to breathe, convinced that the man would hear me if I did so.

"Marvin?" came a woman's voice. "I've called the police. They should be here any minute."

"Good, Nancy!" he called. "Stay upstairs with David."

Nora detached herself from me and slipped backward down the hall. She motioned for me to follow, and after a moment, I did.

"You hear that, you bastard?" came the man's voice. "The police are on their way. We'll have you out in no time!"

I had almost reached the end of the corridor before the man threw open the sitting room door. His eyes widened when he saw me.

"Stop!" he said, and raised the gun. "Stop right there!"

I hesitated for a moment. His gun was pointed directly at my chest.

"What's in your hand?" he demanded.

"Nothing."

"You're holding something; let's see what it is."

I slowly raised my hands, but before I could open them, the door burst open behind me.

"Say, mate, put that thing down," came Errol's voice. "Someone's liable to get hurt."

I turned around, and Errol grinned at me.

"Aren't you . . . . Robin Hood?" the man asked, confused.

"Defender of the poor, adversary of the rich," Errol said, then took a small bow. "We've gotten lost on the way to a party."

Before the man could respond, Errol grabbed my arm and yanked me out of the corridor. We crossed through a laundry room and had almost reached the door when a shot went off behind us.

The sound was so immediate and confusing that I thought the gun had been next to my ear. Errol crouched for a moment, throwing his hands up over his head, then leaped up. He grabbed me by the shoulders and made for the door. Bits of plaster rained down around us, and everything was reduced to a static hiss as my ears tried to recalibrate.

"Come on!" Errol yelled.

I felt the door burst open behind me, and the man nearly collided with me as he aimed at Errol.

"You're not going anywhere!" he yelled.

I turned around to charge at him, but the man fired another shot, narrowly missing my hand.

As the man tried to regain his footing, Errol grabbed a box of detergent and threw it at his head. The box burst open and powder detergent filled the air. Another shot went off somewhere in the room, and I heard glass shatter as the bullet hit a window. I couldn't see anything; the detergent filled my nose and eyes, and I couldn't stop coughing.

I felt someone grab me and push me out of the room. Somewhere, someone was screaming, and the sound was more terrible than anything. I held my hands over my eyes, which burned so much I thought I might go blind.

A shock of cold air hit me as we found ourselves outside.

"We have to go back!" I yelled. "Nora's still in there!"

"I'm right here, Theo," she said, and I felt hands pushing me into the car.

"Everyone in? Good!"

I slammed into the side of the car as we went screeching down the driveway. In the distance, sirens split the silence.

"Go, you bastard, drive!" Errol yelled.

My hands were still clapped over my eyes, and I could feel tears streaming down my face from the detergent.

"Theo, I'm sorry!" Nora said. "They don't usually have guns."

I could hear Jules and Errol arguing in the front. I was squashed between the wall of the car and a soft, relenting mass, which I took to be Bill.

"You can't go down Benedict Canyon," Errol argued. "We'll get stopped!"

"We have to get out of here!" Jules said. "Let go of the wheel!"

"This is my car, you heathen!"

"Hey!" Nora yelled. "Turn left up ahead! I know a place where we can hide out."

I was slammed against the side of the car once again as Jules screeched off the road. We hit a rough patch of road, and I felt the car bumping over gravel and dirt.

"Where the fuck are we?" Errol hissed, and Nora shushed him.

"Jules, turn off the car."

Jules pulled over and turned off the engine. We idled in silence, and not a minute went past before the sirens grew in volume. I held my breath, and gradually they faded away.

I rubbed my eyes, then blinked and took in my surroundings. The night sky was obscured by lofty trees, and as my vision returned, I saw that they were narrow eucalypts. The air was cooler here, and everything smelled like blue wood and something medicinal. My heart rate slowed.

"Nora, what is this place?"

"It's an old clinic," she said. Her voice was slightly muffled. She was chewing on her thumb. "It's been abandoned since the twenties."

"How long do we have to wait?"

"Until they leave," she replied. "Stay in the car, if you want. I'm going in."

"Nora!" Jules hissed, but she climbed over him and left the car. I rubbed my eyes once more, then climbed out after her.

"Great, now we've lost both of them," Errol muttered.

"Hey, wait up!" I called. Nora turned and looked back at me. I caught up with her, and we walked toward the dark building together.

"What type of clinic was it?"

"Tuberculosis," she replied. "A bunch of girls wearing masks and white dresses."

The garden had gone completely wild in the years of abandonment. Chamise and coyote brush grew along the gentle slope that led up toward the hulking structure, which I could see more clearly now. It looked like it might have been a large house at one point, a gingerbread Victorian mansion complete with gables, turrets, and rounded windows.

"Why do you sneak into people's houses?" I asked. "Not enough excitement in your life?"

"I spend all my time on a stage," she said. "I never get the chance to watch other people. It's the chance to be anonymous."

"So buy a mask. It'd be a lot safer."

"Don't you get it? Most of these people don't know how they ended up in Los Angeles. They're all buying into someone else's dream. It's so sad."

We reached the front door. Nora walked up and tested the doorknob.

"It's locked," she said. "Should we climb through a window?"

"Not tonight," I said. "Not for me."

"We didn't get a token," she said. "I didn't have a chance to find something."

I smiled at her, then held up my hand. She frowned and tilted her head, confused.

"Take it," I said. "It's yours."

I opened my hand and revealed a brooch. It was shaped like a scarab, with a fat green jewel for the body, and gold-tipped antennae and legs. Nora was speechless for a moment, then took it from me.

"You stole this?" she said, wide-eyed.

I was confused for a moment. "I thought that was the point of the game," I said.

"You're not supposed to take something valuable!" she said, hitting my shoulder. "What if they called the cops or something? You want me to get arrested?"

"But— they did call the cops."

A slow grin spread across her face. "Theo, I'm joking," she said. "I love it. I think it's the best thing that anyone's ever found. Pin it on me."

I stepped toward her and undid the clasp on the brooch. For the first time that night, I was close enough to catch a whiff of her perfume. She smelled like orange blossoms, the sharp, dazzling smell of a lost California, something that existed only between the faded pages of the old city. The smell made me think of a dusty wilderness that had vanished years ago, long before the pepper trees and oleander came to represent the city.

After I pinned the brooch to her dress, she looked down at it. I hadn't stepped away yet, and she looked up and smiled.

"Let's go, hey?" she said. "The cops are probably gone by now."

I followed her back to the car, wondering what the rest of them would say when they saw the brooch. It turned out that I didn't need to worry, because everyone was silent when we climbed into the car. There were no detours on the way back to the Garden of Allah, and when I finally stepped into my bedroom, the strange couple who had unwittingly set me off on the night's journey had disappeared.

TEN

It was three in the morning by the time I finished reading. Theo's handwriting was cramped and elegant, the letters hooked together. The words were difficult to read, and it took me at least ten minutes to read each page, especially since I took copious notes as I went along.

Errol Flynn, Jules, and someone named Bill. Nora was Eleanor Hayes, of course; it only took me a few pages to figure that out. When I finished reading the first part of the journal I went to the wall of my office, where I had pinned dozens of photographs of Eleanor. After scanning through the photos, I found the one I wanted: Eleanor, at the premiere for *My Friend, Roy.* She wore a long black gown, and pinned near her breast was a brooch, shaped like a scarab.

I could hardly wait to get to work the next morning. When I arrived at the office at six o'clock, I was convinced that I would be the first one in. As soon as I walked into the office, however, I smelled coffee. Someone was already there.

I walked into the kitchen and found Brian humming to himself. His back was to me, and he was stirring sugar into his coffee.

"Brian."

"Jesus fuck!" He whirled around.

I leaned against the doorframe. "What are you doing here?"

Brian scowled. "I'm meeting someone."

"Oh? Who?"

He pointed his spoon at me. "That," he said, "is none of your business."

I followed him out into the hallway. He sauntered toward his office, still humming. When he reached the office door, he gave me a smug little smile.

"So, how's that job search coming?"

"I'm not leaving, Brian. Alexa's keeping me on."

"We'll see about that."

"Who are you meeting?"

"Never you mind." He pulled the door of his office shut behind him. I struggled not to kick the door in, and instead contented myself with going into the kitchen and fixing myself up a cup of coffee.

Over the next few hours, the rest of the *Lens* staff trickled in. I lingered by my desk, pretending to do work, until I saw Petra walk into the lobby. I jumped up and walked over to her.

"Who's Brian meeting up with today?"

"Good morning to you, too," she murmured. "Is that coffee for me?"

"Sure, why not."

She took a sip. "It's ice-cold."

"I made it a few hours ago. So, do you know?"

She didn't reply but set her things down next to the desk. I watched as she turned on the computer and then pulled out an appointment book. She scanned it, then tapped the Wednesday column.

"Caleb Walsh," she said.

"Walsh, Walsh." I snapped my fingers. "The dead art student. Wasn't her name something Walsh?"

"Samira."

"He's started writing the article."

Petra looked uncomfortable. "There's something you should know," she said. "I know what he's writing about, and it's probably why they're meeting today."

"What? Tell me."

"Caleb—Mr. Walsh—is petitioning to have Windhall torn down, but it's pretty hard to demolish a historic building. I don't know all the details."

"When did this happen?"

"It's been happening over the last few days. Mr. Walsh wants Brian to write a story about him so that he can garner sympathy and support."

I sighed, frustrated, and ran a hand through my hair. "I know this man's grieving, but Theo was never convicted for murdering Eleanor, so there's nothing to prove that Samira's death is even linked to Windhall. I don't even know where to start with this—I mean, the amount of assumptions behind this maneuver are on par with some sort of really sketchy political scheme."

Petra gave me a wry smile. "I thought you were writing an article about how he got away with murder."

"I am," I said. "He definitely killed Eleanor. I believe in due process, though, and this seems to violate that."

Petra seemed to be weighing her response. Before she could answer, the front door opened and Alexa walked in, followed by a man with a dark complexion and thinning hair.

Alexa nodded hello to Petra and me, and I quickly studied the man standing next to her. Tailored pants and leather saddle shoes, a worn-in cashmere pullover. He hadn't shaven in a few days, but his stubble almost looked intentional. *Grief by Ralph Lauren*, I couldn't help thinking.

"Hello," I said, extending a hand. "I'm Max Hailey."

"Caleb Walsh," he said. "Are you working on the article?"

"I'm researching Theo," I hedged. "Brian and I are doing research from separate angles."

"I heard." Caleb removed his glasses and rubbed his eyes.

Alexa jumped in. "Max is working on a different story," she said. "You're going to meet with Brian today."

"I'd love to sit in on the meeting," I said. "If that's okay with you, Mr. Walsh."

Brian came bouncing into the lobby. "Cal, my man!" he said. "Come and pop into my office."

Petra stood. "I'll come take notes, Brian."

"Good thought, good thought."

We all filed down the hallway, into Brian's office. He frowned when he saw that I had joined them.

"Hailey," he said. "This is a private meeting."

"It's okay, Brian," Alexa said. "I think that Max should be here, too."

I watched Brian wrestle with his emotions for a minute. He gave me a tight smile, then walked over to his desk and sat down.

I hadn't seen it before, but now I realized that Caleb was exhausted. The skin beneath his eyes was translucent and damp, and his eyelashes were clumped together, as though he had been crying at some point that day.

"Let me begin by saying that I don't think Theo killed my daughter," Caleb said. He paused for a moment. "But I think he's responsible, all the same."

"Sure, sure," Brian said. "This whole thing is his fault."

"Nobody thinks of young victims as human; nobody cares about their families. People think of them as goddamned *icons*." Caleb took a deep breath, then closed his eyes. "I'm sorry. It's been a really fragile time for my family."

"You know," Brian said, after a pause, "there might be a movie in this. I have a good friend at Fox, and he'd love to have a sit-down with you. We haven't talked actresses yet, but I could see someone like Emma Watson playing Samira."

Caleb stared at him. "I think you're missing the point."

Brian steepled his fingers. "So, what, exactly, do you want? I think *you're* missing an opportunity."

"I want people to know what happens to the families of the victims," he said. He closed his eyes, and I could see that his hands were shaking. I worried that he might start crying in Brian's office, but he steeled himself enough to speak up again. "The police haven't caught this person yet, but maybe we can prevent future crimes, if they see that it's tearing families apart."

Brian was jotting this down. "Gotcha," he said. "Little vigilante work, I like it."

"There's one more thing," Caleb said. "Windhall. Theo shouldn't be allowed to stay there any longer."

"What do you have in mind?"

He rubbed his eyes, then took a creased piece of paper from his pocket. I felt another pang of pity for the man: the paper looked like it had been consulted, pocketed, then taken out and crumpled up. I wondered if it might be a picture of his daughter.

Caleb unfolded the sheet and cleared his throat.

"I've looked into it, and Windhall has historic status, so it would be very difficult to have it torn down. There's another possibility, however. We could force Theo to sell the building, and then have it turned into a nonprofit that would benefit women."

"Interesting thought," Alexa murmured. "I don't like your chances at getting Theo to sell, though."

"He might not have a choice," Caleb said, then smiled. "Turns out there's a caveat written into the Beverly Hills charter about the ownership of historic buildings. If the council finds that a building has been allowed to fall into disrepair, the owner has three months from the time a complaint is lodged to prove to the council that they intend to restore it, or else they'll be forced to evacuate."

Alexa frowned. "That seems awfully fast."

"There's a stipulation that the building must have been unoccupied for at least seven consecutive years prior," Caleb said.

"Why hasn't anyone looked into this before?"

Caleb gave another faint smile. "Windhall was only recently declared historic," he said. "Something that Theo's lawyer did, to protect it from demolition. A bit of irony that might work in our favor."

Alexa nodded. "We'll write an article to help you gain traction with this petition. Before we delve into this issue more deeply, however, we'll need to discuss exclusivity rights with you."

Caleb looked uncomfortable. "I scheduled an appointment with another editor later," he said.

Alexa shook her head. "This is a lot of work, and we'll be spending a lot of time and resources to research this article. If you'd like to move forward, we'll need you to agree to speak with us exclusively."

He thought for a moment, then nodded. "I don't see why that should be an issue."

"I'll draw up a contract," Alexa said. "In the meantime, can you tell us a little bit about Samira?"

Caleb took a deep breath. "She never used to keep secrets," he said. "She was a quiet little girl, but she always felt like she could talk to us about stuff. That changed once she started art school."

Alexa nodded, and I could see that Petra was busy taking notes. I prayed that Brian wouldn't jump in with another bad suggestion, a different actress who might play Caleb's daughter in a Lifetime Original Movie.

"She was working on something when she died," Caleb went on. "She said that she'd been contacted by a woman who was doing a tribute for Eleanor Hayes. Samira loved Eleanor, grew up watching all her movies."

I felt a shiver as I thought about the dead girls. It had never occurred to me that they might have been tricked into doing something sinister. The murderer had planned this carefully, methodically.

"Did Samira tell you anything about this woman?" I cut in.

"No," he admitted. "She didn't tell me anything, other than that she was a woman."

"Thanks, Cal," Brian said. "I think I have enough to start writing the article. I'll be in touch when I have questions."

We walked Caleb out of the office, and then I took Alexa aside.

"Can we speak privately? There's something I need to tell you."

We stepped into her office, and she closed the door. It was still a little unnerving to have Alexa's full attention, but I tried to set that aside for the moment.

I couldn't tell her about the deal I had signed with Heather, obviously, but I needed to tell her about the meeting I had had with Leland at Windhall.

"I'm meeting Theo tomorrow."

Her face was impassive for a moment, and then she frowned. "You're meeting with Theo tomorrow? Theodore Langley."

I couldn't help grinning. "It's unbelievable, isn't it?"

"It is exactly that. How did you manage to finagle a meeting?"

"I found something that belongs to him, and I bluffed my way into a meeting."

Her expression was still difficult to read. "What do you plan to discuss with him?"

"Look, I think we can all agree that Theo didn't kill these girls," I said. "There's a reason why Theo came back, though. It's been sixty-seven years."

"Unfortunately, journalists don't have the same prerogatives as fiction writers. We have to focus on what the public cares about, and at the moment, they want to see justice for the murder victims."

I mulled this over. "Alexa," I said. "I'm happy to look into the deaths of these new girls, but I can't let Eleanor go. It's not right. It just doesn't sit well with me."

"You're chasing ghosts, Max. Stick to the present day."

"What if I found out *where* he killed her? They didn't have DNA evidence and all that back then."

"I thought he killed her in the garden."

"No, no, that's what everyone thinks, but they proved that the body had been moved after she was murdered. There were still guests. He had to have killed her somewhere inside, then moved the body."

"I see."

"There must still be microscopic bits of DNA, wouldn't you think?"

She was quiet. "I don't think you have enough time to pursue this properly. You won't have police backing, you know. If they go after Theo, they'll go after him for the two new victims."

"Okay," I said, then, "I'll let you know how tomorrow goes."

"There's one more thing," she said. "You don't have much time to find some conclusive evidence. It's going to be very difficult unless you have some help."

"I'm not working with another writer," I said quickly. "I want sole credit for the story."

She sighed. "You're young," she said. "Probably too young to realize that you're making a mistake."

"I'm capable of doing this alone."

"You're not. I can see that you're a talented journalist, but I'd also like to see that you can work well with others. The *Lens* was founded on a spirit of conviviality, not ego and individuality."

I chewed on this. "Fine," I said. I already knew who I was going to use. "I'll take the new girl. Petra."

"Good." She nodded. "You'd better get started right away; you don't have much time."

ELEVEN

"Come with me," I said to Petra after stepping out of Alexa's office.

"Where are we going?" Petra asked.

"You wanted to help research Theo, didn't you?" I gestured to the door. "I need to gather some information, and I want to start right away."

"Okay," Petra said. "Let me get my stuff."

It was noon, so the freeways were quiet as I drove us to my house.

"Has Brian let you write anything yet, or are you just answering the phone?" I asked.

Petra rolled her eyes. "I'm paraphrasing, but he said something about leaving the writing to the writers. I'm just answering the phone."

"I wish he'd take his own advice," I said. "Brian isn't a writer himself. Don't worry—after we finish this story, you'll definitely get promoted."

We got to my house in less than twenty minutes. Petra looked around in admiration as I pulled into the driveway.

"You live here?"

"My grandmother gave it to me," I said. "It falls apart once a year, but it's all I have."

"It looks like an old fairy-tale house," she said. "You must have loved it when you were younger."

"Yes," I said quietly. "I did."

"I never had a grandparent," Petra said wistfully as we entered the house. I led the way to the kitchen. "You're so lucky that you had her. Is your granddad still alive?"

And there it was, the knife that popped up in every conversation involving my gran. It was almost like I couldn't mention her, couldn't honor her memory without roping in the man who had killed her.

"He died a few years ago," I said. "Before you offer your condolences, though, save them. He wasn't a good guy."

My throat felt tight, and if Petra had squeezed my shoulder or looked sympathetic, I might have fucking cried. She said nothing, but her steady eyes were trained on my face, and gradually, the lump in my throat subsided.

"I don't talk about this with anyone," I said. "And I don't want to talk about it after this, but I'm going to tell you, because you deserve to know why I want to take Theo down."

Petra nodded and then reached across the table and touched my hand. "You don't have to tell me," she said. Her touch fortified me, however, and I swallowed before going on.

"Albert . . . Albert killed my gran eight years ago. They'd been married since the forties, and he had always been a violent asshole. I never knew him that well. He was always in and out of jail for minor things, you know, jacking cars and dodging bills. He wouldn't give my gran a divorce, but she owned this house, and she finally kicked him out."

There was a heavy silence for a moment, with just the distant sounds of cars swerving past the house. Then, I said quietly, "I was out of town when the murder happened."

Petra shook her head and flexed her fingers. "Fucking men."

"He was a raging alcoholic," I said. "I don't know if alcohol even made him drunk anymore. When people drink that much, it's worse when they're sober. Anyway. He showed up and they exchanged some words, and a few hours later, I got The Call. He died of liver failure while he was waiting to be tried."

Petra nodded again. "We're going to get Theo, Max," she said. "We'll get him. I promise."

We walked around to the greenhouse. When Petra and I stepped inside, I cleared a few coffee cups off the table, and took a seat.

"We don't have much time," I said. "I need to collect every piece of information on Theo before I meet up with him tomorrow. You don't happen to have a degree in criminal law, do you?"

"I dropped out of UCLA after a semester."

"No kidding," I said. "You should talk to Lapin."

"Who's Lapin?"

"Ford's partner," I muttered. "He lives with Ford, and he's going to law school at UCLA."

Petra gave me a blank look.

"You know, Brian's dad? Former editor—ringing any bells?"

She raised an eyebrow. "Brian's dad is gay?"

"That okay with you?"

"Yes, of course," she said, flustered. "How long has he been gay?"

"His whole life, I would guess," I said. "You want me to email him and ask?"

"No, it's just . . . Brian seems like a conservative asshole. You think he'd be more open-minded, if his dad is gay."

"Gay Republicans are a dime a dozen here," I said. "It's Los Angeles. Shall we get to work?"

Petra didn't answer. Her attention had been drawn to my Theo wall, and she wandered across the room to examine it.

"Wow," she said. "This is an entirely new level of devotion."

"Some people follow sports teams. Soccer doesn't interest me, so I follow Theo."

The wall had every press clipping, every time that someone had claimed to have seen Theo in the last thirty years. There was a map with pins, but there was no discernible pattern or close grouping. There were also photocopies of all the old articles about Theo from the original trial. Most of them had been penned by Hedda Hopper, a gossip columnist who made no attempt to hide her hatred of Theo.

"I started a new wall," I said, leading her to the back of the greenhouse. "It's the murder night, laid out in the simplest way possible. I want to account for every minute of the night that Eleanor was killed."

Petra peered at the wall covered with my notations. My notes were tidy; precision was second nature to me. I watched her move from the game of hide-and-seek to the search for Theo and Eleanor in the garden, the arrival of the police, the medical examiner's brief and perfunctory condemnation.

"You think he killed her with a stake?"

"It would have been the right size."

"What about a tree branch, whittled down to a point?"

"All possibilities."

She paused at *4:20 in the morning*. "Her aunt came up from San Diego to identify the body," she said. "She got there awfully quickly, if Eleanor was found at two."

"Horse farmer," I explained. "She was probably already up when they called."

"Can I ask you something?"

"Shoot."

"You didn't want to share this piece with me at first," she said. "Why'd you change your mind?"

"Didn't have a choice, really. Alexa said it was too much work for one person."

"Okay, why didn't you want to work with me in the first place?"

I scratched my neck, uncomfortable. "I've been obsessed with Theo forever, and I don't like sharing."

To my surprise, Petra laughed. "I get it. To be fair, though, I want my name on the byline with yours. I'm not going to slave away so you get all the glory."

"Fair."

She turned her attention back to the board. "How are you going to fill in the missing pieces?"

I deliberated for a moment. I didn't know Petra, and I wasn't sure if I could trust her. I decided not to tell her about Heather yet, or the missing journals.

"I found a photograph of Theo," I said. "I want to identify the other people in the photo. There's a young woman, and an old lady in the background."

"Can I see it?"

I took out the photograph of Theo and the young woman dancing, which I had put in a protective sleeve. Petra examined it.

"Where do we start?" she asked.

"Bernard Loew," I said. "We start with him."

"Who is he?"

"He's dead now," I said. "But he was a brilliant set designer in the forties and fifties. He worked on every single one of Theo's films, but Theo fired him from *Last Train to Avalon*."

"Why?"

"Nobody knows," I said. "But he was one of the men who saw Theo in the garden with Eleanor's body. They'd been cordial that evening, but Bernard was one of the people who took the stand against him and said that he was absolutely guilty. He has a son, and I want to get in touch with him. His name is Marcus, and he writes music for movies."

"I'll reach out to him."

"I have a partial list of all the attendees at the party, but I want you to help me fill it out. I'm probably only missing a few people; we can see if anyone is still alive, or if they have children who remember their parents talking about that night."

"Got it."

"The medical examiner said that Eleanor's body had been moved that night," I said. "She was killed, her body cooled. Based on the lack of blood in the garden, and the coagulation of the blood around the puncture wound, she was moved at least an hour after the death occurred."

"Jesus."

"You okay? This isn't too much for you?"

"No, I want to do this," she said. "My best friend has an abusive ex, so I know a little bit about it."

We were both quiet for a long moment.

"There was a second set of footprints by the body," I went on. Talking about murder and abuse normally made my chest feel tight, but Petra's presence was strangely calming. "It made the detectives think that Theo had an accomplice. They never found the shoes that made the footprints, but they were men's shoes."

"You've really done your research, haven't you?"

"I've always wanted to solve this case," I said. "Unfortunately, most of the key players are dead."

I dug through my files for a minute until I found what I was looking for. "Here's a list of almost everyone who was at the party," I said.

"Where did you get these names?"

"I've put together a list from the trial transcripts," I said. "Not everyone at the party testified, but Hedda Hopper and Louella Parsons were both there, and they wrote about this case to no end. There's another piece of missing evidence we need to find if we're going to solve this case."

"What's that?"

"Where Theo killed Eleanor," I said.

She hesitated for a second. "I'm going to play devil's advocate for a second," she said.

"Go ahead."

"What if he didn't do it? What if he was framed?"

"Then we'll prove his innocence." I struggled not to roll my eyes. "I doubt it, though."

"All right," she said. "I'll start going through this list. Anything else I should work on?"

"Keep an eye out for women named Connie," I said. "Anything like Conchita, Constance, Connery."

"Why?"

"It's not important right now," I said. "I'll tell you when I figure it out."

"Anything else?"

"There's something I'm working on, but I could use an extra set of eyes," I said. "I'm looking for someone named Ben."

"Is height important, or will you take anyone?" she joked.

"No, I'm looking for a specific Ben," I said. "I don't know his last name. He's a friend of Theo's, and I think he probably knows something."

I took out my phone and texted her all the Ben contacts that I had lifted from Leland's phone.

"He's about five nine, dark hair that's started going gray. He's probably late fifties. I'll tell you once I figure out more, but start working through this list and see if any of them match that description. Hold on, I've got a picture of him."

I scrolled through the images on my phone until I found the pictures I had taken of Leland and Ben at Windhall.

She took my phone and examined the photo. "You think he might have had something to do with the dead girls?" she asked.

"I can only begin to speculate."

"How will I find him?"

I smiled. "Get creative," I said. "This job will take you places you never imagined."

———————————

The next morning, I woke up early. My interview with Theo was later that day, and I hadn't been able to sleep. I had stayed up late the night before, reading through the first of the journals that Heather had given me, taking notes of every single name and place that Theo mentioned. The wall of evidence in my office had grown into something much bigger, crisscrossed with new names and questions.

After reading through the journals, I pictured Eleanor in the garden, wilting against a bed of dead flowers, a bloody hole in her rib cage. I tried to reconcile that image with the voice I heard in my head as I read Theo's journals. Something didn't fit, but I couldn't figure out what it was.

There was something else that bothered me about the journals, and that was the fact that a lot of pages had been torn out. I had kept a sporadic journal of my own throughout the years, and knew that tearing a page out could sometimes indicate dissatisfaction with one's own writing, but I wondered if it didn't indicate that Heather had torn out pages to hide something else.

I glanced at my watch; Leland was going to send a driver over at any minute. I went into my bedroom and quickly got dressed, then glanced at myself in the mirror, wondering if my outfit was appropriate. I had decided on a button-down white shirt and black slacks, but I looked like a caterer. I tossed the slacks and was stepping into a pair of blue jeans when there was a knock on my door.

"Coming," I called.

I opened the door to a diminutive man with salt-and-pepper hair and pale eyes. He frowned when he saw me.

"Are you Mr. Hailey?"

"Max Hailey, yes."

"I am Fritz," he said, staring at my pants. "Mr. Langley's personal assistant. Mr. Bates has drawn up a contract for you to sign, and I have brought it with me."

With a little flourish, Fritz presented the document. I read through it carefully and had to admire Leland's legal parlance. The terms that we had agreed to were outlined at great length: I was to have two full interviews with Theo, both at Windhall, and after one of these interviews Theo would consent to give me a tour of the house. I was not allowed to photograph nor record Theo in any way, even if he gave me consent to do so on the occasion.

After reading the contract twice, I signed it, then handed it back to Fritz.

"Follow me, please."

I followed him onto the street and whistled when I saw an immaculate, cream-colored Mercedes-Benz, an old model in perfect condition.

"Wow, some car," I said. "What is that—1940s?"

"Quite right."

"Where did Theo dig up that beauty?"

"It was new when Mr. Langley purchased it."

"Of course it was."

"Please, get in."

I started to get into the front passenger seat, but Fritz quickly shook his head.

"You ride in the back."

The old car was in pristine condition, but there was a certain smell to it: the rich, oily flavor of polish at the back of my throat, a cold thrill of dust and caught air, the brittle smell of ancient leather. Fritz didn't seem eager for conversation, so I occupied myself by looking out the window as he drove through Laurel Canyon. I had driven down these streets hundreds of times, but I hadn't been a backseat passenger in my own neighborhood for years, not since before my grandmother had died.

The idea of meeting Theo hadn't fully come home to me yet. He was still just a black-and-white flicker, a two-dimensional specter mostly composed of urban legends and hearsay.

We hit Hollywood Boulevard, and Fritz turned left. I waited a moment, then cleared my throat.

"Aren't we going to Windhall?"

He didn't respond, and I tried again.

"Windhall is in the other direction."

Again, there was no response. I waited another minute, to be sure that we driving away from Beverly Hills, then spoke up again.

"Look, I grew up in Los Angeles," I said. "I know my way around. You're going the wrong way."

"There is a traffic accident on Sunset," Fritz said, meeting my eyes in the mirror.

"How do you know?"

"My smartphone tells me," Fritz said. "I have the GPS."

There was no point in arguing, so I sat back again. It had been a while since I had driven through Hollywood; even though I worked less than a mile away, I generally avoided the neighborhoods above Sunset.

Hollywood looked dull and sleepy in the hazy afternoon sunlight. Signs for acting classes and cheap phone plans were plastered over the old banks and high-rises, and men stood on the sidewalks, waving signs for overpriced parking lots. Sunlight pricked the high western windows, which glittered like blind eyes in the depths of the ruins of Hollywood.

The street was clogged with red tourist buses and taxis. Street performers in smeared makeup and matted fur costumes prowled outside a mall, and a swarm of tourists crouched on the sidewalks to take pictures next to the terrazzo stars on the Walk of Fame. Homeless people wandered the sidewalks, and when we pulled up to a red light, one of them approached the car. He wore a leopard-print dress and fuzzy moon boots. His eyes were protected by Kanye West–style sunglasses. Fritz gave him a filthy look, then got in the right lane and turned.

Here the yards were penned off behind metal fences. The lawns were little more than dirty intermezzos between the side- walk and front door, and the plastic spires of children's playhouses emerged from behind dying hedges. It was a sad tapestry.

"The accident is cleared up," Fritz announced. "We will go to Beverly Hills now."

A dismal feeling settled in the pit of my stomach. I had learned to tune out the changes to the city, the tourists and the pollution, but in my mind, there had always been a separation between the old Hollywood and what had come to replace it. Driving around Holly- wood in Theo's old car made it difficult to see the borders anymore, and it was starting to become clear that the old world was really gone, would never come back.

I steeped in melancholia for the remainder of the ride to Wind- hall. We finally arrived on Theo's street, and I waited for Fritz to make a smart comment as we pulled up to the tall gates, but he said nothing. I watched him climb out of the car and laboriously push the gates open, then get back in the car and guide it carefully up the drive.

Even though I had visited Windhall many times before, it was surreal to come as an invited guest. The great house still hid its face, but I caught glimpses of it through the trees. I glanced around eagerly, trying to absorb all the details that I had missed in the darkness. I tried to reconcile the images of present-day Windhall with the black-and-white parties where elegant women draped in white silk strolled through the lawns. Theo had been a part of that world; he had seen Hollywood before it became a town of swollen boulevards and hazy afternoon sunlight.

The driveway wound its way up through the property, bumpy in sections where roots had disrupted the pavement. Fritz pulled up to the front steps and stopped the car.

"Mr. Langley will be waiting, sir."

I gathered up my things and got out of the car, then walked up the steps. At any moment, the fantasy could break and reality could come crashing back in. I was standing at the precipice of two opposing time periods: the delicate, black-and-white world, full of smoky mirrors and tragic women, and present-day Los Angeles, which had steamrolled over every other decade in favor of the future.

I knocked on the door.

A quiet moment expired before I heard a metal *snick*, and then the front door swung open to reveal an old man. It hadn't occurred to me until that moment that I might not recognize Theo, and I wasn't entirely sure that the man standing before me was the same man that I had been studying for most of my life. He was old, certainly, but he looked far too energetic and sharp to be in his early nineties. He was taller than I was, with ramrod-straight posture and long limbs. His white hair was close-cropped, and he peered at me with sharp green eyes.

"It's about time," he growled. "You must be here about the dishwasher."

It took me a moment for the comment to register. "What?"

"It stopped working a few days ago," he went on. "Nasty smell. I think a rat might have crawled into the wires and had a family. You have a problem with rats?"

"No, I don't—"

"I can't guarantee it's a *rat*, you know. It might be something bigger. How do you feel about raccoons?"

"I'm sorry?"

"Do you think you could kill a house cat with your bare hands?" he asked, peering at me closely. "You look like you've got some muscle on you. There's something in there, I tell you, and it sounds mean."

"I don't think I could," I said, baffled.

"Then why the hell did you come?"

"I'm a writer," I said. "I work for the *LA Lens.* Are you Theo?"

The man glared at me. "Do I look like a Hollywood legend? I'm the old butler."

"I'm sorry, my mistake."

The man glared at me for another minute, then threw back his head and roared with laughter.

"I couldn't resist," he said. "I was eating breakfast this morning, and I couldn't remember for the *life* of me what year it was. I'm positively ancient. It would make a great movie, wouldn't it? Hiring an elderly butler who couldn't keep track of hours, days, years . . . he'd answer the door and forget whether you were home or not. He'd go out to get the morning paper and keep walking until he hit Sunset. You'd never see him again."

"Yes . . . that's very good . . ."

"Don't take the joke personally," he said, waving a hand at me. "I'd have saved it for a door-to-door salesman, but we don't get them anymore. I haven't had an unwanted visitor since I killed Eleanor."

I stared at him, unsure what to say.

"A joke! That was a joke."

"Are you Theo?"

"Where are my manners? Yes, I'm Theo," he said, extending his hand. I took it and was surprised at how firm his grip was. "You have to forgive me, Max, I don't get the opportunity to bullshit people the way I used to."

"Call me Hailey, if you like."

Theo raised an eyebrow. "I most certainly will," he said. "Come in, come in. And wipe your feet!"

I stepped into the house, then took a look around in stunned silence. Everything had changed since my last visit; it looked like the entire house had been cleaned with a toothbrush. The black-and-white floor tiles in the foyer sparkled in the shafts of sunlight that came in through the door, and the walls had been scrubbed of cobwebs and swaths of dust.

Theo watched my observations with a little smile. "We prepared the house for your visit," he said.

"I see that."

"I hope you don't mind," he said airily. "The house had gotten a bit . . . stale."

"Had it?"

"Oh, let's lose the pretense! I know that you were in my house; you know that I know. Let's acknowledge it and move on."

Theo had been busy in the last few days. As we moved through the house, I could see that every inch of the great house had been scrubbed, and that was no easy feat. He must have hired an entire team of cleaners. If my whole game plan relied on finding a piece of Eleanor's DNA to prove that Theo had killed her inside Windhall, my task had just become a lot more difficult. By the look of things, it would be difficult to find even a piece of Theo's DNA in the floorboards.

"You will let me know if you have any questions, won't you, Max? Er, Hailey."

"Of course."

"Tell me something," Theo said, as we entered the kitchen. "Did Fritz take you down Coldwater Canyon, or did he drive you through Hollywood?"

"We went through Hollywood."

"That bastard!" Theo said. "He does it on purpose, you know."

"Does what?"

"Fritz thinks I've let Windhall go to ruin, with the yard falling into disrepair and what have you. He's rather theatrical, likes to show guests the seedier parts of Los Angeles before they arrive. He thinks it makes me look good by comparison."

"Guests . . . ?"

Theo waved his hands. "A figure of speech. The only guest I've had in the last week is my lawyer, of course. Halloween's just around the corner—I might get trick-or-treaters for the first time in fifty, sixty years."

"Somehow I doubt it."

"Well, I'll have to content myself with trespassers, then. Would you like some lemonade? We can take it in the garden."

"Yes, please."

There was no fridge, of course, and I hadn't seen any evidence that the electricity had been turned back on. Sunlight streamed in through narrow windows, but the effect was very gothic: furniture cast in shadows, tapestries and rugs bare suggestions against the dim pallor of the house.

A pitcher of lemonade sat on the kitchen counter, next to two glasses.

"Does Fritz know what the house used to look like?"

"Oh, yes. Fritz grew up here."

I was taken aback. "Before the murder?"

"Naturally. He's not some kind of wild thing; he didn't grow up among the *weeds*."

"How old is he?"

"Old." Theo poured the lemonade. "His mother worked for me. Everyone left, of course, when I moved away from Los Angeles."

A thought occurred to me. "Marja," I said. "Your housekeeper. Was she his mother?"

"You've done your homework." Theo picked up the glasses and motioned with his head. "Let's go outside."

Theo walked toward the service entrance and stood next to it. "You wouldn't mind getting the door, would you?"

"Of course not." I went to open it.

"Feels familiar, doesn't it?" He winked at me. "Almost like you've been here before."

I couldn't help laughing. "It certainly does."

Theo led me down the path that wound along the kitchen vegetable patch. Wild magnolia trees stood like disfigured creatures, gnarled and mostly gone to seed. The path was unkempt and ragged.

"Your garden was beautiful," I said. "I've seen pictures."

"It was very beautiful, yes," Theo said. "Once."

As we moved through the garden filled with dead brambles, I glanced up at the house. I tried to imagine that fateful night, the last party that Windhall would ever see, and a shiver ran down my spine. I could almost see them, the beautiful women and courteous men, dancing to the type of jazz that was popular in those days. They would have been so happy, so triumphant, thinking that nobody and nothing could touch them. The second great war was over; the danger should have been behind them.

"Would you like to see the spot where Eleanor's body was recovered?" Theo said, turning to look at me. "The roses died out long ago, of course, but it might be of interest to your article."

His tone was as casual as if he had offered me marmalade with my morning toast. I wasn't sure if it was meant as some kind of test but reminded myself not to get caught up in one of Theo's tricks. It seemed like he might be mocking me, testing my reserve, but I took the bait.

"Yes," I said. "I'd like to see it."

"It was a shame that we had to kill the roses," Theo said. "I was quite fond of them. I had a skilled gardener, one of the best in Los Angeles, but with everyone in Hollywood calling for my head, we had to get rid of them. It was only a small concession, of course, and it wasn't enough to placate the masses. Sometimes I still dream about that rose garden."

"How did you kill them?"

"Boiling water," Theo sighed. "God, it nearly killed me. When all the plants were gone, we burned the ground. The roses became synonymous with Eleanor's death, and we had so many photographers sneaking into Windhall to take pictures."

We emerged into the sunlight, and Theo pointed to an elevated section of ground. Unlike the rest of the garden, the plants there were patchy, as though the ground was still damaged by what had happened there.

He walked up a little stone stairway, and we emerged onto a high terrace. The terrace was lined with brick, and someone had swept away all the leaves and bracken in preparation for my visit. An ornate white table and two chairs sat by the edge of the terrace, which was lined by small, dark trees.

The trees formed a kind of natural border around the brick terrace, and even though they were mere skeletons, I could feel that they had once offered a sense of peace and quiet reflection from the rest of the garden.

"Citrus trees," Theo said. He walked up and put his hand against one of the trunks. "We used to have a small orchard of them. Satsumas, tangerines, lemons, and your average navels."

"Why so many?"

"California wouldn't exist without citrus," he said. "Los Angeles was built on false advertising. It was a desert, but they sold it as an oasis, thanks to orange groves."

"That's awfully sentimental of you."

"I used to think I would live forever," he said. "Norse mythology holds that oranges contain the elixir of youth. Speaking of which, you haven't touched your lemonade."

I took a sip. "It's good," I said. "Homemade?"

"Sure is. We used to grow the lemons right here, but now I have to buy them when I get groceries, like a common consumer."

"Do I taste rosemary?"

"That's right, and arsenic from the local pharmacist."

"You're funny. Quick on your feet." I took another sip. "Do you still have the brooch?"

"Have what?"

"The scarab," I said. "The one you stole from the house that night."

His eyes hardened, but he said nothing.

"You gave it to Eleanor, didn't you? She used to wear it to movie premieres, tucked against her heart. Do you know what happened to it?"

"Fritz thinks I've made a mistake by inviting you into my home." Theo tilted his head. "Leland does, too. It's mostly boredom, I suppose. And I have a terrible ego. Can't resist toying with someone who's taken an interest in me."

"I've always been interested in you."

"So, tell me, Hailey," he said. "How do *you* think I did it? Everyone has their theories, and I never get tired of hearing them."

"Did what?"

"Killed Eleanor, of course. Isn't that why you're here?"

"So, you're admitting it?"

"I'm always happy to hear a good story. The most popular notion is that I killed her in a closet and moved her body outside."

My face flushed, and I looked down. Once again I got the sense that he was baiting me, and I didn't want to give him a reaction.

"You seem awfully convinced that you won't get another trial," I said.

Theo stretched his arms above his head and winced. "Oh, people have been trying for years, and yet here I am."

"Have you considered the possibility that I might be recording you right now?"

He winked. "I have a good lawyer," he said. "I'm aware that in California, you need to inform someone that you're recording them before you actually do so."

"It seems awfully callous of you to joke about the murder of a close friend."

"Let's talk about something else, then. Why Paul de Longpré?" he asked. "If I were going to break into someone's house and steal a painting, I'd probably go for something more valuable."

"My gran liked him."

"It certainly caught my attention. I suppose that's one of the reasons I invited you back. You're not the first one to break in, you know."

I swirled my lemonade. "They want you to vacate Windhall."

"Who's that?"

"People are outraged about the two girls who were murdered. I'm assuming you've heard; it was a tribute to Eleanor, after all."

"Yes, I've heard."

"One of the girls' fathers is organizing a petition. He wants you to leave."

Theo scoffed. "Surely they don't think that *I'm* responsible for those recent deaths!"

"He thinks Windhall stands as a tribute to domestic violence. The death of innocence and all that."

"Eleanor was *hardly* innocent," Theo muttered, then caught himself. "Why are you telling me this?"

I set my glass on the table and looked at him. "I'm here to listen," I said. "You have a voice. If there's anything you want to say, anything to prove your innocence, now's the time."

"My innocence! You should run a full-length shot of me in your paper, that'll be conclusive. As soon as they see these rheumy eyes and arthritic hands, people will draw their own conclusions."

He was making fun of me. I had rehearsed for this moment, and it wasn't going according to plan. I had seen hundreds of pictures over the years: when Theo was a young man, standing in front of a house covered in wild bougainvillea, standing beside Errol Flynn, a crooked grin on his face, and then after the murder trial, somber and gray. I had painted a personality for him, outside of all the press clippings and photographs, beyond Windhall and his brilliant movie career, but during all of that time, I had never granted him wit.

He watched me with a gleam in his eye. I tried again.

"I've been watching your movies my entire life," I said. "I'm willing to bet that the odds were stacked against you. From what I understand, Hollywood can be a prickly place, and if you piss the wrong people off, it can be deadly."

"You can say that again." He cocked his head and thought. "What was the name they gave me? The Thorn King? It's very poetic, wouldn't you say?"

"Don't you want to keep Windhall?" I was starting to get exasperated. "If this man gets his way, you'll be forced to leave."

"Of course, of course." He waved a hand. "I've spent enough time and money on it. Might as well keep the damn thing intact, if I can."

I cleared my throat and tried a different angle. "My editor wants me to run the story about Lucy's," I said. "We haven't spoken to Connie yet, but my editor has a few ideas about how to find her."

Theo was watching me, and I thought I saw the hint of a smile. "Is that so?"

"Yes," I said. "I'd rather write a story about Windhall, and its cultural significance. Maybe we can keep it from getting torn down."

"I was sorry to hear about your grandmother," Theo said suddenly. "She was a lovely woman."

"You actually remember my grandmother?"

"She worked on two of my films," Theo said. "Of course I remember her."

"I have to say that I'm surprised."

Theo gave me a long, patient look. "I know that the film industry has changed a great deal," he said. "Movies are thrown together in a great haste. Studios pick a screenplay at random, then choose their highest-grossing star. They choose a director who will play nice, be a good little puppet. It's all done very quickly, to maximize profit, and at the end of the day, nobody remembers each other's names. Back in my day, kid, things were different."

I could see that he was starting to open up, and I sat back to let him speak.

"We used to be thick as thieves," Theo said. "Film people had to stick together. Everyone in Hollywood hated us, you know. All the original farmers and townspeople wanted nothing to do with us."

I had so many questions that I didn't know where to start, but I had a feeling that it would be better not to interrupt.

"I only spoke to Nadine a handful of times," Theo said, "but I remember her. She was brave. Showed up to work a few times with bruises, but she didn't let it affect her work ethic."

I flinched at the thought of my grandfather. I was humiliated and surprised that Theo would remember such a tiny detail from all those years before. I knew that he was trying to assert control over the conversation, and I moved to take it back.

"It's interesting to hear you say that," I said. "I thought men showed solidarity for their own kind."

His eyes twinkled. "Are you not a man?"

"Not that kind of man, no. Never."

"Nadine raised you well, then."

"I didn't come here to talk about her," I said quickly. "I came here to talk about you."

"You were close," he said. "You lived with her for a while, didn't you?"

I said nothing.

"You still live in her house," he went on. "She's the one who took you to the hospital when you were young. You were there for a while—two years, was it?"

So he *had* researched me. In the past, subjects that I had interviewed for articles had become hostile, aggressive, reticent, or downright petty. It was fairly common for someone in a vulnerable position to try to turn the tables, especially if I asked the wrong questions or made them feel defensive. It never fazed me; since I had become adept at being a nonentity when I interviewed people, the attacks were never personal. With Theo, however, it was different.

He was watching me with an amused little smile on his face.

"A little over two years," I said. "Good times."

"A problem with your spine, was it? I heard that you never learned how to swim. A shame, in Los Angeles."

"With all the sharks and pollution? Hardly."

"That's why you learned to write." He tapped his head. "No strength in your body, so you had to have a weapon."

"That's right."

"And you set a building on fire. We can't forget that."

"It was a youthful mistake." I cleared my throat. "How are we doing on time? Were you going to give me the tour this afternoon?"

"Of course, of course," he said. "Now, I'm not a doctor, but I did some reading about your condition. Do you find it difficult to walk?"

"No."

"You'd think all that spine damage would have a lasting effect. Do you still have scars?"

"Not where anyone can see them."

"We used to have a saying in Hollywood," he said. "Keep the scars out of sight. Never let anyone know that they can break you."

I glanced around the orange grove. The bracken came creeping in at the edges, the dead brambles and tapping branches an eerie reminder of how much time had passed since Eleanor had been killed. All the dead plants seemed to make a slow progression toward the house, tapping their fingers against the panes of glass, eager to see inside. There was something dark about the garden, and I shivered, imagining the plants slowly suffocating the windows and high turrets. No one would even hear the screams.

"So how about that tour?" I said.

Before he could answer, the kitchen door opened, a glint of sunlight slashing across the pane. A man stepped out, and I felt my stomach jump as I recognized him. He wore a button-down shirt and jeans, and he carried an old-fashioned doctor's bag.

It was Ben.

He squinted against the sun, then raised a hand and waved.

"Hello, Theo," he said, and then, seeing me, nodded. "Mr. Hailey."

"Ahh, the good doctor," Theo said. "I'd forgotten that you two had met."

"Not the most auspicious circumstances." Ben came up the path toward us and set his bag down on the table. He turned to Theo. "Did you forget that I was coming?"

"My mind is a sieve these days."

I quickly put the pieces together. "Wait—you're Theo's doctor?"

"We've got an appointment today." Ben nodded. "Theo must not have mentioned it."

"You're welcome to stay," Theo said. "Dialysis is a real hoot, in the right company!"

"How long will this take?" I asked Ben.

"A few hours, at most."

I considered my options. "Would you be able to give me a tour afterward?"

"I'm afraid not," Ben said. "This is a rather taxing procedure, and Theo will need his rest."

I was struggling to make the connection between Ben and Theo's house; why Ben had been upstairs with Leland, and why I had seen Ben at the murder scene of the second dead girl.

"Come back this weekend," Theo said. "Saturday. I'll give you a tour on Saturday."

I could see that my hands were tied. I was eager to see the house, but I didn't want to antagonize my subject more than necessary, and after a moment of deliberation, I nodded.

"I'll see you Saturday," I said.

I made my own way out of the house, somewhat surprised that Theo hadn't tailed me to make sure that I actually left. As I walked through the grand foyer, I stopped and took out my cell phone, then snapped a quick picture of the ruined light coming in through the stained glass windows. Leland's contract prohibited me from taking pictures of Theo, but it said nothing about the house. Seeing that nobody had followed me, I took a few more quick pictures, then stepped outside and took a picture of the garden from the front door.

A Range Rover sat in the driveway, spattered with mud. It hadn't been there when I arrived, so it must have belonged to Ben. The back passenger window was open a few inches, and I glanced around to make sure that nobody was watching me, then went around the side of the car and reached inside. I could just reach the lock. I quickly opened the door and hopped inside, then reached for the glove compartment and picked through the registration papers until I found what I was looking for.

A name, and an address in Burbank. *Dr. Benjamin Lewis.* Bingo.

TWELVE

When Fritz saw me walking down the driveway, he offered to give me a ride home, but I declined. It had occurred to me that the Beverly Hills Public Library might have a copy of the Windhall blueprints from back when it was a tuberculosis facility, and even if they didn't, they might have a copy of the blueprints from when Theo had made his renovations. It might give me some insight into where Theo had killed Eleanor, if there were any dark, secret rooms.

I left Windhall and walked down the street until I hit Benedict Canyon, then called a cab, which dropped me off at the library. I had visited it on a few occasions and enjoyed the art deco architecture but hadn't spent much time there, because it felt more like a museum than a public space. Still, there was a chance that they might have something that could help me.

"Hi," I said, approaching the librarian at the archives desk.

"Help you?"

"I was wondering if you have the blueprints for an old house in Beverly Hills," I said. "It's called Windhall. I can give you the address."

"I know Windhall," she said. She looked suspicious. "We don't have the blueprints."

"Have you ever had them?" I said.

The woman adjusted her glasses and gave me a hard look. "Are you hunting for treasure?" she asked.

"I just want to see the blueprints."

"I know about the reward offered for leading to Theo's arrest. People come in here, no respect for the fact that this is a library, and they take things."

"I'm a writer," I said apologetically.

"And which restaurant do you work at?"

"Sorry, I'm a *paid* writer." I sighed and tried not to seem impatient. I decided to stretch the truth a bit. "Look, I'll be very respectful. Someone is campaigning to have Windhall torn down, and since it's a historic building, I'd like to try to save it."

"Someone is *what*?"

"You've heard about the two girls who got killed recently? The father of the first victim is very upset. Can you blame him? I don't think Theo had anything to do with the murders, but since it was a tribute to Eleanor Hayes, he's trying to get Windhall torn down."

She still didn't look like she trusted me, so I took out my press pass.

"I'm a journalist," I said. "I've just been to Windhall to speak with Theo, and I need to check something."

"Come on." She gave me a dubious smile. "Nobody's seen Theo in fifty, sixty years."

I took out my phone and scrolled through to find the picture of the foyer. I passed it over the desk to show her, and she studied it for a moment.

"Is that . . . ?"

"Look at the date. I took the picture from the inside of Theo's house just a little while ago." I scrolled through the other pictures that I had quickly taken that afternoon.

"How on earth did you get inside?"

"I have my ways."

She sighed and took off her glasses. "I'm really not supposed to let you see the blueprints," she said. "I guess I would feel better about breaking the rules if I knew that you were a member of our library."

I whipped out my library card. There were five or six library systems within Los Angeles, and I had cards for all of them. Upon seeing the card, the woman's face relaxed.

"Come with me," she said. "You'd better not have chewing gum. You're not allowed any recording devices, either, so I'll have to take your phone."

With some reluctance, I passed her my cell phone. She took me down a softly lit hallway, into a spacious room lined with filing cabinets. There was a big table in the middle of the room, and I took a seat while she rifled around in one of the filing cabinets. After a few minutes of searching, she found what she was looking for.

"We have two sets," she said, bringing over two tubes of rolled up blueprints. "One was from the original building, which was a tuberculosis facility in the 1910s and '20s. The other set is from the renovations that Theo did."

"Fantastic."

"Which set would you like to see? I can let you see them one at a time."

"Just the renovations," I said. "If I need the other ones, I'll let you know."

"There's something I should mention," she said, and I could see her biting back a smile. "There are some handwritten notes on the second set of blueprints."

"From the architect?"

"No," she said. "Actually, I think they're from Theo."

"Wow."

"I'll give you ten minutes," she said. She handed me a pair of single-use cotton gloves. "Use these."

I sat down and slipped on the cotton gloves, then carefully unrolled the library's blueprints of Windhall. A grid of tight lines unfolded before me, and I saw the familiar shapes of the dining room, the screening room, and the library.

The librarian had been right. Scribbled in the margins and blank spaces of the blueprints were a set of handwritten notes. Faded green ink, spikes and squiggles. I recognized Theo's handwriting from the journals, and it seemed that he had written what each of the rooms was going to be used for.

This is the conservatory, read one note. *Intended for breakfast, but I'll mostly eat in the kitchen, standing up. Otherwise I'll eat in my office.*

"Office" was circled upstairs; another note indicated that it was meant to be used as a guest bedroom, but Theo had later converted it for his use.

I read through the rest of the notes carefully, and I couldn't help laughing at a few of them. *Here's the music room*, read another. *Absolute best place in the house to get squiffed and watch the sunset.*

Another set of notes indicated that climbing out the windows of the tower at the back of the house allowed for partygoers to smoke hand-rolled joints or cigarettes without having to worry about sharing their stash. I had an image of Errol Flynn precariously balancing at the edge of the roof before climbing up the shingles, monkey-like, then perching beneath the stars to smoke with a gang of wild friends.

And then I paused.

I set my index finger on the room labeled "Upstairs Guest Room," the room in which I had encountered Ben and Leland on the night of my original break-in. Behind the guest bedroom was a maid's room, and the two rooms were adjoined by a door. On the night that I had visited, however, there had been no sign of a door. I thought back in desperation, then remembered that they had been busy working on the wallpaper. I had assumed that they were busy patching it up, but it seemed now that they had been peeling it away to reveal the missing door.

There was something else that caught my attention. According to the blueprints, the maid's room stood in a part of the house that had once been three stories tall, with a second tower and a lower roof extending over the garden. The third story and roof were no longer part of Windhall.

I glanced at my watch. I only had three minutes until the librarian returned and took the blueprints away, and I knew that there was very little possibility of seeing them again.

I took out my pen and a crumpled paper bag from my satchel, and, working quickly, sketched the general layout of the maid's room and the missing tower. There was an additional part of Windhall that I hadn't seen, and if Theo had been trying to hide it, there was probably a good reason for it.

I had just finished sketching and managed to spirit away the drawing before the librarian returned.

"All finished?" she asked.

"Yes," I said. "You've been very helpful, thank you."

It was dark when the bus dropped me off at the bottom of Laurel Canyon. I hated taking the bus and was normally exhausted from the walk up to my house, but that night I was energized by all the new information. I was excited at the prospect of the missing room, and all the clues it might hold. If anything was a damning piece of evidence against Theo, this was it.

I planned to make myself a coffee and head straight to my office, but when I reached my driveway, I stopped in my tracks.

The lights were on in my kitchen. I lingered there for a moment, trying to remember whether I had left them on that morning before Fritz picked me up. Before I could contemplate the thought any further, a silhouette passed before the window and lingered there for a moment before disappearing.

Someone was in my house.

I made my way around the back of the house. When I stepped through the back door, I heard voices. I froze, listening. There were two men—no, three—talking to one another. By the sound of it, they hadn't realized that I had come home. My first thought was to wonder why someone had broken into my house. I didn't even stop to wonder whether confronting them would be a good idea.

I glanced around quickly, then grabbed a wooden plant stand that was by the back door. Wielding it in front of me, I stalked toward the kitchen. The voices were getting louder, and one of the men laughed.

I waited for a moment, then walked straight into the kitchen. I was about to start swinging the plant stand like a pickaxe, but stopped when I saw ladders, tools, and a drop cloth.

"Whoa, what the fuck!" one of the men exclaimed.

"Shit, man, you scared me!" One of the men threw his fists up, but the other two men started laughing. "Jesus Christ!"

"Who are you?" I demanded. "What the fuck are you doing in my kitchen?"

"We're here to replace your skylight," one of the men spoke up, then pointed to the rotting hole in my ceiling. He wore a set of faded green coveralls. "You know, the massive fucking hole above the counter?"

"It's not a skylight."

"I know that, genius."

I backed toward the door, then quickly assessed the situation. Everything that had been on the kitchen counters had been replaced with piles of tools. A stack of wood and sheet metal sat on the tiles, and a box of shingles were placed on top of my coffee table. All three men regarded me warily.

"How did you get into my house?"

"The door was unlocked."

"So you thought you'd let yourself in?"

The men exchanged looks, then turned back to look at me. "She wasn't sure if you'd be home," Green Coveralls said. "She said you worked during the day, and that we should go ahead and let ourselves in. There's a key in the birdhouse out back, right?"

"Wait, what? Who said that?"

"Heather."

My brain did a few somersaults. The men stared at me in confusion, and then one of them covered his mouth to hide a laugh. Green Coveralls narrowed his eyes at me, then rubbed his chin.

"You didn't know," he said.

"No, I didn't."

At this, the other two men burst into laughter. One of them doubled over, and the other one clapped a hand on his back. Green Coveralls looked like he wanted to join in, but he tried to remain professional.

"You've got some friend, buddy," he said. "We're not cheap."

"I'm not paying for this," I said quickly.

"That's the point, you don't have to. Heather's already paid for everything."

"Why?"

"Sounds like you've got an admirer." Green Coveralls winked at me.

"I don't know if I'm comfortable with this."

He crossed his arms. "We're slated for more rain in three days," he said. "I can tell you've had this problem for a while, because the damage is extensive. Miguel went into the attic to do an assessment earlier, and he nearly fell through the ceiling."

Miguel gave me a lazy salute.

"Let me put it to you this way, pal—if you don't get this fixed within the month, you're going to have to tear off the entire roof. You'll have to replace the attic and the support beams, unless you like living al fresco, of course."

Miguel and the third man started giggling again.

"Shut up, you two," Green Coveralls snapped.

"I need to make a phone call," I said. "I'm going out back."

I retreated into the hallway and made my way outdoors. Once I was outside, I called Madeleine.

"Hey, I can't talk long," she said, as soon as she picked up.

"You still mad at me?"

There was a pause. "Why was I mad at you?"

"Because of Heather," I said.

"Remind me."

"It's not worth it," I said. "I think you were right."

"Okay, it's starting to come back to me," she said. "Is this about the contract you signed with her?"

"She sent some men over to fix my roof," I said.

"That's generous."

"She didn't tell me, Mad," I said. "She told them to let themselves in. She even knew where my spare key was. I had completely forgotten about it, until they reminded me."

"Okay, that's creepy. You think she's trying to get into your pants?"

"I think I just threw up in my mouth a little bit."

"Did you call her to ask her why she sent them over?"

"No," I said, then thought for a moment. "You think she's putting bugs in my roof?"

Madeleine burst into laughter. "Now you're being paranoid. I think she's flexing her muscles, Hailey. She's trying to show you how powerful she is. Hey, I need to go."

"Oh, wait," I said. "I have a request."

"Make it quick."

"This is a shot in the dark," I said. "But Windhall is a historic structure. If Theo wanted to make renovations to it, he'd have to get it approved with a historical council, wouldn't he?"

"Today, yes. Back in the day, though, things were probably looser. Wait a sec—I think it's only been considered historic for a few years, which means that he probably wouldn't have had to request them at all."

I gritted my teeth in frustration.

"You still there?"

"Yeah," I said. "Thanks anyway."

———————————

Once I was back inside my office, I was too distracted to sit down and get work done. I was torn between conflicting desires: on one hand, I wanted to call Heather and give her a piece of my mind, but I wasn't exactly sure why I was so upset. I didn't have a concrete reason to mistrust her, and I thought it might be better to wait until I had a handle on the situation to give her a phone call.

Instead, I took out my phone and called Petra.

"Hey," she said, picking up after three rings. "How did the interview with Theo go?"

I quickly filled her in on all the pertinent details, and she listened carefully. After I described Theo and the house itself, I told her about the hidden room.

"I think I know where Theo killed Eleanor," I said. "It's going to be tough to prove it, though, and we've only got one shot at this."

"Which room was it?"

"It was supposed to be a maid's room," I said. "It was on the original blueprints. Here's my theory: Theo killed Eleanor in the maid's room, she bled a lot, and there was a bit of a mess. At some point, he moved her down to the garden with someone's help, which would explain the second set of footprints in the garden. After Theo is taken away, this second person works through the night, boarding up the maid's room and gluing wallpaper up, like the room was never even there."

"Wow," Petra said. "Any idea who the second person might have been?"

"The only person I can think of is Reuben Engel," I said. "Theo's producer. But they didn't seem to get along very well, so I'm not sure."

"I can't believe they didn't find the room in the original investigation," she said. "Oh, that reminds me. I've looked into everyone who was at the party that night, and they're all dead."

"That's disappointing, but I can't say I'm surprised," I said. "At least I found out who Ben is. He's Theo's doctor—Dr. Lewis. That's what I want you to focus on. See what else you can find out about him. If they're hiding something, Dr. Lewis is helping them."

After we hung up, I was tempted to drive to an all-night café somewhere and claim a table, but I didn't want to transport Theo's journals and risk having someone see me reading them. I took a swig from a cup of leftover coffee sitting on my desk, then opened my computer.

If I couldn't find out the truth from a tour of Windhall, my last hope of discovering what had happened was talking to Marcus Loew, Bernard Loew's son. His father might have been an alcoholic and an unreliable worker, but he had also known Theo pretty well. After Petra and I had talked about Marcus the day before, I had downloaded all of his music into my library. Most of the scores Marcus had written accompanied noir-style films about murder and intrigue, and frequently, one of the main characters was bumped off to a dramatic crescendo. I wasn't normally a fan of movie soundtracks, but his scores were haunting and tragic, and I found that I really enjoyed listening to them.

With Marcus's music playing in the background, I took out the box containing Theo's journals. When I opened the next journal, a stiff piece of paper fell out and landed on the floor. I reached down and picked it up.

It was a thick piece of cream-colored parchment, embossed with curly lettering. As I read the words on the piece of paper, I saw that it was a funeral announcement for someone named Walter Thomas. I had to flip through my notes to remind myself where I had read the familiar name before, and when I finally found it in my pages, I was surprised. Walter Thomas had been Theo's mentor when he first moved to Hollywood, and he was someone about whom Theo had written fondly. I had to remind myself that many of the people mentioned in Theo's journals had been dead for quite some time, whether or not Theo had attended their funerals.

The funeral had been held on August 10, 1946. I flipped the parchment over and saw that Theo had scrawled some notes: *That bastard had the gall to show up and pretend like he didn't want this. Saw Hedda leaning on his arm and talking during the entire ceremony.*

And then, beneath that, it looked like he had engaged in a silent conversation with someone else at the funeral, because there was another style of penmanship, one I didn't recognize.

Thinking of having people over at mine after. You game?
    Course. When?
Methinks seven.
    Who?
Rows 8 – 15. Leave out the heads and the gossip writers.
    Let's get squiffed

I had to laugh when I saw that Theo had written a little grocery list beneath that, composed mainly of alcohol. He had written down drinks he planned to serve—*sidecar, gin rickey, French 75, vesper, aviation cocktail*—and I could see that even though his friend's death had probably devastated him, he was determined to make the best of the situation.

I tucked the parchment back into Theo's journal, then turned the page. Theo had glued in a newspaper article, dated only a week after the death notice.

Reuben Engel assumes top producer role at Metro-Goldwyn-Mayer, the article began. I scanned the rest, but I was more interested in what Theo had to say about it. On the next page, he had written, *Only four more years on my contract! Then Paramount?*

Reuben Engel. His name was popping up more and more throughout my investigation into Theo. It was also suspicious that his favorite daughter, Heather, had contacted me right around the time that I had made contact with Theo. Still, I couldn't bring myself to consider him a serious suspect in Eleanor's death, because it was clear that Theo hadn't liked him, and I couldn't think of a reason why Theo would protect someone he hated over someone he had seemed so fond of.

I knew that there was only one way to find out what Theo thought about Engel, however, and that was to keep reading his journals.

July 5, 1947: Los Angeles, California—

She's sick of it, and I don't blame her. Some days we can't even get inside the studio, because the crowd's too big. Most of them are here to see Nora, of course, that's the only thing they want.

"I'm going to quit, Theo, I tell you!" she said, just last week, but she was laughing. Her good humor is starting to wear through,

though. Dozens more bouquets of flowers delivered to her dressing room, none of them from people she knows.

MGM has hired extra studio muscle just to keep them out, but some of them always manage to sneak in. There are men who disguise themselves as janitorial staff and then make their way to Nora's dressing room, and when she arrives, fall at her feet, professing their love.

And then there are the stalkers. Every star at the height of fame has a few stalkers, but some of them do nothing more than send a few fan letters. Most of Nora's stalkers aren't men, either; they're women who are determined to make their own path in the film industry. Young women all over the country have been cutting their hair and staining their kitchen sinks with homemade dye jobs, desperately aiming for Nora's blue-black tint. They've been painting their faces and having their picture taken, then sending them to the studios, hoping to get called in for a screen test.

At first, Nora was good-natured about it. As the fans and stalkers have grown more determined, however, I can see that it's starting to wear away at her resolve. It's unnerving to arrive at the studio gates for work each morning and find a wave of women with similar eyes, faces, hands, and haircuts to Nora's. We've taken to calling them the Glum Noras, with their pathetic makeup and poorly done hairstyles.

One of these women broke into Nora's dressing room last week while we were busy filming a scene for _My Friend, Roy_. By the time we'd found her, she had tried on each one of Nora's dresses before finally throwing up on one of them and then passing out in the bathroom. The studio has promised to take measures to prevent these women from getting into the studio in the future, but if someone like Charlie

Chaplin can get blackmailed by a stalker, it's only fair to assume that the rest of us will have a worse case of it.

July 14, 1947—

Normal gang of misfits came to the party: Errol, Jules, Bill, and Cate Chapelle. Cate's a good friend of Nora's—don't know her too well, but she seems likable. There's the added bonus of the fact that she can't stand our new producer, either.

We all got sloshed on sidecars and stayed out in the garden until the mosquitoes came out. Might still be a bit drunk as I write this— slept it off but woke up at five this morning, couldn't fall back asleep.

Cate stayed in the guest room. Everyone else went home, but we had breakfast together this morning.

"So what do you think of MGM's new despot?"

"He's not so bad," she said. "Probably worse for women than men, though."

"I bet."

She lowered her voice, even though we were the only ones around. "There are rumors about him, you know," she said. "About things he does when no one else is around to stop him."

"What do you mean?"

She studied her plate. "You've heard that Perla Hastings had her contract dropped when they found out that she was pregnant, right?"

"Sure."

"Whose baby do you think it was?"

I slammed a hand on the table, and she jumped. "Sorry," I said. "But if you're serious about this, we need to investigate."

She looked worried. "Forget I said anything," she said. "I don't know what I'm talking about."

July 23, 1947—

Errol threw a party on his boat last night—same crew. Didn't take the boat out on the water, because Errol was sloshed, just kept it in the marina. I wasn't sure if Nora would come, and was quite happy that she did. After the fireworks and the cake, I tracked her down.

"Hello, Theo," she said. "The studio's letting you have a day off?"

"I've told them I'm working. Don't spoil the secret."

"Lord knows you need a rest," she said. "You work harder than anyone."

I took her aside. I'd been meaning to talk to her about what Cate had told me.

"Has he ever threatened you?"

She frowned. "I'm not sure what you mean."

"Has he ever—you know, made a move? Threatened your career?"

Her face went dark. "He's been flirtatious, but that's about it. What are you saying?"

"Nothing for certain," I said. "Just let me know if he does. Keep an eye out, that's what I'm saying. Listen, you want to get out of here?"

"Where to?"

"I've got a surprise. Come on, let's go."

I'd had a few drinks but thought that I was probably still okay to navigate the roads. Nora was quiet and thoughtful as I drove through Brentwood, which was filled with the sound of Joan's neighbors and their merrymaking.

"Where are you taking me?" she asked, as I drove down Wilshire Boulevard.

"It's a surprise."

I drove up through the sleepy little neighborhoods north of Wilshire, which have started to undergo various developments and restorations in the last few years. It's funny to think that I can remember a time when Los Angeles still had a bit of farmland to it. I've never seen a city change so quickly beneath my feet.

When I turned up Benedict Canyon, Nora smiled.

"I know where we're going," she said. "You're taking me to the old tuberculosis clinic."

I smiled but said nothing. We turned onto Sweet Briar Way, then pulled onto the gravel drive that led up to the old clinic.

"You're not planning to kill me, are you?" She laughed.

"This would be the perfect place to do it." I climbed out, then went around and opened the door for her.

It was one of the last places where you could find solace in Los Angeles. The only sound we could hear was that of leaves and branches crunching beneath our footsteps, and as we walked toward the hulking form of the old house, Nora slipped her hand into mine.

When we reached the front door, I turned to look at her.

"You want to go inside?"

"What's your plan?" she asked.

"Well, we could smash the windows," I said, and shrugged. "Then again, someone might hear us and call the cops."

"There's nobody out here."

"That's true. It would make an awful mess, though. It might be easier to just unlock the door and let ourselves in."

I removed a set of keys from my pocket. With a little flourish, I smiled at Nora and then unlocked the door.

She gave me a wide-eyed look. "How on earth . . . ?"

"I know someone."

"Who?"

"He's a realtor," I said. "He sells houses. He sold me this house, actually."

"Theo . . ."

"I needed a place to live," I said. "Not a bungalow at the Garden of Allah, and not a rental in Beachwood Canyon. I need something I can call my own."

She lingered at the edge of the doorway. "Why did you buy this place, though?"

"It's the first time I felt like I belonged here," I said. "That's because of you."

"I don't know what to say."

"I have a favor to ask," I said. "Are you feeling subversive?"

"I usually am," she replied. "What's up?"

"I'm working on a movie with John Cromwell," I said. "It's about the evils of the film industry. If you're willing, we'd like you to play the lead. She goes off the rails at the end."

"Can I act like Joan Crawford?"

"Of course you can," I said, laughing. "Seriously, though, Nor—I want you to consider this carefully. We're going to piss off a lot of people, and if they realize what the analogy means, it could mean the end of my career. I don't want you to agree to do this lightly."

Her face was dark, and I couldn't see her expression. "MGM hasn't done a lot for me lately," she said. "If you're making a movie to criticize them, I'm in."

"Maybe you should read the script first," I said.

"Theo, I said I'm in," she said. "I'm capable of making my own decisions. Now, are you going to show me the inside of the house, or what?"

I flipped over to the next page, and a note fell out.

Theo ~
Can we meet later? Same spot as Monday.
    Cate

I lay the note down next to the journal, puzzling over what it could mean. There was no mention of meeting Cate in Theo's next few journal entries, but when I continued reading, I saw something written on a scrap of paper, which might have been connected:

Mtg w/ Dr. Menz re: CC

It took me a moment to piece together the fact that CC probably meant Cate Chapelle. The appointment was scheduled for about a week after they had planned to meet, but there was nothing in the next few pages about what the appointment had been regarding.

I continued reading Theo's journals for about an hour, until I came to a set of entries that was increasingly dour. The last one ended with an apocryphal line that was not explained:

Our lives are fun, but not for us.

And then, on the next page, an announcement torn out of the *Los Angeles Times*. According to the article, an MGM starlet named Catherine Chapelle had died in her Beachwood Canyon home late one Sunday evening, and a private funeral service was to be held for her the following week.

THIRTEEN

I spent the rest of the night researching Cate Chapelle and trying to determine her cause of death. The only official statement I could find listed it as a death due to "medical complications." My skin went cold as I read through the few journal entries prior, and tried to piece together the relationship that Theo and Cate had maintained.

According to all the research that I compiled, Cate had been a rising star when she died, someone only a few years behind Eleanor. Was it possible that Theo had killed someone else, and nobody had paid attention?

Petra came to my house early the next morning to review the information that we had collected so far.

"I got in touch with the son of the set designer who worked with Theo," she said. "The composer, Marcus Loew."

"Great work, Petra. Will he meet up with us?"

"I actually spoke to his assistant," she said. "Marcus is in Hungary. He's happy to talk to us, but depending on how long production drags on, he might not be back for another two weeks. I suggested a phone call, but apparently he doesn't feel comfortable discussing this over the phone."

"Let's not bet on it, then," I said. "Filming schedules are unpredictable."

I turned on the stove and put the Atomic on. Before the coffee was ready, my phone rang.

Alexa Levine.

"Petra's here right now," I said, as soon as I answered the phone. "What's up?"

"Turn on the news," she said. Her voice was grim. "Call me back when you see it."

I didn't have a television, but I went to the Channel Nine website on my laptop. As soon as I reached their homepage, I saw what Alexa was referring to.

"Shit," I said.

"What is it?" Petra joined me at the counter.

"Caleb is demonstrating outside Windhall."

I clicked on the live stream of the video. It was a shot of Windhall taken from outside the front gate. A crowd of supporters stood outside Theo's house, waving signs. NO MORE MURDERS! read one, while another read, TRIM THE THORNS! ARREST THEO! Most of the supporters looked like your standard, upper-middle-class former hippies, replete with knit hats and frumpish eyeglasses. I spotted a few kids in their early twenties who might have been Samira's friends from art school.

A blond reporter interviewed Caleb.

"Mr. Walsh, you're circulating a petition to have Windhall torn down. Tell us a little more about why you're doing this."

Caleb stared into the camera. "I don't have any evidence that Theodore Langley killed my daughter," he said. "In fact, I doubt that he did it. It doesn't mean he's not responsible, though. Ever since Theo killed Eleanor and got away with it, his house has stood as a monument to violence against women and a lack of accountability!"

The crowd of protesters cheered.

"I have to go over there," I said.

"I'll go with you," Petra offered.

"No can do, sorry," I said. "I'm going to try to get inside. I doubt that Theo would be willing to talk to you. I already have plans to meet up with him on Saturday, but he might be okay meeting me today instead."

She looked disappointed. "Let me know how it goes," she said. "I'll try to find out more about this Ben Lewis character."

I didn't think that there would be any traffic at ten on a Friday morning, but driving through Hollywood was always a gamble. B movies and sequels were usually given daytime premieres to launch the weekend, and judging by the amount of trashy pedestrians and cars stacked bumper to bumper, Robert Downey Jr. was probably making an appearance on the Walk of Fame.

"Fucking Hollywood!" I yelled and hit my horn in frustration. It bleated a meek response. In the car next to mine, a gaggle of teenagers burst into laughter and started making faces at me. It took everything in my power not to leap out of the car and strangle one of them.

I spent an hour getting down Sunset, and another twenty minutes before I was able to disentangle myself from the blur of traffic and pedestrians angling for a glimpse of a mediocre celebrity conga line. Normally I would have taken side streets to avoid the entire catastrophe, but the side streets had been blocked off. By the time I reached Theo's neighborhood, it was quiet, but I wasn't close enough to Windhall to detect whether the protesters were still there. I parked in my usual spot, then walked toward the house.

There were four cars illegally parked on Theo's street when I arrived, across Theo's gate. Two of the cars were unoccupied, and two men with cameras loitered in front of the gate, peering in and chatting to each other. A few protesters lingered, but it looked like the majority of them had disappeared since the televised broadcast with Caleb.

As I moved closer, I saw that Caleb was still standing in front of Windhall's main gate, speaking to two other protesters. The camera crews were gone, but one of the women he was speaking with looked like she might have been a journalist.

"Hey, buddy!"

I looked up to see who was talking. It was one of the two men leaning against the gate, a scrappy looking Hispanic guy with a ponytail and beige cargo shorts. His hat was on backward, and a $15,000 camera hung around his neck.

"Hey, what are you doing here?" he asked.

I didn't respond but walked right up to the gate.

"I think this guy's deaf, Jones," the man said loudly to his friend, a fat redhead with freckles.

I ignored him. I didn't know what I was hoping to do. Theo wasn't expecting to see me until the next day for our tour, and I had no idea how to get into the house on my own.

"Hey." This was from Cargo Shorts, who was walking toward me. His voice had adopted a more friendly tone. "Who do you work for?"

"A division of the *Los Angeles Times*," I said. "It's called the None of Your Fucking Business desk."

"Hey, that's clever," he said. "Lemme guess, you got yourself an iPhone and think you'll make yourself some cash with a photo of our guy here. What kind of range you think you'll get? Fifty feet? You can stick around and try, but you won't get shit with your little phone."

The redhead giggled.

"Tell you what," Cargo Shorts said. "Just go on home, pal. You're wasting your time here."

I walked over to where Caleb stood. He didn't notice me, but continued speaking to the woman with the notepad, who was writing things down.

"Mr. Walsh," I said. "My name is Max Hailey. With the *Lens*."

He looked up at me and nodded his recognition, then turned back to the woman with the notepad.

"I don't want to interrupt," I said. "But you've promised us an exclusive story."

"Look, Mr. Hastings," he said, turning back toward me. "I'm not interested in selling my story to the highest bidder. I just want people to be aware of what's going on."

I tried to hide my irritation. The story belonged to Brian, not me, but for some reason he wasn't there. I didn't know whether Alexa had called him to let him know what was going on, but either way, I was the one who was going to be responsible for protecting the interests of the *Lens*.

"Miss," I said, turning to the woman with the notepad. "Don't you have any journalistic integrity?"

She looked at me like I was insane. "I run a blog."

I swore to myself and then walked back toward the gate. If a rash of articles appeared in publications over the next few days, it was going to lessen the impact of my article about Theo, and by the time I pulled all my facts together, nobody would care anymore. I pulled out my cell phone and dialed Leland's number. He picked up on the second ring.

"Mr. Hailey," he said. "What can I do for you today?"

"You can tell your client to come down to his gate and let me in," I said.

"I thought you were meeting him tomorrow."

"Change of plans," I said. "I'm sure you know about the protesters who have been outside Windhall all day."

I could almost hear him rolling his eyes. "Yes, Mr. Hailey. I'm aware."

"Caleb Walsh has been gaining public sympathy," I said. "It's only a matter of time before Theo gets ousted from Windhall, thanks to some legal bracket you probably didn't consider when you had Windhall declared historic. If you want me to get Theo's story out there, I need to run my interview. Tell Theo to let me in."

"All right, Mr. Hailey, I'll give him a call. Give me a minute, would you?"

Five minutes passed, and there was still no sign of Theo. I was about to pull out my phone again when a police car pulled up the street and rolled to a stop in front of Theo's gate.

Two police officers stepped out, and one of them approached the small cluster of remaining protesters.

"You've had your fun," the first cop said. "It's time to clear out, now. We've had complaints from the neighbors."

"I'm well within my right to protest here," Caleb replied. "Sweet Briar Lane is public property."

"We've had noise complaints," the cop replied. "Two or three calls in the last half hour."

I leaned against the fence and watched them spar. Cops still made me vaguely uneasy, and even though I knew that I was well within my legal rights to be there, I didn't want to attract their attention.

I took out my phone and called Brian, but it went straight to voice mail.

"Sir, you can't stand here."

I looked up to see one of the cops approaching me. I gave him an innocent look, then raised my hands. "I have an appointment to be here," I said. "I'm waiting for someone inside that house."

The cop followed the direction of my finger, toward Windhall.

"Sure you are. Let's move along."

"I'm not a protester, and you won't find anyone who's had noise complaints from me. I can call my editor right now and have him verify that I'm meant to be here."

Before I could call him again, I heard the sound of rattling chains. I turned to see that Fritz was struggling with the padlocked chain holding the gates of Windhall together, and when he saw everyone outside the gate, he scowled.

"Sir, do you live here?" the second cop said, approaching the fence.

"No questions, thank you."

"Is this man disturbing you?" the cop indicated me.

Fritz considered me. "Yes," he said. "I find him very disturbing. He's an invited guest, however, so please let him through."

The cops weren't sure how to respond. I walked toward the gate and helped Fritz with the chains, and he finally managed to unlock them.

"Thanks for coming down," I said to Fritz.

He acknowledged the comment with a slight incline of his head.

"Has anyone come up to the house today?"

"No one."

"I imagine it's been a circus with photographers outside your gate," I said, hoping to get some kind of response from him, but Fritz said nothing until we reached the front door.

"I told Mr. Bates that Mr. Langley was not at home," he said. "He said that you may wait inside until he returns."

I frowned. "When will he be back?"

"Within an hour, Mr. Hailey."

He climbed the steps up to the front door. Before he could open the door, however, it swung inward, and he stepped back in surprise.

"Oh! Hello, Fritz—you startled me." A woman stepped out onto the front steps and noticed me. "Hello, who's this?"

My first thought was that the woman was one of the most beautiful people I had ever seen. She could have been anywhere from forty to sixty, with light brown skin and almond eyes. A light spray of freckles across her nose set off her complexion in a pleasant way. Her hair was pinned loosely atop her head with an antique silver pin, and she removed a pair of gardening gloves as she looked between Fritz and me.

"I'm Max," I said.

"Max *Hailey*," Fritz added.

"Ahh, you're the famous Hailey," the woman said, giving me a wry smile. "My name is Flannery. Are you meeting with Theo today?"

"Yes," I said. "There's been a change of plans."

"Theo's in town, but he'll be back soon."

I followed her down a path that led through the garden.

I couldn't figure out Flannery's relationship to Theo, but I didn't know how to make the question seem innocuous. "How long have you worked for Theo?" I tried.

She stopped walking, then turned around and gave me a bemused look. "I don't work for Theo, Max," she said. "We're old friends."

"How did you meet?"

"Through a mutual acquaintance."

The path led around the back of the garden, and we emerged into the little citrus orchard. Flannery brushed some leaves from the table and pulled out a chair.

"Have a seat, Max," she said. "I'll go inside and get some lemonade."

She went inside, and I wandered around the garden. It must have been so peaceful, back in the '40s and '50s, when Theo had invited guests back for a bit of respite from their world of red carpets and flashbulbs. When I was sure that Flannery was gone, I walked around to get a look at the back of the house.

The windows of the upstairs guest bedroom glinted in the sunlight, but they revealed nothing. I took out the drawing that I had made in the Beverly Hills library and quickly consulted it. According to the blueprints that I had seen, the hidden maid's room would have been on the northern side of the house. I glanced up again and saw that there was a dusty little window on the second story, one that I hadn't noticed before.

There was no way to know what was inside that room unless I was able to see it for myself, but in order to see it, I had to pretend that it didn't hold too much interest for me. I decided to occupy my time waiting for Theo by exploring the garden.

I meandered down the brick path that wove through the ancient orange trees, and to my surprise, saw that the path led out of the garden and branched off toward a wall at the edge of Theo's property. There was a tall hedge, overgrown and wild, which bordered the garden. I followed the brick path and saw that buried in the mess of the hedge and weeds was a little wooden door.

The door only came up to my shoulder, and the wood was badly cracked. The hinges and door were done in an old wrought-iron style, and I ran my hands over the metal, wondering how old the door was. The handle was locked, of course, but I was still disappointed.

"Max?" Flannery's voice came floating out through the orange trees. I stood up and walked back down the path to go find her.

"There you are," she said, when I reappeared. "Where did you go?"

"I was looking around the garden," I said. "Did you know that this path ends in a little door?"

Flannery poured the lemonade and didn't respond. She handed me a glass, then looked up to meet my eyes.

"Fritz has told me all about you," she said, taking a sip. "He's not very happy about your visits."

"There's only been one, so far," I said. "And what exactly has he told you? I haven't interacted with him at all."

"Fritz has ways of getting information," she said, then gave me a rueful smile. "He and Theo are thick as thieves. What exactly are you hoping to find? Why are you here?"

"I've been fascinated by Theo and Eleanor since I was a kid," I said.

"You've bought into the fairy tale."

"It's not exactly a fairy tale," I countered. "Director finds his muse and kills her in the rose garden."

"That was never substantiated, Max."

"You haven't answered my question."

"Which question?"

"Do you know about that door?"

She smiled. "It's been out of use for years," she said. "I'm told that movie stars used to sneak between each other's yards when they didn't want to interact with the outside world. It got a lot of use during parties."

"Who lived next door?"

"Some old silent star," she said. "If you know anything about film, you know that a lot of silent stars were ruined when film started using sound technology."

"So I've heard. Who lives there now?"

"Who knows? Old Hollywood got chopped up and sold a long time ago. It's probably some reality star, maybe a young pop idol."

"I like the idea of a secret door."

"They were all over Beverly Hills, at one point," she said. "I've heard that Harold Lloyd had a secret road under Greenacres, but of course, it's probably a rumor. Old Hollywood was very much a private world—if the old stars didn't want to interact with the commoners, they didn't have to." She said *commoners* with disdain.

"Somehow they always managed to get inside, though!"

I turned to see Theo at the edge of the garden. He pointed at Flannery.

"Flannery's the perfect example," he said. "I can't remember for the life of me how she got onto my property. Windhall used to be so well guarded."

"Theo's an old recluse who can't stand change," Flannery replied. "He's been out of touch with reality for years, unwilling to move beyond the glory of the old days."

"Tell me, Hailey," Theo said, walking toward the table. "Have you ever heard of a Mexican named Flannery? Her parents must have had some sense of humor. Or maybe they wanted everyone to think that she was Irish. Let me tell you, kid, you ain't fooling anyone."

"Oh, Theo, I'm not sure that Fritz passed the message along, but please stop leaving your denture glue in my passenger seat. I had a foster kid in there yesterday, and he was mortified on my behalf. I had to explain that I'm too young for dentures."

Theo burst into laughter, then squeezed Flannery's shoulder. "Look at Hailey, he's so embarrassed," he said. "We like to exchange barbs, Hailey; it's how we stay young."

Flannery stood up. "I'm going into town," she said. "Please behave yourself while I'm gone."

Theo kissed her cheek, then took a seat across from me. "So, Bob Woodward," he said. "Back for another round."

"You're very funny," I said. "You don't think I'll write the story?"

He shrugged. "You aiming for a Pulitzer, or something more on par with a *TMZ* spread?"

"You should fix up your garden," I said, looking around.

"It has its charms," he replied. "You know how some people start to resemble their dogs after a while? My garden is a reflection of my inner self."

"Come on."

"It's a waste of water," he said. "With Los Angeles dying of thirst, I don't need to add to the problem. Besides, what makes you think I'm going to stick around?"

"Where would you go?"

"I've always wanted to visit Tokyo. Greece? Ethiopia?"

"While we're on the topic of travel, where have you been this whole time?"

Theo looked at me, then burst out laughing and slapped his knee. "You don't really think it's going to be that easy, do you?"

"Not at all. I had to ask, though."

"I travel a lot. But I don't like the cold."

"I have a feeling you're going to stick around. Flannery said she's been working on the garden."

"Bless her."

"How did you two meet?"

Theo opened his mouth, then gave me a sly grin. "A mutual friend," he said. "No questions about Flannery. Leave her out of our dealings."

I pointed toward the hedge. "Who was your neighbor? When you still lived here, I mean."

"Tom Mix," Theo replied.

"Good relationship?"

Theo shrugged. "Sometimes his guests would get drunk and sneak into my yard," he said. "I found a few strangers in my pool. They were always completely top-heavy with booze."

"How'd they get over here?"

"There's an old door in the hedge."

"You still have the keys?"

"Long gone." Theo picked up Flannery's glass and finished off the remainder of the lemonade. "Let's go on that tour. I've got other things to do today."

———————————

A long time before meeting Theo, I had come to know his house by heart. With the help of the feature in *Architectural Digest*, as well as numerous society columns, photographs in *Time* and opaque shots in the *Los Angeles Times*, I had memorized everything there was to know about Windhall. I knew about the gold and avocado tiles in the master bathroom, the stained glass roses frozen in the windows above the eastern garden, the stone faces peering down from the shade of the tennis court.

For years, I had imagined the parties that began at twilight and lasted well into the dawn, the champagne glasses shattered against the garden walls. I could almost hear the music of parties long since faded drifting down the drive, but as I grew older, I knew that no matter how well I knew the house, it was something that would never belong to me. And in all that time, in all those daydreams, I had never imagined that there was an entire section of the house that had been hidden.

Theo took me into the house through the back entrance, which led out onto the garden.

"Any place in particular you want to see?"

"All of it."

He waved a hand. "In case there's not enough time," he said. "Upstairs? Downstairs?"

"Upstairs." I didn't want to lead him directly to the upstairs guest bedroom, but I could get him close without leading him to suspect anything. If Eleanor had been murdered there, there must be faint spatters of blood, perhaps a single strand of hair. It would be enough.

He hummed as he led me up the stairs.

"Golly, it's been a while since I've done this," he said, pausing in front of the stained glass window on the landing. "I'm forgetting a few details, Hailey. The rear foyer used to be the medical dispensary, back when this place was a clinic. The kitchen was actually where they stored bodies, while they waited for the coroner to come. They used the counters as cooling boards. We could never get those stains out—bodies leak a *lot*, you know. My kitchen staff prepared the Bolognese alongside bloodstains."

"Really?" My ears perked up.

"Of course not. How morbid do you think I am?"

He made a sweeping gesture with his hand, and I walked down the hallway ahead of him. The late-afternoon sunlight cast spokes of light against the wall, a slanting mosaic that made the house seem even more unearthly. My brain glazed over as Theo opened various doors and showed me the conservatory, the laundry and linen closet, the upstairs study and secondary library, and the twin bedrooms. He skipped over the upstairs guest bedroom as though the room weren't there at all.

"Well? Anything else before I show you downstairs?"

"Nothing." My heart rate accelerated. I didn't want to risk calling him out on skipping the room, because it was already our second visit, and he had promised me two visits. If he chose to kick me out of the house then, there was nothing I could do about it. I had a different idea, though, for how I could see the room.

"Let's go downstairs, then," Theo said.

I followed him downstairs and patiently listened as he recited the function of each room. I could tell that he was boring himself, doing exactly as he had agreed upon in the contract, not a flowery sentence more.

"Any other questions, Mr. Hailey?"

"You've done what I asked, so thank you."

"Not at all," he said, inclining his head. "I wish you the best of luck with your article."

We started walking toward the front door. I stopped, then patted my pockets.

"I had a notepad," I said. "I was taking notes."

"Perhaps you left it in the garden."

"No, I had it after that," I said. "I think I left it somewhere in the house. Give me a moment, I'll be right back."

Before he could protest, I took off down the hallway. I had reached the stairs before I heard him calling my name. Taking the stairs two at a time, I reached the top in less than thirty seconds. I ran down the hallway, toward the guest bedroom where I had encountered Ben and Leland that first night.

My hands shook as I turned the doorknob. I wasn't sure exactly what I was hoping to find—a bloodstain on the far wall, or all the furniture moved out, maybe—but there was nothing. The room was just as innocuous as the others that Theo had shown me.

It was a mirror image of the first guest room. As with all the rooms in the house, it had a dark wooden floor and white walls, with quaint decorations at intervals around the room. The windows offered a view of the rose garden and the mountains beyond. I closed my eyes and tried to remember where Ben and Leland had been standing when I had encountered them that night, and then reopened them.

The armoire. It was standing on the north end of the room, and it hadn't been there before. I crossed the room in three paces and grasped the edges of the armoire, which was a heavy, antique thing. Grunting, I managed to shift it slightly to the left, just enough to see the peeling wallpaper and scrape marks, the edge of a doorframe behind the wood.

Someone cleared his throat behind me. Slowly, I turned around. Theo stood in the doorway, a tight smile on his lips.

"Did you find your notebook?" he asked.

I stepped away from the armoire. "No."

"You thought rearranging the furniture might be of some assistance, I see."

I wondered what he could possibly do. If it were a match of physical strength, there was no question that I would win. Still, a brief thought crossed my mind, and that was that Theo had the entire house rigged with trapdoors, sliding chutes down to buried cellars, nails and screws and horrible things that would slice and cut and kill. He had been the best set designer, a kind of magician, and for the first time since coming to Windhall, I wondered if I was safe.

But there was one more thing I needed to know before I could leave Windhall.

"What happened to Cate Chapelle?" I asked.

There was a flicker of recognition in his face—it was quick enough that if I hadn't been expecting a reaction, I might have missed it.

"Who?"

"I know about Cate," I said. "I know how she died."

His face closed, then, and I realized that I had pushed my hand.

"All right, Hailey," Theo said softly. "You've had the tour. I think it's time to leave."

Resigned, I crossed the room and slipped past him, out through the door. He remained five paces behind me as we walked down the hallway, back down the stairs, and then out through the grand foyer.

I paused at the front door.

"I always wanted to meet you, you know," I said. "All those stories, all the different nursery rhymes and urban legends. I knew that there had to be something more."

"And? What are your conclusions?"

"I think people were right," I said. "It was always just a big illusion."

He was silent as I crossed the threshold and made my way down the steps. The garden had a curious, buzzing stillness about it as I walked around the roundabout, past the fountain, and made my way down the steep drive.

In fairy tales, there are warnings not to look back one final time. If you make it out of the forest, don't test your luck, don't glance over your shoulder and look to see what's waiting behind you.

I couldn't resist.

As I reached the hedge where the drive started to turn, and Windhall would disappear from sight, I looked back to the house one last time. The door was still open, and Theo was still standing inside, watching me. The interior of the house was steeped in darkness, but Theo was standing in the sunlight, lit up like a phantom.

He raised a hand and held it in greeting, or in warning, it was too far away for me to tell. He stayed there for a moment and then vanished into the house once more, closing the door behind him. I stood there for a minute longer, feeling the gardens creep up around me, the dying hedges and the withered agapanthus, and I knew that it was over. The house had managed to survive for so long by being invisible, by becoming forgotten. People had forgotten about Theo, and the world had moved on.

I had come in with my tools and poked around, and in doing so, I had exposed a fragile, dying thing to light. And now it was too late. The garden felt like it was closing all around me as I made my way down toward the front gate, feeling for the first time that I might not be able to get out again.

FOURTEEN

I waited until I was halfway back to my car before I took out my phone. Two missed calls from Petra, one missed call from Alexa. I selected Alexa's number and waited as the phone rang.

"Hey, Max," came Alexa's voice. "You get in touch with Theo?"

"I'm leaving his house now," I said.

"So he hasn't fled the city?"

"I don't think he's going to," I said.

"Any leads?"

"There's a missing room," I said. "There's definitely a missing room. I think that's why Theo came back to Los Angeles, Alexa. I think he was worried that the police were going to find a way to get into his house, to try to connect him with these two new dead girls. If there's something he's trying to hide, he probably wants to destroy it before the police find it."

"It's a good thought."

I had to tell her about the journals, but I didn't know how to admit that I had them without telling her about Heather. If I mentioned Heather, I would have to admit that I had signed a contract with Heather, and I had promised not to publish anything until I had given Heather forty-eight hours alone with the information.

"There's something else I need to tell you," I said. "I have Theo's missing journals."

It took her a moment to put the pieces together. "You're not talking about the famous journals that got the case thrown out, are you?"

"Those are the ones."

"Hailey, where did you find those?" She sounded shocked.

I had to be careful where I stepped. "I'm going to pull the source card," I said. "For the moment, I need to protect her."

"'Her?'"

"They're legitimate." I ran a hand through my hair. "Look, there's something else. I've been reading about a producer Theo worked with. Apparently there were rumors about him making passes at some of the actresses, and one of Eleanor's friends confided in Theo. I think it was Reuben Engel, the man who was set to produce *Last Train to Avalon*, but I can't prove it."

Alexa leaned back in her chair. "This is coming from Theo," she said. "You're reading a firsthand account from Theo's perspective. Try to keep that in mind."

"Of course."

I hung up without telling her what my real plan was. I was going to have to find a way to break into Windhall, because unless I knew what was inside the room, there was no chance that I would be able to figure out what happened to Eleanor.

———————————

The next morning, I went over to Petra's apartment. Even though I had dropped her off a few days before, I hadn't gone inside her apartment complex. It was the standard '70s-style two-story block complex, complete with an over-chlorinated pool and brown and yellow shingles. Petra's apartment was on the second story.

She looked surprised when she opened the door, then stood aside for me to come in.

"Am I early? We did say eight o'clock, didn't we?"

"Yes, sorry," she said. "I'm easily distracted."

Petra's apartment was tidy and sparse, with a few newspaper clippings on the walls. An aquarium against a wall added a little color to the room. I peered inside and saw a somber-looking fish doing laps around the tank.

"Who's this?"

"Todd."

"Pleased to make your acquaintance, Todd," I said.

"You want some coffee, or something?" Petra hovered at the edge of the room.

"Sure."

"It's instant," she added.

"That's fine."

I did a quick inventory of the room while Petra busied herself in the kitchen. Her apartment was filled with mismatched, slightly apologetic furniture, the type you rescue curbside on garbage day or else pick up from a thrift store and carry home. All the pieces of furniture were small enough that they could be carried onto public transportation or lifted by one person into a small car.

I read through the spines of Petra's books, all of which looked like they'd been scooped up for a few bucks at Goodwill. I stopped when I saw the edge of a photograph peeking out from between two books and picked it up so I could look at it. Petra had her arm slung around an older woman with brown hair and a candy neck-lace, shorter than Petra by a few inches. I was still looking at the picture when Petra came into the room, holding two cups of coffee.

"Janet," she said. "Not a great story."

"Recent?"

"Bay to Breakers in San Francisco," she said. "We flew up for the race last year."

"People almost never print photos anymore," I said. "She must have been special."

"She was," Petra said, shrugging. "She is. Not talking to me, though."

"I've been thinking about the maid's room," I said, putting the photograph back. "I'm convinced that Eleanor died in there."

"How will you prove it?"

"I'm going to break into Windhall."

She gave me a cool look. "Don't you already have some kind of criminal record?"

"Why does everyone keep mentioning that?"

"I thought Theo was supposed to give you a tour of his house," Petra said. "What happened to that? Change his mind?"

I briefly detailed the events of the day before. Petra nodded, but she seemed distracted.

"I thought you'd be all over this. What's on your mind?"

She gave me a shy smile. "That movie set," she said. "The special city that was made for *Last Train to Avalon*."

"You mean . . . Avalon."

"It still exists," she said. "I found it."

It took a moment for her comment to register. "What do you mean, you found it?"

"Just that. The whole set is intact, it's all together. It was bought up by a private collector a few years ago."

I stood up so quickly that I splashed coffee all over my jeans. "Shit, sorry. Where did you get this information?"

"Well, I went down to the Los Angeles courthouse to look at the remaining documents from the trial," she said. "It turns out a lot of them have been stolen over the years, since it was such a popular case. After Theo was acquitted, the remaining pieces of Avalon were packed up into crates and sent to MGM."

"And?"

"They were stolen over the years," she said, frowning. "I went to talk to someone in the props department, and apparently there's a bit of a conspiracy theory surrounding the whole movie. God, you should have heard what this one guy told me about actresses who went off their contract. Supposedly the studio had ways of making people disappear."

I could only think about the movie set. "If the pieces of Avalon were stolen over the years, how did one guy end up with the whole set?"

"He had to track them down," she said. "I called a few antiques dealers, and I finally got in touch with the man himself. He lives in Eagle Rock. I called him. Wouldn't leave him alone, actually. When he found out that you've spoken to Theo, he opened right up. He told me that Theo was framed, and then he said he could prove it."

"So who did it?"

"He wouldn't tell me over the phone."

"You still have his number? Can I have it?"

"I'll give it to you, on one condition," she said. "When you meet him, I'm coming with you."

"That's fair."

"He said he can meet up with us tomorrow."

"Great work," I said, and I really meant it. I was on the verge of telling her about Theo's journals, but something told me to be a bit cautious. It wasn't because I didn't trust her, but nobody else knew about the contract that I had with Heather, and I didn't want Petra to be complicit with that information.

Shit, Heather, I realized. I was going to have to reveal the maid's room in Windhall to her, or else risk breaking my contract.

"You okay?" Petra asked, tilting her head to look at me.

"I just realized what we're up against. It's not going to be easy."

"Are you still serious about breaking into Windhall?"

I scratched my head. "This does change things," I said. "But Theo's definitely hiding something."

"What happens if you *do* manage to break in to Windhall? What are you looking for?"

"I'm going to go in there with a black light," I said. "Theo might have done a bit of cleaning up in the last few weeks, but there's bound to be something. I mean, even if someone framed him, there could still be blood spatter, evidence, something."

"How are you going to get in there?"

"I have my ways."

"Oh," Petra said, going over to her desk. "Before I forget. I looked into that doctor of yours—Benjamin Lewis. I found out a few things about him, not too much information, but it might be of some help."

She glanced down at her notes, and hesitated. "I had a crazy thought," she said. "What if Dr. Lewis is actually Theo's son? Not just his doctor, but an actual blood relation?"

I almost laughed. The idea was so absurd that it might actually be *possible*.

"Holy shit, Petra," I said. "What did you find?"

"Ben was born in 1950," she said. "A little over a year after Eleanor was killed."

"And who's the mother?"

"Someone named Rebecca Lewis," she said.

"Was she on the guest list for the party?"

"No, she wasn't, and I can't find anything about her. I couldn't find a death certificate, so there's a chance she's still alive."

My hands were tingling. "That's a great lead," I said. "Maybe Rebecca Lewis was some unknown actress. She had an affair with

Theo, got pregnant, and had Ben. If Eleanor and Theo were an item, it would give Theo motive to kill her."

"That's a stretch."

"Maybe she attacked him. Maybe she was really angry. Things escalated, before Theo knew what was happening, she died. Petra," I said, sitting up. "Maybe Rebecca was the second person in the garden. Maybe she helped Theo kill Eleanor."

"Jesus."

We both stared at each other for a long moment.

"Right," I said. "Well, keep looking for this Rebecca Lewis. We don't have much time, so you should make her your main priority."

"Hailey," she said. "I don't want you to treat me like your secretary. We're partners in this."

"I've never treated you like a secretary."

"You might not realize it," she said, "but you have. *Look into this, research that.* You didn't let me come to interview Theo, and you never tell me what you're working on. That needs to change. We're in this together."

"You're right, Petra, I'm sorry," I said. I hesitated a moment, and then said, "I found something else."

"Oh?"

"There was another actress," I said. "Someone else who died. She was also close to Theo, and I'm wondering if he was responsible for her death, as well."

She looked intrigued. "Who was she?"

"She was never very famous," I said. "Her name was Cate Chapelle. It's another angle I'm going to look into, though."

"Thanks for sharing that, Hailey," she said. "I'm glad you feel like you can trust me."

I was on my way home when Heather called.

"What do you have for me, Max?"

"I'm still working on a few leads," I said. "I'll let you know when I have more."

"It's been a week," she said. "Your contract means you're obligated to share findings with me."

"It hasn't actually been a week," I started to point out. "It's only Saturday."

She made an impatient noise. "Time is irrelevant. Do you have anything, or not?"

I racked my brain for something I could share with Heather. "You've heard that Caleb Walsh wants Theo to leave Windhall?"

"Of course, everyone knows."

"If he leaves," I said, "we might lose track of him. He could disappear forever."

"I've taken care of it."

"What do you mean?"

"I have someone watching the house," she said. "If Theo leaves, he won't get very far."

"Great," I said. "Look, my phone battery's getting low, and I don't have a charger handy. Do you mind if I call you later?"

She sighed irritably. "I haven't heard anything from you yet, Max. I hope you know I expect to get something for my money. And that new roof I put in."

"I didn't ask you to do that." I was annoyed that she had brought it up.

"I wanted you to know that I was serious about my offer." The way she said it made it sound more like a threat than a gift. "I need to see something by the end of the weekend, or we're going to have to reassess the situation."

"Thanks, Heather." I hung up before she could respond.

I was pulling into my driveway when I received another text. I thought it might be from Heather, so I parked and got out of my car, then went into my house and put the Atomic on the stove. Once I had made myself a cup of coffee, I took out the phone and looked to see who had texted me.

Dr. Ben Lewis. I knew that much without opening it, because ever since I had saved Leland's contacts to my phone, Ben's number had been under his own name.

I sat at my kitchen counter, running my thumb across the screen, wondering if I should open it. The only reason that Ben would be contacting me now was if something had gone wrong. Perhaps Petra hadn't been discreet enough when she was looking into him, and he knew that we had found out about his mother. There was a chance he knew that I had found the room, and perhaps he was planning to take actions against me.

I opened the text.

Hello, Max, it read. *You have no reason to trust me, but consider this a friendly warning. Heather isn't telling you everything. If you want to know the truth, ask her what happened to Lola DeWitt.*

I was on the verge of replying, when I remembered that my contract with Heather was supposed to be secret. I had no idea how Ben could have found out that I had been speaking to her, but I wasn't about to find out. I went to my computer and searched for "Lola DeWitt."

There were a few results for modern women with the same name, or names that were similar. After scrolling through the results, I finally hit one that I thought might be the woman Ben had referenced. The page led me to Lola DeWitt's IMDb profile. There were a few results under her filmography, and I was surprised to see that she had acted in a few movies with Eleanor. The last movie that she had been in was one that Theo directed, called *The Man Who Death Forgot.* According to the profile, Lola had died in 1951, three years after Eleanor's death.

After her IMDb page, Lola's trail disappeared. I scrolled through the Google search results for almost thirty minutes before admitting that I wasn't going to find anything. I thought about texting Ben back to ask him but thought that it was probably not a good idea to acknowledge his text until I figured out what his angle was.

Instead, I decided to continue reading Theo's remaining journals. If he had directed Lola in a movie, there was a chance that he would say something about her, especially if Ben thought that she was someone important. Even if there was nothing about Lola, I might find some gem of information about the mysterious Rebecca Lewis.

I finished my coffee, then went out to the greenhouse and sat down with the next journal.

―――――――

August 3, 1947: Los Angeles, California—

"You'll be lucky if they don't try to kill you," John Cromwell warned me, when we told him about my new script. "People who piss off the studios have a way of disappearing."

It turns out that all my obnoxious scribbles between rehearsals have served me well: we're making a movie about Hollywood. I've got plenty of documentation from the last few years, all these journals and conversations jotted on the backs of paper bags. We're going to use all of it when we piece together our script.

Nora and I went round to see John and tell him about the project, which I've been working on the last few weeks.

"Just tell me if you're interested in the project. I've already decided to make it."

"I stayed up all night, reading your script," he said. "It's probably the best thing you've ever written. But I noticed a few problems."

"Tell me."

John shook his head and gave me a weary smile. "You lack finesse," he said. "You're young. Subversion is all about subtlety."

"I'm the highest grossing director at MGM, John."

"For the moment, you are," he agreed. "But don't you remember all those silent stars who couldn't get a script after films went to sound? All those empty houses up in the hills? They thought they were gods."

"The studios think they're too big to fail," I said. "They're run by the most egotistical men in Los Angeles. If we don't say something against them, we're only part of the problem."

"You can't mock them outright, you know," he said. "Unless you're going to fund the entire picture yourself."

"It can't be too subversive, or the audience won't understand."

John looked at me. "Even if you do decide to go forth with this script, labeling all your collaborators ingrates and cannibals, you can't expect to find a cast willing to put their own careers on the line. The Sophia character is a strong role, but what actress would be willing to put her life on the line?"

"I will," Nora said. "I'll play the part."

"You haven't read the script yet."

Nora shrugged. "I'm not afraid to be controversial."

John steepled his fingers and thought for a moment. "I'll help you make this movie," he said. "We'll make Los Angeles a mythic city. We'll call it Avalon. Travelers and tourists have to arrive by train, and there's nothing but desert for a hundred miles in each direction."

"The desert," I echoed. "Okay."

"Your main character," he said. "This Jody. He comes out west, hoping to make it big, but instead of movies, let's say he works at a newspaper . . ."

"And Sophia?" Nora spoke up again.

"A talented journalist," John said. "This Manfred character is a bit on the nose, don't you think? A character everyone will completely hate, but perhaps too obvious."

"It's apt."

John gave me a curious look. "Was he inspired by someone?"

"Can't say."

John looked at the script, flipping through the pages. "Don't make the parallels between the newspaper and MGM too obvious," he said.

"I'll try to be more subtle."

"The studios won't make a film that mocks them," he said. "And listen to me carefully, Theo. This is about more than your career. If you piss off the wrong people, they'll come for your head."

As the script progresses, so does Windhall. My manager thinks that having a big house will be good for business. He's already hired a small army of gardeners and cleaning people. He's a bit too excited about the whole thing, but he's hired a good staff. He's found a Swiss German woman to run my household, and from our initial meeting, she seems to have a good head on her shoulders. She's a pretty little thing, but she seems very serious. I don't know if we'll have much of a relationship outside our professional capacities, but I don't mind that. I need someone I can trust more than anything else.

September 27, 1947—

Nora keeps refusing to film. Poor darling. She's taken it harder than most, and it's lasted longer than I thought it would. Trying to figure out how we might skip out on our contracts. Also wondering who might be willing to show <u>Last Train</u> once we're done filming.

October 12, 1947—

That monkey came to visit me on set today. He hasn't been around much, but then again, most producers are only good for the wet bar at the premiere. He won't be the first one who's surprised when they announce that a movie has finished filming, because he hasn't shown up on set once.

Today, he wasn't happy.

"I read the script," he said.

"Congratulations, we've only been filming it for six weeks."

His next move caught me off guard. He threw a fist so quickly that I didn't have time to defend myself, and I staggered backward. But the fist didn't connect. He laughed while I recovered, and I realized that he must have been drinking.

"Just fooling around," he said. "Can't you take a joke? You're known for your sense of <u>humor</u>, Theo."

I tried to keep my voice even. "Is there something you wanted? I'm in the middle of editing."

"This script," he said. He took a folded packet of papers from his pocket and waved it at me. "Is this meant to be funny?"

He was still laughing, but his eyes were red. He was clenching a fist, and I knew that in his state of inebriation, he was liable to be dangerous.

"Talk it over with Mayer," I said. "I don't have time for this."

I started to walk away, but the monkey reached out and grabbed my shoulder. He's known as studio muscle, but his grip surprised me.

"You think you can get away with this? You think I wouldn't find out what you'd done?" He moved closer, and I smelled whiskey. His proximity was alarming, but I managed to hold my ground. "You're finished, Langley."

I laughed the comment off. "Thanks for the warning."

"You should watch out for your friends," he called after me, as I walked away. "Have you seen Eleanor lately? You think she can take care of herself?"

October 15, 1947—

Well, it's over now. John came to see me this morning with bad news. I was surprised to see him show up at my house, since we had plans to see each other later in the day, when we were going to start looking at the reels together.

"They're cutting us off."

The full weight of the statement didn't sink in right away.

"What do you mean?"

"The studio wants us to stop working on Last Train to Avalon," he said. "No more editing, no more stills. It's finished."

"But we've already finished filming," I argued. "All the scenes are done, and we'll be done editing in a few weeks. We're doing fine on budget."

"It's done, Theo."

I ran a hand through my hair. "Look, is it because of the script? Did Mayer read it? I don't understand."

He shook his head, holding up a hand to stop me. "The funding's gone. It's over. These things happen all the time, you know. Accept it. We gave it our best shot."

"I'll pay for it myself," I said quickly, and John gave me a long, cold stare.

"Even if you could pay for every single person on that set, you're forgetting the One Rule," he said. "Thou Shalt Not Piss on the Studio's Feet. We tried, and we failed. The studios are everything in this town. Everything. They own the film-editing labs. We finished filming, but your story will sit undeveloped on some shelf, rotting away in the darkness, with no eyes to see it, because the studios own all the movie theaters, too. They own the audiences, whether the audiences know it or not. They own all the equipment you've been using these past few weeks, and, hell, Theo, they own all the roads and buildings we've been using as locations. As long as they're paying you a salary, they own you, too."

I must have looked shocked, because John patted my shoulder.

"Better you should hear it from a friend," he said. "You'll move on from this."

"Is there anything they _don't_ own?"

"The desert," he said thoughtfully. "No one owns the desert. I suppose that's why I wanted to set your story out there, come to think of it. Cheer up, old boy. You'll get over this."

October 21, 1947—

I've never seen her like this. She came over last night when I was asleep, and I found I had to talk her down.

"I'm going to tell everyone," she said.

"They'll kill you if you do."

"I don't care anymore, Theo! I don't care about anything. We're living in a cage, can't you see that?"

FIFTEEN

I woke up early Sunday morning. My head was still buzzing from reading Theo's last journal, and I was lost in my thoughts as I made myself coffee. I had completely forgotten my plans for the day, which is why I didn't hear the doorbell at first.

When I opened the door, I found Petra. "You forgot, didn't you?" she accused.

"Forgot what?"

She brushed past me. "Are you making coffee?"

"Yeah, do you want some?"

"We're supposed to head to Eagle Rock in twenty minutes," she said. "He's a busy man."

It took me a moment to put the pieces together. "Avalon!" I said. "You're right, I did forget!"

She gave me a strange look. "You seem distracted."

"I'm fine, it's nothing."

"Are you ready to leave?"

"Yeah, just give me a minute to get dressed," I said.

———

I was a bit of a snob, so I didn't admit it easily, but I secretly loved Eagle Rock. It had the faded '70s vibe that Los Angeles was famous for, and on a clear, hot day, when the pavement was singing and there wasn't a hint of haze in the air, you could almost forget you were living in a modern city. There had been a bit of modernization in the last few years, but since Glendale and the eastern suburbs were still considered pretty uncool, the surrounding neighborhoods like Eagle Rock had been largely ignored. You could still find quaint little diners and bizarre antiques shops on every corner.

We took Petra's car, and I looked out the window. Even though I loved East Los Angeles, I hadn't been past Silver Lake in the last year, except to visit Heather in Pasadena.

"What's his name again?" I asked.

"J. Montgomery Dean," she said. "He goes by Monty."

"Is he a porn star?"

"He collects antiques."

"What sort of shop is it?"

"You'll see."

We turned down Colorado, onto Eagle Rock Boulevard. "You know you can get some of the best food in Los Angeles in this neighborhood?" I said.

"Yes, I did know that."

Petra turned down a little side street lined with a mix of Craftsman and cinder-block houses. We parked, and I followed her down the street. We stopped outside a quaint old sandstone building that looked like it might have been built in the early 1900s.

"It was an old bank," Petra said. "I thought you might appreciate that."

I looked up at the sign. 'The Last American Trading Post,' I read.

"Come on," Petra said, then opened the door and stepped into the cool interior of the shop.

It took my eyes a moment to adjust to the gloom, but once they did, I took an appreciative look around. The shop had a square, blocky feeling, appropriate for an old bank. The ceilings were lofty, and light filtered down from high windows. Against one wall of the shop were the old teller windows, with wooden slats and iron rungs. CASHIER was painted in blocky gold letters above the till.

Two wide, wooden tables were set up in the middle of the room, and they were stacked with an array of old books. Stock shelves along the sides of the shop boasted every manner of antique oddity, from apothecary jars and glass lamps to fur-trapping materials. I paused before an unidentified skull, preserved beneath a glass dome.

"It's an Eskimo skull," came a voice.

I turned around and found myself face-to-face with a young woman with black and purple hair. It was pinned in a lazy knot on top of her head, and the bottom half of her head was shaved. She wore old-fashioned horn-rimmed glasses, but her face was decorated with several intricate piercings. She blinked at me.

"I think you're supposed to say Inuit," I said. "Eskimo is racist. Besides, it looks more like a mountain lion."

"Bravo, gold star," she said. "You looking for something in particular?"

"We're here to see Monty," Petra spoke up. "Are you Raquel?"

"That's me," the young woman said. "Monty know you're coming?"

"Yes," Petra said, then hesitated. "It's about old Los Angeles."

Raquel narrowed her eyes. "Are you Petra?"

"Yes, and this is Max Hailey."

"Avalon." Raquel nodded. She took out her cell phone and dialed, then spoke into the phone. "Yeah, they're here. Should I send them down?"

She hung up the phone and then turned around. "Right," she said. "I'm going to need to take your cell phones. You can leave them up here with me; it's perfectly safe. Literally. We have a nineteenth-century safe behind the till."

I rolled my eyes, but Petra laughed.

"Do you have cameras or any other kind of recording device?" Raquel asked.

"Nothing."

"I'm going to need your bags and jackets," she said. "Put your stuff down here, and then I'll give you a little pat down."

"I don't think I'm comfortable with that," I said.

Raquel gave me a hard look. "You're about to step into one of the most elusive properties in Los Angeles," she said. "Most people don't even know this place still exists. You don't have to submit to any of our security measures, but if you don't, I'll direct you toward the exit."

I gave her a wary look, then stripped off my light jacket and handed her my satchel. "I have some confidential writing in there," I said. "Don't go through it."

"Relax, Hemingway, I've got plenty of reading material to pass the time." She stepped toward me and gave me a quick, efficient pat. Petra stepped forward and got the same treatment, then Raquel put our bags behind the counter. She glanced around the store and looked up at a clock on the wall, then crossed the room and flipped the OPEN sign around to CLOSED.

"Right," she said. "Let's go meet Monty."

We followed her through a door at the back of the bank. I expected a dank basement but was surprised to see that the stairs led down into a well-lit room filled with cool, clean air. There were no windows, since we were underground, but the room had the efficient, pleasing light of a museum. Various pieces of art hung on the wall at even intervals, each one bearing a plaque beneath it. As with the room above, this underground chamber held plenty of bizarre artifacts, from Victorian vascula to musical instruments that looked about two hundred years old.

A man emerged from a corridor at the back of the room. My first thought was that we had come to Eagle Rock and somehow wound up standing in Stanley Tucci's basement, that's how close the resemblance was. Unlike Stanley Tucci, however, this man was missing all of his top teeth.

"Welcome. My name is Monty," he said, adjusting his glasses. I was surprised that the missing teeth had very little effect on his speech. "I see you've been deemed worthy by my lovely assistant."

"Yeah, whatever," Raquel said. "I'd better go back upstairs. Oh, Tim called. He found that skeleton you were looking for."

"Are they willing to sell?"

"It's stuck in Yuma," she said. "Looks like a ton of paperwork to get it across the border. You'll have to call him yourself."

"Is he wearing the original clothing?"

"Yeah." Raquel saluted us, then retreated back upstairs.

"So, where were we?" Monty said, rubbing his hands together. "Petra, lovely to see you again."

"Wait, you've already met?" I glanced between them.

"We've done business together," Monty said, raising an eyebrow. "When was that—last year?"

"July."

"I'm confused," I said.

"I used to run a catering company," Petra said. "The event was at Heritage Square, and it was small, so I got the chance to talk to a lot of people."

"Wow," I said, impressed. "I had no idea you ran a company."

She gave me a wry smile. "Everyone has a backstory, don't they? You shouldn't make assumptions about unpaid interns."

I knew that I was being rude, but I was starting to feel anxious. "You said you'd show Avalon to us?"

Petra and Monty exchanged a look.

"Come with me," Monty said. "I don't have a lot of time."

We followed him through the basement, toward a reinforced steel door. Monty entered a code into a number pad and the door gave a satisfied beep, then released with a compressed *whoosh*. Monty gave us one final look, then stepped inside.

The room was steeped in darkness, but Monty flipped on the light. I gasped.

The second room was about the size of the first, which was slightly smaller than my living room. The walls were bare and freshly painted, and there was a wide walkway around each of the walls. In the center of the room, lit up by six stage lights hung from the ceiling, was Avalon.

"Before you approach, let me tell you the rules," Monty said. "First of all, no touching. That should go without saying. I know that Raquel took your phones, but if you have some hidden cameras, you're not allowed to use them. You can get close enough to see the buildings, but you must be extremely careful." He frowned. "You haven't been drinking alcohol today, have you?"

"No," I said, my eyes focused on the miniature city.

"Just covering my bases," Monty said. "I don't want you to stumble or vomit on it. Go ahead, you can take a closer look."

Petra and I walked toward the miniature set, both of us taking extreme caution not to make sudden movements. The buildings came up to our waists, and The streets were wide, so that a movie camera could move between them. Some of the streets had camera trolley tracks laid into them.

"Is this the original setup?" I asked, turning to look at Monty.

"Yes, it is," he said. "I bought up all the pieces separately, but I took painstaking efforts to make it just the way that Theo intended."

It was surreal to stand and look at a set that I had imagined for most of my life. It was more beautiful than I had imagined it to be, and I could see that an extraordinary amount of work had gone into it. Each detail was perfectly crafted, from the tiny Victorian mansions on Bunker Hill to the glittering palace in the center of the set. The light glinted off the domed windows and the curving spires, and despite Monty's warning, I longed to touch it.

"I don't suppose you've read a copy of the script," I said, distractedly. "Do you know what the movie was about?"

"Great script," Monty said. "Pity it didn't get released. The story's about a young female journalist who finds out her boss has been extorting his employees for sex. Lots of metaphors and allusions, of course—this was during the Hays Code–era of filmmaking. Really limited filmmakers. It'd be like telling Michelangelo to paint the Sistine Chapel with crayons."

I frowned. "That's right," I said. "They changed the story halfway through."

Monty looked impressed. "How did you know that?"

"I've done some research on my own. You don't happen to have a copy of the script, do you?"

Monty shook his head. "I read a copy, but that was years ago. I've been trying to find it again for years. There are rumors that Theo finished filming *Last Train* before leaving Los Angeles. If that film exists, it would prove everything."

"'Everything'?"

Monty adjusted his glasses once more. I could tell he was enjoying talking about Theo.

"I have a theory," he said slowly, "that the film was full of studio secrets. All lightly veiled, of course, but enough to send a number of people to jail. Racketeering, bribes, conspiracy to murder."

"Come on."

"Why do you think they killed Eleanor?"

Petra and I exchanged a glance. "Theo killed Eleanor, you mean," I said.

"He's innocent. I guarantee it. The studio framed him because they were scared of his film. He'd threatened to release the thing under his own name—you know it was his money, don't you?"

"No."

"Sure, sure. He lost everything after the trial." Monty shrugged. "That film would have proven his innocence, but nobody could ever find it."

A thought came to me. "Have you ever heard of someone named Lola DeWitt?"

He shook his head. "Name doesn't mean anything to me. Who is she?"

"An actress who worked with Theo and Eleanor," I said. "Someone told me that I should look into her, but I can't find anything about her online, other than an IMDb page."

Petra cut in. "Who do you think was responsible for Eleanor's death, if not Theo?"

"I can tell you that with complete certainty, too," he said. "Reuben Engel. You do any kind of research on him, and you'll see that he was the studio bitch. Trust me."

———————

Once we were back in the car, I burst into a cold sweat.

"Are you okay?" Petra asked. "You look awful."

"Do you think he's telling the truth?" I asked. "Do you think that Theo was framed?"

"Monty's a bit extreme," Petra said. "People who withdraw from society tend to be paranoid."

"He made some good points."

"Look, prominent unsolved murders always lead to a bunch of conspiracy theories. I'm sure Monty isn't the first one to suggest that the studio was behind Eleanor's death. Don't you think there would be more evidence, if that were the truth?"

"Evidence," I said, then frowned. "Oh, holy fuck. The film clip."

"Film clip?"

"That clip! We have to get the clip back from Heather!"

"Hailey, what are you talking about?"

I sank my head in my hands. "Oh God, it's too late."

"You have to tell me what you're talking about."

I badly wanted to tell Petra about the contract with Heather, but I also knew that it was impossible. Nobody could know about the contract. I chewed on my fingernails for a moment, thinking. There was something else that I could tell her about, even if I couldn't tell her about the magician's film, now in Heather's possession, or the contract that I had signed.

"There's something else I should tell you," I said. "You probably won't believe me."

"Try me."

"Theo's missing journals," I said. "You've heard of them, right?"

"Everyone's heard of them. They're like F. Scott Fitzgerald's pen collection, or Babe Ruth's baseball bat. They're legend."

"I have them."

"Bullshit."

"Petra," I said. "I'm not lying to you. I found a source close to Theo, and I can't tell you who this person is, but I made a deal. I have the journals."

Petra was quiet for a long moment. "Why didn't you tell me?"

"I didn't know whether I could trust you," I admitted. "I also thought that I could do all the research by myself, but you've just shown me that I was wrong about that."

"We talked about this the other day," she said. "How can you expect me to do my job if you don't share crucial information with me?"

"That's a little unfair," I said. "I've never worked on a story with anyone else, and I do tell you a lot."

"Can I see them?" she asked finally.

"Yes," I said. "They're back at my place. Let's go there now, and you can catch up on what I've already read. I'm almost at the end."

SIXTEEN

We drove back toward my house without hitting any traffic. My kitchen ceiling was almost fixed, and the men Heather had sent were gone. Their tools were strewn around the kitchen, but it was possible that they had just gone out for more supplies without leaving a note.

The hole in the ceiling was gone from sight, but the roof wasn't completely finished yet. They had replaced the inside of the kitchen roof with sheet metal and covered it up with paint and spackling paste, but the damage to the attic roof was a lot more extensive. The lead builder had communicated this all to me very slowly, because he could see that my technical knowledge was virtually nonexistent.

"Should take a few more days," he'd said. "We'll be done by the end of next week. Heather paid us to work quickly."

Before heading out to the greenhouse with Petra, I put the Atomic on the stove, and when it was ready, I carried the coffee cups out with me. Petra and I sat side by side at the large table, and I gave her the stack of journals that I had already finished. I saved the last one for myself.

"Have you read all of these?" she asked, carefully turning the pages.

"Yeah, his handwriting's a bit tough," I said. "Just ask me if you get stuck."

"What are you up to?"

I opened the last journal. "Nineteen forty-eight," I said. "A few months before Eleanor was killed."

"You think the journal will tell you what happened?"

"Only one way to find out, I guess," I said.

––––––––––––

February 19, 1948: Los Angeles, California—

The premiere for Susan and Her Small-Town Band *is in four days. I should be excited, but I have so much on my mind that I can't really wrap my head around it.*

Nora's still a mess, even after all this time. We've been trying to find ways to move past it, but she's having trouble.

Today I met with the production designer for Susan.

"This movie is going to be huge," he said. "The early reception we've gotten from critics tell us that this could be as big as Gone with the Wind, *if not bigger."*

He crossed himself.

"Now, let's talk logistics. The whole day is going to be about the premiere, from the morning to night. We've rounded up all the extras on contract, and they'll be walking around Hollywood during the day, dressed up as small-town citizens. We're going to have barbershop quartets and musicians making music. We want everyone to get in the mood, see? In the evening, we'll have Tommy Dorsey and his orchestra stationed just outside the theater, playing something good and peppy."

"Sounds great."

"That's not all," he said. "Here's the kicker. We've hired six low-flying airplanes to circle Hollywood Boulevard as the premiere is starting, and they'll drop magnolias from the sky. Just like in the scene from the movie! The crowds will love it; it will make them feel like they're part of the film."

"Isn't that some kind of traffic hazard?"

He gave me a strange look. "We're not normal people, Theo. Normal rules don't apply to us."

"Right, right."

I was leaving the studio when I ran into John Cromwell. We haven't spoken since the studio canceled _Last Train to Avalon_, but he didn't look surprised to see me, and he took my hand.

"Congratulations," he said. "I've heard _Susan_ is poised for success."

"Thanks," I said. "Will you be at the premiere tonight?"

"Oh, no," he said. "I like to avoid premieres."

"Why's that?"

"We encourage madness, don't we? I don't need to see it firsthand."

"Eleanor said something similar once."

"Ah, Eleanor," he said faintly, and his expression was difficult to read. "How is she?"

I had an automatic pleasantry at the ready, but then I remembered that if there was one person in Hollywood with whom I could be honest, it was John.

"I'm worried about her," I said. "I haven't seen her in a few weeks, and I'm not sure she'll show up for the premiere."

"It happens to everyone sooner or later."

"What's that?"

"The pressure," he said. "The difference between the character they play on-screen and their true personality. If you don't break free from the studios altogether, you'll end up going crazy."

"She's got three more movies on her contract."

"And I hear that this one's going to be one of the. biggest," he agreed. "They won't let her go easily after that. Eleanor makes a ton of money for MGM."

I toyed around with an idea and decided to come out with it. "I'm going ahead with the story," I said. "I've decided to finish editing Last Train to Avalon. There are a few scenes missing, but it's almost ready. If the studio doesn't want to finance it, it's fine; I have enough money to pay for the rest myself."

"I see."

"Oh, tell me what you really think."

"I'll be surprised if they don't tear Eleanor apart," he said.

"Who?"

"The studios, the audience," he said. "Does it matter? Surely you know the old adage about people offering their gods up for a feast. We must destroy our gods eventually; every religion dictates it."

"I disagree."

"Stick around," he said. "They can't exist without us, and for that, they come to resent us. It's the infinite struggle, Theo, the reason why nobody can ever be truly happy when their gods are within reach. They must destroy us, possess us, or watch us die."

March 14, 1948—

The word's out. Apparently half of Hollywood knows that we're planning to release Last Train to Avalon, but if my head's on the chopping block, I haven't realized it yet.

Raoul had a party last night. I didn't want to go, and I tried to stay home, but Errol and Jules came over and strong-armed me into it.

"You don't get to hide, boyo," Errol said. "You're still a part of the group."

We watched all the houses south of Mulholland disappear beneath the bends of the road as we drove over.

"Why do we do this?" I asked, turning to Jules.

"Do what?"

"Pretend."

"Because we can't face ourselves, obviously," he said. "Don't worry, Errol brought plenty of alcohol."

We took shots in the garden, and by the time we walked up to the front door, I was nicely sauced. I asked, "Where's Nora?"

There was a long silence. I was drunk, but not too drunk to see that Errol and Jules exchanged a glance.

"Have another drink, pal," Errol said, turning to pass me his flask.

"He's had enough."

"Have one more."

"You haven't answered my question," I said.

"She's not here," Jules said. "Nobody's seen her in a month."

"We need to go to her house," I said, suddenly adamant. "She could be in trouble, and nobody would even know."

"We're staying at the party," Errol said. "You might have written a nice little treatise against Hollywood, but you can't just disappear, or your whole career will be sunk. Look sharp, sit smart, and we'll be there in a minute."

The night was a masquerade, filled with bowing gods and starlets in silk dresses. They drifted past me in a haze of smoke and expensive perfume. I couldn't focus on any of them; they all faded together into a blur.

I had been to Raoul Walsh's house once before, but I had never been to one of his parties. There were so many people that I was hoping to lose myself in the crowd, but that quickly proved to be impossible. Before we had even reached the front door, I felt sharp fingers digging into my elbow. I turned around to find Hedda Hopper.

"Theo," she drawled. "How lovely to see you. One would almost think you were set to vanish completely."

"Hedda," I said, trying to gather my wits about me. I hoped she couldn't tell that I was absolutely blitzed.

"It doesn't bode well for a leading lady's career when she can't participate in the social scene," she went on. She had an unpleasant little smirk on her face. "Where is Eleanor this evening?"

"Tell me, Hedda," I said, reaching out to touch her face. "Did you use words like 'bode' before you adopted that fake British accent, or is that a new thing?"

Errol burst into laughter and then quickly tried to disguise it with a coughing fit. Jules looked scandalized, and then he too looked like he might collapse into laughter.

"You haven't achieved the kind of grandeur necessary to become an alcoholic wreck," Hedda sneered. "And neither have your friends."

"Good God, who needs grandeur?"

"You're pathetic, Theodore Langley."

"Coming from you, that almost seems like a compliment."

She jabbed a finger in my chest. "I own the eyes, the ears, and the lips in this town," she said. "You forget yourself."

"People keep claiming the anatomy of Los Angeles," I said, and sighed. "But if we're dividing up parts, I think a colon is more in line with what your career represents."

"Bastard!"

"Write whatever you want about me, Hedda," I said. "I'm a director, nobody gives a damn about me."

"What about your friends?" She gave an evil look to Errol and Jules, who were choking on their fists in a desperate bid to disguise their laughter.

"They seem to like me."

"No, you idiot," she said. "You seem to forget that they have careers, too. You're going to regret tonight, Theo, mark my words."

And with that, she swished off.

It might have been a good idea to leave after that, but we couldn't resist going inside for one more drink. We found Eddie Mannix, who was standing at the bar and giving a wary eye to the people dancing inside. He caught sight of me before I had a chance to do so.

"Get your ass over here, Langley," he said.

"Aye, aye, sir." I gave him a mocking salute.

He turned to Jules. "You should tell your friend not to be such a smart-ass," he said. "He's liable to get himself in trouble."

"I'll relay the message, sir."

Eddie turned back to me. "Where's Eleanor?"

"Ladies' room?"

"What did I just say about being a wiseass?"

"I don't know where she is."

"You're her director," he said. "It's your job to make sure that your leading lady shows up nice and pretty for parties, whether or not she's under the weather."

"I can't control her."

He laughed. "Good to know," he said. "Maybe it's time I take responsibility for that."

"I didn't mean that."

"I'd like you to pass along a message," he said. "You think you can remember, or will you be too drunk?"

"I'm not drunk."

"There's a thousand girls out there who look just like her," he said. "She's not that special. If she can't look sharp and show up on time, we'll get rid of her."

"What is that supposed to mean?"

"Let's go, Theo," Jules said quickly.

Eddie gave me one final look, then returned his attention to the rest of the guests in the room.

Once we were back in the car, I turned to Jules.

"Why'd we leave?"

"That was a threat, Theo," he said quickly, putting his car in gear and then easing down the street. "I don't know how serious he was, but I don't think we should test it."

———

I flipped through the rest of the pages, but they were blank. Along the inside spine of the journal were the riffled edges of torn pages. The rest of the journal was missing.

"Shit," I said.

Petra looked up from her stack. "What's up?"

"That's the last one," I said. "It just . . . stops. It looks like the rest might be missing."

"Shoot. What do you think happened to it?"

"Maybe Theo got rid of it," I said. "Or maybe someone else did, after the journals were stolen." I stopped a moment short of mentioning Heather's name. "This isn't the first piece of the journal that's missing. I mean, I've seen other pages that were torn out. But it seems like the next piece might have been something crucial."

Petra looked stumped, and I ran a hand through my hair.

"I'm starting to get a bad feeling about this," I said. "What if I was wrong about Theo?"

"About his innocence?"

"We have a very narrow portrait of what actually happened in the months leading up to Eleanor's death," I said. "We know what the news has told us. We know the urban legends, all the myths that have been mutated over the years. What if Theo's not guilty?"

"Slow down. What did you just read?"

There were voices outside the greenhouse. I turned to look through the window and saw the roofing men entering the house through the back door.

"I don't think we should talk about this here," I said. "Let's go see Alexa."

I gathered up my things and shoved them into my satchel. As I stepped out through the greenhouse, I heard another voice.

"He must be here somewhere; he's not at work."

Heather.

"Isn't that his car in the driveway? He has to be here." It took me a moment to identify the other voice, and then I realized that it must have been Barney, her assistant.

I put a hand on Petra's shoulder to stop her, then considered my options.

"What's wrong?" Petra asked.

"*Shhh!*" I motioned for her to be quiet.

"We haven't seen him today," said a male's voice, which I thought must have been one of the builders.

"Has anyone checked out back yet?"

"We have to go," I told Petra. "We'll cut through the neighbor's yard."

I led her around the back of the greenhouse. The fence in the back of my yard was weak and rotting, and it had started to slope down at the back. My neighbor and I had exchanged a few emails about banding together to fix it, but he was a travel photographer who was frequently out of town, and we hadn't gotten around to doing it yet.

Petra gave me a strange look as I climbed over the fence and then motioned for her to follow me.

"What are you doing?" she asked.

"Look, I'll explain later," I said. "Did you park on the street?"

"Yeah, a few blocks from here," she said.

"Thank God for that," I said. "Let's go to the office and give Alexa an update on what we've learned."

SEVENTEEN

Once we were out of Laurel Canyon and heading toward the office, I turned to Petra.

"Thanks," I said.

"Thanks for what?"

"I know I sound like I'm being paranoid," I said. "But I think she's spying on me."

"I don't know what's going on," she said. "Didn't you hire those men to fix your roof?"

"Look, forget I said anything," I said. "I'm probably just imagining things."

Petra was quiet as we drove up to the office and parked out front. We walked up the stairs together, and I tried to think of something to say.

"I'm really glad to have your help, you know," I said.

She didn't respond.

"It's a lot more work than I thought," I added.

Still no response.

"Hey, is everything all right?"

We reached our floor, and Petra stepped into the office. It was late Sunday afternoon, so the office wasn't completely full, but a few writers lingered by their computers.

I followed Petra down the hall, confused at her sudden mood. She knocked on Alexa's door without looking at me, and Alexa called, "Come in."

Petra stepped inside, and I followed her.

"Max, Petra," Alexa said. "Have a seat."

"I'm not staying," Petra said. "I'd like a different assignment. I wanted to tell you in person."

Alexa looked stunned. "Did something happen?"

"Petra, what's going on?" I asked. "I thought we made a break-through today."

Still not meeting my eye, Petra addressed Alexa. "I know that interns are treated pretty badly in Los Angeles," she said. "There are so many aspiring writers, actors, models that there simply isn't room enough for everyone. I thought that the *Lens* would be different, but I can see that I was wrong."

"Petra, please, have a seat," Alexa said. "Max, what's going on?"

"I have no idea! Petra, what are you doing?"

"Can you find me a different assignment?" Petra asked Alexa.

"I'll have to check with Melissa," Alexa said. "She's taken over the interns. Do you want something on the culture desk, or do you want something different?"

"It doesn't matter," Petra said.

"Can I ask why you'd like to leave, halfway through an assignment?"

Petra turned to look at me for the first time since we entered the office. "Hailey, you make me run around, doing errands for you, and you keep me in the dark most of the time. I'm done."

"Petra, please."

"Who was the woman in your yard?" she asked. "Why did you want to sneak out the back?"

I faltered. "It doesn't matter."

"See what I mean?" Petra turned back to Alexa. "He wants my help, but he won't tell me anything."

"She's not important!" I said. "She has nothing to do with the article."

Alexa frowned. "Have you two been sleeping together?"

"No!" Petra and I said as one. Petra gave a slight shudder.

Alexa focused on me and asked, "Max, what's going on?"

"This was supposed to be my article," I said. "I appreciate her help, but I can choose what information I share."

Petra threw her hands up in the air. "I'm going home," she said. "Alexa, please let me know if you find something that I can work on. Otherwise, I guess I'm done here."

She turned and walked out of the office. After a second's hesitation, I followed her.

"Petra, wait!"

She had reached the stairs. With a sigh, she turned to face me.

"Please don't do this," I said. "We're doing great work together."

"I know, Hailey," she said. "I know that was Heather Engel-Feeny in your yard. Why was she there, and why were you avoiding her?"

"She's . . . a friend."

"You're lying to me!"

"It's not relevant," I said, my tone pleading. "Why do you need to know?"

She opened the door.

"You remember what I said this morning, about catering a lot of fundraisers?" she said. "Heather was at the Heritage Square fundraiser last year. I've seen her all over town."

"What are you talking about?"

"Do you know what she's working on?"

"Some conservation projects." I shrugged. "What do you mean?"

"Have you ever heard of someone named Linus Warren?"

It took me a moment to remember who he was. The man from the *Vanity Fair* article, and the one I had seen at Heather's house.

"I've seen him once or twice," I said. "Why?"

"I'd take a closer look," she said. "I'm not sure you realize who you're dealing with." She stepped into the stairs, closing the door behind her.

The articles that came up with a Google search for Heather were mostly pages that I had already seen. There were charity events and philanthropic fundraisers, cases of Heather visiting underprivileged families in South Central and bestowing her famous smile upon them. And then I started digging into Linus Warren, and I realized what Petra had meant when she said that I should be careful.

The article was about a suspicious double homicide that had happened on some land that Linus Warren was trying to develop. According to the article, Linus had been in the process of buying an apartment complex when an old couple had put their feet down and refused to sell the apartment they had lived in for thirty years. A month later, they turned up dead.

The police and medical examiner determined that the deaths were the result of a botched home invasion, but the local community wasn't satisfied. Six months after their bodies were found, Linus bought their apartment and went ahead with his plans to raze the entire complex. The murderer was never apprehended, and if Linus was questioned, the articles weren't very conclusive.

And then I found the article about Highland Park.

Highland Park was a neighborhood in East Los Angeles, tucked underneath Pasadena. Madeleine and I used to spend a lot of time there, before we both started working full-time. We would drive over on a weekday afternoon, when we knew that things would be quiet, then walk through the sloping streets, pausing to stare up at the slender palms. Afterward, we'd stop at one of the little bodegas and buy mango sodas, tamarind candy, salted plums, and dried apricots. I loved that Highland Park felt like the last vestige of a civilization before the unruly desert, with all the old Victorian homes sighing against the shifting landscape.

Highland Park wasn't a wealthy neighborhood, and even though most of the houses were either done in a Victorian or a Craftsman style, most of them were unrestored, rambling homes. Most of the houses around North Figueroa were owned by Latinx families, and despite the slow gentrification that had started to creep in during the last few years, the area still had a charming, unrefined feeling. There had been a lot of talk of historic conservation in the last decade, and that's why I wasn't surprised to read in the article that Heather was interested in developing an entire street of Craftsman houses.

When I saw Linus Warren's name mentioned, I paused, and then I realized that the article's focus wasn't about the development. It was about two more unsolved deaths, both Latina protesters. *Magda Flores* and *Linda Echevaria*, I read, scanning the article for more detail. A third man had been injured, but his family requested that his name be kept out of the article, for fear of repercussions.

The details of the women's deaths were unclear, and it seemed that the publication wasn't willing to speculate on whether or not they had been murders or accidents. The deaths had occurred earlier that year.

I tried calling Madeleine, but her office told me that she was busy. Without any other leads, I decided to head over to Highland Park and visit the local city council.

The address that I found led me to a rambling Craftsman behind North Figueroa Street. I parked and went up to the door, which read SE HABLA ESPAÑOL, followed by COME IN. I opened the door and stepped inside.

The house had been converted into an office, and it was crammed with file cabinets, mismatched furniture, and stacks of boxes. Handmade posters and flyers were pinned to the walls, and the sound of someone typing on an old computer filled the air. A young man with a starched collar and gray slacks stood behind a table in the corner of the room. He spoke into a cell phone and jotted things down on a sheet of paper.

I waited until he was finished with his call, then approached.

"Welcome to the Highland Park Neighborhood Council," he said. He looked harried and distracted. "Can I help you?"

"Do you live around here?"

"Yes."

"What is this place?"

"Well, we're the neighborhood council," he repeated. "We do a lot of things for the community, including lobbying for Latinx council members."

"You do any kind of conservation work?"

"Not really," he said. "Are you looking to buy an old house?"

"I'm new to the area," I said.

"Buying or renting?"

"Visiting. Can you tell me a bit about the neighborhood?"

"I'm pretty busy," he said. "If you want, I can set you up with someone who can give you a tour. You can also visit the library. They have some resources there."

"Does the name Heather Engel-Feeny mean anything to you?"

All traces of politeness disappeared from the young man's face.

"I know who she is, yes," he said. "Please, excuse me. I have a mountain of work ahead of me."

"Who is she?"

"A gold-plated cunt," a new voice said. I turned around to see a Latina woman of ample proportions. She wore a tight-fitting USC sweatshirt over wool slacks, and her makeup was flawless.

The typing had stopped, and I realized that she must have been the one working at the computer in the other room. "Anything else you want to know?"

"What do you have against her?"

"Excuse me, who are you?" This was from the young man. "Do you work with Heather?"

"I need to know what her involvement in Highland Park is," I said.

"We don't want to talk to you."

I sighed. "I'm a journalist," I said. "I know who Heather is, we've met face-to-face, but I have no allegiance to her. If you have something you want to say, you're safe."

"She's a terrible person," the young man said. The color rose in his face. "She ruins lives."

"Manny can be extreme when he's emotional," the woman said, walking over to pat him on the shoulder. "Heather is trying to buy up tracts in Highland Park, but the offers haven't been approved yet."

"They'll get approved," Manny said bitterly. "She's got the whole council in her pocket."

"Is this about her conservation project?"

The woman started laughing. "Boy, you're so far off-base that you don't even realize it," she said. "Conservation has nothing to do with it."

"She's evicting families," Manny said. "She's bought up leases and lapsed mortgages. It's a slow process, but she's evicting one Latinx family after another."

"People can't afford to pay rent anymore," the woman added. "In a few years, this whole neighborhood will be white and upper middle class."

"I thought she was trying to preserve old homes," I said lamely. Both of them stared at me.

"You're the perfect consumer," the woman said. "You believe exactly what they tell you to believe. Heather's counting on people like you, people who don't know how to think for themselves."

"I almost hate to ask," I said. "But have you heard of someone named Linus Warren?"

They both stared at me.

"He's a white dude, probably a bit shorter than me," I said.

"What are you doing here?"

"I'm working on a story."

"If you're a journalist, you should know all about Linus Warren," the woman said. "Unless, of course, you've been living under a rock."

"Enlighten me."

"You ever hear of someone named Cesar Gavaria?" the woman said.

"Sure. Political activist who bombed a building downtown."

"Uh-uh," she said, shaking her head. "He was a peaceful protester. Linus and his cronies set up those bombs. Three men got killed, but that was all pinned on Cesar. What about Magda Flores? Linda Echevaria?"

I felt a slight chill. "They died a few months ago," I said. "I just read about them."

"Same thing happened with them. Unlike you white people, Latinos believe in a sense of culture and community. We believe in self-sacrifice and longevity. Our communities are more like coral reefs, thriving and building upon themselves. Linus and Heather want to tear these communities to the ground and replace them with shiny, single-family homes."

My phone rang. Aware that I was being rude, I slipped it out of my pocket and glanced at the screen, hoping it might be Petra. *Unknown caller.*

"Sorry," I muttered, hitting ignore and slipping my phone back in my pocket. "What were you saying about Heather?"

"Who do you work for?"

"I'm a writer with the *Los Angeles Lens*," I said. I pulled out my press pass and handed it to Manny. "I'm working on a different story, but this might be worth writing about."

"I've heard of the *Lens*," the woman said. "You just got purchased by Time, didn't you? As part of a big media package?"

"Yes," I said, perplexed. "How did you know that?"

"You're not going to write about this," she said. "It'll never get past your editor. Who do you think Time Inc. is owned by?"

"Let me guess, Heather?"

"This isn't a Hollywood movie, genius. No neat ends like that. But you're not far off base—your news conglomerate is run by the same wealthy taxpayers who will vote to allow Heather to buy up all these homes. She's got dozens of influential investors, and she thinks nothing of killing off a few protesters to advance her cause."

My phone rang again. I took it out and saw that the same blocked number was calling again.

"I have to take this," I said. "I'll just be a minute."

I picked up the phone and stepped outside. "Max Hailey," I said.

"Max, this is Isabel Perkins," came the reply. "I work for Marcus Loew."

It took a moment for the name to register. "Marcus Loew."

Isabel sounded irritated. "You called to speak to him about Theodore Langley," she said. "His father was Bernard Loew. Does any of this sound familiar?"

"Marcus, of course! Is he still out of town?"

"No, he's back," she replied. "He's filming over in Griffith Park today. His schedule is a little bit tight, but he said that he could probably slot you in this afternoon."

"He wants to meet today?"

"Otherwise it'll have to be next month."

"No, no, today's fine," I said. "Look, I probably won't get over there for another hour, but I'm definitely coming. Where should I find him?"

"Do you know where the abandoned zoo is in Griffith Park?"

I dug into the recesses of my memory. "I think so," I said. "I've been there before."

"Drive past the train tracks, you can't miss it," she said. "I'll let him know to expect you this afternoon."

———

My head was spinning as I drove toward Griffith Park. I was having trouble keeping track of all the new information I had learned about Heather and Linus, but I knew that I was in over my head. It was clear that Heather's father had been responsible for Eleanor's death, to one degree or another, but I wasn't sure how that fit in with all the recent deaths that had happened near Windhall. I hadn't figured out who Connie was, either, and I had no idea how she fit in with the whole crooked picture.

I wondered how I could get out of my contract with Heather without incurring her wrath, or if there was a chance I could simply give her false information. A part of me knew that would be impossible; according to the contract I had signed with her, I wouldn't be able to run any kind of article unless I had shown her the information first.

Griffith Park was always busy on weekends, and even though it was cold and blustery, this Sunday was no exception. I drove past the Southern Railroad and the merry-go-round, and then saw that security barriers had been set up to block the road. I pulled into the parking lot and got out, then walked toward the barriers.

A man in a black baseball cap saw me coming and held up his hand. "Can't come this way," he said. "Private event."

"I was invited."

"You have a pass?"

"Call Isabel, she'll tell you."

He narrowed his eyes at me, then spoke into a walkie-talkie. "You got a read on Isabel? Yeah, send her to the front."

He put the walkie-talkie back in his belt, then stood with his legs spread and his hands clasped.

"You enjoy your job?" I asked, but he ignored me. I knew that I was being an asshole, but I was starting to feel paranoid about what I had learned about Linus and Heather, and pleasant small talk seemed beyond me at the moment.

A few minutes passed, and then a woman came walking down the footpath toward us. She had short dark hair, and I guessed that she had Chinese heritage. When she saw me, she nodded.

"Max Hailey?" she said.

"Are you Isabel?"

"It's fine, Scott," she told the security guard. "He's with me."

I followed Isabel down the path.

"Marcus is excited to meet you," she said, as we walked. "Theo has always been a bit of an obsession with him."

"What are you guys filming?"

She gave me a tight smile. "I can't say," she said. "Confidentiality, and all that."

"Of course. I don't know very much about the film industry, but is it normal for composers to visit a film set during production?"

"I can't say whether it's normal, per se, but Marcus feels that he can't get a good feel for his subject matter unless he's involved in every aspect of the movie."

The old zoo came into sight. I had visited it on a handful of occasions, sometimes with Madeleine, and sometimes by myself, but it had been a few years. The cages were rusty and disused, and piles of leaves collected in the corners of the enclosures. The bear and lion enclosures were made to look like caves, with big, blocky rocks, but the spaces were small and dingy. Every time I had visited, the zoo had been completely empty, but now it was crawling with film crew and actors. I narrowed my eyes.

"Is that Bérénice Bejo?"

"Wait here, please," Isabel told me. "I'll be right back with Marcus."

I watched her as she disappeared down the path. She went over to a pair of men and addressed them. One of the men towered a foot above her, and he looked like he was in his sixties. He bent his head to listen to her and adjusted his little glasses, then nodded and looked toward me.

A moment later, the pair of them approached me.

"Marcus, this is Max Hailey," Isabel said. "I'll leave you to it."

"You're the kid who's hunting Langley," Marcus said.

"That's me," I said. "And you write music for movies about dead people."

He laughed. "Come on, let's go for a walk."

I found myself liking Marcus. He was taller than everyone on set, looming over all. His hair floated above his head in a wispy fringe, and his round glasses made him look like a cross between Bacchus and an old-fashioned British accountant.

Marcus led the way toward one of the old enclosures, and we sat down on a little precipice.

"I've been listening to your music," I admitted. "It's really haunting."

Marcus closed his eyes and nodded. "So, Theo," he said. "How did you get an interview with him?"

"We came to an understanding," I said, deciding to skirt around the topic of the photograph. "I know his lawyer."

"You know, my dad never liked Theo," Marcus said. "He was always convinced that Theo had something up his sleeve. He wasn't surprised when Eleanor was killed, and he wasn't surprised when Theo got away with it."

"What do you think of Theo?"

"He was a brilliant man," Marcus said. "Well, is, I guess, since he's still alive."

"What do you think really happened that night?"

"I've been in Hollywood long enough to know that I'll never know." Marcus winked. "Nearly everyone who was at that party is dead now. Theo probably won't be around much longer, either."

I was dying to tell Marcus about the journals.

"It seems like Theo really cared about Eleanor," I said, instead. "Why would he kill her?"

"Maybe he didn't."

"Do you think he was framed?"

"I've considered that possibility," he said. "It certainly wouldn't be the first time a star was punished at the height of success. When a star becomes too powerful, the studios get scared. In some ways, that's still true. You're old enough to have seen a young actress rise quickly and then get toppled by some minor scandal. We crave stories of success, but we don't want our stars to be *too* successful. We want them to remain within reach. You see?"

"Do you know about *Last Train to Avalon*?"

Marcus nodded. "I do."

"Do you think that's why Theo got framed for Eleanor's death? I've heard that people in charge were trying to teach him a lesson."

Marcus sighed. "The one thing that has remained constant in my entire tenure in Hollywood is that the studios will do whatever it takes to protect themselves. Anyone who threatens that will be jettisoned without thought."

I could tell that he was dodging the issue, and I couldn't exactly blame him. I was a journalist, and if he said anything too damning, he was running the risk that his name might end up next to an unsavory quote in the *Lens*.

"Marcus, this is off the record," I said. "I'm not going to write about anything you tell me. If you want me to put that in writing, I will."

"Very well," he said after a pause. "You asked me if I thought that studio has something to do with Eleanor's death. Yes, Max, I think they had a hand in it."

"Do you think Reuben Engel was the one who actually killed her?"

He thought for a long moment. "Engel had a reputation for being studio muscle, even if his official title was producer. I'm sure the studio knew what was going on, but he made them so much money, they looked the other way."

"What do you mean? What was going on?"

Marcus studied me for a moment. "Do you know anything about Engel?"

"A lot of women around the studio didn't like him."

"Yes, but do you know *why*?"

"Well," I said. "I know that he made advances toward a lot of actresses."

"He was a rapist." He spoke quietly, matter-of-fact. "I've heard different accounts about how many women he assaulted, but he had a habit of blackmailing women who didn't give him what he wanted. I heard that *Last Train* was about how Engel raped a woman and she had an abortion, then died from it."

I was dumbstruck. "You're not talking about Cate Chapelle, are you?"

"That sounds familiar."

"And Eleanor? Did he . . . I mean, was she one of his victims?"

"That, I can't say. I don't know. I would venture to suggest that he would probably be angrier with someone who stood up to him, though."

I sat there, numb and disbelieving. "Are you saying that Theo was prosecuted for a crime he didn't commit, and then spent his life in hiding as a result?"

"He wasn't ever convicted, remember?"

"But he disappeared," I said. "He had to leave a life that he worked so hard to build."

"'We destroyed our gods; we tore them limb from limb.'"

"What's that?"

"It's a line from *Last Train to Avalon*," Marcus said. "I got to read the script a few years ago. Shame it was never released, it's probably the most honest movie ever written about Hollywood."

"Where on earth did you get a copy of the script?"

Before Marcus could answer, Isabel materialized beside him.

"Sorry to interrupt," she said. "We're ready to start filming, and David needs a word."

"I have to go, Max." Marcus rose to his feet.

"Just one more question," I said. I had to frame it so that I didn't reveal my contract with Heather, because I didn't want it to get back to her.

"It seems like people know about this," I said. "They know about Engel. Why hasn't it gotten out yet?"

"His children, I would assume," he said. He looked thoughtful. "His daughter doesn't work in the industry, but she has a lot of political sway. Works in city planning, or something like that. I'm sure her own career would suffer if the truth got out, so she's probably invested in making sure that it never does."

EIGHTEEN

I stopped for Vietnamese takeout from Silver Lake on my way home. While I waited for my order, I pulled out my phone and called Petra. It went straight to voicemail, and since I wasn't sure exactly what to say, I hung up.

The roofers' cars were gone when I pulled into my driveway. I walked up my path, fumbling for my keys, then tucked the bag of food under my arm while I let myself in.

It wasn't until I was halfway across the living room before I realized that I wasn't alone in the house. A light was on in the kitchen, and I could hear the clink of ice cubes. For a moment I thought that Madeleine might have stopped by for a surprise visit, but as soon as I walked into the kitchen, I saw that I was wrong. My stomach sank.

"Hello, Max," Heather said. She raised her glass to me, and I saw that she had helped herself to the bottle of Macallan.

I sighed. "You hired men to fix my roof without consulting me, and now you've taken the liberty of letting yourself into my house. Did you make a copy of the spare key?"

"Don't be so ungrateful!" She laughed. "You're doing me a favor by looking into Theo, and I did a favor for you, by having the roof fixed."

"It's been a long day," I said.

She took a sip of Scotch. "Oh, I see, you'd like me to leave. You're trying to be polite. Is that it?"

"Please leave my house, Heather."

She stood and closed the distance between us. "I'm not leaving until you show me all the evidence you've collected," she said. "You've been to see Theo twice now. What have you learned? Can we open a new case against him?"

"I've gained some insight into a development project in Highland Park," I said.

It took her a moment to gather my meaning. "You've been to Highland Park? Good for you! What do you think?"

"Have you killed anyone yet, or will you leave that part to your friend Linus?"

"Don't be naive, Max," she snapped. "It's not as black-and-white as that."

"What happened to those protesters? All those girls who died?"

"You'll have to ask someone who knows."

"I'm tired. Please don't make me ask you to leave again."

"We signed a contract, and so far, you've given me nothing. I gave you Theo's journals, and now I'm calling to collect on our agreement."

"I haven't found anything." I spread my hands. "The house has been scrubbed, from top to bottom."

"What about that doctor? You must have learned something about him."

Rebecca Lewis. The name came back to me, then, but it meant nothing to me. I could offer it to Heather, but something held me back. I didn't want to give her that information until I had decoded it myself.

"Let's talk in the morning."

"That's not good enough."

"Do you know what my next story will be about? It's going to be about the unsolved death of two protesters in Highland Park. Do you even know their names?"

She put a hand to her chest and pretended to look hurt. "It's not for me, Max. I'm doing the Highland Park project for the sake of posterity."

"So the rumors are true? You're responsible for those deaths?"

"Of course not," she snapped. "The problem with your generation is that you're too idealistic. Let's go for a drive sometime, and I'll show you the state of those houses. The better houses are afflicted with mildew, rot, bad infrastructure. The worst of the lot are crammed with illegal immigrants, crack whores, and unwed mothers. They tear down the interior walls and fill them with cots, then rent them out for five hundred a week to pregnant illegal immigrants, so they can give birth in America as a way to stake their claim on a green card."

"I'm tired," I repeated. "I'd like you to leave."

"You're shortsighted," she said. "I bet you've lost sight of Eleanor, too. Has Theo convinced you of his innocence yet? He will, I can assure you of that! He's a charming bastard, that Theo, and he managed to convince a judge."

"I heard something about your father," I said slowly. "He had quite the reputation around Hollywood."

She narrowed her eyes.

"Did your father kill Eleanor, Heather?"

She tilted her head, then burst into laughter. "God, you're all alike," she said. "You meet someone high up on the food chain and he spins a pretty theory for you. Next thing you know, you've dropped all your convictions and sterling evidence, and you end up swallowing the tastiest pack of lies."

"So it's true."

"My father had nothing to do with Eleanor's death! I could sue you for even suggesting it. Now, I'd like to see what evidence you've collected. You're bound by contract, or did you forget?"

"It's at the office," I lied. "Well past business hours now, though. You'll have to wait until morning."

"You expect me to believe that? Let's see what's in that green-house of yours."

"You can't go in my office, Heather."

"It's made of glass, Hailey," she said, wagging a finger at me. "Not very secure, is it?"

"Threats are beneath you."

"It's not a threat," she said. "I'll give you one more chance to hand over your evidence."

I remained silent, and she shrugged.

"Suit yourself," she said. "You can expect to hear from my lawyer in the next few days. You haven't realized that you're nothing more than footnote in history. You can't stand in the way of prog-ress, Hailey. Theo's going to have to pay for what he did eventually."

I didn't sleep well that night, and when I reached for my phone the next morning, I saw that I had a list of text messages, asking me if I had seen the headlines. Before I could wrap my head around the onslaught of communication, I went to my computer and opened up a new browser.

MURDER SUSPECT APPREHENDED, read the top result. Beneath that, the caption went into more detail: *Pasadena woman responsible for two deaths, third attempted murder.*

It took a solid minute for the concept to gel in my mind, and I had to read another article to be completely sure that the news was true. The Beverly Hills murders had nothing to do with Heather, or Linus Warren; the woman responsible was a narcissistic performance artist. *A fucking performance artist.*

The woman hadn't been formally charged yet, just held for questioning. The articles were as definitive as they could be, given the fact that there had been no trial yet. There didn't seem much room for doubt, however, given that the woman had reportedly provided the police with details nobody but the murderer could have known.

"Shit."

I got my things ready and then headed out the door. I was going to have to talk to Alexa about everything that happened, even if it meant breaking my contract with Heather.

If I was going to break into the hidden maid's room at Windhall, I was going to have to do that soon, too. I decided to wait until Friday to make my move. According to the website for the Beverly Hills Council, the neighborhoods along Benedict Canyon had banded together to set up various cordoned-off areas with an assortment of festivities. According to the announcement, there would be bands, costume competitions, and treats galore for young children who wouldn't fare well with all the mayhem of teenagers on the real Halloween.

"Amen for helicopter parents," I muttered, then turned off my computer and gathered my things up to go to the *Lens* office.

I hadn't even made it to my desk before Alexa found me.

"We need to talk about your story," she said.

"They found the murderer," I said. "I know people will probably lose interest in Theo in a week, but I should be able to finish this story either today or tomorrow."

"Come to my office."

I followed her down the corridor and stepped into her office, prepared to tell her about what I had learned about Highland Park and Linus Warren. Even if I didn't have a great story to write about

Windhall, I might be able to scrape something together about the protesters.

When we stepped into Alexa's office, Brian was sitting in a chair. He grinned at me.

"I have some good news," I said, ignoring Brian. "But first, I'd like to come clean about something. Petra was upset because I didn't treat her with the respect that she deserves."

"Petra quit altogether. She won't be coming back."

"Shit." I said, and ran a hand through my hair. "It's probably my fault, to be honest. I really wasn't fair to her."

Alexa nodded and pressed her lips together. "Anything else you want to come clean about?"

Brian leaned forward in the chair. "Hailey, we know. There's no point in lying anymore."

Alexa held up a hand to silence him, then turned back and waited for me to answer.

I briefly wondered if Alexa knew that I was planning on breaking into Theo's house. "Did Petra say something to you?"

"We haven't spoken since she quit," she said. "Hailey, I have a lot of respect for your work ethic and I'm sure that there are reasons for why you do things the way that you do. It comes as no joy to me, therefore, to tell you that you're fired."

Her words didn't register with me right away.

"I have two more weeks to find information on Theo," I said. "I'm going over there on Friday."

She shook her head emphatically. "You're not," she said. "Leland called me yesterday to inform me that your contract was severed due to a breach in terms. He sent a courier with the nullified document."

My heart was pounding so hard that I thought Alexa must be able to hear it. I swallowed hard to try to dispel my panic, hoping that my fear wasn't evident. "That's still under dispute," I said.

Brian stood. "There's no room for dispute on this one," he said. "We've spoken about it. It's final."

"Leland told me why the contract was void," she went on. "Apparently you signed a different contract with Heather Engel-Feeny. Something to the effect that you would allow her to pick through your evidence as she wished?"

"That's not exactly true," I argued, but she held up a hand to silence me.

"You don't have to tell me, Max," she said. "I know exactly what your contract with Heather says, because her lawyer called, too. She's suing the magazine because you've failed to live up to your end of the contract."

I felt all the blood drain out of my face. Alexa shook her head and looked so disappointed that I tried to summon words sufficient to express an apology. None came.

"You haven't been coming to the office very much in the last few weeks," Alexa said. "It doesn't seem like you want to be here, anyway. Perhaps this news isn't as bad as it seems."

"Alexa, I have a new lead," I pleaded, but the words were pale and insignificant.

"Please clean out your desk," she said. "I don't want to see you in here after today."

———

I could feel everyone staring at me as I went back to my desk. There was a pregnant stillness in the office as I gathered up everything that I could carry, and I willed myself not to look up and make eye contact with anyone. Brian lingered behind me as I packed my things, and I willed myself not to turn around and punch him in the face. I finally glanced up and saw my colleagues gathered, in groups of two or three, whispering to each other as they waited for confirmation of the obvious truth.

"What?" I snapped, throwing a hand in the air. "Can I help you with something?"

The crowd moved back a little bit but didn't completely disperse. Brian gave me a sideways grin. I was filled with anger and humiliation as I stalked toward the door and left the office, then got in my car and headed home.

As soon as I got there, I went into the greenhouse. I had burned through every last opportunity and connection; there were almost no leads left to follow. But there was one last thing that I hadn't investigated: Lola DeWitt.

The only information I had on Lola so far was that she had been in one of Theo's movies, *The Man Who Death Forgot*. The movie was about a wealthy railroad heir who was presumed dead after a violent train accident. He wakes up in a hospital several weeks after the accident, disfigured and unrecognizable to his family. Rather than trying to reclaim the life he'd led before the accident, he sets out to build a new life for himself, despite his new physical deformities.

I went onto IMDb and checked out the cast list for *The Man Who Death Forgot*, reading through the biography of every actor and cast member. Most of them had died or moved to Montana, but there was one woman (listed as Dancer #6) who was still alive, and when I did a little bit more digging, I found that she was living in a trailer park near Palm Springs. According to her scant IMDb page, she hadn't acted in anything since '82, but I decided to drive out and see if she remembered anything from her experience filming a movie with Lola. At the very least, she might be able to give me new information about Eleanor. I gathered up my things and got in my car, then headed east, toward Palm Springs.

The desert was strange, and I remembered reading old interviews with actresses who had come out in the '30s and found it to be so exotic. Back in those days, trains heading west had stopped in Arizona and New Mexico, and the only vendors for miles were

Native Americans selling turquoise and silver jewelry. I recalled what I had read in Theo's journals, about the desert being the one last place that the studios didn't own.

Heading out there now, I could begin to understand why. The trailer park was on a little dirt road on the outside of Palm Springs, away from all the resorts and spas with their luxurious swimming pools. After driving down a nondescript road, I parked in a dirt parking lot, then walked up to a trailer painted with sunflowers and enormous ladybugs. A splintered wooden sign designated the trailer as the reception.

The trailer park manager turned out to be a tan, broad-faced woman in stained denim coveralls. When I told her what I wanted, she stuck a toothpick in her mouth and chewed on it.

"You're looking for Tammy Brewer?" she said. "You her kid or something?"

"No, I'm a writer. I live in Los Angeles."

Her face broke out in a big grin. "A writer, huh? I always knew that Hollywood would come knocking. You write for the flicks?"

"Not at all, ma'am. I'm on the bottom of the feeding chain, more or less."

"You know, we can rent this park out," she said. "People come down from the movies all the time. Brad Pitt and Angie came down one weekend."

"To your trailer park?"

"No, they stayed at one of the resorts in Palm Springs," she said, waving a derisive hand in the direction of town. "You need a filming location? The nicest trailer we got is probably number eight."

"I think you misunderstand," I said patiently. "I don't work for movies. I don't know any celebrities. For the last three years, I've worked for a dying magazine in a dingy part of Hollywood."

At the word "Hollywood," she perked up again.

"What's Hollywood like?"

"It's not as glamorous as people think," I said, and cleared my throat politely. "Can you direct me toward Tammy's trailer, please?"

Tammy's trailer sat at the edge of the park. The scrub and desert were on the other side of a barbed-wire fence, and in the distance, a low range of mountains squatted against the horizon. I remembered a story I'd read in Theo's journal, about a luxurious weekend spent in Idyllwild, retreating to a beautiful wooden cabin in order to get some peace of mind. I wondered what he would have made of the trailer park.

I knocked on Tammy's door and waited for a minute. There were the sounds of shuffling inside, and then someone called, "Just a minute!"

A moment later, the door blew open. A shirtless man stood before me, blinking into the sunshine. His skin was the deep, rich brown of desert citizens who spend most of their time outdoors. He wore a pair of old boxer shorts, and, strangely enough, a bolo tie.

"Howdy," he said.

"Is Tammy here?"

The man stood aside and motioned for me to enter the trailer. I stepped into a cloud of cigarette smoke, and saw a woman slouched over at a little kitchenette table. She had a cigarette clamped between her teeth, and she looked up when she heard me come in.

"I think Chet's dead," she said, without preamble.

"Who's Chet?"

"The goddamned lizard," she said, moving aside to show me a terrarium. "He hasn't moved for three days."

"I told you to take him out of the aquarium," the man said, coming over to join us. "Maybe he's lonely."

"It's not an aquarium, Harv, it's a *terrarium*."

They both peered in through the glass.

"What do you think?" Harv asked, turning to me.

"Uh," I said. "I'm probably not the best person to ask. I think that type of lizard looks dead on a good day."

"Well, golly," Tammy said. "Maybe we should add another lamp. These lizards like heat."

"Told you not to go catching things in the desert," Harv said.

"I didn't catch it, you silly man," Tammy said, grabbing a handful of his stomach. "Chelsea gave it to me when she moved to New Mexico."

I realized they'd both forgotten about me, and I cleared my throat. "You're Tammy Walsh, aren't you?" I asked.

"Well, I *was*," Tammy said. "Before I married that bastard from Pennsylvania."

"You used to be a dancer," I said.

They both broke into wild laughter, and Harv patted Tammy on the back.

"Say," Tammy said. "You want to play a game of bullshit with us? Isn't much fun with only two players."

"She's right," Harv joined in. "You deal out all the cards, and then of course you know what the other person's got."

"Harv's a lawyer," Tammy piped up, unnecessarily.

"Look, I don't want to bother you," I said, "but I was hoping you could tell me something about *The Man Who Death Forgot*."

They were both quiet, for once, and Tammy tapped a cigarette on her hand. She had suddenly turned serious.

"What are you doing here, kid?" she asked.

"I'm a writer. I'm working on a story."

"You work for MGM?" she said, giving me a wary look.

"No, I'm a journalist."

"I didn't see a penny of those royalties," she said. "They screwed us over."

"Oh?"

"Sure, they paid us fifty bucks for a day of dancing, and that's all we got," she said. "It's not even legal, the way they treat their actors."

"I'm sorry to hear that," I said. "My gran was an actress."

A light came on in her eyes. "What was her name?"

"Nadine Shaw."

"Don't know her. Sorry, kid."

"Do you remember working on that movie? Do you remember Eleanor Hayes?"

Tammy stuck another cigarette in her mouth and lit it. "'Course I remember her," she said. "Not very well—we weren't supposed to talk to her—but sometimes she'd come and hang out with us. The studio heads didn't want the chaff mixing with the big stars, you know."

"Was she nice?"

"Weird kid," Tammy said. "Down-to-earth and all that, didn't have a big head about her. But she was a tin-stamped weirdo."

Harv giggled.

"She had some problems on that film," I said. "Some personal problems. Do you know what happened?"

"Say," Harv said, poking my shoulder. "You ever meet Bob Mitchum?"

"Hush, Harv!" Tammy said. "I'm trying to remember. There was something that happened. God, it's been a while."

"I like the boxing pictures," Harv said. "And the old Westerns."

"There was a dancer," Tammy said slowly. "One of the girls we danced with. She was with us partway through the film, and then they kicked her off. Real nice girl, but kind of strange. Had a real thing for Eleanor."

"Thing?"

"Yeah, the girl was obsessed. She even broke into Eleanor's dressing room, tried on some of her dresses. Eleanor was real upset, threatened to walk off the film if they didn't do something about it."

A chill ran down my spine. "Can you remember her name?"

"It was one of those cute names, like Dolly or Sally. Lucy, maybe."

"Was it Lola DeWitt?"

Tammy's gaze went distant. "Yeah, that was it," she said. "Lola. Crazy little thing, that girl."

"How do you mean, crazy?"

Tammy looked at me, and then her face hardened. She stood up and grabbed the ashtray from the table, then started collecting butts that had collected around the trailer.

"I don't wanna talk to you," she said. "I have nothing to say."

"Wait, what's wrong?"

"Get out of my trailer. I got things to do."

I stood up. "I'm sorry if I said something to offend you," I said. "I'm just writing a story."

"You work for them?" She turned and glared at me. "You work for the studios?"

"I work for a magazine," I said, then recanted. "I just got fired. I don't work for anyone."

"Yeah? Then why are you down here, asking questions?"

I took a step forward, but Harv stood up and put his hand on my shoulder. "Easy there, champ," he said. "Gotta respect the lady's wishes."

"Please, listen to me," I said. "I'm a writer, working on a story. That's it."

"Why are you looking for Lola?" Tammy said.

"Someone mentioned her name."

"She was a bad seed." Tammy lit another cigarette. "Always bragging about climbing up the chain, getting famous, and all that. Some producer told her that she was going to be the next Eleanor Hayes, and I guess she believed them."

"Did you believe her?"

"I thought she was talking air, at first. But then there were days when Eleanor refused to come to work, I don't know why. Guess she had a problem with a director, or a producer. They'd call Lola in to stand for her. It went to the girl's head."

"Do you think she might have become violent?"

"God, I don't know, kid," Tammy said, and she looked tired. "Everyone was pretending to be someone else back then. I don't think I ever really knew who anyone was, or what anyone was capable of."

NINETEEN

It was nine days until Halloween, and yards were decorated in grand style. Some of the decorations around my neighborhood had been up for a month already, and as the days crept closer to the holiday itself, more and more went up. For the last three days, I had been toiling around my house, by turns listless and filled with new enthusiasm at my chances of catching Theo. I didn't shower once, and the only things I ate were cold pad thai and cereal.

I finally forced myself to shower and shave, then have some coffee and get dressed. There was one more thing I had to do before executing my plan.

The decorations around Petra's apartment building were a little bit more subdued, but one of her neighbors must have had kids, because a trio of poorly executed jack-o'-lanterns sat beside their doormat.

When Petra opened her door, she gave me a droll look.

"A bit early for trick-or-treating, don't you think?" she said. "Your costume sucks, by the way."

"I figure if I start now, all the good houses will still have candy."

"Good thinking." She leaned against the doorjamb and folded her arms.

"You gonna let me in?"

"I'm busy," she said. "Polishing my résumé."

"Alexa told me you quit," I said. "I hope it's not because of me."

"It's not your fault," she said. "I realized that I was wasting my time as an intern."

"I'm sorry," I said.

"You've already said it. It's unnecessary to say it again, Hailey."

I spread my hands. "You were my partner," I said. "I'm not very good at accepting help, but you helped me. I told you that I was going to break into Windhall, and I'm going to go through with it."

I couldn't read her expression. "Have you thought about the consequences?"

"I don't have anything left to lose," I said. "I've already lost my job. Alexa fired me. I don't know if you've heard."

"I heard." She picked at her fingernails. "I'm still friends with some people who work there, you know. There have been a few changes to the *Lens*."

"Brian get fired?"

She gave me a half smile. "Alexa canceled the Time buyout. It's gone independent again."

"When was that?"

"Not sure. In the last few days, I guess."

I thought about Heather's lawsuit against the magazine, and my heart sank. Alexa's decision must have been before that, because the lawsuit would push the *Lens* even further into the red.

"There's something else you should know," I said. "You were right about Heather and Linus Warren. They're up to something. I know the papers are saying they caught the woman who was killing those girls, but I think they might have had something to do with it, anyway. It's another crazy theory, and you probably don't want to hear about it."

"I have a minute before I need to keep working on my résumé."

"I think Engel was responsible for Eleanor's death."

"I see."

"But I know Theo is hiding something, too. There's gotta be a reason why Theo came back, after all these years away. I mean, he just showed up, out of the blue. There's something in that maid's room, and I'm going to find out what it was."

"Job or not, you're taking a huge risk."

"It's my last shot."

I took out my phone, and when I found what I was looking for, I scribbled something down on a piece of paper.

"Here," I said. "This is my friend's number. I know it's a big ask, but if I don't call you by tomorrow morning, would you let him know that I've been arrested? His name is Thierry. Tell him to find me at the Beverly Hills police station."

"Hailey—"

"Don't try to talk me out of it. Just, please—call him."

She looked sad for a moment, then nodded and took the piece of paper. "I know that I'm not going to talk you out of it," she said. "So I'll just wish you luck."

———————

Friday was a crisp, perfect day. Laurel Canyon smelled like crushed eucalyptus, woodsmoke, and a fine haze of dust. I spent the afternoon packing up my notes on Theo, trying not to get frustrated or emotional about the turn of events. Heather hadn't asked to have the journals back, but I put them into the original box in which she'd given them to me, along with the all the papers and photographs that had been tucked between the pages.

Last of all, I picked up Theo's satchel. I took down the photo of Theo and the mysterious Connie from my bulletin board and studied it once more. The strip of numbers on the back were still a jumbled bit of nonsense to me, and they offered me nothing new at that moment, either. Instead of putting it back in the satchel, I put the photograph in my pocket and started packing up my bulletin board.

Eventually, four o'clock rolled around, and I packed what I would need for the evening. Since I was a massive nerd and a true-crime junkie, I had prepared for the evening by spending hours on the Internet, digging up Reddit posts by crime scene techs and coming up with a way to find old bloodstains. It turned out that blood doesn't glow underneath a black light: that's a bit of creative fiction endorsed by decades of television. The only way it would glow was if you sprayed the site with Luminol, a compound that would also assist in highlighting particularly old samples. I had supplemented my research by purchasing a small black light from the hardware store, and a vial of Luminol off Amazon. It had been a lot more simple than I anticipated, and I couldn't help feeling like a rock star as I left the house.

In addition to the black light and Luminol, I had purchased a skeleton outfit. Since the entire street was going to be cordoned off for the pre-Halloween festivities, I needed to blend in, and there was no better way to do that than by wearing a costume. I would be able to disappear among the happy trick-or-treaters and parents, and even if someone did see me, they wouldn't be able to see my face. Before heading over to Benedict Canyon, I changed into the getup, then tucked my mask and black light into my backpack. I knew that the entire neighborhood would be under scrutiny, and that parking would also be a nightmare, so I left my car in an all-night parking lot off the Sunset Strip, then took a cab back toward Beverly Hills.

Theo's neighborhood was decked out in fine style. Children dressed up as demons, princesses, and goblins wandered through the streets, holding the hands of their parents. One of Theo's neighbors had filled their entire yard with elaborately carved jack-o'-lanterns, and the next yard boasted a very realistic-looking cemetery. Children ran among the gravestones, and a fog machine set the ambience.

It was almost sunset, which meant that I still had some time to kill. I stood in front of a house down the street from Windhall and admired the decorations. A group of people dressed as zombies were playing music in front of the house, much to the delight of the gathered audience. A few private security officers mingled among the crowds, keeping a wary eye on things, and I spotted a pair of cops on horseback.

I let myself get carried down the street by the current of people. There were hundreds of people that night, which meant that I would easily disappear among them, and as long as I didn't do anything too crazy, I wouldn't call attention to myself. Windhall came into view, but it was submerged in darkness, not a single light illuminated in the windows. It carried the same kind of resolute stature as a dying tree in the middle of a garden; while everything else blooms and flourishes, the wood slowly shrinks into itself before disappearing into the ground.

As the crowd of merrymakers flowed around me, I slowly moved toward the wall surrounding Windhall. The sunlight was slowly dying, and the shapes on the street began to merge. I waited to be sure that nobody was paying attention to me, then shrank into the vines growing over the wall. A few minutes passed, and then I started climbing up the vine limbs, and then reached the top of the wall and swung a leg over.

This time I was careful to lower myself down until I was in a position to drop without hurting myself. The sounds of children laughing and shouting were muted by the wall that was now between us. I listened closely to make sure nobody had seen me climb over. After satisfying myself that my ascent had gone undetected, I stood up and made my way toward the house.

Windhall was eerily silent against the backdrop of dark hills and the ragged lawn. The sounds and lights of the neighborhood party beyond the gate only served to emphasize the juxtaposition, and once more, I felt that I had stepped back in time to visit. The house was lifeless and more bereft than I had witnessed it in the past, and for one brief, stark moment, I wondered if Theo had packed up and fled Los Angeles once more.

I didn't let the thought deter me from moving forward. Even if Theo had departed, there was still a chance for me to prove what had happened. I hadn't come to any conclusions about whether Theo was truly innocent in Eleanor's death, but whether or not he had had a hand in what had happened, I needed to know the truth. Heather might still sue the *Lens*. I was still unemployed and was probably going to end up writing captions for a crappy real estate company, never to use my journalism degree again. I had nothing to lose.

I walked around the side of the house, past the swimming pool and the rotten gazebo, and made my way through the ruined citrus grove. The black windows of Windhall looked down on me, and I kept waiting for a light to come on inside Theo's bedroom, but there was still no sign of life. The second-story window of the boarded-up room was above the rose garden. I took a deep breath and steeled my nerves.

The door to the back porch was locked, but it only took a few tries with my credit card to get it open. I let myself in and stood for a moment, listening. The house was just as quiet as it had been when Madeleine and I had paid Windhall a visit. That had only been a few weeks before, but it felt like an entire century had passed since then.

I was more familiar with the layout of the house now, but not so familiar that I knew which boards would creak if I stepped on them the wrong way, and I still hadn't abandoned the possibility that Theo was somewhere in the house, waiting for me to make a wrong move. I reached the empty ballroom, where the Venetian floorboards retained their luster despite the years. There was an understated beauty about the place. For one heartbreaking moment, I pictured how things might have turned out differently for Theo and Eleanor if things hadn't gone so badly: a trio of children growing up among the oranges, growing old and inheriting the house, wearing down the tradition and allowing the ghosts to fade into the woodwork. Instead, the ghosts had the run of the house.

I made my way through the west stair hall, past the library and through the grand foyer, and then up the stairs. My heart was in my throat with every wind shudder, every jump and creak of the house. I reached the top step, and the hallway yawned before me, the open doors standing like sentries along a sinking ship.

The upstairs guest room hadn't changed since my second visit with Theo. I stood in the doorway, perplexed. The fact that Theo hadn't changed anything felt like pretty damning evidence that I had been wrong about the whole thing—if there really was a hidden room with critical evidence, Theo most certainly would have tried to cover it up, or to destroy the evidence.

Conscious of time, I donned my headlamp and then turned around and locked the door of the guest bedroom. I didn't think that anyone would come, but I didn't want to take any chances. I crossed the room to the armoire that was standing in front of the door to the maid's room and gently grasped it with both hands. It took quite a bit of maneuvering, but eventually I was able to move it enough to see the edge of the doorframe. Bolstered by this, I took a small rest, and then used the last of my strength to shove with my shoulder.

For one dizzy moment, I could see what was going to happen, but I still thought that I might have enough time to prevent it. The weight of the armoire stood unevenly, and I had pushed it too hard. I reached out to try to grab it, but it was too late, and the entire thing toppled forward, and then, with a terrible, jarring noise, went crashing through the window.

The reverberations of the sound went through the whole house—or at least, that's the way it seemed to me. The armoire was much too big to fit through the entire gabled window, so half of the piece of furniture remained in the room. I could feel my blood shooting through my veins as I waited for the eventual aftermath, the police and security guards, the footsteps pounding up the stairs and grabbing me, the arrest. But there was nothing.

When I had finally caught my breath, I turned my attention back to the edge of the maid's room door. Now that the armoire was out of the way, I saw what I was dealing with: the edge of the door was visible beneath peeling wallpaper, but there were pieces of plaster and wooden boards covering the door itself. The room had clearly been boarded up and covered in a layer of plaster, and when that had dried, someone had slapped wallpaper over it.

I took hold of one of the pieces of wood that was blocking the door. It had been nailed down, but after wrangling with it for a minute, I managed to pry it loose. The rest of the pieces of wood came away with a similar amount of struggle. I piled them carefully on the floor, then dusted my hands off and stood facing the door. It was a traditional Victorian door, two squares of inlaid wood painted white; a brass handle. I reached for the handle.

I heard voices. It wasn't the children on the street or snatches of laughter; these voices were closer. I edged toward the window and peered out over the toppled armoire. *Four flashlight beams coming across the grounds of Windhall.* Someone was inside the grounds.

As I stood there, a beam shot up and illuminated the upstairs guest bedroom, dazzling me. I ducked backward so quickly that I stumbled and fell, but it wasn't quick enough. I knew that I had been seen.

My mind churned through all the possibilities. There was the possibility of someone else who had decided to break in, but I knew that was unlikely. The festivities of the Halloween party were still in full swing, and I didn't think that four people would be able to slip into the grounds undetected. They had to be police, or worse, people who worked for Heather.

I didn't have much time. I tried the doorknob of the maid's room, but it was either locked or completely rusted shut. After a moment of hesitation, I shoved my shoulder against it. The door didn't budge; it was much heavier than it looked. I lifted my foot and kicked the doorknob, which took a few tries, but the door finally yielded.

I stumbled into the maid's room, coughing as waves of dust rose up. My light illuminated billows of dust and sediment, and then, as the dust settled, the room itself came into focus.

The wallpaper was different here. A pattern of tiny flowers drifted against a cream background, the perfect, quaint design typical of old-fashioned nurseries. The room was empty, but the walls bore evidence of furniture long gone: ghost patches where sunlight had never penetrated, the faint shape of a pair of twin beds and a dresser.

The window was hung with tattered curtains, silk organza gone to seed. A snatch of moonlight filtered in through the gaps, illuminating the floor. I could hear the voices more clearly now and knew that they must have reached the house. Men's voices, I could hear that much, though I couldn't distinguish anything they were saying.

Adrenaline had gotten me this far, but now I was convinced that it was a foolish venture, fruitless and pointless. I had given up everything to be here, but I wasn't sure what I was doing, and I was almost convinced that I was going to be arrested before I found anything.

Still, I pulled out the black light, which revealed pirouettes of dust, ghostly columns in the air. Nothing. And then, just as I was beginning to lose hope, a faint shimmer of blue.

There were noises downstairs. I could hear them coming through the house. And then, two voices I recognized: I could hear Ben and Leland.

"I know where he is," said Ben. "He's up in the guest bedroom."

"This way, gents," Leland said. The group was coming up the stairs.

My heart pounding in my chest, I went over to the window and sprayed the area with Luminol, then turned on the black light. The patches of blue glowed faintly under the window, and I could see that the wallpaper had been peeled away here, but it looked like an old wound. The patches of wood and glowing blue marks showed underneath this. I dropped to my knees and started to peel away the wallpaper, then took out my knife and scraped away at the wood.

They were in the hallway now. I could hear their footsteps marching toward the guest room, but with the house's strange acoustics, it seemed that they were all around me.

I was almost done. I picked away until I had a piece of wood about the size of my thumb, which glowed faintly blue under the black light. I wrapped it up in a plastic bag, and then wrapped that up in a second bag. There was only one option, and it wasn't appealing, but I knew that I didn't have a choice.

I had left the maid's room and was waiting in the adjoining guest bedroom when they found me. Leland opened the door of the bedroom with a key, then stepped inside and glanced around. He took in the armoire and then saw me sitting on the bed. He almost looked disappointed.

"I told you to stay away from Windhall," he said. "Why didn't you listen?"

Ben didn't say anything, but when he met my eye, he looked sad. He was followed into the room by two policemen, a man and a woman.

"Are you aware that this is a private residence?" This was from the woman.

"He's aware," Leland said.

"And you're aware that breaking and entering is an offense?"

"Yes, yes, he's aware," Leland said. "Search him. He came here to steal something."

The male cop came over and frisked me. He turned over the black light.

"What's this?"

"It's a black light."

"I can see that," he said. "And the liquid?"

There was no point in lying; any idiot detective would put it together eventually.

"Luminol."

"What are you doing with it?"

Ben cleared his throat. "You don't have to answer that, Hailey," he said. "I don't think you should say anything at all."

Leland made a hand gesture to the cop. "Anything else?"

The cop continued to frisk me. "He's got a mask," he said. "Creepy skeleton. Keys, both car and house, a wallet." He opened it and looked through my cards. "No driver's license."

"We know who he is. Anything else?"

"That's it."

"All right, let's go," Leland said. "Take him to the station."

TWENTY

It made a great finale. The officers frog-marched me down the driveway of Windhall and made a big show of unlocking the gates, then escorted me toward their waiting car. Children looked on in shock and delight as I was pushed into the cruiser. I have to admit that I must have made quite a sight; I was still dressed as a skeleton, other than the mask, and now I was covered in dust.

"I have to go to the bathroom," I announced, but nobody listened to me.

Before the officers put me into their car, Ben put his hand on my shoulder. "Don't say anything," he said. I was confused that he was being so nice to me. Weren't we on opposite sides of the equation? "Wait for your lawyer."

It had been a while since I had been booked, but I remembered the routine. Once we got to the station, I had to sign some paperwork, and then the two cops took me into a room and jogged me for details about what I was doing at Windhall. I politely told them that I wasn't willing to talk until I had a lawyer. Jail isn't really like what they show on television; it feels more like a bad hospital with really shitty nurses.

They kept me in the room for three hours, leaving me to doze at one point, until a different officer appeared.

"You Max Hailey?"

"That's me."

"You're free to go."

I blinked and rubbed my eyes. I was so exhausted that I was delirious, and I wasn't feeling very perceptive. "And then what?"

"Then what, what? Then nothing. You're done."

"That's it?"

"No charges filed. We need this space for the next shithead who gets a brilliant idea."

I followed him down the hallway and emerged into the booking room. Petra and Thierry were standing there, waiting for me.

"All right, asshole," Thierry said. "What kind of mess did you get yourself into this time?"

"I'd love to fill you guys in," I said. "Let's get out of here, though."

"Let's get breakfast or something," Petra suggested.

"You okay?"

"There's something I need to tell you," she said. "It's about Rebecca Lewis, Ben's mother. Not here, though. Let's wait until we're somewhere else."

———————————

Thierry refused to stop at any of the cafés in Beverly Hills, and he made me wait until we'd reached Venice. "You know I hate Beverly Hills, Hailey, don't test my patience." He stopped at a hole-in-the-wall Mexican joint, populated by salty surf bums and grizzled beachcombers. I ran to the restroom while Petra and Thierry sat down and ordered. I was gone for about fifteen minutes, and by the time I got back, Thierry had finished his breakfast burrito.

"Your coffee's cold," he announced. "What, they don't let you use the bathroom in jail?"

"I didn't want to go there," I said. "It was of a rather sensitive nature."

"What, you some kind of princess now? Can't shit with an audience?"

I turned to Petra. "You said you found something out about Rebecca Lewis?"

She glanced around and then lowered her voice. "I've been looking into her a lot," she said. "Trying to figure out when Theo could have been with her. Trying to figure out if Theo could be Ben's father, if he and Rebecca had an illegitimate child together. Also, Hailey, you mentioned that the second set of footprints in the garden might have belonged to her."

"What footprints?" Thierry leaned back against the booth and drank his coffee. "This shit's way over my head. I thought we were here to talk about how you ended up in jail again."

I knew that if I didn't answer Thierry, he would sulk. I decided to give him the abbreviated version. "When Theo was arrested, there was a second set of footprints found in the garden, near Eleanor's body. There was a long-standing theory that he had an accomplice, but they could never figure out who it was."

"I haven't proved that the footprints belonged to Rebecca," Petra went on. "Not yet. But here's where it gets interesting. She spent some time in Vermont."

"I don't see the connection."

She took out her notebook. "I wrote down that strip of numbers from the back of the photograph of Theo dancing with that woman," she said, then read out, "Oh-two-one-six-six-four, G-F-N-V-T."

"I've been mulling over them for a few weeks now. What do you think they mean?"

"My mom was really into photography for a while when I was growing up, always had tons of sleeves of photographs that she'd gotten developed. I went to visit my parents after I quit the *Lens*. There's not much to do at their place—bad Internet—so I was looking through old family photos. There were similar numbers and letters on the back of these photos, except these ones all started with CA. I realized that the letters were state abbreviations."

I felt goose bumps on the back of my neck.

"Fuck, Petra, you're incredible."

"V-T is for Vermont," she said. "The numbers are a date in February, nineteen sixty-four. And that meant that G-F-N was a town in Vermont. I pulled up trusty old Google and went through all the town names in Vermont. The only one that makes sense for that configuration of letters is a little town called Grafton."

Thierry let out a low whistle. "Your girl has mad skills, Hailey. Maybe instead of subjecting her to the ritualistic slavery of an unpaid internship, you can give her gainful employment."

"He was in America the whole time," Petra said quietly. "All those stories about seeing Theo in another country were lies. Why do you think he'd stay in America, rather than leave?"

"It's easy to hide in plain sight," I said.

"Maybe."

I reached into my bag and dug around until I found the photograph of Theo dancing with the woman. I studied the small patches of snow on the ground, the caps of white on the roofs.

"I looked into Grafton," she went on. "There used to be a corner drugstore that developed film, but it's been razed and turned into a Starbucks. They were probably the ones who developed this film. It's too bad we can't ask them about Theo.

"But I did a little more digging," she said. "To try to find out where the picture might have been taken. Apparently, in the sixties, there was a controversial center run by nuns. It was at the edge of town. Unwed mothers and their children were sent there until they were able to get back on their feet."

"Any idea what it was called?"

"Saint Lucia's."

It took a moment to connect the dots. "Do you think—I mean, that has to be Lucy's," I said. "With Connie, at Lucy's. Right?"

Petra tapped the photograph. "I think Rebecca was at the women's center, and that's why Theo went out there."

"Where does Connie fit into all of this? Have you figured out who she is yet?"

"Maybe there's a way to find out," Petra said. "The buildings are still there."

"Is it still a home for unwed mothers? Those don't exist anymore, do they?"

"I don't think so. The center went bankrupt and the original owner passed it onto her kids, but according to what I could find, now it's filled with squatters. Grafton's one of those cutesy, picturesque Eastern towns where people go to see the fall leaves, and everyone *hates* those buildings."

I looked at Petra in admiration. "Did you find all this through Google?"

"I called a few places in Grafton."

"We have to go out there," I said. "Tomorrow, if possible."

Thierry had looked bored by our conversation, but he perked up at this. "You allowed to leave the city and all? With your new arrest record?"

"They let me go this morning. Said nobody was pressing charges."

Thierry gave me a hard stare. "You know what that means, right? They're planning to finish the job themselves."

"What job?"

"H, you've been pissing these guys off for weeks. They're going to kill you."

"Shut up, Thierry."

"I'm serious." He stared at me with flat eyes. "Maybe it's a good idea for you to leave town after all."

Petra watched us without saying anything.

"What do you think?" I asked her. "Want to take a quick trip?"

"You go," she said. "I'm looking into something else. I need to stay here."

"Come on, you're as much a part of this story as I am."

She gave me a sly grin. "I'm chasing a different dead girl," she said. "Two of them, actually. I'm going to find out the connection between Linus and all those girls who died in Beverly Hills."

"How do you plan to do that?"

She shrugged. "I found out a little bit more about that performance artist. Deborah Mann. Once she realizes that Linus and Heather can afford the top criminal attorneys and she can't, she'll want to get her side of the story out there as quickly as possible."

"All right, enough of this," Thierry said. He leaned across the table and fixed me with a stare. "I want to know why your ass was in jail last night."

"I went to Windhall to find something."

"You broke into Windhall and stole something, then got arrested for it. Genius move. I'm guessing they didn't let you keep it."

"They didn't know about it."

He gave me a hard look. "You hide it somewhere on the grounds?"

"Nope." I grinned at him. "I swallowed it. That's why I took so long in the bathroom just now."

I dropped the pair of Ziploc bags on the table. Thierry frowned, and then he realized what he was looking at. His eyes widened, and he leaped out of his seat.

"Jesus, get that away from me! That's vile!"

Petra peered at the plastic bags with curiosity. "What am I looking at?"

"Proof," I said proudly. "That's a piece of bloody wall that I took from Windhall. I had to swallow it, because I knew that if they found it while they were searching me, it would disappear."

"You're telling me that bag just came out of you?" Petra stared at me.

"I have to get it tested," I said. "If it's Eleanor's blood, we have enough evidence to reopen the trial. We can find out what really happened."

"How are you going to get it tested?"

"I'm friends with a blood tech at Cedars-Sinai," I said. "I spent a few years there when I was a kid."

"Seriously, Hailey, there's something wrong with you." Thierry took a swig of his coffee and gave me a dirty look. "Let's get out of here."

———————

My cell phone had died, but when we pulled into my driveway, I could hear the landline ringing. I stretched as I stepped out of Thierry's car; the night in jail had kinked up my neck.

"You gonna answer your phone?" Thierry asked.

"Why bother? Only people who have the number are telemarketers."

We went into the house as the answering machine kicked in.

"Hailey, pick up." It was Madeleine's voice. "Seriously, *pick up.*"

I crossed the room and grabbed the phone. "Mad. What's going on?"

"Where are you?" she sounded anxious. "I've been calling you for an hour."

"I was otherwise engaged," I said. "You okay?"

"Hailey," she said, and her voice sounded oddly electrified. "Oh my God, Hailey. It's Windhall. The whole thing has gone up in flames. It's all over the news."

TWENTY-ONE

Thierry tried to stop me from leaving the house, but I wouldn't take no for an answer. Since my car was still parked near Windhall, I finally managed to convince Thierry to drive me and Petra toward Beverly Hills.

There's an odd quality about fire, that you can sense it several miles away. The air above Beverly Hills was white and ashy, and tendrils of smoke reached up toward the heavens. There was a sweet smell in the air, and as I passed Sunset, I could see a dark plume of smoke above the hills. The road was blocked at the bottom of Benedict Canyon Road, three streets below Theo's house.

"Residents only past this point," one of the officers told me.

"You don't understand, I need to see Windhall. I know Theo personally."

"You hear what I said? Move along."

A collection of rubberneckers and photographers had gathered at the bottom of the blockade, and a few news crews were filming the occasion. Two helicopters circled overhead. I felt tension in my chest, and Petra put a hand on my shoulder.

"What do you want to do?" she asked.

"There's another way," I said. "Come on. We need to get closer."

Ignoring Thierry's protests, I got back in my car and reversed, then headed back toward Sunset. The fire trail where the dead art student's body had been discovered was far enough away that I doubted they had blocked it off, and we would be able to see Windhall from above. We had to move quickly, though, or they might realize the vantage point had been missed.

"You know that you can't get anywhere near Windhall, don't you?" Thierry was saying. "You just got arrested for breaking in. You want to get yourself arrested again, fine, but this time there won't be anyone to bail you out."

I parked on an offshoot of San Ysidro Drive.

"Look, you don't have to come with me," I said. "But I'm going to get closer."

I made my way down the path toward the outlook. I could feel Petra and Thierry behind me, but nobody spoke as we moved through the overgrown path toward the peak with the view of Windhall.

The branches above us cleared, and I made my way onto the rocky outlook. Several hundred feet down the embankment stood Windhall, engulfed in flames. A veil of smoke hung over everything in Theo's yard, and the house stood in ruins. Even at that distance, I could feel the heat, and it felt like a caress. I could make out the frames of the windows and saw that the skeleton of the house had been exposed. It was beyond saving.

"Shit," I whispered.

The upper turret had caved into itself, a collapsed skull. The smoke was so thick that it hung in tatters around the sooted windows, the broken glass, and the ragged woodwork. I could see firemen forming a brigade from the street, unwinding hoses to combat the flames, but I knew that it was futile.

Petra and Thierry stood on either side of me, and for once, they were completely silent.

"What do you think happened?" Thierry said.

"I'm guessing it was Heather," I said, after a moment. "She said that Theo was going to pay for what he did. I didn't know that she was going to burn his house down. Unless, of course, it was Caleb Walsh. He *was* determined to tear Windhall down."

The sun dazzled above the eastern ridges, and the house stood defiant against the hills. The suggestions of what the house had once looked like were still there, but it only existed in pieces: the tallest tower was still *there*, only it had been carved out by flame, and the glass in the windows had shattered. The lower domes and cupolas had collapsed into themselves, and daylight shone through in places where there had once been roof and shingles.

"I did this," I said. "I started digging, and this is what happened."

"You can't blame yourself," Petra said. "Besides, if it *was* Caleb, then this had nothing to do with you."

"Blame himself? He's trying to take credit," Thierry retorted. "Hailey, you're not that influential."

I felt hollow. "You don't think Theo was inside, do you?"

"You were there last night," Thierry said. "Did you see him? *Hear* him?"

"No, but I wasn't there for very long." I pinched my eyes shut. "Let's see if we can find out what happened. Maybe the firefighters will talk to us."

We picked our way down the fire trail. The crowd on Benedict Canyon had grown, and I could see an ambulance through the fray.

"Why is there an ambulance?" I turned to Thierry.

He didn't respond. The crowd was surging forward around us, and I could hear snatches of conversation.

"Can't believe he was still alive," a woman behind me muttered. "I grew up here, there were always stories about him. I always thought my mom was lying."

"Yeah, well, he's not alive anymore," a man replied. "They're saying he was inside."

I edged closer so I could listen in on their conversation.

"Creepy place," the woman said. "Whoever set that fire did a favor to the whole neighborhood."

"A dried-up corpse," the man said. "He probably went up like a stack of matches."

The ambulance siren started up, and the crowds parted slightly to make room for it. Firefighters came through the crowds, pushing people aside until there was enough room for the ambulance to reach the street, then take off down Benedict Canyon toward the hospital.

Once it was gone, the crowds began to disperse, and I pushed my way closer to the house. A pair of firefighters were talking next to the gate.

"Is it true?" I asked.

They turned to look at me.

"Was he inside?"

"You can't be here," one of them said. "We need you to stand back in case the fire spreads."

"Was Theo inside?" I repeated. "I need to know if Theo was inside."

"We retrieved a body," one of the firemen finally replied. "Someone was inside when it happened."

"It was a man," the other said. "We're not at liberty to say more than that. Really, you need to leave."

———————

Thierry dropped me off at my house. Before I got out, he put a hand on my shoulder. "You can drop this," he said. "You can leave this story behind. It's done, Hailey."

I went into the kitchen and poured myself a shot of Heather's whiskey, then sat down. I was shaking so hard that I could barely lift the shot to my lips, and when I swallowed the amber liquid, I didn't really feel any better.

I called Leland's phone, but he didn't answer. Another thought occurred to me, then, and I ran over to my computer. I hadn't used Theo's email address since I'd contacted him, trying to get an interview. Now, I found the address among my notes and penned a quick email to Theo:

> I know you don't want to talk to me, but please give me some sign that you're okay. I saw the fire.

After pressing "send," I poured myself another shot of whiskey and tried to calm myself down.

With all the insanity of the day, I had almost forgotten about the blood sample that I had collected from Windhall. It was difficult to believe that twenty-four hours before, I was planning how to break into Theo's house. Now, I had been arrested and seen Windhall burning down.

After a few more shots, I booted up my computer and checked various news sites, then watched as Windhall collapsed in on itself, taking all the years of layered history along with it. At one point, some photographers managed to sneak past all the fire barricades and climb the walls of Windhall. Their photographs turned up on the *Huffington Post* a few hours later.

The fire was the only thing on the news that evening. I couldn't turn on my computer without seeing images of Windhall, a burned hull devoid of beauty. The hedges surrounding the yard were also badly damaged, and the whole property was exposed, once and for all. It was as though the fire had peeled away the protective sealant that had managed to keep out trespassers and curious bystanders for years.

I had drifted off to sleep when I heard a soft tapping on my door. The sound intersected with my dreams, at first, and then I gradually woke up and realized that someone was outside. I rose to my feet and padded across the room to open the door.

It was Madeleine.

"Hey," she said softly. "Are you okay?"

"I honestly don't know."

"Did you find what you were looking for?"

It only took a few minutes for me to catch her up on everything from the last twenty-four hours, from the stolen piece of wall to the fire, to Theo's body.

"I still have the sample," I said. "I was going to have it tested against Eleanor's DNA, but now I don't know if I can."

"How would you get Eleanor's DNA?"

"I have some of her hair," I said. "It's part of some stuff I got from this crazy collector. I'm sure they'd have a record of it somewhere, since all of the original tests were done on Eleanor at Cedars-Sinai."

She leaned against the doorframe. "You need to take it in," she said. "It's the only way you'll ever get peace from this."

"I know."

"Let's go," she said. "I'll drive."

Petra answered right away when I called, and Madeleine swung past her apartment to pick her up.

"Where are we going?" Petra asked when she climbed into the car.

"You said you wanted to be part of the story," I replied.

It was approaching six o'clock, and traffic was heavy. I knew from experience that Claudia spent most of her time at the lab, though, since she was a workaholic. If she wasn't at work, there was a chance that she was at her home in Studio City. I'd been there a few times, and I knew that she wouldn't be upset if I showed up at her house with an emergency request.

When we got to the hospital, one of the night-shift nurses told me that Claudia was on break.

"She's probably in the courtyard," she told me. "Go out there and see, if you like."

Sure enough, we found Claudia leaning against the wall of the courtyard, eating her sandwich. I had always liked Claudia—back when I was in the hospital, she had had green streaks in her hair, but now it was cut short and shaved on the sides. She was a curvy black woman who wore horn-rimmed glasses, and it was widely acknowledged that she was the best blood technician at Cedars-Sinai. Even though we didn't see each other too often, we made a point of getting in touch at least once a year. The last time we'd seen each other, we'd both gotten shit-faced at a bar in downtown Los Angeles.

"Hailey," she said, nodding a greeting. "What do you need?"

"Can't this be a friendly visit?"

She rolled her eyes. "You have a carefully curated network of friends all over Los Angeles. Out with it, Hail. What do you need?"

"I need a blood test."

"You been promiscuous lately? Worried you might have picked something up?"

"It's not my blood."

Claudia nodded at Petra and Madeleine. "Are you going to introduce me to your friends?"

"Petra, Madeleine; this is Claudia."

"Pleasure's all mine." Claudia bowed her head. "Let me finish this sandwich and then we can go inside. Jesus, Hailey, you're seriously starting to owe me."

When she finished her break, we followed her into her office, which was crammed with blood slides and test tubes. Claudia heaved a breath and sat down, then adjusted her glasses and folded her arms across her chest.

"Tell me what's going on."

"I just need a match."

"Okay," she said. "Are you breaking any laws? Am I going to get in trouble for this?"

"I'm not breaking laws," I said. "This is an ancient case that the Los Angeles murder squad failed to solve."

"Is this about Eleanor Hayes?"

"Maybe."

She beckoned. "Maybe. Like you ever talk about anything else. Let's see your sample."

I took out the plastic bag and handed it to her. "It's a piece of wood."

"I see that," she said, peering at the piece of wood.

I handed her the locket. "I don't know if this helps," I said, "but this is a locket of Eleanor's hair."

"It's not going to happen right away," she said. "Probably at least a week."

I ran a hand through my hair. "Any chance you could do it faster than that?'

"What's in it for me?"

"Dinner at the Magic Castle?"

"I'm not *twelve*, Hailey."

"Who doesn't like magic?"

"I'll let you sit on it and get back to me." She tilted the piece of wood under the lights. "I like Brazilian food and Korean spas, by the way."

"See you, Claud."

———————————

It was almost eight by the time we left the hospital.

"Home?" Madeleine said, turning to me. "Or do you need to drown your sorrows at some shitty bar?"

"I was hoping you could take Petra home," I said. "I'm going to the airport."

Madeleine gave me a long look. "You're not kidding."

"Afraid not. I need to go to Vermont."

"Probably wise."

"I thought you might try to talk me out of it," I said. "You're really supporting this?"

"Hailey," Petra said slowly. "They're going to come looking for you."

"Who?"

"The fire," she said, giving me a look I couldn't decipher. "They're going to think it was you. And if Thierry's right, that the only reason they're not pressing charges is so they can come after you personally . . ."

"I couldn't have set the fire," I argued. "I was in jail last night."

"But the fire started today," she said. "They're going to think it was you. You have a record."

"Jesus, I wish people would stop reminding me," I said. "I didn't set Windhall on fire."

"We know that, but who else does?"

"I'm not going to jail until I finish this story. Otherwise I risked it all for nothing."

TWENTY-TWO

I didn't sleep on the plane, and felt jittery and anxious during takeoff and landing. The flight was a red-eye, and I imagined all the amorphous states collapsing against each other beneath the plane as we headed east. I had always had a strange affection for these places, the self-contained towns where everyone knew each other, where you could settle into a slower pace and know your own place in the world.

By the time I arrived in Burlington, I was starting to get paranoid from dehydration and lack of sleep. I made my way to the rental car counter, rubbing my eyes to feel more alert.

"What's the cheapest car you have?" I asked the girl behind the counter.

"How long do you need it?"

"Today."

"It's going to be around a hundred. Sedan okay?"

"That's fine."

"You need chains."

"Chains?"

"For your wheels." She looked at me like I was an idiot. "It's fall, but you never know what weather you're gonna get, not with global warming. There's a chance it could snow in the mountains. Do you know how to put them on?"

"I'm from Los Angeles," I said, and she rolled her eyes.

"Come with me."

"Look, how long is this going to take? I don't have much time; I'm flying home later today."

"Your rental insurance is no good if you get into an accident without chains," she said.

Thirty minutes later, I was heading toward Grafton. Clouds of yellow and russet-colored leaves rose above the bends of the highway up into the mountains, shifting from apple green to crimson. Even though I was sleep-deprived, I couldn't help but feel entranced. Growing up in Los Angeles meant that I hadn't seen very many real autumns, apart from my college tenure. The air felt crisper and fresher than it had even in Burlington, and as I rose up through the mountains, I started to feel more optimistic.

I knew that it was irrational for me to feel rushed about getting to Grafton. Whatever information lay in wait for me there was already several decades old, and another few hours wasn't going to harm anything. Still, an incomplete picture was beginning to form in my mind, and as a writer, I knew that if I didn't act on my impulses quickly, they were liable to evaporate completely.

Grafton was just as lovely as all the pictures that I had seen of it: white houses with red caps, American flags crooked in the wind. Sugar maples and green firs, little white churches and apple orchards. I didn't know where Saint Lucia's was, and my phone was having trouble picking up a signal. I spotted a bed-and-breakfast up ahead and parked outside.

When I climbed up the steps, the woman behind the desk looked up and smiled. "Reservation?"

"I was hoping you could help me with something," I said. "Have you ever heard of Saint Lucia's?"

Her smile faded. "Are you law enforcement?"

"No, I'm a journalist," I said.

She raised an eyebrow. "What have they done now?"

"Who?"

She shifted in her seat and glanced around to make sure that nobody else was listening.

"Last month, it was an overdose," she said. "Apparently both parents were hooked on meth, and they let their little children run wild. Two of them had to go to the hospital for inhaling the fumes."

"Are you talking about Saint Lucia's?"

"That's why you're here, isn't it?"

"I'm looking for these buildings," I said, and I passed her the photo of Theo and Connie.

She adjusted her glasses and examined the photos. "Oh, honey," she said. "The buildings don't look like that anymore. This was when it was a home for single mothers."

"What happened?"

"They meant well," she said, passing me the photo. "The nuns set up a home for women who had nowhere else to go. For a while, things were going well, but then the nuns ran out of money. They left town, and the squatters moved in. It's not Christian to judge, so I won't, but you don't find anyone in Grafton who's glad they're here."

"The squatters?"

"The buildings have been derelict for years," she said. "No power, no water or gas. It's awful in the wintertime—they burn anything that will catch a light. You're not planning to go out there by yourself, are you?"

"You don't need to worry about me, ma'am."

"Some of them have knives. It's not technically in Grafton, so our police don't go out there unless they really have to. Unincorporated land, you understand."

"Can you tell me how to get there?"

She hesitated.

"Please, I've flown all the way out from Los Angeles."

She paused. "All right. I'll draw you a map."

Once I was back in my car, I looked at the hand-drawn map. There was no sense of scale, but I gathered that the old buildings were some distance outside town. I shivered, not from the cold but from what the woman had told me. I knew that connecting the dots between the broken-down women's facility and the burnt shell of Windhall was going to be a stretch, but I didn't see any other paths opening in front of me.

The drive out to Saint Lucia's was pastoral and lovely. Cathedrals of trees intersected over the narrow road, which wound past acres of apple orchards. It was at least a half-hour drive from Grafton, which was remote enough as it was. I was starting to wonder if the woman had given me wrong directions when I saw an old wooden sign in the distance.

SAINT LUCIA'S, it read, and nothing more. The sign was wind-battered and derelict, hanging off its screws. A few more minutes passed, and then I came upon some overgrown hedges leading down a long drive. I turned the car carefully down the drive, aware of several large potholes in the pavement. Piles of leaves had blown into some of them, so I was able to drive down the road without too much difficulty, but it still made slow progress. At the end of the hedges, I emerged into a wide parking area, and I saw what the woman had meant about Saint Lucia's falling into ruin.

In the photograph, the buildings had been crisp white Victorian buildings, tidy as ironed shirts. There had been signs of life and ebullience here and there, a bit of rebellion in the form of wildflowers shooting up from between stoops and in the cracks of sidewalks. I had painted an entire narrative around the two dancers in the photograph, Theo and the unknown Connie, but this was not what I had been prepared for.

The original buildings were still there, all six of them, but they were nearly beyond recognition. No longer painted white, each house was a different shade of sherbet: lime, mango, rose. The new paint was evidence that at some point, someone had taken the initiative to restore life to the place, but now, all that life was gone. The houses had seen better years, the paint peeling and the porches sagging.

I climbed out of my car and glanced around. There were two cars parked at the far end of the lot, but neither looked like it still ran, and the undisturbed layer of leaves on the ground indicated that nobody had left or arrived since it had fallen. The peeling paint on the buildings exposed bare wood underneath, and the effect was similar to seeing a skeleton beneath a grinning face. I could see that the buildings hadn't been completely abandoned; as I walked across the parking lot, a curtain moved aside to reveal a white face. When I waved, however, the curtain was snatched back into place.

I went up to the first door and knocked. The sky-blue house had a dilapidated door and a rotting front porch. There was an odd grinding sound from within the house, and I leaned forward to see if I could detect anything through the window, but I couldn't see past the lace curtains.

The door opened to reveal an old woman dragging an oxygen machine behind her. She gave me a sharp look, then shook her head and waved a hand in my face.

She was starting to shut the door on me when I moved forward and put a hand on the doorjamb.

"Excuse me," I said. "Have you ever heard of Theodore Langley?"

She didn't respond but took her cane and tapped it sharply against my fingers. I jerked my hand away, and she quickly slammed the door in my face. I heard the sound of laughter behind me.

I turned around to find myself facing a man in a plaid shirt and a heavy denim jacket. He had dark skin, light eyes, and white hair. He carried two bags of groceries and shrugged when he saw me looking at him.

"Tough luck, kid," he said.

"I'll try someone else."

"Ain't no one here willing to talk to you."

"Why not?"

"You come from the outside."

"All right. Thanks for your time."

I could feel his eyes on me as I trotted down the woman's steps and crossed the small patch of dead grass that sat between the houses. I walked up to the next house, a salmon-colored Victorian, and knocked on the door. A pair of curtains was snatched back, a dirty look passed out at me, but nobody came to answer the door.

I cast a quick glance backward to see the man leaning against the railing of one of the houses, amused. He looked like he was lounging and watching something funny on TV, and the expression on his face annoyed me.

"What do you want?" I asked, irritated.

"Maybe I know something," he said. "Unless you'd like to try some more doors. Go on."

"Talk to me about what?"

"Oh, someone like you comes along every few years," he said. "I'm usually the one who ends up answering the questions."

"Then let's talk," I said. I wasn't willing to be grateful to him, not yet. He almost certainly had an angle of his own, something he wanted from me. "I'm Max Hailey. And you are?"

"Thibodeau Bisset. You can call me Tibo."

"Okay. Tibo."

"Tell you what. I'll make you some tea. It's not great stuff, but it's what they have on markdown over at the supermarket. Sound good?"

More curious than anything, I agreed. Tibo turned down a narrow path behind the buildings, and led me into the back garden of the last house. He knocked on the door, then tried the door handle and let himself inside. Without hesitation, I followed him into the house.

The interior was dry and smelled like dust, but it was surprisingly warm. It was very dark and felt claustrophobic since the windows were blacked out with garbage bags. We were in a kitchen, but the counters were covered in cardboard boxes.

Tibo hummed as he made his way through the kitchen and out into a sitting area. The windows here were also blacked out, but the room was illuminated by a collection of lamps of all different sizes: retro lamps, tall standing lamps, miniature lamps in the shapes of flowers.

The room was very clean, but also tight, since it was walled in by more cardboard boxes. There was a little woven rug on the floor, and a low table. The free space in the room was about half the size of my kitchen.

Tibo was watching me with an amused expression on his face. "What do you think of Vermont?"

"Where do you get the electricity for all these lamps?" I asked. "I thought you were . . ."

"Squatters?"

"Yes." I blushed.

"We sure are. The county shut off our power about three years ago. I work at the dump, see, and we see a lot of car batteries go through."

"And you light your house with them?"

He shrugged. "I like light."

"Why not take the bags off the windows?"

"Not safe. These buildings have to look empty, or we get child protection and other county services coming by. Sit. Have a clemen-tine." He took a paper sack from his pocket. "Go on."

I accepted one of the fruits, then peeled it, watching his face.

"Probably surprised to see oranges in the freezing cold."

"Someone told me that they're winter fruit," I said.

"That's right, very good. Where you from?"

"Los Angeles."

"Sometimes they come further than that."

"Who?"

"The visitors," he said. "We are the custodians of ghost stories, those of us who still remember. These rooms have seen a lot of heartbreak. Now that the children are grown, they come back looking to make sense of what happened. My mother was a nurse for the women, so I remember. I assume you've come because you're looking for someone."

"I am looking for someone," I said. "Two people, actually."

He nodded.

"Do you know who Theodore Langley is?"

The man went on peeling his clementine, managing to uncloak the entire fruit without destroying the skin.

"You do, don't you?" I pressed.

The man didn't respond, or perhaps he didn't hear. "What can I help you with?"

"I need to know if he was here," I said. "Actually, I know that he was. I'd like to know why."

"Maybe it was before my time."

"You do know who he is. What was he doing here?"

"There's a certain kind of confidentiality around here," he said. "We keep to ourselves. You probably noticed yourself, outside."

I passed him the photograph. "Do you know who this is?"

The look of surprise that passed over his face was so immediate and fragile that I almost reached out to steady him. He passed his thumb over the face of the young woman, ignoring Theo.

"You know her," I noted.

"Where did you get this?"

"Let's trade information." I laced my hands together. "Tell me who she was, and I'll tell you what I know."

"I didn't know what happened to her," he said. "She left without saying anything."

I rubbed my hands together. "Connie?"

"No," he said, and then gave me a perplexed look. "Connie was her friend."

I stabbed the photograph with a finger. "Who is she?"

"That's Flannery."

The surprise on my face must have been evident, because the man stared at me, and we were both quiet for a long moment.

Finally, he broke the silence. "Do you know her?"

"Yes. She's friends with Theo." I thought for a moment, then tried again. "Who's Connie?"

"Look, I need to know who you are. Tell me who you *really* are."

"I was writing a story about Theo," I said. "But I got too involved, and everything went to shit. I'm not working for anyone but myself at this point. I just need to know what happened, even if nobody believes me when I go home. I need to know, because this story has turned my life upside down, and I still don't understand it."

He was quiet for a long moment, then nodded. "Flannery was my friend," he said finally. "We were kids together. Flannery was in love with Theo's son."

The story was getting more and more complicated. Finding out that the woman in the photograph was Flannery didn't clarify anything, either.

"Was Theo in love with Connie?"

He looked confused and I immediately realized that it was the wrong question. Before I could backtrack, however, he shook his head and set the photograph on the table.

"Connie," he said slowly, "was Theo's son. Short for Conrad."

My head was spinning. "And who was the mother?"

"Rebecca," he said. "Rebecca Lewis. It was a home for unwed mothers, remember. Rebecca and Connie lived in the house at the other end, the one that's painted peach now. Theo used to come and visit them."

Rebecca Lewis. I had a sick feeling in my stomach, and suddenly realized that I had been chasing the wrong person all along. I took out my phone and scrolled through until I found a picture of Ben.

"He's probably older than when you remember him," I said. "But do you think this could be Connie?"

He took the phone in his hands and pulled out a pair of glasses, which he slipped onto his nose. After staring at the photo for a moment, he smiled, looked sad, then handed the phone back to me.

"Yes," he said. "I'd say that would have to be him."

———————

I was back at Burlington Airport when my phone rang. I glanced at the screen. *Petra.*

"I've been calling you for hours."

"Hello to you, too," I said. "I haven't had service. I've been up in the mountains."

"So you haven't seen the news."

"What are you talking about?"

"I was too late," she said. "It's about Linus and Heather."

"Tell me."

"Turns out I was right about the dead girls," she said. "There's a connection after all. Someone talked—I think it was a disgruntled former employee from Heather's Getty Art Trust."

I was starting to feel excited. "What did they say?"

"The first victim was incidental," she said. "The art student near Windhall, it was supposed to be some kind of tribute to Theo."

"By the performance artist?"

"Exactly. When Linus and Heather caught wind of it, they paid her something obscene to kill more girls, and make it look like it was Theo. It all tied back to the development in Highland Park. Heather knew that her father had something to do with Eleanor's murder, and she was worried that if it ever got out, she wouldn't get the political support she needed to get started on the development."

"Did Heather actually admit that?"

"No. Nobody can find her, of course."

"How are you going to proceed with this?"

"Deborah hasn't been willing to talk to any male journalists, thinks they're all chauvinist pigs. I managed to get in touch with one of her friends, and she says Deborah might be willing to talk to me."

"Good work, Petra."

"When are you coming back?"

"Soon. They're calling my flight right now."

By the time I got back to Los Angeles, I was so tired that I was almost hallucinating. I had gone four days on fractured sleep, not getting more than two hours at a time, and the picture in my head was getting blurrier with each new piece of information. I was about to crawl into bed and fall into a coma when Claudia called.

"Hailey," she said, and I was surprised by how serious she sounded. "I need you to come in and see me."

I felt weird and jumpy. "Can you tell me what's going on?"

"Come in. Let's have a chat."

"Claud, what's going on?"

She sighed. "We need to talk about the results," she said. "Just come in. I'll be around until four today."

I got in my car and drove toward Cedars-Sinai, knotted up with anxiety. Claudia was incredibly frank, and it was a surprise that she didn't tell me what was going on over the phone.

I found her in her office, and she motioned for me to close the door.

"I did the tests," she said. "I ran them twice. I had a friend check the DNA sequence against Eleanor's DNA, and I've got some bad news."

"It's a match."

She held up a finger. "It's *not* a match," she said. "This blood belongs to someone other than Eleanor Hayes."

I shook my head. "That's impossible."

"Is it? Sorry to hear that." She handed me a file. "This is your paperwork. I can't offer you help on your Jane Doe without a contrasting DNA sequence."

"Can you tell me how old the blood was?"

"Afraid not," she said. "You can't date blood through standard DNA processing."

I must have gone pale, because she reached over and grabbed an apple, then offered it to me.

"You eat today?"

"How is that possible?" I said, ignoring the offer. "You think the results could have been tainted by dust, or paint, or something like that? Maybe the fact that it's an old sample means that the results are inaccurate."

"DNA is smaller than dust, first of all," she said. "It's a pretty good sample, all told. You want to tell me what's going on?"

"I don't want to implicate you."

"Suit yourself," she said. "You can buy me dinner next time we see each other."

TWENTY-THREE

After leaving the hospital, I didn't even bother going home. It was a little past three in the afternoon, and I took out my phone to text Petra.

Want to know how the story ends?

A few minutes later, a response came through.

Yes.

On the way to her apartment, I stopped at a doughnut shop to pick up a bag of glazed doughnuts and two cups of coffee. Petra was already waiting outside her apartment when I pulled up to the curb. She climbed inside and took one of the cups of coffee.

"Where are we going?"

"Burbank."

I followed the directions on my phone, which took me past Griffith Park and the Los Angeles Zoo. Burbank had always felt strange to me, the way the sky seemed to zing with electricity, the pregnant stillness of a valley beneath a crest of mountains. The only errands I had ever done in Burbank involved IKEA and a bad acupuncture session.

After double-checking the address on my phone, I parked outside a little row of bungalows that had been converted into offices. They were all cute and perky, with flowers in boxes outside every window.

"Where are we?"

I still felt some of the lingering insomnia, but I was more clear-headed now. My heart was beating quickly, though, and I hoped that Petra could take the information well.

"Dr. Lewis is Theo's son," I said.

"We always thought that was a possibility, but do you have proof?"

"Here's the really tricky bit," I said, nodding. "I don't think Eleanor died."

"What?"

"I don't think she died that night." I took a deep breath. "I think it was part of an elaborate cover-up."

"When did you decide this?"

"It makes sense," I said. "Theo was a magician. People never knew how he pulled off those elaborate sets."

"A set is different from a human body, Hailey. Think about the medical examiner, all the police. Do you think Eleanor played dead long enough to fool them into thinking she was dead? Or are you suggesting that Theo paid them off?"

"This is the really crazy bit," I said. "I think . . . I think it was someone else's body."

She stared at me.

"The blood in Theo's maid's room didn't match Eleanor's DNA. What if they killed someone else, then dressed her up like Eleanor and told the police that there had been an accident?"

"Jesus."

"Let's go talk to Ben."

We got out of the car and walked down the path between the bungalows. There was a directory board in a little courtyard, and I consulted it.

"He's in three," I said. "Let's see if he's in."

We entered the bungalow, where we found an empty waiting room and a receptionist.

"Hello," she said. "Do you have an appointment?"

"No, I thought I'd just drop by," I said. "Is today busy?"

"Is this a medical emergency?"

"No, I'd just like to ask Dr. Lewis a few questions."

"You have insurance?"

"Not since I quit my job."

She looked at an iPad. "He's on a house call," she said. "But I imagine he's on his way back to the office now. Take a seat, I can squeeze you in for a quick appointment when he gets here."

I took a seat, glancing around the office. "Nice place," I said. "It looks like a house."

"It was," she agreed. "These were bungalows for the Disney studio, back in the fifties and sixties."

"So I'm sitting in someone's living room?"

"Yes," she said. "The bookshelf is actually a fireplace."

Petra and I were quiet as we waited. Three patients cycled through, exchanged words with the receptionist, glanced at us, and left. After an hour, the front door opened and Ben came in.

He didn't see me at first, but went straight to his receptionist's desk, then checked the mail.

"You have a walk-in," she said, and gestured at me.

Dr. Lewis glanced up with a polite smile, then realized who I was.

"Hailey," he said. "What are you doing here?"

"I was hoping that we could talk."

Petra stood up and glanced at me.

Ben addressed her. "Did you come together?"

"Yes."

"I'll see you, Hailey, but your friend will have to wait here."

"No insurance," the receptionist said in a low voice, but Dr. Lewis waved a hand.

"Don't worry about that, Sandy," he said, then motioned for me to follow me into his office.

I was so high on adrenaline and nerves that I had lost the ability to make small talk.

"Thanks for not pressing charges," I said.

He frowned.

"You know, the other night," I said. "When I broke into Windhall."

"Leland wanted to, but I managed to talk him out of it."

"Any idea who set that fire?"

"It was electrical." His mouth twitched.

"I know who you are," I said.

He put his bag on his chair, then turned to me and raised an eyebrow. "How about that."

"You're Theo's son."

He occupied himself with some papers by his computer, and for a moment, I thought that he hadn't heard me.

"You're Connie," I added.

He set down his papers and then slowly turned to face me. "Hailey, I'm not willing to talk about this with you," he said. "If you're feeling unwell, I'm happy to give you a diagnosis, but otherwise, I have real patients to see."

"Eleanor didn't die that night, did she?"

He was quiet now, watching me.

"Theo loved Eleanor," I went on. "He would have done *anything* for her. They wanted to leave Los Angeles, but she couldn't, because she had two more movies on her contract. She was threatening to expose Reuben for the things he had done to her friends, and they even wrote a movie about it. When they found out that Reuben Engel was planning to kill her, they decided to run away."

He still didn't say anything. I was on a roll, and my heart was beating so quickly that I thought I might start hyperventilating.

"That's why you asked me to look into Lola DeWitt," I said. "She was the girl in the garden, wasn't she?"

"Who's your friend?" He nodded toward the reception area.

"Her name is Petra," I said. "She was helping me research the article."

"What have you told Heather?"

"Nothing at all."

"I know about your contract with Heather, Hailey. I have trouble believing you haven't told her anything."

"I was planning to report to her," I said. "But when the story started to unfold, I realized that I didn't trust her."

"I don't know which of the journals she gave you," he said. "Not exactly. But I do know Heather, and I know that she's incredibly manipulative. If she gave you something, it would have been a distraction from what really happened. Theo's real journals detailed what really happened, and that's why the prosecution went after them."

"Tell me what really happened."

"I thought you knew everything." He raised an eyebrow. "Didn't you come here to tell me that?"

"I came here to tell you that I have information," I said. "Information that's come at a great cost to me. I can run half a story with that, and you can sue me for misinformation. We'll go back and forth for a few years, and eventually the real story will leak out. In the meantime, however, Heather will go forward with her development in Highland Park, and by the time everyone realizes that her father was a murderer, it will be too late."

Ben's face was impossible to read. He hesitated for a moment, then crossed the room and went out into the reception area.

"Lucy, please cancel my next few appointments," he said. "I have to step out for a minute."

He came back into the office, then closed the door. "We can talk," he said. "But not here."

I was suddenly wary. "I think I'm more comfortable talking here," I said.

Dr. Lewis folded his arms across his chest, annoyed. "You came here to talk to *me*," he said. "If you want to talk, we can talk, but I'm not willing to have such a personal discussion in my place of business. Yes? No?"

"Fine."

"We'll take my car," he said. "I could use a coffee."

We exited into the reception area. Petra looked up from the book that she was reading.

"Can she come with us?" I asked.

"Absolutely not."

"It's okay, Hailey," Petra said. "Go without me."

"I don't know when I'll be back," I said. "It's probably best if you go home. I don't want to keep you here."

"I'll wait."

"Thanks, Petra."

Ben was quiet as we drove out of Burbank, toward the city. I didn't want to ask where we were going, because I didn't want him to know how anxious I was. Finally, he turned off the freeway and down Los Feliz Boulevard, and I realized where he was taking me.

"Griffith Park?" I asked.

"You know a better spot for a private conversation?"

"What about all the tourists?"

"They won't pay attention to us," he said. "They came for the view of the Hollywood sign, the city. We could set something on fire and they wouldn't pay attention."

It was similar to something that Theo had said, about distracting someone while presenting them with the truth all along. The most gifted storytellers were the ones who didn't have to work to hide their secrets, they simply presented you with another option.

We stopped at the Trails Café for coffee, then got back in the car and headed up to the Observatory. It was a quiet Sunday, and Ben found parking near the beginning of the hiking trail.

"Here we are," he said, climbing out. "Let's take a walk."

We walked side by side in silence, until we reached a bench overlooking the city. The trail was quiet at that time of day; it was cold enough that most of the tourists had flocked to the safety of the observatory.

"I guess there's no harm in me talking to you," he said. "Not now."

It took me a moment to realize his meaning. "The fire," I said. "I heard that Theo was inside. Is it true?"

"He was dead before they reached the hospital."

"I'm so sorry." I wondered if Ben had gone through Theo's emails after his death, and seen the message that I had sent him after the fire. I decided not to ask him.

"Tell me what you know," Ben said, facing Los Angeles.

"Reuben Engel was a monster, and Eleanor threatened to expose him," I said. "They wrote a movie and started production, but Reuben found out the movie was really about him. Theo and Eleanor didn't have a lot of options, so they faked a death."

"Not quite."

"It wasn't her body, I know that much," I said. "I found the blood, had it tested."

He shook his head, incredulous. "You've done your job, I'll give you that much."

"It was Lola's body, wasn't it?"

"They didn't plan to kill her," he said softly. "It was never part of the plan."

"Right, so this perfect Eleanor doppelgänger turns up dead, and the real Eleanor doesn't appear to set the story straight."

"Have you seen pictures of Lola?" he asked, turning to give me a cross look.

"Just the shots of Eleanor's dead body. Lola's dead body, I guess."

"She looked exactly like Eleanor. If you've seen *The Man Who Death Forgot,* you've seen her. She was in most of the second half of the movie, because Eleanor refused to come to work. She didn't want to work with Engel."

He was quiet for a moment. "Lola was unstable, though. Nobody would deny that. Eleanor tried to take the girl under her wing, but she was like a parasite. Eleanor found her in her dressing room, going through her things. She would show up at parties, pretending to be Eleanor. It was funny for a while, but Eleanor was already feeling paranoid and trapped."

"So they killed her?"

He cut me another look. "Let me finish telling the story," he said. "No more interruptions."

"Sorry."

"They had been planning to escape for a while," he said. "Eleanor's aunt Penelope had a horse farm in San Diego, and they were going to stay there for a while, then head down to Mexico. Theo wanted to finish making *Last Train to Avalon,* because it was about what really happened—the fact that Reuben Engel was trying to have her killed, that the film industry was corrupt, et cetera.

"They threw a party. It was supposed to be one last chance to say goodbye to friends, without really saying goodbye, of course. But then Lola showed up."

He rubbed his neck and took a sip of coffee. "The producers had been making her promises for a while," he said. "They said that she could be the next Eleanor. They wanted another pretty, bright-eyed starlet, and one they could control. They'd spent all this time and money on Eleanor, but she refused to let them control her life. Lola wanted to be Hollywood's sweetheart, but she couldn't take Eleanor's place unless Eleanor was actually out of the picture."

"Where does Reuben fit into the story?"

"He took Lola to Windhall that night," he said. "I don't think anyone was supposed to get killed. There are conflicting stories about this, but I think Lola was planning to disfigure Eleanor. Cripple her, maybe. They found out that Reuben had the whole thing planned. There was a fight, and Theo stepped in to help Eleanor."

I pictured Lola's famous injuries, the hole through the heart, the black eye.

"Did Theo punch Lola?"

"Theo would never," he said. "But there was a struggle. She fell off the balcony on the third story and landed on the second-story roof."

I frowned. "There was no third story balcony on Windhall."

"There was," he said. "It was part of the renovations when Theo moved into Windhall. They had it removed after Lola died."

"The spike," I said. "I thought they stabbed her through the back."

He shook his head. "She fell from the balcony and landed on the roof," he repeated. "There was a row of gothic Victorian spikes. She landed on one, and while the party continued, Theo moved her inside."

"Into the maid's room," I said. "That's why there was blood on the windowsill."

"You should have been a cop. You figured it all out."

"They must have taken the spikes down," I said, thinking. "That's why there was a delay."

"Eleanor panicked."

"What about the dress, though? Lola was wearing Eleanor's famous green dress."

"The dress never belonged to Eleanor," he explained patiently. "It was an iconic image that the press seized on."

"Why didn't they tell the police what really happened? If Lola was really the aggressor, Eleanor had an excuse."

He looked sad. "It wasn't that simple," he said. "For one, Los Angeles was completely owned by the studios. Eleanor had been receiving threats, notes from stalkers, for years. Without the studio's protection, she wouldn't have been safe."

"Awfully cavalier, to just let someone die."

"Lola was dead," he said softly. "There was nothing they could do for her. And she was the one who attacked Eleanor."

"What about the medical examiner? Didn't he realize that it wasn't Eleanor?"

"The man was a drunk," he said. "Besides, Eleanor's aunt Pen was in on the plan. She drove up from San Diego straightaway, identified the body. She was hysterical, they couldn't contain her. She was calling out for Theo's head. All an act, you see."

"And Theo was willing to risk going to jail over a crime he didn't commit?"

"It happened so quickly, I don't think they even considered the consequences."

"So that's why Theo came back," I said. "It was because of the new death. He was worried that people would break into Windhall and find out what really happened."

Ben nodded.

"But why did he leave the house alone for so long? Wasn't he worried that someone would break in earlier?" I asked. "I mean, why didn't he destroy the house as soon as he left Los Angeles?"

"There were attempts," he admitted. "At first, Theo considered having the house torn down, but Leland said that the construction crews might find the hidden room. Instead, Leland filed a petition to have it declared a historic monument. It's one of the oldest remaining buildings in Los Angeles, as I'm sure you're aware. Or *was*, I should say, since it's gone now."

I cleared my throat. "There's something else," I said. "Something I never figured out. There was a film."

Ben frowned. "What film?"

"It was just a clip, really," I said. "Shot in Eleanor's dressing room. Less than thirty seconds long. A man walks toward her and starts to attack her. I couldn't figure out who made it."

Ben closed his eyes. "Ahh, yes. I know what you're talking about."

"Was it Engel? The assailant, I mean."

He nodded. "It was good timing. Engel showed up to set drunk half the time anyway, and from what I've heard, he was wasted that day. Jules was behind the camera, and he turned it on Engel."

I was taken aback. "If they had proof that Engel attacked Eleanor, wouldn't that force the studio's hand? They'd have to deal with the problem."

Ben held up a finger. "They couldn't prove it *was* Engel," he said. "His back was to the camera. That film was one of a chain of events that led to the creation of *Last Train to Avalon*."

I had been studying Eleanor for years, chasing down someone I thought had been her assailant and murderer, but all along, her studio had been the one to betray her. I couldn't believe that they would treat her as a prized commodity and yet do nothing to ensure her safety.

"How did you feel when they told you about all this? Were you still a kid?" I asked.

"We lived on a farm back east. Of course, those were the days before Internet, so I was a young man before I even knew that they had been famous. Our telephone barely worked most of the time." Ben paused. "How did you find out that I was Connie?"

"I went to Vermont."

He looked confused for a moment, then seemed to realize what I was talking about.

"They were so careful," he said quietly. "They thought of everything. How on earth did you find out?"

"I didn't, actually," I admitted. "Petra is the one who figured it out. There was a lab developing number on the back of a photograph. Grafton, Vermont. I went there and met someone there who remembered Flannery, and you, of course. He called you Connie."

"You know, a part of me always thought this day would come," he said quietly. "I thought that someone would find out the truth. I used to imagine what I would say to them, how I would explain it. It's not my job to explain it, though. It's Theo's. But I guess it's too late for that."

"Didn't you want people to know the truth?" I said. "If you knew that Theo was innocent, and you knew what really happened, wouldn't you want others to know?"

He seemed to be at a loss for words. "Theo was always the storyteller, not me," he said. "Nobody could take a narrative out of his hands. He was adamant that we keep living our lives the way we always had. I knew that revealing the truth would have been a violation of his trust. Privacy was so important."

"That doesn't seem to leave you with much agency."

"They didn't tell me until I was fifteen." He took another sip of his coffee. "By the time I realized, I didn't see what good it would do to change things around. I thought they were ordinary people."

"And why did he agree to talk to me?"

Ben gave me a rueful smile. "He wanted to see how much you knew," he said. "If you knew about me, about my family. That's part of the reason he's kept this charade up, you know, all these years. He didn't want anyone else's name to get dragged through the mud."

"Dr. Lewis—"

"Really, Hailey, call me Ben. I think we've been through enough to have passed formality."

"I looked up Lola," I said. "It said that her date of death was 1951. If Lola's body was the one they used, how is that possible?"

"When the studio realized what had happened, they fixed things. They didn't want it to lead back to them. By then, Theo had been long gone. They couldn't find him."

"And Eleanor changed her name to Rebecca Lewis."

"Yes." Ben closed his eyes.

"She died recently, didn't she? That's why Theo was ready for the story to come out."

"Last year. Throat cancer."

I cleared my throat and rubbed my hands together, unsure of what to say. I had been around enough death to be squeamish with shallow condolences, but Eleanor's death truly did feel like a loss, and Ben had been extraordinarily compassionate with me.

"It's hard. It must have been hard, I mean," I said.

"It's fine."

I finished my coffee, which had gone cold. Los Angeles glimmered in the distance, a flat bas-relief of the city I thought that I knew so well.

"There were so many people," I said. "They looked everywhere, that night, if you can believe the articles. How on earth did they hide Eleanor?"

Ben gave me a rueful smile. "You've been to the house," he said. "You must have seen it."

"Seen what?"

He drew a shape in the air. "There was a little door in the wall, leading to the neighbor's house. He was away, filming something in Italy. They stole through the garden and disappeared, and then Theo came back."

"Wow. Of course."

We were both silent for a moment. It almost felt companionable.

"I used to imagine meeting him," I said. "I spent my whole childhood wishing that I could have grown up in that world of movie stars and glamour. I didn't know whether I should fear him or want to be his friend. But I definitely wanted to be a part of that gilded life."

Ben nodded.

"One last question," I said. "The second set of footprints in the garden. Who did they belong to?"

He sighed and shifted in his seat. "I guess it doesn't matter anymore," he said. "She died twenty years ago. He never wanted the truth to get out about her."

"It was Marja," I said, slowly realizing the truth.

"Yes, Fritz's mother," he said. "She was the one who helped Theo move the body to the garden, and afterward, she was the one who boarded up the maid's room and covered it with wallpaper. That's why Fritz was always so unfriendly to you; he didn't want you asking questions. I don't think they would have gotten away with any of it without her."

All of the details I had collected over the years went flipping through my head like playing cards loosed from a deck. There was one detail that stuck in my head.

"The shoes," I said. "The second set of footprints. They belonged to a man."

Ben gave me a sad smile. "What did they always say about Theo?" he asked.

"That he was a murderer . . . ?" I was drawing a blank.

Ben gave me a look of infinite patience. "Every detail," he said. "He thought of every detail, in all of his films, down to the rip in a pair of stockings. He knew that all the household staff would be questioned about that night, and he didn't want to implicate Marja. He gave her a pair of men's dress shoes."

"And it never occurred to anyone that it wasn't actually a man?"

"No, never," he said. "Not until you came along. Theo was so close to getting away with it."

TWENTY-FOUR

It was three days before Halloween. Hollywood and Sunset bore the usual traces of the season: the advertisements for pumpkin patches, witches and orange streamers hanging from light posts, children running around in partial costumes, giving them a test-drive. The air was unseasonably warm and dry as the inside of a clay kiln. I parked on De Longpre Avenue, then walked toward the *Lens* office.

Petra was waiting for me in the courtyard of the building.

"You ready?" she asked.

"Only one way to find out."

It was a typical Monday in the office, writers milling around each other's desks and slouched over computers and stacks of papers. We got a few nods as we walked down the hall toward Alexa's office, and I knocked on her door.

She answered a moment later. "Max," she said. Her expression was cool and distant. "Petra. What can I do for you?"

"I have a story for you."

"I'm not interested." She folded her arms across her chest. "I'm in the middle of something, and I've got an appointment at three o'clock."

"That gives me fifteen minutes."

"Max—"

"I know that I don't deserve a second chance," I said. "I wasn't completely honest with you. But, please, Alexa, hear me out."

She glanced between me and Petra. "All right, come in," she said. "You've got two minutes."

I followed her into the office and pulled out my satchel. "I know this is going to sound crazy," I said. "But please let me explain. I know what really happened to Eleanor Hayes."

Alexa folded her arms and leaned back against her desk.

"Eleanor Hayes," I said, "matinee idol and American sweetheart, died in Maine last year. She had throat cancer, and she passed away surrounded by family and friends."

She shook her head. "If this is a conspiracy theory, then this meeting is over."

"You've always been interested in stories about corporations against individuals," I said, speaking quickly. "This is one of those stories. Eleanor Hayes was threatening to reveal Reuben Engel's crimes against women, and the studio wanted to get rid of her. They couldn't just fire her, or there would be an outcry from the audiences who loved her. Reuben was scared that even if they fired her, the story would still get out. He sent someone to disfigure her."

"Max—"

"Theo found out what was going on," I said. "There was an actress, Lola DeWitt, who looked just like Eleanor, and who had also been stalking her for months. *That's* the body they found in the garden. Lola showed up to the party and something happened, I think she attacked Eleanor, anyway, she died—and they pretended that it was Eleanor's body."

"I think I've had enough," Alexa said. She crossed the room and opened her door.

"He's telling the truth, Alexa," Petra said. "I can verify all of this."

Alexa raised a hand to stop her. "You're new at this," she said, then turned back to me. "Hailey, I know you've done some great coverage, but that doesn't mean you're not susceptible to believing a wild theory."

"I've done my research on this. I have the paperwork to show that Eleanor changed her name to Rebecca Lewis. I can take you to where Lola's body is buried—"

There was a knock on the door, and Jordan poked his head in.

"Your three o'clock is here," he said. "He said that he has information about Heather Engel-Feeny."

"You need to go, Max."

"I have someone who can verify all of this," I said.

Alexa folded her arms across her chest. "Who could possibly verify all of this, other than Theo?"

"That would be me."

We all looked to see Ben standing in Alexa's door. Alexa frowned.

"Are you Dr. Lewis?" she asked. "My three o'clock?"

"Yes."

She glanced between us, uncertain. "And you two know each other?"

Ben closed the door behind him. "That's why I'm here," he said. "I don't think we can keep the truth hidden any longer."

"Remind me why we're meeting," she said, frowning.

"I wanted to validate a few points."

She glanced between us, then threw up her hands, exasperated. "All right," she said finally. "Have a seat. I'll give you a chance to explain yourselves, but be warned, I'm very weary of sensationalist bullshit."

We all sat down.

"Now, tell me—succinctly—why you're both here," Alexa directed.

I began slowly, telling her all the disparate pieces of evidence I had gathered, from the blueprints showing the hidden maid's room, and finally the blood stains that had seeped into the wood of the windowsill. I told her about Lola DeWitt and the missing journals, about Reuben's threats toward women and the fact that Eleanor wanted to expose him. And finally, I told her about going to Vermont and finding the man who remembered Eleanor, not as a matinee goddess, but simply as a woman looking for redemption.

When I had finished telling her everything, Alexa turned to Ben.

"How do you fit into this?" she said. "If you're Theo's doctor, aren't you bound by confidentiality?"

"I'm not here as Theo's doctor," he said. "I'm here as Theo's son."

"Excuse me?"

"Theo and Eleanor were my parents."

Alexa glanced around the room, looking at each of us individually. "Come on."

"I know you're a busy woman, and I respect the work that you do," Ben said. "I wouldn't dream of wasting your time."

"Can you prove this insane paternity claim?"

"Absolutely," he said. "If you want DNA evidence, I can provide it. In the meantime, however, here's an album of family photographs. All of them taken after Eleanor was supposed to be dead, of course."

He passed her a photo album, and Alexa quietly flipped through the photographs. I watched as Alexa pored over shots of Eleanor and Theo working together in a garden, sometimes accompanied by Ben, sometimes not. There were pictures of meals, of dancing, of quiet moments of reflection. None of it matinee quality, all of it the boring rituals of everyday life that most celebrities never got to have.

"I heard that Theo died when his house caught fire," Alexa said. "Is that true?"

"I'm afraid it is."

"If you're really Theo's son," Alexa said slowly, "why would you give us all this information? Why now?"

"It's not fun to grow up with a lie. I've always wanted the truth to come out, to have the world stop hating my father for something he didn't do. I couldn't do it while my parents were alive, though, because the world would come rushing in. They would have sacrificed everything for nothing."

She seemed lost in thought for a moment, and then she stepped outside and cleared her schedule so that we'd have an hour free to talk. At the end of that hour, Jordan knocked on her office door to say that her next appointment was there, but she waved him away. In all, we sat in her office for four hours, talking and explaining everything that had happened.

I could see that Alexa was deciding whether she could trust me. Ben promised to give her whatever she needed to publish and verify the story, stipulating again and again that his name was to remain out of it. When she had asked all her questions, and sat patiently through all the answers, she said that she was going to think about how to proceed. She promised that she would call us the next day, and if she decided to commission the article, that she would draw up contracts for both of us.

"Just one more question," she said, as we stood to leave. "People pay homage to Eleanor Hayes's tombstone at the Hollywood Forever Cemetery every day. Whose body is *really* buried there?"

Ben cleared his throat. "It's empty."

"And what did you do with Lola DeWitt's body? I hope you didn't just dump it over a cliff somewhere."

Ben looked offended. "Ms. Levine, please remember that I was not complicit in any part of this affair. And I can assure you that my parents were not barbarians. She's buried in Glendale."

"Under her own name?"

"No," he said. "But Theo's lawyer allocated some funds so that she could be buried under her own headstone, should the time come."

"I'd say that time has come."

"There's one more thing," he said. "It's about Theo's last movie." He reached into his briefcase and removed a blank DVD case, then set it on Alexa's desk. "It survived, you know. And it reveals everything that happened."

Alexa stared at the DVD.

"I was thinking," Ben said. "If you wanted to show it, that's your prerogative. It might go nicely with the release of the story. I heard that the *Lens* is struggling to make ends meet."

The room was silent as Ben stood and gave me a small smile, then nodded his head and left.

———————

Things happened very quickly over the next few days. A few hours after my meeting with Ben and Alexa, Leland called to update me on Lola's body.

"We've purchased a plot for Lola at Forest Lawn," he said. "We decided it would be best to move her body into a new space, rather than just giving her a new headstone. I don't think she has any remaining family, but we're still going to give her her own headstone."

"When will it be ready?"

"Two days," he said. "You're welcome to write about it, if you like. We'll have a small ceremony."

"I'll be there," I said.

Alexa got in touch with me the next morning. "I found a venue to show the movie," she said. "I've watched it three times now. I think it's one of Theo's best."

"Where are you going to show it?"

"The New Beverly," she said.

"Quentin Tarantino's movie theater? The one near Milk Bar?"

"Apparently Tarantino's always been a big fan of Theo's movies."

"Are you going to run the story?"

"Yes," she said. "And I'm going to let you write it."

"Thanks, Alexa."

"It's not a job offer," she said. "I'd like to be very clear on that. You're writing it as a freelancer."

"I understand."

"Heather's lawsuit against the *Lens* is going forward," she said. "For your breach of contract. It's going to be very public."

I waited.

"The *Lens* has never been one to back down from the threat of power, though," she went on. "I think it might actually be good publicity. It'll lend an air of veracity to the story we're trying to tell. Plus, Heather seems to have absconded from the city, so that might look bad in court."

"So the lawsuit is a good thing."

"I didn't say that," she warned. "But you're off the hook, for now."

———————

The next day, I went to meet up with Leland at Forest Lawn Cemetery, and was only slightly surprised to see that Ben was talking with Leland. Leland waved when he saw me.

"Did you know?" I asked Leland. "Did you know about all of this?"

He inclined his head but said nothing.

Forest Lawn was quiet at that time of the morning, only a few families come to lay flowers on the graves of their loved ones, as well as groundskeepers mowing the grass. I doubted that Lola's grave would have ever gotten much traffic even if it hadn't been anonymous.

We were quiet as the old coffin was lowered into a fresh grave, this time with Lola's name on it, and then the three of us left the cemetery together in silence. When we reached the parking lot, Leland turned and offered me his hand, which I shook.

"I don't think I'll be seeing you again, Hailey," he said. "Take care of yourself. I hope the rest of your career is a little less . . . illegal."

"Thanks," I said. "Thanks for facilitating all of this."

When he was gone, I turned to Ben.

"Do I get to know where Rebecca was buried?" I said.

He shook his head. "I'm afraid not," he said. "I'd like for her to remain anonymous."

"Can you give me a hint?"

"She's somewhere that she loved," he said.

I knew it wasn't fair for me to ask, but I couldn't resist. "And what about Theo?" I asked. "Will he be buried next to her?"

Ben hesitated. "You don't need to worry about them anymore, Hailey. Just write a decent article."

I didn't think that the New Beverly would be able to arrange a screening for *Last Train to Avalon* for at least a week, but after returning home from Lola's burial, Alexa gave me a call.

"The theater's really excited about Theo's new movie," she said. "They want to do three screenings this weekend. The first is going to be tomorrow. Sort of a Halloween special."

"You're kidding."

"I'd like to release the article tomorrow, too," she said. "Article in the morning, movie at night. Do you think you'll be finished by then?"

"I just need a few more hours."

"I had a meeting with the district attorney this morning," she said. "I wanted to let her office know about the article before our story was published."

The legal ramifications of the story hadn't even occurred to me; I had been so busy chasing my own answers.

"She would like me to pass along a message," Alexa went on. "No more vigilante work. She quoted a figure, some amount of money that you've cost the Angeleno taxpayers with your little escapades, but I can't remember it off the top of my head."

"Sorry."

Alexa gave a dry laugh. "No, you're not," she said.

"I'm glad the truth is out," I said. "Nobody deserves to have that kind of blame on their head."

"Well, don't get all hung up on that," she said. "Not yet. We need you to focus all your energy on the upcoming article, if we're going to publish it tomorrow."

The article was published the next day. I had gone on several days of fragmented sleep in order to finish it, but in the end, it was worth it. Ben and I had sat down for hours to go over all the missing details, and the result had been a fifteen-thousand-word feature on the *Lens* website. I had been incredibly explicit about certain things—the years in Vermont, Reuben's threats against women, the way Marja had helped move the body into the garden—and skimped on other details. We had decided to only identify Ben as Conrad.

When the article was published, I decided to give myself a well-earned day off. I hadn't had time to do laundry or clean the house in weeks, and I was looking forward to sitting down in the garden with a pot of coffee. I turned off my Internet and ignored the copy of the *Los Angeles Times* that had arrived in my driveway earlier that morning. There would be time for all of that later.

I took my time doing my chores, cleaning every surface and purging all my waste baskets, then plumping up my couch cushions.

I threw open all my windows and gathered up the old newspapers that had been collecting in bins around the house, then did a thorough dusting job.

I went out for a late lunch on Franklin Avenue, enjoying the fact that I had time to sit and watch the stream of people walk past. Hipsters, fashionistas, aspiring young comedians who hadn't shaved or exercised in months. All of them eager for recognition, eager to make a name for themselves in Los Angeles. There was a kind of obtuse snobbery present in all of that, and I was slightly sickened to reflect that that had been me, once, not too long ago.

That evening, I got ready at my house, then drove over to Madeleine's, where I would meet up with Thierry and Petra. We had all decided to head over to the premiere together.

Everyone was already there when I arrived, and they quietly climbed into my car. Nobody spoke as we drove toward Melrose, and I found parking a few blocks away so that we could walk.

"So, Hailey," Thierry said, breaking our silence. "This movie any good, or what?"

"I haven't actually seen it yet."

"You gotta be kidding me," he said. "You spent years of your life chasing down any kind of information about Theo, and when you finally get the most important piece of the puzzle, you don't seem to care?"

"I've had a lot on my mind lately, T," I said. "I'm here to watch it tonight, aren't I? I didn't need to see it first. Alexa watched it; she said it was good. I trust her."

As we approached the cinema, I saw that there was a crowd on the sidewalk. It didn't register until we were nearly within shouting distance that the crowd seemed to be for the New Beverly. I glanced at Petra, and she shrugged.

"You really think Theo had that many fans?" I asked.

"I think people like a spectacle," she replied. "The theater did a pretty good job of promoting the movie, considering they only had a few days to get this together."

The line of people was so big that we had to elbow our way through. Someone was calling my name, and I turned to see Brian, standing with Ford and Lapin. He came over and grinned.

"Well done, my man," he said. "Never thought you'd manage to pull something like this off."

"Thanks." That was Brian for you—last time I had seen him, he had been celebrating the fact that I was getting publicly fired, but now that I had a tiny bit of celebrity, the past was forgotten. I was surprised to find that I didn't care one way or the other.

He turned to Petra. "You can have your job back, you know," he said.

"I've already spoken to Alexa."

Brian leaned in and gave me a conspiratorial grin. "Have you heard about Heather?"

"What about?"

"Conspiracy to commit murder," he said. "They can't find her anywhere, man, but they will. You should write the story when they do."

"I'll think about it."

Once we were inside the theater, we ran into Marty, the *Lens* photographer. He gave me a big hug and clapped me on the back.

"You're a legend," he said. "This is going to bring in a ton of revenue for the magazine. Looks like we're not going to get evicted for at *least* three years, thanks to you."

Praise had always made me squeamish, so I diverted the conversation. "You working tonight?"

"Officially, yes," he said. "I'll have to show you my pictures later. There are some seriously famous people here. Marion Cotillard was standing in the lobby a minute ago, but I think you missed her. And then there were three old ladies with walkers and oxygen tanks. Turns out they were debutantes in *Gone with the Wind*. And speaking of *Gone with the Wind*, Olivia de Havilland is here."

"Oh my God," Madeleine said. "I forgot she was still alive."

"She's a riot," Marty said. "Still a babe. You should go talk to her."

"Afterward," I agreed. "I think they're going to start soon."

We found our seats in the little theater, and the lights dimmed to announce that the movie was about to begin.

There was no studio card at the beginning. The opening credits began right away, and I felt a chill when I saw Eleanor Hayes's name imprinted over the shot of a train traveling along tracks through the desert.

Last Train to Avalon appeared after the last of the names had rolled, and a wave of applause spread throughout the theater. People clapped and cheered, and someone behind me whistled so loudly that my ears rang.

Madeleine squeezed my arm. "You did this," she said. "Everyone is here because of you."

"I'm the reason everyone *isn't* here, too," I whispered back.

It took her a moment to decipher my meaning. "Theo's death is not your fault," she said. "Heather set fire to Windhall, and Theo was old. He probably didn't have much time left, anyway."

"You know that Olivia de Havilland is pushing a hundred, right? Theo could have had another ten years in him."

"You exposed what really happened," she said. "That matters. Theo might have died, but if you hadn't stepped in, he would have died without letting the truth come out."

I turned my attention back to the screen without saying anything else. I had been so distracted that the first ten minutes of the movie had been nothing but images: black-and-white cacti, oil derricks reeling against a turbulent sky, a young girl clutching her skirt as a wind threatened to spirit her away.

Eleanor's love interest, played by Robert Taylor, arrived at a nondescript building that resembled the front of MGM. He pushed back his hat and grinned.

"Never thought I'd make it," he said. "But I'm here now. Wait'll they see me back home!"

The movie was fast-paced and surreal. The cinematography was beautiful, with gray expanses of land punctuated by diagonal shadows and winding rivers. It captured the feel of old California, the black-and-white images I had imagined as I read through Theo's journals.

Eleanor was ravishing, no longer a sweet, girl-next-door type, but a tough businesswoman who made it clear that she wouldn't let anyone push her around. Things appeared to be going well for her at first: she scored a major scoop on a murder that happened in Malibu, and gained popularity with the other writers at her paper. As her star began to rise, however, the new editor in chief, played by a menacing Charlton Heston, began to bully her.

It took me a while to realize that Robert Taylor's character was meant to be Theo. There was a scene where Eleanor and Robert conferred together, trying to figure out how they could show the world how awful the editor in chief truly was, and Eleanor turned to Robert.

"Nobody will believe us, you know. This is a life that everyone wants, and we're on the verge of throwing it all away."

He stroked her face. "Our lives are fun, but not for us."

Petra sat next to me, and I felt her hand close down on my arm.

———————

When the movie was over, I let myself get carried out of the theater by the crush of people moving toward the exit.

"There's a party," Petra said, turning to me. "I think it's at Ford's house. Should we drive together?"

"I think I'll meet you there," I said. "I need a bit of fresh air first."

I drove around for an hour, too wired to stop anywhere for longer than five minutes. First I drove up to the Franklin Canyon Reservoir, but the silence was too eerie, so I headed down Mulholland and studied the skyline from a distance. I got back in my car and started driving again, and I didn't realize where I was going until I was almost there.

I hadn't been to see Windhall since the fire, and I was surprised by how quiet the neighborhood was. It had been almost a week since my arrest and the fire, followed by my trip to Vermont, but I still expected to find someone waiting for me when I pulled up in front of Theo's gates and parked. Instead, I was the only one there.

The main gates had been thrown open at some point during the fire to allow the firefighters access to the house, and nobody had bothered to close them. They hung open like broken wings. The swaths of vines that had once strangled the wall surrounding the property had been singed in patches, and great chunks had been burned out of them; most of the gardens had burned and black patches were carved into the ground.

The house itself was difficult to look at. It hardly looked like Windhall anymore: the gaping holes where the windows had once been were hollow and cruel, and all the paint on the exterior was streaked with soot and smoke. The moonlight was bright enough that I could make out a fair amount of damage, and it reminded me of the dreams that I used to have about strolling up the main drive to find a ghostly procession of guests and champagne.

The front of the house was caved in, and there was no clear way to get inside. I decided to try my luck entering around the back of the house, and took the little garden path flanked by singed figs, where I had once followed Flannery.

I had almost reached the desiccated orange grove when I realized that I wasn't alone. A man stood at the edge of the ruined orchard, hands in his pockets. His back was to me, and in the darkness, for just a moment, I thought it might be Theo. Then the man turned; Fritz.

"So," he said. "You've come back to see the damage you caused."

"I didn't do this," I said. "I was in jail that night. Don't worry, the police are going to figure out who was responsible."

"You're the one responsible," he said without venom. "The world had forgotten about him. They would have left him alone, if you could have let the story rest, just the way it was. You couldn't leave it alone, could you?"

"I'm sorry," I said.

"I don't want your sorries," he said. "Theo doesn't need your pity. You think you fooled him into inviting you into his house, but he was smarter than you. He was always smarter than you."

I glanced up at the facade of the old house, the trailing roses now scorched to twigs; the gaping windows and the crumbling old roof. I thought about all the old orchards that had been razed to make way for film, and in turn all the old silent stars who had been left in the dark when they became useless, mute.

"Did you follow them to Vermont?" I asked. I wondered if Fritz knew that his mother had helped Theo with the body in the garden. "Or did you stay here?"

"No more questions, Mr. Hailey." He reached into his pocket and produced an envelope. "Theo wanted you to have this."

"What is it?"

"I'm sure I don't know. It belongs to a locker at Union Station. Goodbye, Mr. Hailey."

I waited until he had disappeared around the side of the house before I slipped a finger under the envelope flap. A key fell out into my hand. I studied it for a moment, then looked inside the envelope. There was a note, and when I took it out, I saw that it was written in Theo's familiar, spidery handwriting.

I read the note two, three, four times before the meaning registered with me. With shaking hands, I took out my cell phone and called Marty.

"Jesus, Marty, pick up!"

When he finally answered, I could hear that he was somewhere crowded. There was a lot of background noise.

"Hailey, my man! Where'd you disappear to?"

"Where are you?"

"We're at the Top Hat in Silver Lake. Everyone's celebrating."

"You have your camera?"

"Sure, what's up?"

"Stay there," I said. "I'll be there in ten minutes."

I tucked my phone in my pocket and took off at a sprint, nearly tripping over the ruined garden path in my haste.

TWENTY-FIVE

I drove down Benedict Canyon Road so erratically that I was surprised nobody pulled me over. I slowed down a bit when I hit Beverly Hills proper, but still managed to get to the bar in record time. People spilled out onto the sidewalk, and I had to push my way through the crowd to look for Marty.

Someone grabbed my arm, and I turned to see Madeleine.

"Where did you go?" she said. She almost had to shout to be heard over the din.

"He set me up!" I said. "Theo set me up!"

"What?" She pointed to her ear to indicate that she hadn't heard me.

"Where's Marty?"

"I think he's by the bar!"

It took another five minutes of pushing through the thick crowd to find Marty, and when we did, it was clear that he was beyond sloshed.

"I need to see your camera!" I shouted.

"Man, have a drink! You've earned it."

"Your camera! Where is it?"

Marty was so drunk that I had to repeat the request three or four times, but he finally agreed to lead me out to his car. His camera was in the trunk, and he got it out for me.

"I'm gonna boot and rally," he said, swaying on his feet. "You help yourself to my darkroom."

He wandered off into the bushes to vomit. Madeleine and I leaned on the trunk of his car, and I started going through the pictures.

"What are you looking for?" she asked.

"Theo planned this whole thing," I said. "Marty took shots of the event tonight. I'll show you."

"What do you mean?"

I gave her the note and the key that Fritz had given me.

You see? Everything works itself out by the end of the film.
P.S. Did you get a look at Olivia? Not all of our friends fade away into dim obscurity.

She read it, then frowned. "What does that mean?"

I slowly shook my head. The only thing I could do was laugh. "It means that he was at the theater tonight. Theo was at the premiere."

"You don't sound like you're joking," Mad said quietly.

I didn't reply, trying to piece together everything that had happened after my last visit with Theo. I had broken into Windhall, been arrested for it, then returned home to find that the house had gone up in flames.

"Fuck," I whispered, rubbing my temples. "How far back does it go? Did he plan this whole thing?"

"What are you talking about? Hailey—take a few deep breaths. Are you *sure* Theo sent you this note?"

I looked at her. "I'm a moron. I want that on the record."

"Theo died in the fire," Mad insisted. "There was an ambulance—paramedics . . ."

I gave a wild laugh. "You don't think he could have arranged that? I didn't exactly check their credentials. Theo could have arranged this whole thing."

She put a grounding hand on my arm. "What does this key belong to?"

"It's a box at Union Station," I said. "He left me something."

"Any idea what?"

"I have lots of ideas."

I passed her the camera. Madeleine squinted at the screen. "What am I looking at?"

"At the back of the theater," I said. "Zoom in."

She toggled the zoom button until she could see what I was trying to show her. "Jesus," she said. "Is that really Theo? How on earth did he come to the premiere without anyone seeing him?"

"It's what we always said about him," I said. "It's easiest to hide in plain sight. Everyone had already mourned him, they'd already moved on."

"I thought he died! Isn't that what you wrote in your article?"

"I'm so fucking stupid," I said. "I can't believe I fell for it twice."

Petra came out into the parking lot and spotted us.

"Hey," she said. "I thought you left." She came over to join us and glanced between me and Madeleine. "What's going on?"

"The story isn't over," I said. "Theo didn't die in the fire."

She didn't laugh. "What are you talking about?"

I quickly filled her in, and Madeleine passed her the camera. Petra's eyes widened when she saw the picture of Theo.

"What's in the locker?" she asked. "Have you told Alexa what's going on?"

"Not yet."

"We could still find him," she urged. "He's probably somewhere nearby."

"What's the point?"

"This makes an even bigger story than we thought," she said. "He escaped the fire that burned his house down."

"He's gone," I said quietly. "He wouldn't write me this note unless he had already planned his escape. He's long gone."

"What's in the locker?" Madeleine piped up. "We need to find out."

"Sure," I said, without much enthusiasm. "Let's go to Union Station."

Union Station was one of my favorite buildings in Los Angeles. The gorgeous art deco building was flanked by palm trees, and the high ceilings and decadent floors always made me feel like I had stepped back in time to the 1930s. Even late at night, the station wasn't quiet; as the main hub of Los Angeles transportation, there were always people arriving, leaving, and lingering in the hallways.

Marty had disappeared from the bar's parking lot by the time we were ready to leave, so we took his camera with us. Once we were at Union Station, we found the locker that corresponded to the key that Theo had left for me in the envelope. I hesitated before sticking the key in the lock, and turned to look at Petra. She nodded.

The key stuck for a moment, and then it turned and I opened the locker. Inside was a parcel wrapped in brown paper. It was about the size of a coffee table book, and I had an idea of what it might be before I undid the tape and removed the paper.

"It's a painting," Madeleine said, once I had unwrapped it. "Why would he leave you a painting?"

"It's not just any painting," I said. "It's a Paul de Longpré paint-ing. It's a joke. Theo told me that de Longpré was the first real celebrity in Los Angeles."

"That must be worth a fortune."

I didn't respond, because I had noticed that there was another envelope inside the locker. I opened it and found another note: *That which burns brightly burns quickly, but oh, see how it burns.*

"Wasn't that the last line of the film?" Madeleine leaned over my shoulder.

There was something else in the envelope. I slid it out, and it took a minute for the meaning to sink in.

"Hailey," Petra said. "Is that . . . ?"

It was a single, spent match.

"The fire at Windhall," I said slowly. "I thought for sure it was Heather."

"So . . . Theo planned this whole thing?" Petra asked.

"My God," Madeleine said.

"Why would he do that, though?" Petra asked.

"He'd wanted to get rid of that house for years," I said. "Ben told me so himself."

"You think Dr. Lewis was in on this? I thought he was helping you write the article."

"I thought so, too," I said. "Maybe this whole thing was about revenge against Reuben."

"He must have been looking for a writer. You thought you were looking for him, but he was waiting for you," Madeleine said.

"But why?"

"Because of her," Petra said. She was holding Marty's camera, and she was looking at a photo. "Look."

Madeleine and I moved to stand next to her, and she showed us the picture. It was one I had skipped past while looking for Theo. Marty had taken it before the film started, when everyone was milling around in the lobby. It was a throwaway snap, or at least I would have thought it was. It was the type of shot you take when you're too busy to focus on a single subject.

Standing to the left of the doors, arms around herself against the cold, was a face that I had studied so many times that I could see it in my dreams; indeed I had, many times. The years had been kind to her, or at least, kind enough. So many years had passed that I wouldn't have recognized her if she had passed by me in the lobby, but on her face was one of the most famous smiles in the world.

It was Eleanor Hayes.

ACKNOWLEDGMENTS

Books may get written in the privacy and solitude of dark rooms, but they do not exist as the efforts of a single person.

First and foremost, I owe a huge debt of gratitude to my agent, Annie Bomke. Thank you for taking a huge risk—and for investing weeks, months, years—on an unknown writer. Thank you for your honesty, your fast responses, kind words of encouragement, and all the hours you spent helping me scrape my ideas into a digestible form. I am constantly humbled and honored by your sharp memory and how much effort you dedicate to the work of others.

Huge thanks to fellow noir and Los Angeles history enthusiast Katie McGuire, who was my wonderful editor. Thank you so much for choosing my book. Thank you also to Claiborne Hancock for your encouraging words, and thank you to all their colleagues at Pegasus Books.

I am hugely indebted to my family, both near and far: all the Barrys in Northern California, the Christens-Barrys in Maryland, the Leones in Minnesota, the Hinshaws in Michigan and Georgia. Even though our geographical distance means that I see some of you only once every few years, I feel lucky that I am related to each and every one of you. Thanks and love especially to Owen Christens-Barry, a cousin who is more like a brother, and his wonderful parents, Bill and Carol. You all mean a lot to me.

Thank you to Marsh's extended family (especially Suellen) for welcoming me into the fold. I am grateful to have been accepted by your wonderful group.

Special thanks to Christine and Tony DeMaria for dinners and for checking in. Thank you for reminding me, again and again, that nothing creative thrives in a vacuum. Thanks and love go to Natalie Carmen, my earliest extended family. I love your family and appreciate everything that you've done for me. Pierre Bienaime—I'm not sure you realize how much your enduring friendship has meant to me over the years. Thank you for inspiring me when we were at university together, then visiting me once we no longer lived in the same zip code, then continuing to reach out and call when we weren't on the same continent.

I would have been lost without the direction and encouragement of some incredible teachers at UC Santa Cruz: J. Guevara, who introduced me to Richard Brautigan and the power of short stories; Kate Schatz, who taught me how fun writing can be in a group of like-minded people; Natasha V., who championed my freakish ideas and crossed out 70 percent of the work I turned in. All of you made me a much better writer.

Love and thanks to my local writer friends: Louise Wakeling, Linda Moon, Becky Head, and Rebecca Lang. I deeply appreciate all the time and effort you give in critiquing each piece I hand in each month. Thank you to everyone in our community who has shown me how wonderful the people of small towns can be, especially Paulina Kelly, whose warmth and generosity continues to amaze me. Thanks for short shifts, possum noises, and Jason Momoa references. Thanks also to my dear friend Bec Carr—and her partner, Rich Cass—for their warmth and hospitality.

Endless love and gratitude to my adopted family, Don Allinson and Melanie Ivanhoe. You are a port in a storm. I don't think I can ever repay how much you have given me over the years.

Leslie Plesetz: I think you know how much I love you, but I know that I don't say it enough. You mean the world to me.

A big thank-you to my parents, David and Camilla Barry, who taught me the love and joy of stories, who told people I was a writer years before I was comfortable using the label myself. Dad, I would give absolutely anything to be able to share this with you. You championed my creativity before it was even there. Thanks to my mom for making up stories and sharing them with my brothers and me.

I have a lot of gratitude for my older brother, Nico, who continues to inspire me with his intelligence and patience. Thank you for sharing my weird sense of humor. Thanks also to Elyse, the newest member of our family, for contributing her own humor and compassion. Clive, I miss you.

Tilda and Huon: thank you for letting me join your family. I am always proud to tell people that I have the best stepchildren that anyone could ask for. I love you both very much.

For being there for me each morning, each distracted afternoon, I owe enormous thanks to my supportive partner, Marsh Wilkinson. Thank you for listening to rambling thoughts and half-formed ideas. Thank you for traveling with me, quarantining with me, reading next to me in silence. You make this lonely type of work quite a bit less isolating.